PRAISE FOR KERRY ANNE KING

Praise for *A Borrowed Life*

"In this vivid and triumphant tale, a woman loses her controlling husband and discovers she's been tightly contained in a cocoon for decades. Learning who she is, one step at a time like an unsteady toddler, means challenging everything and every relationship in her life—and grappling with surprises that will turn her world upside down. Is she Elizabeth, the tight-laced pastor's wife, or Liz, the thespian who has a point of view all her own? Earthy, unpredictable, and wildly enjoyable."
—Barbara O'Neal, *Wall Street Journal* and *Washington Post* bestselling author of *When We Believed in Mermaids*

"Watching Liz Lightsey come back to life after years of letting her identity slide away is a treat. *A Borrowed Life* shows Kerry Anne King at her empathetic best, writing a tale of passion, meaning, and growth at any age, and leaving this reader touched and delighted!"
—Kelly Harms, *Washington Post* bestselling author of *The Bright Side of Going Dark*

"Written by Kerry Anne King with humor and heart, *A Borrowed Life* is the story of Liz, a woman who finds herself at a midlife crossroads and bravely decides to reinvent her life by taking a giant leap outside her comfort zone. At times hilarious and cringe inducing, heartbreakingly sad and bursting with joy, Liz's unpredictable journey will have you gasping at every turn. I loved this book!"
—Loretta Nyhan, bestselling author of *Digging In*

"Kerry Anne King's *A Borrowed Life* is both beautifully written and unflinchingly honest. A cautionary tale about the insidious ways we allow others to keep us small, it's also a lesson on the enormous power of love and friendship, and how the people in our lives can lend us strength as we grow, cheering us on to be our best lives and who we are truly meant to be. This story with its wonderful cast of characters is one that will grab you by the heart and refuse to let go."
—Barbara Davis, bestselling author of *When Never Comes*

"Life has a way of coming up with surprises, even for people who know themselves to be settled. In Kerry Anne King's latest wonderful novel, Elizabeth is a mother and dutiful pastor's wife, serving the needs of her family and the church. But when Thomas suddenly dies, Elizabeth embarks on a journey of self-discovery that awakens her to life's joys and losses, risks and magic. With *A Borrowed Life*, King has written a heartrending, page-turning novel that zips along with twists and turns, humor and poignancy, and will have you cheering (and gasping) as Elizabeth-now-Liz rediscovers the meaning of freedom and creativity and love."
—Maddie Dawson, bestselling author of *Matchmaking for Beginners*

Praise for *Everything You Are*

"Hopeful at its heart and sincere to its core, *Everything You Are* is a testament to the power of connection."
—*Booklist*

"*Everything You Are* is a fresh, imaginative story about the power of dreams and our hunger to be who we really are. Kerry Anne King orchestrates a fluid, emotional, and wholly original tale of families, secrets, and the power of our gifts to free us. I loved every magical word."
—Barbara O'Neal, author of *When We Believed in Mermaids*

"Real and raw, King's *Everything You Are* is a gorgeous tale of life told between those lines too often blurred. Love and sorrow, regret and hope are woven into every aspect of the story by music—not just any music, but the magical kind that leaves both creator and listener, for better or worse, irrevocably changed."
—Terri-Lynne DeFino, author of *The Bar Harbor Retirement Home for Famous Writers (and Their Muses)*

"Writing sensitively about characters struggling to overcome tragedy and loss, Kerry Anne King has delivered a beautiful, soulful novel that hits all the right notes—especially for music lovers. It will leave you with tears in your eyes and sighs of contentment when you reach the satisfying, emotional conclusion. A richly rewarding read."
—Julianne MacLean, *USA Today* bestselling author

Praise for *Whisper Me This*

"Rich in emotions and characters, *Whisper Me This* is a stunning tale of dark secrets, broken memories, and the resilience of the human spirit. The novel quickly pulls the reader onto a roller-coaster ride through grief, mystery, and cryptic journal entries. At the heart of the story is an unforgettable twelve-year-old, who has more sense than most adults, and her mother, Maisey, who is about to discover not only her courage, but the power of her voice. A book club must-read!"
—Barbara Claypole White, bestselling author of *The Perfect Son*

"Moving and emotionally taut, *Whisper Me This* is a gut-wrenching story of a family fractured by abuse and lies . . . and the ultimate sacrifice of a mother's love. King once again proves herself an expert with family drama. A triumph of a book."
—Emily Carpenter, author of *Burying the Honeysuckle Girls* and *The Weight of Lies*

"Kerry Anne King writes with such insight and compassion for human nature, and her latest novel, *Whisper Me This*, is no exception. The families on which the story centers have secrets they've kept through the years out of concern for the damage that might be done if they were exposed. But in the end as the families' lives become intertwined and their secrets come inevitably to light, what is revealed to be the most riveting heart of this book are the gut-wrenching choices that were made in terrifying circumstances. One such choice haunted a mother throughout her lifetime and left behind a legacy of mistrust and confusion and a near-unsolvable mystery. Following the clues is an act of faith that sometimes wavers. There's no guarantee the end will tie up in a neat bow, but the courage of the human spirit, its ability to heal, is persistent and luminous throughout the pages of this very real and emotive story. I loved it."

—Barbara Taylor Sissel, bestselling author of *Crooked Little Lies* and *Faultlines*

Praise for *I Wish You Happy*

"Laugh, cry, get angry, but most of all care in this wild ride of emotions delivered by Kerry Anne King. Brilliant prose inhabited by engaging characters makes this a story you cannot put down."

—Patricia Sands, author of the Love in Provence series

"Depicting the depth of human frailty yet framing it within a picture of hope, *I Wish You Happy* pulls you in as you root for the flawed yet intoxicating characters to reach a satisfying conclusion of healing. King's writing is impeccable—and her knowledge and exploration of depression and how it affects those it touches makes this a story that everyone will connect with."

—Kay Bratt, author of *Wish Me Home*

"Kerry Anne King's Rae is a woman caught between the safety of her animal rescue projects and the messy, sometimes terrifying reality of human relationships. You'll never stop rooting for her as she steps into the light, risking everything for real friendship and love in this wistful, delicate, and ultimately triumphant tale."

—Emily Carpenter, author of *Burying the Honeysuckle Girls* and *The Weight of Lies*

"Kerry Anne King explores happiness and depression [and] the concept of saving others versus saving ourselves in this wonderfully written and touching novel populated by real and layered people. If you want to read a book that restores your faith in humanity, pick up *I Wish You Happy*."

—Amulya Malladi, bestselling author of *A House for Happy Mothers* and *The Copenhagen Affair*

"It's the horrible accident that forms the backbone of the plot at the beginning of *I Wish You Happy* that will take your breath and have you turning the pages. The hook has a vivid, ripped-from-the-headlines vibe, one that will have you wondering what you would do, how you would respond in a similar situation. But there are so many other treasures to find in this story as it unfolds. From the warm, deeply human, and relatable characters to the heartbreaking and complex situation they find themselves in, this is a novel to savor, one you will be sorry to see end. Sometimes funny and often very wise and poignant, *I Wish You Happy* is a reading journey you do not want to miss."

—Barbara Taylor Sissel, bestselling author of *Crooked Little Lies* and *Faultlines*

"Kerry Anne King has written a novel that will grab you right from page one and then take you zipping along, breaking your heart and making you laugh, both in equal measure. It's a lovely story about how we save ourselves while we try to save those around us. I loved it!"

—Maddie Dawson, author of six novels, including
The Survivor's Guide to Family Happiness

Praise for *Closer Home*

"A compelling and heartfelt tale. A must-read that is rich in relatable characters and emotions. Kerry Anne King is one to watch out for!"
—Steena Holmes, *New York Times* and *USA Today* bestselling author

"With social media conferring blistering fame and paparazzi exhibiting the tenacity often required to get a clear picture of our lives, King has created a high-stakes, public stage for her tale of complicated grief. A quick read with emotional depth you won't soon forget."
—Kathryn Craft, author of *The Far End of Happy* and
The Art of Falling

"*Closer Home* is a story as memorable and meaningful as your favorite song, with a cast of characters so true to life you'll be sorry to let them go."
—Sonja Yoerg, author of *House Broken* and *Middle of Somewhere*

"Kerry Anne King's tale of regret, loss, and love pulled me in, from its intriguing beginning to its oh-so-satisfying conclusion."
—Jackie Bouchard, *USA Today* bestselling author of *House Trained*
and *Rescue Me, Maybe*

"King's prose is filled with vitality."
—Ella Carey, author of *Paris Time Capsule* and *The House by the Lake*

A
BORROWED
LIFE

ALSO BY KERRY ANNE KING

Closer Home

I Wish You Happy

Whisper Me This

Everything You Are

A
BORROWED
LIFE

A NOVEL

KERRY ANNE KING

LAKE UNION
PUBLISHING

Published by Lake Union Publishing, Seattle

www.apub.com

Amazon, the Amazon logo, and Lake Union Publishing are trademarks of Amazon.com, Inc., or its affiliates.

ISBN-13: 9781542019484
ISBN-10: 1542019486

Cover design by Faceout Studio, Spencer Fuller

Printed in the United States of America

In memory of my mother, who inspired me with her own quest for creative freedom and taught me early that I could be anything that I wanted to be

I hope one day you say "yes" to everything that ever scared you. I hope you look back and laugh in the face of all those monsters that put fear in your hands and hesitation on your tongue. I hope you look at yourself and see your own heart staring back at you, and I hope you believe the way it pounds.

—*Stephanie Bennett-Henry*

As though to breathe were life!
Life piled on life were all too little.

—*Alfred, Lord Tennyson*

Chapter One

Thomas is snoring.

Which means there's a problem with his CPAP, which means that I, as the dutiful wife in this equation, should gently shake him awake lest he suffer brain damage from oxygen deprivation. But it's very nearly five a.m., and if I wake him, that will be the end of all hope for time alone with my thoughts.

How much does a little bit of oxygen deprivation really hurt a person, anyway? Surely he'll be fine.

With the finesse of long experience, I slide out of bed without jiggling the mattress. The room is full dark, but my questing fingers easily locate my bathrobe, draped over the foot of the bed. I tiptoe out of the room and ease the door closed behind me, reveling in the solitude as I pad, barefoot, down the hallway.

I love the soft mystery of the shadowy kitchen illuminated only by the streetlight outside, but I love the peace and quiet even more. This is my time, this thirty minutes stolen from the demands and expectations of the day.

First thing, I withdraw a single-serving packet of tuna from the pantry and stealthily open the back door. A disreputable orange cat sits at a wary distance, watching me. One ear is half missing, and he's thinner than I'd like, but he looks better than he did when I caught him digging through my garbage can a few months back. Since then, we've come to an agreement. If I provide him morning tuna, he will leave my garbage alone. Beyond that concession, he is unwilling to go. I can't get near him or touch him, and he won't eat as long as I'm watching.

When I go back inside, I drop the telltale evidence into the trash can in the kitchen, wash my hands, and retrieve my journal from its hiding place in the cupboard by the stove. Thomas is clear that a man's place is never in the kitchen, so my secrets are more safely hidden behind the baking sheets than they would be under lock and key. Sometimes I stash novels in that cupboard, as well. There are things a pastor doesn't need to know about his wife's choice of reading material.

Unlike the covers of the novels, fantasy romance featuring adventurous characters in scandalous states of inappropriate dress, my current journal appears demure and church-sanctioned. I won it as a prize at a women's conference. *Prayer Journal* is printed in large letters across the front, followed by a scripture: *A word fitly spoken is like apples of gold in pitchers of silver. Proverbs 25:11.*

But what is inside strays far from the teachings of what I privately call the Church of Thomas, decidedly not fitting to my role of Pastor's Wife and Helpmeet.

Rendered solid and real by the magic of ink and paper, the thoughts I jot down here remind me that I am something more than Mrs. Thomas Lightsey. It's not the first journal I've kept, and it won't be the last. When all of the pages are filled, I'll shred it, as I've shredded all of the others.

Sitting on the floor in front of the window, letting the light from the streetlamp illuminate my page just enough to make out the lines, I write:

> *January 3, 2019*
> *Hey you, are you still in there?*
> *I feel that I'm losing you, no matter how hard I try to hold on. I've resorted to small acts of rebellion. Yesterday*

I hung one of Thomas's green shirts in with the blues. Moved that hideous vase on the coffee table two inches off-center. I wondered if he would even notice, but of course he did. And instructed me, oh so kindly, about the need for perfect order and the whole cleanliness-is-next-to-godliness doctrine.

I'm not so sure God is big on perfect order. Surely even He would get bored with that. Maybe that's the reason for entropy. Imagine if everything just was perfect and stayed perfect and He had absolutely nothing to fix or do for eternity? Give me hell before that sort of heaven.

And yes, God, I know You're reading this because even my thoughts don't really belong to me. So since You're reading along, I want to ask You something. You know what I want, more than anything in the world?

A room of my own, à la Virginia Woolf. Like Thomas's study, only mine. I'd paint it soft blue, I think. And have one of those antique writing desks with the roll top. Wouldn't it be lovely to sit and think and write like this in the middle of the day and not just first thing in the morning?

I hear Thomas waking. Gotta go.

Stay with me, Inner Liz. Please don't ever leave me.

I slide the journal back into its hiding place and shift smoothly into a routine perfectly orchestrated over the course of thirty years of marriage. Lights on. Slippers on my feet. I turn the burner on under the frying pan to heat the potatoes I prepped last night. Start the preloaded coffeepot.

Precisely ten minutes later, I fix Thomas a mug of coffee with one scant spoonful of sugar and the perfect dollop of cream. I give the sizzling potatoes a stir. Lift the mug and turn, smile in place, to welcome my husband with fragrant coffee and a morning kiss.

Chapter Two

Click-clack. Click-clack. Yarn over, slide the stitch.

My fingers itch with boredom. The clock on the wall says 4:15. Another hour and forty-five minutes until I'm released from this slow torture, and I'm already stuffed to the gills with gossip and innuendo. My butt aches from the hard wooden chair I've put myself in, having left the softer seats for my knitting circle guests. The baby blanket I'm knitting is only two inches long, with hundreds of dreary rows left to go.

"Really, I can't believe Marjorie asked to head up the committee," Earlene is saying, her knitting needles clicking her righteous indignation. "Every week she's at church, as it should be, of course. But surely she knows she can't be in leadership when we all know what she's up to. She doesn't even try to hide it."

Earlene is my across-the-street neighbor, and was unofficially running our congregation long before my husband took over as pastor. If God were bossable, she'd likely take Him on as a project, but since He's out of her reach, she contents herself with managing people. Since Thomas isn't any more open to her opinions than God is, she generally presents them to me.

"We need to love her back to Jesus, not cast stones." Kimber's tone is pure holier-than-thou. "I invited her over for dinner after church last week."

"And got all the salacious details, I'll bet. Come on, spill." Annie's eyes, alight with mischief, meet mine. I want to grin at her, but it's my responsibility as the hostess of this Blankets for Babies Knitting Circle and the wife of a holy man of God to curb wagging tongues.

Personally, I have sympathy for Marjorie, the gossip meal of the day. Her husband is a lout. I know, but can't say, that he beats her. I've watched the two of them come in for marriage counseling, heard Thomas advise him to love his wife the way Jesus loves the church, and reassure her that her love in Christ will save the marriage. He's prayed over them more than once.

Prayers are useless over a man like that. God's not going to smite him down, no matter how often he smites his wife. If she's left the brute and moved in with an unbeliever who, reportedly, has a gun and is willing to use it in order to protect her, she has my sympathy.

I steer the conversation toward safer waters.

"Tell us all about the wedding, Amy. Has Lisa chosen a dress?"

It's not the smoothest segue in the world, but none of them notice. Weddings and babies are the only topics that rival juicy gossip, and fortunately we have a wedding coming up.

Amy drops her knitting so she can gesture with her hands. "Oh, the dress is beautiful, although it is a little too revealing in the neckline, I feel. I spoke to Lisa about that. I said, 'Honey, it's best to leave the treasure out of sight until the wedding night,' and she laughed at me. Laughed! I'm worried about what the two of them are already up to."

"Wouldn't be the first time a premature baby weighed eight pounds," Annie murmurs, and Amy bristles.

"How dare you imply—"

"You implied. I was just being comforting."

"She's young." Earlene's needles click nearly as fast as her tongue. "And she's a bride. I'm sure the dress is beautiful. That groom of hers, now . . ." She shakes her head, indicating that she could say things if she wanted to but is holding her tongue.

"What about him?" Amy demands.

"Well, there was that incident with alcohol . . ."

"He was sixteen! A lot of kids experiment as teenagers. He's got that great job now, at Vaagen's."

"Easy now," Earlene says. "I didn't mean to start a war."

She did, of course. Earlene thrives on teapot tempests. Bored as I am, spats and hurt feelings are not diversions I am fond of.

This time, Felicity changes the subject. "Do you think next time we might try a pattern for the blankets? Or maybe some prettier yarn?"

She's the new youth pastor's wife, a pretty little thing, all big eyes and enthusiasm. She's not yet indoctrinated in the unwritten bylaws under which the knitting circle operates, but she's about to be educated. Amy and Earlene drop their feud and turn on her, instant allies in the face of this threat to the status quo.

"Fancy yarns are more expensive," Earlene says. "The idea is to make these blankets as cheaply as possible so that the babies of drug-addicted mothers will have one special thing."

"If some are nicer than others, some babies will feel left out," Amy chimes in.

"And the idea of just making all of the blankets cute is preposterous, of course." Annie's voice holds an edge, half humor and half something darker that connects with my own mutinous soul. If I weren't the pastor's wife, Annie and I might be friends.

I glance at the clock. Four twenty. I've accomplished two more rows. At this rate, I'll still be knitting this blanket when I'm eighty. How many minutes, how many seconds, is that?

Felicity's blunder has opened the door to a hazing.

Amy, mother of the young and hopefully still-virginal bride-to-be, leads the charge. "So, Felicity—Lisa tells me that your husband has a . . . different way with the young people."

"How do you mean?" Felicity asks, walking right into the trap.

"More contemporary. Less . . . biblical."

"The music they've been playing!" Earlene adds. "Drums and guitars and such. No offense, but I'm not entirely sure it's appropriate within the house of God."

"God is probably grateful for the change." Annie keeps her eyes on her knitting, not looking at me this time. "Think about it. All of the congregations, year after year, singing the same old songs. He's probably bored to tears."

"You are entirely too flippant about the Almighty," Earlene snaps.

Felicity huddles deeper into her chair, bending her head so that her long chestnut hair hides her face, but not before I catch a sheen of tears in her eyes and a flush of embarrassment on her cheeks.

Church gossip has it that Annie is part of a growing faction agitating to replace Thomas with a pastor who is a little less repressive and a lot more open minded. Felicity's husband is a step in that direction. It's easier to bring new blood into the youth group than the general congregation, half of which is old and set in their ways.

Laying aside my knitting, I get to my feet. "Anybody ready for tea and cookies?"

It's way too early for refreshments, but these are dangerous waters we've strayed into. I've got to stop this now before the tension escalates further, and I can't think of any topic of conversation that will serve the purpose.

"Not for me. It's not even five o'clock." Leave it to Earlene to point out the obvious.

A loud crash cuts across my reply.

"What in heaven's name?" Earlene exclaims, the clacking of her needles pausing as she listens for more.

We're suspended in an oasis of silence. No clicking of tongues or needles. No rustling of knitting bags or unrolling of yarn. We all wait for Thomas to step out of his study. To say, "All is well, ladies. I caught a book with my elbow. I hope nobody was alarmed."

Seconds tick by.

The silence continues. Thomas does not appear.

No footsteps. No indication of Thomas tidying up. He would never just leave a fallen item to its fate, any more than he would overlook the opportunity to save an erring soul.

After what seems like a small eternity, Earlene's needles resume clicking and the rest follow her lead. A strange sensation coils in my throat, right above my collarbones. It's difficult to breathe past it.

"Excuse me," I murmur. "Let me just make sure Thomas doesn't need any help."

My shoes whish over the carpet of the living room. Tap-tap on the hardwood in the hall.

The study door is closed, and I hesitate, listening.

I know better than to disturb him when he's behind a closed door. He'll be preparing a sermon. Engaged in prayer. Maybe on the phone with a troubled parishioner.

But I hear nothing.

Lightly, I tap on the door, braving his displeasure. Whisper, "Thomas?"

No answer.

I tap louder, say his name out loud, even though I know all ears in the living room are tuned in this direction. Even though they will all hear his patient reprimand.

But he doesn't answer. Doesn't say, "Elizabeth. Can it wait?"

The doorknob feels cold and dangerous in my palm. I turn it, then stare in confusion, trying to make sense of what I see.

Thomas lies on the floor of the study, eyes closed.

For one confused instant, I think he's decided to take a nap.

My eyes take in the details. The office chair tipped over on its side. The cup of chamomile tea I'd fixed before the circle, spilled, little rivulets of greenish liquid spreading toward the computer keyboard. Thomas's legs bent at an awkward angle, his arms flung wide.

His Bible is splayed open on his chest, the pages bent. It's this disrespect for the Word of God, more than the fact that he doesn't seem to be breathing, that finally wakes me up and tears a scream from my throat.

I hear a stampede of feet in the hallway, feel bodies jostling in the doorway behind me.

"CPR," Earlene commands. "Who knows CPR?"

I wait for one of them to run forward, drop to her knees, start resuscitating their fallen shepherd.

Their faces are shocked, stricken. Nobody moves.

"Always skipped those classes," Annie moans. "Didn't think I'd need it."

"Me, too," Kimber admits. "Somebody *do* something!"

"I'll call nine-one-one," Felicity says. "Oh my God. What's the address here? I can't even think."

"I'll call," Earlene overrides.

I turn back to Thomas. He's no longer the slim man he was when I married him, and there's no room to kneel between his body and the bookcase on one side, or the desk on the other. I pick my way forward and sit astride his belly.

My skirt rides up over my thighs, and I wait for his reprimand. *"Elizabeth Lightsey, the world can see China."*

But he says nothing.

His face is a color skin was never meant to be.

I hear Earlene's voice behind me, talking to somebody on the phone. "I don't know. Just a minute. Elizabeth, is he breathing?"

"No." There is no movement of his chest, no sound of air moving in and out of his lungs. I press my fingers to the skin of his throat, where the pulse is supposed to be, but it's pointless. I can feel the way he isn't here, the absence of him.

"Does he have any medical conditions?" Earlene shouts. Too loud, as if I'm in the backyard instead of just a few feet away from her.

I position my hands over his breastbone. Press down. His chest doesn't even give. I push harder, put all of my weight behind it. This doesn't feel at all like the resuscitation dummy I practiced on.

"Tanya wants to talk to you," Earlene shouts.

I look up, confused, compressing Thomas's chest again. Surely even Earlene knows I'm not free to chat right now.

But she holds the phone out toward me, then says, "Wait. What am I thinking?" and pushes a button.

A voice comes through on speakerphone.

"Mrs. Lightsey? Elizabeth?"

"It's not a good—"

"This is Tanya. From church. What's happened to Pastor?"

I stop compressions, staring at the circle of pale, stricken faces gaping back at me. They all expect me to answer, and that finally jars loose the important detail. Tanya works for dispatch. Colville is a small enough town that I know half the people in it. Tanya is my 911 contact.

I take a breath. "He's—lying on the floor. I found him this way."

"Is he conscious?"

"No, he's just lying here."

"Did he fall? Hit his head?"

"He's not breathing, Tanya. His heart isn't beating. I don't know—"

"An ambulance is on the way. Now, I need you to start CPR. Okay? Can you do that?"

"I think so."

"Good, that's good. Oh, dear God help us. Okay. I'll count with you. Are you ready? One-one-thousand, two-one-thousand . . ."

Somebody is weeping, and from the strange place my brain has wandered off to, it feels irrational. If I had any breath left over, maybe I'd say, "What are you crying about? He's not *your* husband."

My arms feel like jelly. My breath burns in my lungs, my heart is laboring.

10

Guilt sets in. This is all my fault. Just this very morning I asked God for a space of my own, and He's punishing me for my selfishness.

"Time to give him a breath," Tanya says. "Tilt his head back, seal his nose with your thumb and forefinger . . ."

I try, but Thomas does not cooperate. His skin is clammy and his neck is stiff and I'm doing this wrong, all wrong. I pinch his nostrils and get set to deliver a breath. His lips are cold and taste sour, and my stomach lurches.

Nausea is a luxury I don't have a right to.

I take a new breath and try to blow it into him. It feels like blowing up an overly stiff balloon. My own lungs burn with the pressure, and I don't think any of the oxygen is transferring from me to him.

Which means his head isn't tilted back properly, but any time I take to try to fix his airway will be time that his heart isn't beating.

"All right, back to compressions," Tanya's voice says, and I abandon the botched breathing thing and resume my inadequate chest compressions.

If Abigail were here, she'd know how to do CPR, would probably already have her father up and talking and requesting a fresh cup of tea.

One-one-thousand, two-one-thousand, three-one-thousand, four . . .

Thomas is an annoying breather. At night he snores, sighs, makes puffing noises. In the daytime he tends to snuffle and snort even when he's reading or watching the news on TV. It irritates me some days until I want to scream at him to stop.

And now he has, and I'd give anything for him to start again.

My own breath is coming hard and fast. My heart is pounding. The ambulance has begun to feel like a myth.

"Are they coming?" I gasp.

"Just a few more minutes. Keep going. One-one-thousand, two-one-thousand . . ."

My arms and shoulders are beyond aching. I can't do this anymore, but I also can't stop.

"They're here," Annie's voice says. I hear footsteps in the hallway and look up to see a woman in uniform, a man behind her.

"We'll take it from here," the woman says.

"There's no room to work," the man responds. "We'll have to move him." His hand rests on my shoulder. "Ma'am, you can stop now. We've got this."

I keep going, like a mechanical toy, but he hauls me up to my feet and passes me off to Earlene's none-too-steady hands out in the hallway. We squeeze into the space between a wheeled stretcher and the wall. I notice a trail of muddy snow on the hardwood floor. Thomas will have a fit about that when he wakes up. Maybe I should wipe it up, now, while we're waiting.

The EMTs shove the visitor chairs against the wall and drag Thomas out from behind the desk. The man resumes CPR, brisk, professional. The woman puts a mask over Thomas's nose and mouth and starts breathing for him with a bag, then stops to slap sticky pads on his chest and hook him up to an EKG machine.

A heady rush of relief flows through me. These people are so competent. Everything will be fine after all. Later this evening, Thomas will be gently chastising me for my failure and suggesting CPR refresher classes, and this time the resuscitation doll will get my full and undivided attention.

But my rush of hope disintegrates rapidly. The EMTs are intense, focused. They speak to each other in short, abrupt words that sound like code.

Not one of them speaks to me. Not one of them says, "It's okay, Mrs. Lightsey. We've got this. Your husband will be just fine."

"No rhythm," the woman says. "Let's shock him."

I hear footsteps running in the hallway. A pair of warm arms circles my waist, gently tugging me back away from the door.

"You don't need to watch this," a familiar voice says. "Come away."

"Val. He's . . ."

"I see. Come on now."

Val's voice is reassuring, calm. She works in a nursing home; this isn't her first encounter with a medical emergency. I let her lead me down the hall, into the living room. When she puts her arms around me, I lean into her, bury my face in her shoulder, and she rubs slow circles on my back, making small shushing noises as if I'm a child. Her hair smells like bacon and tobacco, oddly comforting.

Val is my neighbor to the left, not a member of the fold. Thomas has tolerated our fraternizing because I've told him I'm witnessing, trying to save her soul. He knows nothing of the clandestine friendship that has sprung up between us. Coffee in the backyard on summer afternoons, or in one of our kitchens in the winter. Shared excursions to the grocery store. An occasional movie night when he's out late at a meeting.

I hear the stretcher wheels in the hall and turn to watch it roll by. One EMT continues chest compressions while another propels the stretcher with one hand, squeezing the breathing bag with the other. I follow them out the door and into the cold dark of a January evening.

The stretcher wheels leave tracks in the snow between the porch and the ambulance.

A small crowd of neighbors has gathered across the street. The knitting circle ladies huddle together on the porch. Both groups are whispering, gawking. Thomas has become entertainment. A spectacle. They shouldn't see him like this. He's a holy man of God, not a resuscitation dummy.

Val's arm steadies me as the ambulance team loads Thomas into the ambulance. Earlene prays aloud, hands clasped.

"Our Father, please be with our pastor in this moment. You are the Almighty Healer, you have the power to work miracles, and you know how he is needed here on this earth. We ask that you work a miracle now on his behalf, and yet we bow to your will . . ."

"You can ride with us if you'd like," the woman EMT says. Something is wrong with my brain and my muscles. I can't bring myself to say a single word, to do anything more than blink at her.

"I'll bring her," Val says. "That will be better."

The EMT nods and closes the doors on her partner, who is still delivering compressions, then springs into the driver's seat. Lights and sirens start as they drive away.

I'm shivering. Snow is drifting down, swirling in the light of the streetlamps. My feet in my slip-on pumps are wet, my toes burning with cold. The gathered crowd has turned their stares on me.

Val's arm tightens around my waist, and she tugs me into motion. "Let's get your coat and some boots, and then I'll drive you to the hospital."

Grateful that somebody has taken charge of me and is telling me what to do, I let Val lead me into the house. I sit on the sofa when she tells me to. Drink the glass of water she gives me.

The ladies of the knitting circle collect their belongings in funereal silence, tucking unfinished blankets into knitting bags, returning their chairs to the dining room, putting the unused cups and plates back in the cabinet

Val wraps an afghan around my shoulders, and only then do I realize how my body is trembling. "Is there anybody I can call?"

I blink up at her as if the words are in a foreign language. Who would I call? My parents are dead. Thomas's parents are both in a nursing home, his father so far gone with dementia he won't comprehend what's being said to him, his mother not much more coherent.

As for friends, a pastor's wife can't have friends, not really. Inside the congregation, it looks like playing favorites when I'm supposed to love everybody equally and unconditionally. Friends outside the fold are off-limits. Val is the closest thing I have to a real friend.

"Liz?" Val kneels down on the floor, puts her hands on my shoulders. "Do you want me to call Abigail?"

My stomach lurches, rises. I press both hands over my mouth. Val's kind face blurs and swims in front of me.

I will need to call my daughter and tell her . . . tell her . . .

I can't do this. I can't face this new version of the world, this new version of myself.

The house looks strange, as if I've never seen it before. The greens in the throw rug in the living room grate on my nerves. I hate green, at least in that color, would have chosen blues if I'd had a say. Everything is so freakishly neat, it looks like a stage set. There is not one thing in this room that I love, that belongs to me. My entire married life feels like a book I read, a movie I watched.

Outside of Thomas, I don't have a life. Outside of Thomas, I don't even exist.

I hear myself laughing wildly, the lunatic laughter of a crazy woman.

Kimber and Amy exchange glances and hustle out the door together. Felicity is already gone. Annie hesitates, touches my shoulder. I want to thank her, but the insane laughter doubles me over, and I can't stop, can't speak.

"What is wrong with her?" Earlene demands, hovering, an expression of outright horror on her face.

"Hysterics," Val retorts. "Perfectly normal given what she's just been through. I'm sorry, but do you need something?"

Before Earlene can come up with a response, my laughter shifts to weeping, great tearing sobs that feel like they're going to turn me inside out. Over the horrible, humiliating sounds I'm making, I hear Earlene's voice, clear and authoritative, praying for both my soul and my sanity.

"Do you have to do that?" Val challenges, interrupting.

"I'm seeking intervention—"

"Pretty sure He can still hear you if you pray silently." Val turns back to me, her voice softening from commanding to coaxing. "Come on, Liz. Let's get you to the hospital."

She fetches my coat and drapes it over my shoulders. Kneels down and slips my shoes off my feet, sliding on my warm winter boots in their place. I feel oddly comforted by this small action and sit there like a child, letting her dress me.

Somehow Val even manages to shoo Earlene out of the house. She drives me to the hospital. Walks with me to the reception desk. Asks about Thomas.

"Someone will be right out to speak with you," the receptionist says. Her expression gives nothing away, and I try to guess whether this is good news or bad news. If Thomas is alive, miraculously recovered, surely she'd just say, "Go on in. He's been asking for you."

Val and I settle into chairs, side by side. She holds my hand the whole time, her hand soft but capable, the skin a little dry and red on the back, nails trimmed short. In the chair across from me, an elderly man reads a magazine while the woman beside him rocks slightly, her face clenched in pain.

When the double doors open and a bearded man in green scrubs comes out, a giant hand seems to squeeze my chest, stealing my breath.

"Mrs. Lightsey? I'm Dr. Blaise."

I get to my feet, even though I know without him telling me that I'm not Mrs. Lightsey anymore. In order to be a "Mrs.," there needs to be a "Mr.," and the doctor's expression tells me plainly that the "Mr." part of this equation has passed into the great beyond.

Chapter Three

How do you tell your only child that her father is dead?

That I should do this monstrous thing—break into her ordinary day with such shattering news—seems as possible as climbing Mount Everest or flying to the moon. How will I even begin?

My instinct is to shield her from danger, to kiss her hurts and make them better, and everything in me recoils from being the one to hurt her. If I must deliver this blow, I want to be able to hold her as I tell it. But as Val points out, very gently, if I wait, if I drive to Spokane, given the small town and church communication network that Abigail and I are both connected to, she is likely to hear it from somebody else.

So I call her, even though she's in the middle of a shift in the emergency room at Sacred Heart.

"Hey, Mom," she says. "We're expecting an onslaught any minute. Can I call you back?"

"No, honey. We need to talk now."

I take a breath and steel myself. She likes facts and abhors emotional scenes. I try to keep my voice even, as if I'm reporting on the weather.

"Your father had a heart attack earlier this evening."

A space of silence. A quiet breath.

"Abigail. Honey. I'm—"

"What time? Has he had TPA? Are they life flighting him here or to Holy Family?" She sounds as calm as if she's taking report on an incoming patient.

"They're not sending him anywhere. He's . . ." Despite my best intentions, a sob escapes me, my voice breaking.

"Mom. Take a breath. Just tell me."

"He's not . . . he didn't . . . honey, I'm so sorry, but he's dead."

"Oh," she says, still in that professional voice. "I should probably come home. I'll need to get my shift covered."

And then she hangs up before I can even suggest that she get somebody to drive her. No tears. No I-love-yous. Just the silence of my own thoughts and all of the time in the world to think them. Maybe this is what hell is, I think. Being given the thing we think we want and then having to live with it.

News travels fast, and members of the congregation come and go. Many of them bring food. Some offer comfort, but most seem to expect it from me.

"God has a plan, even if we don't understand it," I tell them, because it's the sort of thing Thomas would say, not because I believe it. Val stays with me, quietly making decisions. She carries the food into the kitchen and tactfully herds anybody toward the door who stays too long or cries too hard. All the while, I'm worrying about Abigail.

The stretch of road from Spokane to Colville is treacherous, even in the summer. Corners, deer, idiot drivers who are in too much of a hurry and try to pass when they shouldn't. This time of year, there could be packed snow or black ice. She was in shock on the phone. When that breaks, she'll be distraught, maybe not safe to drive.

I watch the clock, mentally tracking her progress. An hour, maybe, before someone can be called in to cover the rest of her hospital shift. Half an hour to drive to her apartment for an overnight bag. Another hour and a half for the trip home, maybe longer depending on the road conditions.

It's half past ten when I finally hear her car in the driveway. I run to the door, wrench it open. She's standing on the porch, a duffel bag in one hand, the other clenched into a fist.

All I want is to draw her into my arms, to comfort her, but Abigail hurt is Abigail defiant. She's sealed herself off into a self-contained module, untouched and untouchable.

I reach out a hand but let it fall when I see her stiffen. "Abigail. Honey . . ."

She brushes past me into the house, and I watch her take it all in. Her father's recliner, empty, when at this hour he should be comfortably ensconced with a cup of tea, absorbed in his bedtime reading. The kitchen, where a plastic-wrapped fruit basket sits on the counter next to an array of desserts and a simmering Crock-Pot. Still wordless, Abigail proceeds down the hall, past her own old bedroom, stopping at the open door of Thomas's study. The inner sanctum, a threshold neither of us ever cross without invitation.

Empty. Desecrated.

Seeing it through my daughter's eyes, I'm struck by remorse that I didn't clean it up before she got here. I should have thought of this. The office chair lies on its back like a dead thing that could no longer support its own weight. There's a litter of discarded packaging on the floor, left behind by the EMTs.

Abigail drops to her knees in exactly the place where her father fell. She picks up his Bible and smooths the crumpled pages. Her body heaves as if trying to rid itself of some terrible toxin, and then she begins to weep, the choking, tearing sobs of a woman who hardly ever cries, forced beyond her limit of endurance.

No Band-Aid will fix this hurt. I can't kiss her and make it better. Helpless, I sink down beside her and lightly touch her head. When she doesn't push me away, I stroke what I can of her hair, which is twisted up so tightly into a bun that it pulls the skin of her forehead into tiny hills and valleys.

I long to loosen it, to see her beautiful hair free, to be able to soothe her by running my fingers through it like I used to do when a nightmare woke her. But it's been years since she's allowed me that liberty. We sit in that small space, physically pressed together, so that every one of her cries travels through my own body.

Gradually, her weeping subsides to gentle sobbing. She draws in a deep breath, and I get up and bring her the box of tissues that always sits on Thomas's desk for use by emotional advisees.

"It doesn't seem possible." Abigail plucks tissues from the box, mops up her face, blows her nose.

"I know."

"This room . . ." Her face crumples in on itself, and my heart crumples with it. I don't want her to feel grief or heartbreak. I want to go backward in this day and press pause somewhere, anywhere, before Thomas died. But I can't shift reality for either of us.

Soft footsteps in the hallway. "Is there anything I can do?" Val stands in the doorway, an unlikely angel of salvation with her frizzled hair and overdone makeup, a serpent tattoo coiled around her forearm.

"Thank you so much, but please don't trouble yourself," Abigail says.

She corrects her posture. Neutralizes her expression. Puts on a polite veneer. My heart twists again as I watch her, knowing I'm the one who taught her this.

"Everybody is watching you, honey. You need to be an example for the others."

The words nearly choked me then. Now the thought of them burns like acid.

Val smiles, kindly. Her mascara is smeared black around her eyes from tears of sympathy. "I was about to put the food away, but you really should come and eat a little something, Liz. Just a little soup."

"I'll take care of it. I'm sure you'd like to get home." Abigail's words are polite, but her tone is dismissive. It's the sort of thing Thomas would have said, and it stings me.

"Oh, I don't mind." Val either doesn't notice Abigail's coolness or she's deliberately ignoring the hidden message. She reaches down a hand to me. "Come now. Your body needs food, at least a few bites."

"All right. Thank you, Val. For everything." I infuse all of the warmth I can find into the words, remembering her arm around me, her hand holding mine. All of this day, she has been here for me. A rock. A tobacco-scented angel. I let her pull me to my feet, then reach out to my daughter. "Come. Let's eat something."

Abigail gets to her own feet, ignoring my outstretched hand. Adjusts her blouse and skirt. Smooths hair that doesn't require smoothing. "I'm not hungry. I'm going to ask one of my docs to call in a sedative and pick it up for you. Which pharmacy are you using?"

"I don't need—"

"I guess it's really a question of what's still open," she says as if I've never spoken.

I glance at the clock. "Nothing, at this hour."

"Maybe I can pull some strings." She taps her phone, searching for something.

"Abigail. I don't want to take a pill."

"It's just for a few days, until you get over the shock."

A thread of anger winds through my grief. If I'm guilty of teaching her to hide her feelings, it was Thomas who taught her this sense of superiority masquerading as concern for my well-being. Always the two of them, riding over my words, discounting my opinion, knowing what I need better than I do. But Thomas isn't here now, and Abigail is my child, and the shadow of my inner self bristles at the condescension.

"What about you?" I ask. "Are you going to take Valium, too?"

Abigail's forehead creases as if I've asked her a puzzling riddle. "Why would I do that?"

"Grief. Shock. All of the reasons you want to get the pills for me."

"I've never needed sedatives," she says. "Okay, here we go." She taps the phone and then holds it up to her ear. I walk away. If Abigail thinks I need to take pills right now, she'll find a way to get them. If that will take her mind off her grief, I can be the grown-up and let her.

I follow Val to the kitchen, where I'm met by a warm, savory aroma that fills my mouth with saliva.

"Mmmm. That does smell good. Maybe I could eat a little. God. What am I going to do with all of this food?"

"We'll freeze most of it. What doesn't fit in your freezer, I'll store in mine. I've still got a big old freezer from before my son moved out. It's nearly empty now. Why don't you go sit in the living room and I'll bring you a mug of soup?"

"I can't let you—"

"Why ever not?"

"It's asking too much. It's late. You've given up your evening—"

"Are you kidding? What sort of friend wouldn't be here? What else would I possibly be doing?"

Friend.

The word sends little tendrils of warmth running through me.

The closest person I ever had to a friend was back in high school, before Thomas. Everything in my life has been marked by that dividing line. Before Thomas. After Thomas. On one side, Liz, wild and fierce, looking for love to compensate for parental neglect. On the other, Elizabeth, tamed and subdued and half killed by kindness. The thought of having a real friend brings fresh tears to my eyes.

"Liz?" Val queries.

"Sorry, I got lost there for a minute."

She touches my arm. "That's to be expected. You're shivering. Go curl up on the couch and let's get something warm in you. And maybe we can turn up the heat a little? It's cold in here."

I am shivering. I feel cold to my bones, as if I'll never be warm again, but it hasn't even occurred to me to turn up the heat.

"Women and thermostats," Thomas says in my head. *"Up, down, up, down. Somebody gets a hot flash or has their monthly and the setting goes down. Or it looks cold outside and the setting goes up. I'm sorry, ladies, but I'm the boss of this piece of household equipment."*

But Thomas isn't here. I can turn the heat up if I want.

I walk to the thermostat and boost it up, from sixty-eight to seventy. And then, in an extravagant burst of rebellion, all the way to seventy-two. Then I snuggle into the couch underneath the afghan.

Val brings me soup in a mug, and I cradle it in my hands, letting it warm me.

Another rebellion. We do not eat in the living room in this house. We take our meals as a family, at a set time, at the table. Routine is right next to the gospel. But there are no more routines, there can't be, because Thomas was at the center of all of them. It feels good to be eating here, where I won't expect to look up and see his face across the table.

"Thank you, Val. For everything."

I want to get up and hug her, but I have the mug, and my body feels too heavy to manage the effort. Instead I reach for her hand and squeeze it.

She squeezes back. "I'll leave you alone now, but I'll check on you tomorrow. Call if you need anything, okay?"

I feel an unexpected loss when the door closes behind her, a reluctance to be alone with my daughter. Things have never been easy between the two of us, and we are now in completely uncharted waters.

When Abigail walks down the hallway a few minutes later, she's completely put back together. She's washed her face, put on a touch of makeup. The only thing that gives her away is the puffy redness of her eyes.

She eyes my mug with disapproval. "Coffee? At this time of night? You'll never sleep, even with a sedative."

"It's soup."

"You've spilled." She says it like I've emptied an entire tanker of oil into a pristine ocean.

I follow her gaze to a slop of soup glistening on the surface of the coffee table, a noodle curled at the center like an obscene worm.

Abigail bustles into the kitchen for a cloth and wipes up the table. Sets down a coaster.

"I'm going to go pick up your meds."

"From where? Everything's closed."

"I worked something out with the hospital pharmacy. Will you be okay alone? I could ask Earlene to come over."

"Please don't. Just stay here yourself. I don't need a sedative."

She puts her jacket on. Reaches for her boots. "I've already called in favors to get them. Earlene will—"

"Oh fine, then. Go get your pills, if you must. But I do not want Earlene over here."

"They're not *my* pills, Mom."

I take a breath, astonished by my rising anger and my inability to shove it back down.

"Oh, for God's sake. I can't stop you if you want to go, but Earlene is not coming over. Do you hear me? You will respect my wishes, Abigail."

I've uttered one of Thomas's phrases. Abigail's body jerks as if I've struck her, and for half an instant, I see the vulnerable child gazing out at me, wounded. Already I regret the phrasing, but before I can call it back, she's gone, slamming the door behind her.

Chapter Four

April 4, 2019

Dear Inner Liz,

Monday was April Fools' Day.

Remember how it was when you were a child? The kids at school all playing jokes. The time Mom said, "Guess what? Your dad quit drinking and went to rehab," and then when you believed her said, "April fools! He's in jail again," with that ugly, sickening laugh.

That's what my whole life feels like. When Thomas died, I thought maybe I could resurrect my old self, which now seems as likely as Dad ever quitting the booze before it killed him. I'm bored. So terribly, horribly, sickeningly bored. Whatever I thought grief would be, it isn't this. I don't even know what I want to do, except that it isn't to keep going on in this dreary, dull way.

Thomas and I had a business arrangement more than a marriage—we were in the church business. And now I'm still in the church business as the sole remaining partner. I want out. Only, where would I go? What would I do? Today is Thursday. Thursday will be knitting circle day until hell freezes over, but I'm sick to death of these women and their same old gossip, and I just want to climb into bed and stay there . . .

Outside, at least, it is spring, even if my interior life is caught in an endless winter.

In the front yard, my maple tree is covered with tiny red flowers. Daffodils and tulips are blooming. The first exploratory bees are out, ambassadors for the hive. The lawn is already green and growing, in need of the lawn mower I've never used and don't know how to operate. Thomas was big on the division of labor between what is a man's work and the place of a woman. Yard work was his. Mine was the house.

He also managed the finances and vehicle maintenance and a thousand other things I've had to figure out on the fly. Over the last three months, I've dealt with life insurance, Social Security, and bank accounts. Nearly escaped having the power shut off because I never thought to pay the electric bill. At least that learning curve gave my brain something to do. Abigail came home every weekend, and the two of us maintained a sort of truce as we worked things out together.

But now that I'm set with a monthly budget and there's some distance between us and the initial grief, Abigail has been coming home less and less. Why should she? We have little to say to each other. All we seem to have in common is Thomas, who somehow is still managing to run my life for me from beyond the grave.

I slam the chair I'm carrying onto the floor with unnecessary force, taking pleasure in the clatter and crash. My soul rises up in rebellion at the idea of working on a blanket that looks exactly like the last blanket, and the one before that. I've come to believe that the road to hell is paved with boring baby blankets, all worked in stocking stitch either in baby blue or pink, never both. Maybe I'll be a total rebel and insist on knitting in variegated yarn.

A tap at the door, and Val breezes in, carrying an essence of a wider world with her.

Val is the one thing in my world that has changed. She drops by for coffee. She drags me out for lunch dates, even whisked me off to a movie one night. Now she skids to a halt, taking in the circle of chairs. "Oh dear Lord. Again? Which thing this time?"

"Knitting circle."

"Tonight?"

"It's Thursday, Val."

"And?"

"Thursday is knitting circle. Every Thursday, since Eve ate the apple. Maybe before that."

"Not tonight." Val clasps her hands and assumes a pleading expression. "I need you. Tell them you had to cancel on account of a soul in peril."

I adjust the chair to be more in line with the others. Earlene likes to come over early and fine-tune my chair arrangement. If she does that today, given the level of pressure built up inside of me, I might snap and wrap my knitting around her throat.

An idea for an irreverent screenplay pops into my head.

Strangled by a Baby Blanket, *a one-woman play in a single act, written and performed by Elizabeth Lightsey.*

These bits of ideas have been dropping by with increasing frequency lately. I've thought about writing them down but never do. It all seems so pointless. Writing was something the younger me, Liz, aspired to do. It's too late now. I opted for Thomas.

"What's up?" I ask, trying to shake off my mood. "You don't look in peril." She looks like she's dressed for a date. Her hair is curled, her makeup piled on even thicker than usual, which is saying something. She's wearing a low-cut blouse that reveals plenty of cleavage and jeans that leave not a single curve of her butt or hips to the imagination.

"Oh, but I am. I'm going to audition for a play. I'm frightened half to death, and I need a wingwoman. You. I need you."

I catch a tantalizing whiff of freedom. In high school, I lived and breathed theater. Onstage, I could be somebody else, a girl with an interesting life. A girl who mattered. The other drama kids felt more like family than anybody waiting at home.

But that's all part of my pre-Thomas life. I sigh.

"I can't, Val. Not on such short notice."

"Of course you can. You can do whatever you want."

I snort at that. Right. That's me. Free and easy and charting my own course. "Earlene will be here any minute. I can't just leave."

"I beseech thee," Val intones, dropping to her knees and clasping her hands in an exaggerated stage gesture.

Earlene enters, right on cue, as if she's been waiting in the wings for her line. As always, she is perfectly, but primly, put together. A neat blouse and skirt, modestly falling just below her knees. Black flats. No makeup or jewelry or anything about her that speaks of a concession to vanity. Except her hair. No woman who has been around as long as Earlene has hair that is perfectly raven black.

"What *are* you two doing?"

Val, still on her knees, collapses onto the floor in a fit of irrepressible laughter. The corners of my own lips twitch at Earlene's scandalized expression.

"One of those things," I say, trying to find a safe place to look. Not at Val. Not at Earlene. "You would have had to be here."

"Good thing I came over when I did." Her eyebrows, sparse and decidedly more gray than raven, draw together. "You're a chair short. You've forgotten that Amy's daughter is joining us."

Right. The new bride, about to be initiated into the joys of charitable needlework. I had forgotten, but the oversight is an opportunity I seize before the second thoughts have time to catch up with me.

"Actually, it's the perfect number of chairs."

"No," Earlene corrects me patiently. "There are seven of us. You've only set up for six."

"I'm not going to be able to make it this evening."

"I don't understand."

Val gets to her feet and smooths her hair. "I'm afraid I'm dragging Liz off tonight on a mission of mercy that is much more pressing than the knitting. She said the circle couldn't run without her, but I told her, 'Liz, Earlene can totally manage without you for one evening. She's so good at managing, and you're needed elsewhere.' So it's all my fault, but you *can* manage, can't you?"

The play of emotions over the old woman's face would make the perfect study for a portrait painter. Val's shameless manipulation does the trick.

"Well, of course, I can manage," Earlene says. "But what in heaven's name do you need Elizabeth for?"

"I'm afraid I can't tell you," Val says. "It's private."

I cringe a little. Earlene is likely imagining everything from a court date to an abortion. She has frequently admonished me to cut off all ties with Val, referencing her as "no better than she should be" on a good day and "that shameless hussy" when her gossiping tongue is at its sharpest.

"Thank you, Earlene," I say. "I'm so sorry for the short notice. But if anybody can manage, it's you."

Val grabs my hand and tows me toward the door. I follow, giving Earlene breathless instructions while I put on my shoes and coat. "There's a vegetable tray in the fridge. The cheese is in there, too, already cut up. Crackers on the island. You know where to find the tea and sugar."

As soon as the front door closes behind us, Val bounces up and down like a child. "You did it! I'm so proud of you!" She throws her arms around my neck and hugs me like I've won a medal or done something heroic. She smells of perfume and smoke and hairspray, all melded together to make a Val fragrance of which I'm growing increasingly fond.

"Come over to my house for a minute. Let's fix you up."

"Wait. Val! I'm going to watch, I don't . . ."

She's already crossed the yard and is holding the door for me. I glance over my shoulder and see Earlene peering out the living room window. I can either backtrack and endure a knitting circle made even more odious by her iron-fisted control, or seek refuge in the forbidden territory of Val's house.

I choose Val's, feeling like a teenager sneaking out for a night of underage partying.

Every house has a smell. Val smokes outside, so tobacco is only an undertone to coffee and fried food and a light lemon air freshener. There's clutter everywhere. Books and mail on the kitchen counter. Magazines on the coffee table in the living room. Her shoes by the door are not lined up precisely. It smells and feels like the home I never had, and I always feel more relaxed over here.

But not tonight.

"What did you make me do?" I demand, only half joking.

"I am rescuing you. Sit down. Here." She drags a kitchen chair away from the table, and I drop obediently into it.

"I thought we were leaving immediately."

"No way. We're early. I never could have pried you loose if we'd waited any longer."

"Has anybody ever told you you're brilliantly manipulative?"

"Ha. Hang on. I have barely begun with my evil master plan." She disappears into the bathroom, and I figure she's off to do some more primping, but she reappears almost immediately with a mirror, a comb, and a cosmetic bag. Misgiving pricks up its ears in warning, followed by full-on emergency alert sirens when she drops the bag on the table, shoves the mirror into my hand, and moves behind me.

"Val. What are you doing?"

"You are so tense. Relax a little." Her fingers massage the knots in my shoulders. It hurts, but it's the good kind of hurt, and I feel my body easing under her touch. Her hands work their way up my neck to the base of my skull. "Even your hair is tight. I bet it makes your head ache."

I tug my head forward, away from her meddling hands, but she's already removed two heavy combs and is loosening the tight French braiding. I can't contain a sigh of relief as my hair loosens and cascades down over my shoulders.

"You have such beautiful hair," Val says. "Mine's already full-on gray if I don't dye it; yours hasn't even got a thread of silver. I don't know why you keep it tied up so tight."

"Vanity," I whisper.

"Earlene dyes hers, in case you didn't notice."

"I noticed."

"And that young one—Felicity—she's got a different style every week."

"You don't understand." My hands are shaking, my breath catching in my throat. Tears are about to follow.

"Thomas again?" Val asks.

Thomas again. Thomas always.

Getting my hair done was one of my last outward rebellions. Abigail was a baby, and the disconnect between the Liz I'd always been and Elizabeth, the wife Thomas was shaping me into, was beginning to frighten me. I'd dropped into a hair salon on impulse, carrying Abigail asleep in her car seat.

"What do you want done?" the hairdresser asked, running her fingers through my hair.

"I don't know. Something different."

"Let's go short," she said. "That's the new look. It will bring out your beautiful eyes and be so easy to maintain. Lots of moms go short."

I was feeling reckless and wild, a little desperate. "Do it," I told her.

But I didn't love it. I looked even less like me in the mirror, my head too small. My ears too big.

"What have you done?" Thomas demanded when I walked in the door.

Tears welled up in my eyes and spilled over, beyond my ability to hold them back.

"Vanity," he said. "I thought you were above that, Elizabeth, but I suppose all women are prone to it."

I cried harder, humiliated and broken, and his face softened. He drew me into his arms and stroked my shorn head. "Hush now. It's just a lesson. Forget your hair and the things of this world. Focus on what we are called to do. God gave you to me as a helper. So be that, Elizabeth. That's what you're here for."

His words sank into my vulnerable soul. As soon as my hair was long enough, I started braiding it without a word from him, a reminder to myself of the dangers of vanity.

Now, as I look in the mirror, I see a shadow of my younger self. I run my fingers through my hair. It feels decadent and luxurious. My face is softened by the waves. I look younger.

"How about a little makeup?" Val asks.

"I'm in mourning. The hair is more than enough."

She holds out a tube of lipstick. "Of course you're in mourning, darling, it's only been three months. But this isn't the eighteenth century. It's not like there are rules."

I laugh at that. "Are you kidding? There are rules, all right. It's just that they're invisible and nobody ever wrote them down." I'm shocked by the amount of bitterness in my voice. If I continue as I am, I'll end up like Earlene. A bitter, wretched, resentful old woman.

Lipstick is such a small thing. I uncap the tube and smooth a touch of color onto my lips.

"*Remember Eve and the apple,*" Thomas says inside my head. "*She had the whole garden of paradise, and yet she wanted more. Look where that got her.*"

"If this is paradise, you can have it," I retort.

"What's that?" Val blinks at me, and I laugh, shaking off a nearly physical sensation of bondage.

"Never mind. Are we going, or what?"

"I'll get my keys." She dances her way toward the door. I look at myself one more time in the mirror, guilt raising its ugly little head.

"It's only the one time," I whisper, just in case God and Thomas are listening.

Chapter Five

I hesitate at the back of the theater, lagging behind Val, enveloped in a haze of sensory memories. The hushed murmur of a waiting crowd filling the seats. The heat and glare of the spotlights. The controlled chaos behind the scenes. And a clear vision of my old self standing in the spotlight. She spreads her arms wide and smiles at me. *You're here. You came back.*

The vision shatters as a large man strides out to center stage. "New blood!" he booms, no need for a microphone, his voice projecting to the far corners of the room. "Excellent, excellent. Come on in, ladies. Have a seat. We were just getting started."

"Hey, Val! Come sit over here." A small woman waves at us from the second row. It's hard to guess her age. Her hair is snow white but thick and wavy, pulled back in a casual ponytail. Her eyes, black and inquisitive, belie the crow's-feet around them. The woman beside her is her polar opposite, well above average height, with drooping jowls and more than enough weight for the two of them. Her hair is short, thin, and mousy, but her eyes are a startling green and her smile reveals straight, very white teeth and a deep dimple in one cheek.

"Meet Tara and Bernie," Val says, settling into a seat beside the small woman. "Ladies, this is Liz."

I'm about to ask which name goes with which face when the large woman's gaze slips away from me and to the back of the theater.

"Ohhhh, there we go," she murmurs. "I could look at that until the cows come home."

A man stands at the back of the theater, not hesitant or undecided, just surveying the scene. I guess his age at fifty, mostly from the lines in his face. He's fit enough to be much younger, dressed in well-worn jeans and a flannel shirt.

"Bernie. Stop objectifying the poor man." The small woman, who must be Tara, elbows her in the ribs.

"Poor man, nothing. And you're just as bad."

"He's off duty," she says virtuously. "You can only ogle him when he's in uniform. There are rules."

"Volunteers as an EMT," Val supplies in response to my raised eyebrows. "Bernie has a thing for a man in uniform."

"Or preferably out of uniform." Bernie waggles her eyebrows.

"Lance, stop your dillydallying," the man on the stage booms. "Sashay on up here. We were waiting for you."

The man laughs, easily, and saunters up the aisle in no particular hurry, settling into the seat behind me.

Val squeezes my hand. "I'm so nervous!"

"You'll be great."

"For those who don't know me"—the man on the stage pauses for the wave of laughter that runs through the small group scattered through the front seats—"my name is William Shakespeare. Oh, I'm just kidding. Don't we all wish? William Smith, but my friends call me Bill. I'll be running the audition today. The play is *Just Say Yes* by Imelda D. Bainbridge. It's a romantic comedy about a woman having a midlife crisis. She makes a resolution to say yes to any opportunity that comes knocking, which gets her into all kinds of trouble and into an unexpected relationship. It's also a musical, so there will be some choral singing, and we'll be working with the community orchestra."

Bill claps his hands. "Okay, let's get started. We only have a few women of a certain age here, and we're going to have all of you read for Lacey, our female lead. We'll audition for the male lead at the same time. Anybody have a monologue you're dying to perform? No? Great, let's dive in. Val, come on up."

"Me?"

"Yes, you, young lady. And, Lance, why don't you get yourself up here since you're an old hand at this. Not that I'm calling you old, mind, har har."

The man behind me gets to his feet. Bernie whistles, and he turns toward her and bows, laughing, then skips the stairs and vaults up onto the stage.

I squeeze Val's hand. "Go on. They're waiting."

"I can't. I'm literally paralyzed." Her face beneath her makeup has gone white, her eyes are wide. I have a spark of fear that she's going to tip over sideways and I'll be compelled to try another round of fruitless CPR.

"Well?" Bill calls down. "Are you here to audition, or is this a spectator sport?"

"Yes. I—I just don't want to go first."

"Fair enough." His eyes slide over Val and rest on me. "I guess you're up. What's your name?"

"This is Liz," Val supplies when I don't answer.

I gaze up at him in dismay. I can't say no right after Val. Everybody is staring my way. Lance grins at me conspiratorially as if the two of us share a secret.

"Don't be shy," Bill booms. "We're all friends here. Come on up."

"Well, go on." Val's face is a study in innocence, but I have my doubts. This is not her first encounter with this theater crowd, and I suspect she knew exactly how this was going to play out.

"You and I are going to have a long talk later," I whisper.

She laughs. "Go on. You'll be great."

It's just an audition, I tell myself. I'm not going to actually get or take a part. Tomorrow I'll go back to my regularly scheduled life. I feel a shift and transformation as I climb the steps. My spine straightens, my head comes up. I feel my gait smooth and lengthen into a forgotten confidence.

Lance meets me at center stage, and reaches out to shake my hand. "Welcome to bedlam."

Up close, his eyes are blue. His hand is warm, calloused, and he shakes mine with conviction, as if I'm an equal.

"Okay, you two, let's get started." Bill hands us each a dog-eared script, open to act 1, scene 2. "Take a minute to scan the lines and start when you're ready."

I feel like I've developed super senses. I hear the once-familiar rustling and whispering from the theater seats. The buzz of overhead lights. Bill is in my peripheral vision, just off to my right.

"Ready?" Lance asks.

I glance up from the paper. He's relaxed, easy, and I nod.

Let's get this over with, Elizabeth says.

Bring it on, I'm ready, Inner Liz counters.

Lance takes a step toward me, bringing him inside my comfort bubble, front and center and dominating my senses. Bill fades from my peripheral vision. My awareness of whispers and buzzing lights goes with him. I breathe in the scent of clean sweat and fabric softener and a hint of cologne. My eyes travel up from the page and encounter a broad chest, the shirt open at the collar revealing a sunbrowned neck. His eyes gaze into mine with an intensity that flutters my breath and brings blood rushing to my cheeks. An almost-forgotten sensation whispers awake, low in my belly.

Guilt follows hard on its heels, and I twist the wedding band on my finger. What is wrong with me? I should not be feeling this, not toward a stranger, not so soon after Thomas's death. It's not proper.

"I don't see what propriety has to do with anything," Lance says, his voice passionate, intense.

My eyes widen. My lips part. It's as if he's read my mind, and I'm desperately searching for something to say when he continues, "We're here now. We've met. Neither one of us is getting any younger."

All of the breath leaves my body in a sharp exhale of relief and embarrassment. I am an idiot. He is only reading lines from the play. I take a small step back and put a hand over my heart.

"Are you telling me I'm old?"

"You're not young."

"And you're an ass." I turn half away from him, take a step to the side. He intercepts me, puts a restraining hand on my arm.

"Lacey. Don't be that way. I'm only saying—"

"What? Please. Enlighten me." I infuse years of pent-up sarcasm into my voice.

Lance's tone shifts to pleading. "Don't be like that. I'm saying that you *will* be old. Someday. And maybe you'll wish, when you're rocking in a nursing home chair, that you'd said yes to something. Anything." Lance takes a step closer so we are separated by no more than a breath. My eyes are drawn up again to meet his. "Say yes to me. That's a start."

I can see the dark stubble of whiskers along his jaw, a shaving nick on his chin. Can feel his breath on my face, warm, coffee scented. His eyes have tiny flecks of amber mixed into the blue, and they look startled, as if something about me has surprised him.

The moment shatters in a burst of applause.

"Nicely done, Lacey," Lance says, bowing. He swings down off the stage with a flair, once again bypassing the stairs, to applause from the seats below.

Acting. It was all just acting. So why are my knees trembling, and why can't I catch my breath? I manage to make it down the stairs and back to the safety of my seat. Val hugs me, laughing. "That was amazing!

How am I supposed to follow that performance? Fess up. You've been in plays before!"

"It's been so long, Val. In another life."

"Total chemistry between you two," Tara says. "That was awesome!"

"Will it burn if we touch you?" Bernie reaches behind Val and Tara and pokes at my shoulder, then shakes her fingers while making sizzling noises.

I press my palms against my hot cheeks, embarrassed but exhilarated, loving the easy camaraderie.

"You ready now, Val?" Bill booms from the stage.

"After that? Totally wishing I'd gone first." But she gets up, laughing, and takes center stage together with a soft-bellied, balding guy named Geoff.

Val does well, although Geoff stumbles over his lines and has nowhere near the stage presence of Lance. When everybody has had a chance to read, Bill leads us through some choral singing and simple choreography. All of it is familiar, easy, except for my husband's voice, which is ever present in my head.

"You don't belong here, Elizabeth. This is not the Lord's work."

Just this one time, I answer back, over and over. *Just tonight.*

"Ladies, gentleman," Bill says when the last notes of music fade away. "That is it for tonight's festivities. Thank you for coming out to audition. Parts will be listed on the website by Saturday night. If you don't get a role, please help us out backstage. We can use everybody somewhere."

Outside it's cold and moving into dark, the last colors of sunset vivid in the west. It feels like it's going to freeze tonight. I get in the car, snuggling into my jacket.

"You were so awesome!" Val says, starting the engine and turning up the heat. "You are totally landing a role!"

"And you set me up! You knew they'd ask me to audition."

She giggles. "I can neither confirm nor deny the truth of that allegation."

"Look, Val. I see what you're trying to do. It was fun. But you know I can't really be in the play."

"You can if you want to."

I feel tired, all at once, all of the excitement evaporating and leaving me with the heaviness of my same old life.

"The rehearsal schedule is impossible. To run off for one night is one thing. But it's not just the knitting circle. There's the women's prayer meeting, and the nursing home singing group, and hospital visitation, and—"

"Do you really like doing all that shit?"

"It doesn't matter what I like."

I watch the colors leach out of the sky as night rolls in. My time to play around with theater is over and gone. I'm not Lacey, the character in the play, shaking up her world by saying yes to everything. If there was a time to break out of this life I'm living, I missed the turnoff. It's too late for me.

Chapter Six

Saturday morning, Val shows up at my door with fresh doughnuts, lattes, and another plan.

"Let's go shopping," she says, licking sugar off her fingers.

I know she doesn't mean groceries. I also know she hasn't given up on dragging me into the theater production. My mouth is full, and I chew slowly, following it up with a swallow of coffee to buy me time for the right response.

"Not in the budget," I say.

"Come on, Liz," Val persists. "We're not talking a complete new wardrobe. You need a pair of jeans. A new shirt. How long has it been since you bought something for yourself just because?"

Temptation stirs.

"Beware vanity," Thomas warns. *"You have plenty of clothes."*

A visual of his closet jolts me. The row of quality suits. The multiple pairs of mirror-gloss shoes. "I represent God," he'd said once when I remonstrated about the price of a shirt and tie. "It's important to look my best."

My job was to represent humility and sacrifice, to look neat and practical but never beautiful. I have two pairs of perfectly serviceable shoes and a wardrobe designed to mix and match, all in sober shades of brown, gray, and black. All boring. All old.

I feel my inner Liz stir and perk up her ears at the idea of buying new clothes. The audition caper woke her up, and she's been restless ever since. *Let's do it,* she whispers. *Every woman deserves new clothes once in a while.*

The truth is that our house and car are paid for, and I have no other debt. With the widow pension I get from Social Security, along with the funds from a life insurance policy Thomas bought years ago, I've been able to pay all of my bills and put a little bit aside. The only reason clothes aren't in the budget is because they've never been in the budget.

"All right," I hear myself saying, shocked at my own words. "Let's go shopping."

~

"This is one time I wish we lived in Spokane," Val laments as soon as she gets me in the car. "Our choices here are so limited."

"Our choices here are Walmart. And no, I am not letting you drag me off to Spokane."

"Fine. But we are not going to Walmart, either." She drives into the parking lot of North 40, and I stare at her, confused.

"Are we buying farming supplies?"

"Oh my God! You've never even been in here. Come on." She drags me into the store, and I'm surprised to discover jeans, shirts, even a few casual dresses hanging on racks at the far end of the store.

I don't know what size I am, but Val looks me over, grabs up an armful of jeans and shirts, and herds me into a changing room.

A few minutes later, I'm looking in the mirror at a woman who resembles the long-ago Liz more than I ever thought possible. Faded jeans rest low on my hips, paired with a soft plaid shirt, open at the throat, rolled up at the cuffs. My fingers reach to fasten the top button, but Val pulls my hands away. "Even you are allowed to reveal your throat. Well, what do you think?"

"You look like a floozy, Elizabeth."

It's growing increasingly easy to ignore Thomas's commentary.

I don't look like a floozy at all. I look . . . free. Unfettered. About twenty years younger.

"I can't possibly wear this," I say, but I can't take my eyes off my image in the mirror.

"You keep saying that. I don't think it means what you think it means."

We both laugh, and then Val says, "Either you buy these, or I'm buying them for you. You need a change."

"I don't think—"

"People wear jeans, Liz. Even that Earlene woman from your church wears jeans."

"Not this kind of jeans."

"You want mom jeans? I mean, you could, but you don't need to. You have a body people twenty years younger would be happy for."

The woman in the mirror looks alive, awake. Inner Liz has become Outer Liz. The thought of changing back into my skirt and blouse fills me with loathing and a hot rebellion. I don't want to lose that self again.

"Can I wear this home?"

"Of course you can! People do it all the time."

I buy two pairs of jeans. The plaid shirt and another flowered one. Two T-shirts.

When we walk out of the store, I feel different. Stronger, more adventurous. When Val suggests a detour into the hair salon right next door, I agree to that, too. I let the stylist chop my hair off so that it just grazes my shoulders.

"Feels good, right?" Val asks in the car.

I run my fingers through my silky new curls. My head feels so light, like I might float up out of my seat if the belt weren't anchoring me.

"It's not about what I love. It's about—"

"Duty and sacrifice and self-immolation. Only it's not, Liz. You don't have to do any of that shit if you don't want to."

I shift in my seat and study her profile. I know she works long hours, that the ends barely meet. This car is probably twenty years old. But she seems so fully alive, so very much Val. As if she knows who she is and is happy being that woman.

"What's your story?" I ask, breaking my rule of never pushing into other people's business.

"What do you mean?"

"You sound like you know something about duty and sacrifice."

Val grimaces. "Oh, that. Yeah. When I was young, I married a guy who believed he was the center of the universe. He didn't think much of women. All the clichés. Come when I call, do what I tell you, and don't cry or I'll give you something to cry about."

"And?"

"Oh—I left him. I was tired of him giving me something to cry about. And Lenny was in the middle of it. One day, when he was about four, my sweet little boy looked up at me with his chubby cheeks and his innocent face and said, 'Give me a cookie now, woman. Or else.' His father laughed like it was the funniest thing in the world. But I cried. I could see the kind of man Lenny was going to be if I stayed. I packed us both up, moved us out. I couldn't get full custody, but I did what I could, and the boy respects me. And now he respects his wife."

I'm silent, absorbing this.

Val shoots me a sideways glance. "I know your church isn't big on divorce. I hope you don't think less of me."

"Val! Of course not."

"I've overheard some of your friends and what they think of me." A tinge of bitterness darkens her tone.

"They are not my friends. Honestly? I was just thinking how strong you are, and how much I admire you."

"You? Admire me? That's crazy, Liz. I'm a nobody."

A strong, resilient nobody. Thomas preached against divorce, exhorting women to stand by their men and their marriages because it was the godly thing to do. So many weeping women came to him for guidance, some with black eyes and swollen lips. He sent them home to their husbands, advising them to pray for a better marriage. I disagreed with him, willed them to run away, far and fast. But I said nothing. Did nothing.

What would my relationship with Abigail be like if I'd walked away from my marriage? Would she have grown to respect me? Or would we be worse off than we already are?

As if I've somehow summoned her, Abigail's car is parked in the driveway. A rush of joy shifts immediately to dark foreboding. She calls nearly every day to check on me, to ask how I am eating and about my health, but I haven't seen her in a month.

"Think about the play," Val calls after me as I run toward the house. I wave, but my mind is on anything but a drama production. Abigail here, today, means something terrible has happened.

Chapter Seven

I burst through the door with words already escaping my lips.

"What's the matter? Are you okay?"

My eyes scan my daughter, looking for the hurt. She's too thin, but then, she always has been. Her hair, darker than mine, is neatly braided as usual. She looks tired, but other than that, I don't see a mark on her. While I'm looking her over, she's also assessing me. Her lips tighten in disapproval.

"You've changed your hair."

I touch a guilty hand to my head. "You like?"

"I liked it the old way. Where have you been?"

"Getting my hair cut." I turn away to hide my hurt at her criticism and the defensive anger that rises with it, setting down my shopping bags in the hope she won't ask to see what's in them. "If I'd known you were coming, I would have been here. Did your schedule shift? I thought you were working this weekend."

Abigail has been cleaning. The afghan I left rumpled on the couch is precisely folded. My novel has disappeared, along with all evidence of doughnuts and latte cups. And the ugly vase that I tucked into the corner of the bookcase has been moved back to its place at the precise center of the coffee table.

More criticism, but at least of the silent variety. I wait for her to tell me why she is here, but she maintains her silence, and I finally am the one to break it. "What's going on? How long are you staying?"

"Earlene called. She was worried."

"You came to check on me because of Earlene?" Laughter bubbles up but fizzles out before it reaches my lips. Thursday evening. Auditions. The abandoned knitting circle. "Oh, honey. I'm perfectly fine. You know how Earlene is."

"In this case, she seems to have a point."

"Really? Enlighten me."

Inner Liz is closer to the surface than she used to be, and I turn to face my daughter, long-dormant defiance stiffening my spine. I can pretty much guess what is about to come. She'll lead off with one of her father's favorites, consorting with unbelievers, followed by commentary on my hair and my inappropriate new clothes, and end with my irresponsible behavior around the knitting circle.

Abigail hesitates, which is completely unlike her, and I brace myself. Maybe I'm wrong. Maybe it won't be the usual lecture at all, but something worse, something I can't see coming.

"There are pickles in the refrigerator," she says in a scathing tone.

"Earlene called you about pickles?" I was prepared to defend myself, but I'm disarmed by bewilderment.

"Dad hates pickles. You never buy pickles."

I can't think of a single word to say. All I can do is stand there, wishing things were different between us, that we knew how to communicate like normal people. Thomas was our anchor; without him, we are adrift in uncharted seas.

Abigail clenches her hands into fists. Her voice rises. "My entire life, there has never been a jar of pickles in the refrigerator. Why now?"

Anger rises, hot and bitter, born of years of being told what I can and cannot do, even to the extent of what I can eat and when and where. At the same time, I feel the grief underneath her words; I want to soothe and comfort her. So I keep my tone as level as I can and offer an explanation rather than a retort.

"I was at the grocery store last week, buying mustard, and I walked by the pickle section. Bread-and-butter pickles. Hot pickles. Sweet. Gherkin. Dill. And I remembered that before I got married I loved pickles. When I was a kid, they were my favorite food and I ate them with everything, even for breakfast. How could I forget something like that? People all over the world eat pickles every day. It's not like they are . . . *evil* or something. The apostle Paul never mentioned them, even once! There is absolutely no reason in the world why I shouldn't eat them, too, other than that your father didn't like them."

As soon as I'm done, I'm sorry.

Abigail's whole body is one clenched muscle of grief and resistance. Tears trickle down her cheeks, and she brushes them off with the backs of her hands.

My anger vanishes as rapidly as it appeared, leaving a dull gray weariness in its wake. "I know you miss him," I say, gently now. "But he's not coming back. Everything has changed, and we have to change, too."

"*You* don't. You don't, and the house doesn't."

"But I do, Abigail. It's inevitable. Listen—"

"There's absolutely no reason why you can't do things the way you've always done them, keep the house the way you've always kept it. None."

"What you're saying is that you want the house to be a museum and me to be a wax sculpture. That's not fair, Abigail."

"I didn't say you had to be a sculpture. I'm just asking that you conduct yourself—"

"The way he would have wanted me to. Is that it?"

"Yes! Why is that so hard?"

"Because I'm a human being."

"Oh, for heaven's sake, Mother. Don't be so melodramatic. Just . . . behave with some decorum. Is that too much to ask?"

I want to tell her that it depends on what she means by "decorum," but I already know the answer. I'm the widow of a godly man. I am expected to live out the rest of my days quietly doing good works. And Abigail, who has always worked so hard to control her world, will fight to keep me and the house from changing.

Abigail retreats into professional mode. "Don't be too hard on yourself," she says. "Grief affects people in all kinds of ways. Are you sleeping? Eating?"

"I live on a diet of pickles and French fries. Haven't slept in a week. Is that what you want to hear?"

She flings her hands up in frustration. "Oh, good grief! I'm just trying to take care of you. You're acting like a child."

"Maybe it would help if you stopped treating me like one. Has it occurred to you that I can take care of myself?"

"You're not making a very good case for that, I have to say. Don't take this as criticism, Mother. You've been very brave, but you're not young anymore, and I know this has been a terrible stress. But you are not yourself right now."

"You think all there is of me is Mrs. Lightsey, your mother, the pastor's wife."

"But that *is* who you are! You're not making any sense."

"I prefer to go by Liz, did you know that? Your father was the first one to call me Elizabeth. I was a tomboy who loved to climb trees and run barefoot. I was going to write plays, and maybe be an actress when I grew up."

"When I grew older, I put away childish things," Abigail says.

"Don't you quote scripture at me." I'm the one who is shouting now. If I hear one more quote from the ubiquitous apostle Paul, I am going to scream. Straightening my spine, standing as tall as I possibly can, I reach for a voice of authority, rusty with disuse, and plant my hands on my hips. I have something to say, and for once, I am going to say it instead of keeping it to myself or writing it in my journal later.

"Now you listen to me. Your father's death was sudden and tragic, and there is nothing we can do to change that, or to bring him back. But you and I are still alive, still here. And if I'm locked into spending the rest of my life never changing, never growing anywhere except old, then I might as well be dead and buried in a grave beside him."

A loud silence swirls around us. Abigail's face pales. She takes a step toward me, one hand outstretched. "Mom. Are you thinking about—harming yourself?"

"Oh, for the love of God, no! You aren't listening to me!"

She draws a deep breath. Her hand drops to her side and her jaw tightens. "That settles it. I'm moving home."

I stare at her with my mouth open, emotions rattling through me like a freight train.

Excitement at the idea of the chance to build a relationship with my daughter.

Doom for the tiny bit of freedom I've garnered.

Guilt at the idea that she is going to sacrifice her life and come home to play the martyr.

The guilt wins. "You don't need to move home, Abigail. I'm fine. You have a life in Spokane."

"It's not open for discussion. I should have done this right away. You need me. I'll give notice and apply at the clinic and the hospital. Colville is always short on nurses."

"But you love your job! We don't have a trauma center here."

She shrugs as if this doesn't matter. "Honor your father and your mother," she says. "I promised Daddy I'd take care of you if anything happened to him. I haven't done that."

"That doesn't mean you have to give up your life, Abigail. Do what makes you happy."

It's like I haven't even spoken. "I'll move back into my old room. I'll apply on Monday. I already work for Providence, so it shouldn't take long."

I can't let her do this. Having Abigail home won't improve our relationship; it will cement us both into the adversarial positions we've developed over the years. But how can I tell my daughter that I don't want her here? Maybe she needs this. Maybe she even needs me.

Before I can think of a single thing to say, Val knocks and barges in without waiting for an answer. "Audition results are already up! You are not going to believe this!"

She flings her arms around me and spins me around, laughing and squealing.

"Did you get the part?" I ask when she lets me go and I can breathe again.

"Me? Oh, I got a part. But so did you. You got Lacey! You're going to be the lead!"

I cling to Val to steady my head, still spinning from our wild whirling.

"I'm sorry, what?"

"You are Lacey! Lance is Darcy. And—"

"But, you wanted to be Lacey."

Val shrugs. "I don't have time for all of the lead rehearsals. I'd have to miss for work. But you can totally do this. We just need to cancel all of your shit!"

"Cancel what, exactly?" Abigail's tone is frosty, disapproving.

Reality settles onto my shoulders, heavy and dull. "I'm not canceling anything. You know I can't do this, Val. I never even meant to audition."

"Right? That's the total fun of the thing! And you and Lance will be perfect together. Come on, Liz, it will be good for you."

Just for an instant, I entertain the possibility. This is my chance to break out of my stifling routine, to get back to a world I have always loved. Weeks of rehearsals in place of drudgery. Me and Lance, onstage together. I'm dizzy again for a whole different reason.

Abigail glances from me to Val and back again. "You auditioned for a play?" She says it as if I'd auditioned to be a pole dancer instead of for community theater. "Mother! What will people think?"

She turns on Val. "This is your doing. Mom's vulnerable, and you've taken advantage of that, dragging her away from her friends and her support system. Leading her into temptation. This needs to stop."

Val looks like she's been slapped. Abigail breathes like a bull about to charge.

I put my hand on Val's arm. "Thank you. For everything. But I really can't. Will you explain to Bill?"

Her eyes meet mine, and I shrink away from the hurt and disappointment I read there.

"No," she says. "You can tell him yourself."

Chapter Eight

The next morning, Abigail is up before me. When I shuffle into the kitchen, oatmeal bubbles on the stove. The coffeepot is on, and I pour myself a mug, add cream, and take my first sacred morning sip. It tastes all wrong, flavorless and thin. My face twists into a grimace.

"Which beans did you use?"

Abigail, busy slicing an apple, doesn't look up. "It's decaf."

"Well, that explains everything." I set the mug down on the counter with a little more force than intended.

"Sleep is important," she says. "Caffeine is—"

"Necessary to both of us surviving the morning. Did you want some of this before I dump it? Because I am making real coffee." I open the cupboard door to grab my usual blend, but it has been replaced. New bag. New brand. 100 percent decaffeinated.

"I've made you a healthy breakfast," Abigail continues. "Come eat. And then we'll get ready for church."

My future plays out before my eyes. Life with Abigail will be as regimented and controlled as it was with Thomas, only—healthier. Without caffeine. The room closes in around me. I can't breathe. My hand goes to my chest, and I'm aware that I'm gasping.

"Mom?" Abigail queries. "Mom? Are you okay?"

I look at her, the kitchen, the hijacked coffeepot. My throat clogs with the smell of oatmeal, a food I've detested since I was a child.

I have to get out of this house.

Without another word, I scoop up my purse and make a break for the front door, Abigail on my heels. I snag my keys on the way out and flee to my car, slamming the door behind me and hitting the locks. I'm in my pajamas and slippers, hair uncombed, but I don't care about anything except getting away.

Abigail pounds on my window as I start the car and back out of the driveway. I watch her in my rearview, growing smaller and smaller. And then I turn a corner and she is gone.

I drive aimlessly, windows open, even though it's still too cool for that and I'm not properly dressed. The wind helps me feel free, makes it easier to catch my breath. When the panic passes and my heart settles to a reasonable rate and rhythm, I head into town.

First thing, I grab coffee and a breakfast bar from Ritzes drive-through. Coffee, real coffee, the way God intended it with caffeine included, switches on my brain. The sugar from the breakfast bar feeds my inner rebel, and I begin to feel human again, a woman with at least the illusion of control over her own life. But I am not ready to go home and have a come-to-Jesus conversation with my daughter, and I am certainly not going to church.

Instead, I drive all the way out to Bradbury Beach, losing myself in the twists and turns of the drive, the forests, the occasional vistas of the Columbia River. I park in the lot, wishing I had decent clothes, and shoes instead of slippers, so I could get out and walk. But I just sit in my car, gazing out at the river and sky, breathing, searching for the magic answer that will free me and my daughter from the tangle we're in.

It feels like Thomas has reached out from the grave to control us both. I don't want to live the life he foisted on me. And I don't want my daughter to give up the life I know she wants and deserves. But she's as stubborn as he was, and has the desperation of grief, youth, and indoctrination behind her.

My phone rings. Again.

It's been ringing and chiming at intervals since I left home, and I know that Abigail is worried and I'm being selfish. I should at least let her know that I'm alive.

So I answer without looking at the call display.

"Elizabeth Lightsey?"

I try to be polite to telemarketers, telling myself they are just people trying to make a living, but today politeness comes hard. "Please take me off your list."

"Your daughter asked me to call."

My thumb hovers over the disconnect button.

"Maybe it would help if I introduce myself," the caller says. "My name is Mavis, and I'm a counselor at NEW Hope."

A jolt of electricity goes through me, like lightning from on high.

"Abigail is worried about you."

"Abigail is a worrier."

"Mrs. Lightsey. Elizabeth. Your daughter says you told her you want to die, and that you drove off this morning in a highly emotional state and she has no idea where you are."

"You have got to be kidding." I lean my head back and take a breath.

"Can you tell me where you are right now?"

"No. I mean, I could, but I'm fine. There's no need. Seriously. Abigail has completely overreacted."

The woman's voice, warm, compassionate, professional, is relentless. "Your daughter tells me she's a nurse and knows the signs of suicidal behavior. We would all feel so much better if you—"

"This is not about her, or you, or how any of you feel!" I snap, my emotions finally deciding which direction they want to go. Not laughter, not grief, but pure, unadulterated anger. At this moment, what I want more than anything in the world is to turn my meddling, controlling daughter over my knee and spank her.

"Of course not," the woman says soothingly. "And I'd love to help you."

"I am not planning on dying anytime soon."

"Can you tell me more about what 'soon' means to you?"

I take one breath, and then another. I know how the mental health crisis system works. I've called them at Thomas's request, listened as they interviewed suicidal people right in my own living room. If this woman on the phone isn't satisfied that I'm safe, she could get a trace on my cell phone. Come after me with a deputy, drag me in for a psych evaluation and maybe even detention. Given that Abigail is a professional, they'll give her word more weight than mine.

I have to tell this woman something, but I resent the intrusion into my life. I don't want to rehash the morning's scene with Abigail or get into my untapped reservoir of guilt or talk about my lack of proper grief over my husband's death or the crushing boredom that threatens to consume me. I choose my words carefully, laying them out in my mind before I speak.

"Listen—it's Mavis, yes? Let me be very clear, Mavis. What I said to my daughter was that I would rather die than continue to live my life as I have been. But I have no intention of doing that, do you understand? What I meant to tell her is that I am choosing to explore life and expand my horizons. I do not think about dying. I have no plan to end my life."

I hear typing on the other end of the line as Mavis records my comment. Perfect. A chunk of my life is now documented in the mental health crisis system.

"I'm glad to hear that, Elizabeth," she says after a moment. "I'm sure your daughter will be relieved—"

"My daughter needs to mind her own business."

To my surprise, the woman laughs. "Chances are good she's having difficulty with her own grief process, and so is hypervigilant about yours. Good for you, for expanding your horizons. Maybe you could let her know you are all right? She sounded quite frantic when she called."

"I will do that, forthwith."

"And if you ever need to talk, we do have counseling available. And I have a crisis line number I'd like to give you, as well. Just in case."

"Sure. Thank you." I pretend to write down the number that I have no intention of calling, even asking her to repeat it for clarification.

When the call disconnects, something hot and fierce bubbles up inside of me at the thought of being forced back into the old, monotonous life. This is no flash of anger, no transient emotion. I feel bigger, more alive, and I can't—won't—go back to that small, pale existence. Not for the sake of the church, not even for Abigail.

I dial Val, and when she answers, I say one single word.

"Yes."

Chapter Nine

When I get home, Abigail meets me at the door, not tearstained and worried but imperious and outraged. "I can't believe you ran off like that! Do you want to explain yourself?"

Her tone sparks my own anger. "I don't need to explain myself to you." I brush by her and drop my purse on the couch.

"You've been gone for hours! I didn't know where you were!"

"I'm all grown up, Abigail. I'm not required to tell you where I'm going."

"You were upset. You skipped church. You left the house *in your pajamas!*"

I raise my eyebrows, making a point of looking her over from head to toe. "*You're* upset. You are in *your* pajamas."

Abigail runs a hand over her nightshirt, eyes widening, as if startled to discover this is the truth. "But *I'm* not . . ." She stops, clearly biting back words.

"Let's get something very clear." I kick off my slippers, leaving them where they fall instead of lining them up in the expected orderly fashion. "I'm not planning suicide. And you will not, ever, invade my privacy like that again."

Abigail blinks, takes a step back. I realize I've been shouting and that it feels good to shout. I'm tired of silencing my emotions, tired of letting everybody tell me what to do.

"I'll do my own thinking. I will drink my own coffee and eat whatever the hell I feel like for breakfast. Do you hear me?"

"I'm just trying to—"

"I know what you're trying to do. I have enough people in this town with their noses in my personal life. If you're planning to live at home, you'd better get that straight right now. You're not going to tell me what to do."

Abigail's own temper flares. "I don't appreciate your tone or your language. I'm only trying—"

"You're trying to live my life for me."

"That's ridiculous!"

"Is it? Where's my coffee? What happened to the novel I left on the couch last night?"

Abigail lifts her chin. "It was a trashy romance. I'll buy you something more—"

"Fitting?" I laugh, bitterly. "You're going to control my reading material, too? What did you do with my book?"

"I threw it away."

"You did what?"

"Daddy would—"

"He's not here! What did you do with it?" I stomp into the kitchen, open the trash can. Sure enough, there is my half-finished book, a blob of oatmeal glommed onto the cover.

"I can't believe you threw away my book!"

"I can't believe you were reading that garbage! It's disgraceful."

"How do you know? Did *you* read it?"

"I looked at the cover. An objectified woman, broadcasting her wares for the men—"

I laugh again, this time for real. "That is a very strong woman with magical powers. Any man who dares to objectify her is probably going to be very sorry. And maybe dead."

Last night I'd left said heroine in the middle of a life-and-death dilemma, and I really want to know what happens. There's no bookstore in Colville, and the soonest I can get a replacement is through two-day delivery from mail order. I don't have an e-reader, although I can suddenly see the appeal. Abigail would think three times before throwing away an electronic device.

I fish out my book.

"Mother! It's covered in germs."

"I don't see any germs." But I do see oatmeal. And coffee grounds. Decaf coffee grounds, insult to injury. The cover and half the pages are soaked and turning brown.

Abigail snatches the book from my hands and shoves it back into the trash. Turns on the water in the sink and scrubs her hands with soap.

"This is all the influence of that Val person. You need to stop hanging out with her."

"Val is my friend, and I will hang out with her as much as I want."

Abigail glares at me, both hands on her hips, and all of a sudden, the whole scene strikes me as funny. We've switched places somehow, she and I. She's acting like the mother, I'm the rebellious teenager. The more I think about it, the funnier it gets, and I burst out in the sort of belly laugh I didn't know I was capable of.

"I don't see anything funny."

I wipe my eyes and draw in a steadying breath. "Honey, I've been reading these books since before you were born. I used to hide them from your father, but I'm not going to hide them from you, because you are not the boss of me. You know what Val reads? Science fiction. Hard-core. Wouldn't touch a fantasy romance if she was stranded on a desert island."

Emotions chase themselves over Abigail's face, visible for once, and I wait to see which one is going to land. She traverses through bewildered and worried and winds up right back at anger.

"You—you hypocrite! All those Bible storybooks you made me read as a child. The true-life inspiration stories when I was a teenager. And all the time you were reading fantasy?"

A memory hits, as clear as if it happened yesterday.

Abigail sits in her father's lap in the big chair in the living room, watching the words as he reads. It's the story of Peter walking on the water, a story she's heard a hundred times and knows from memory.

All at once, in the middle of the part where Peter begins to sink because of his lack of faith, she dares to interrupt, laying her little hand flat over the page and looking up into her father's face.

"How come there are no girl disciples?"

Thomas, in a relaxed and indulgent mood, laughs and hugs her tighter, planting a kiss on top of her head. "Women can't be disciples."

I'm sitting in my chair across from him, knitting, because it makes him happy when I knit and I love the moments when he reads to our daughter. My fingers fumble, and I drop a stitch, sensing what is coming, feeling it already like a strike to my heart.

Abigail looks up into his face. "Why?"

"Women are meant to take care of men—"

"Well, then, if there had been a woman there, she could have taken care of Peter."

"He had Jesus to take care of him."

"But," Abigail says again, "there are no girls in any of the stories."

"There's Mary and Martha," I say quietly, trying to forestall where this conversation must, inevitably, end.

"But they don't do anything interesting. I want to walk on the water," Abigail says. *"And feed the people the fish and bread. And—"*

"Are we going to finish the story or not?" Thomas's limited supply of patience is up. So is Abigail's.

"Not." She slams the book shut with her little-girl hands. "I want to read a story about a girl who does something interesting."

"Do something with this, would you, Elizabeth?" Thomas says, leaving me with a bag I didn't pack and do not want to carry.

I keep my eyes on my knitting. "Well, there's Esther—"

"That's a stupid story!" Abigail says. "All she does is get dressed up and talk to the king. I want to be like David and kill giants. Why can't I be a man?"

"Unfortunately, you are not." Thomas bites these words off, one a time, and I know they're meant for me. I, the woman put on this planet to be his particular helpmate, have failed to give him a son. "A woman is on this earth to be a helper for men." He's not shouting, but it's his angry voice. His arm isn't around Abigail anymore, and she's perched unsupported on his lap. She starts to cry, but silently, because even at four she knows that her tears will not be tolerated.

"Women who try to be men are a disgrace and an abomination. I will not hear words like this from you again, you understand?" Abigail nods, but it's not enough. Thomas grabs her chin and forces her to look up at him. "Tell me."

"I understand." Her voice is crumpled with tears.

My heart is breaking, breaking, and breaking again.

"Go to your room," he says. "Elizabeth, go read her the story of Adam and Eve. It's time she understands her place in this world."

Abigail flees the room and burrows, sobbing, into her bed. I sit down beside her and smooth her hair, stroke circles on her back.

"Are you going to read me the Eve story?" she asks after a long time, rolling over to look up at me. Her little hand touches my cheek and comes away wet with tears. "Why are you crying, Mommy?"

I'm about to tell her that I'm sad, too, about the lack of girl disciples. I'm about to suggest a different kind of story, about a girl named Joan of Arc, but I hear approaching footsteps, and then Thomas looms in the doorway.

"You're not reading," he says.

And the best I can bring myself to do for my daughter in that moment is to say, "I think she's had enough of stories for tonight."

Now my little girl is all grown up, so very much the woman I was complicit in raising her to be. I would give anything to have that moment back. I'd tell her about Joan of Arc, and the warrior queens of the Amazon. I'd find her books about women who were doctors and missionaries, explorers and scientists. Women who went to space and to war.

"I'm sorry," I whisper, the only thing I can do, and, of course, she takes that all wrong.

"I forgive you. Just don't read them anymore."

"Oh, I'm not remotely sorry for reading the books," I clarify, tilting up my chin. "I'm sorry I hid the books from you. I'm sorry I didn't insist on other things for you to read. But it's not too late! We can both read whatever we want to, now."

She stands there, hands on her hips, looking at me, and I begin to hope we'll have a moment of breakthrough, of connection.

"You don't understand the first thing about anything," she says. Then she turns her back and stalks away, off to her bedroom, slamming the door behind her.

Chapter Ten

Abigail doesn't come out of her room all afternoon.

Three times, I walk to her door and raise my hand to knock, wanting to tell her I'm sorry, to make things right between us. But what would I be apologizing for? I can't say what she wants to hear—that I'm sorry about reading novels, or changing my hair, or finding a different way to be. And it doesn't seem like the right time to tell her I'm going to be in the play.

I'm staring into the fridge, trying to think of something to fix for dinner, when my phone chimes with a text message.

Val: Some of the cast is meeting for dinner to celebrate. Rancho Chico. 5:30. Be there.

Liz: I don't know. Abigail is here.

Val: She's a grown-up. Pretty sure she can find herself some dinner.

Val: Or you could bring her leftovers.

I flirt with temptation. Abigail is barricaded in her room, and even if she comes out, dinner will consist of an awkward truce, at best. More likely it will turn into another battle. Besides, this is as good a chance as any to signal that I'm a free and independent woman living her own life.

I leave a note on the counter. *Sorry to abandon you, but I've gone out for dinner. Leftovers in the fridge. Love you.*

~

When I walk into Rancho Chico, the group is already there, seated around a long table. Tara and Bernie are both nearly to the bottom of what I think are margaritas. Lance holds a glass half full of beer. I just have time to hesitate, shy and uncertain, before Bernie shouts, "Lacey! Our leading lady has arrived!"

Val gets up and hugs me while the rest raise their glasses and cheer. There is one empty chair between Lance and Geoff, a fat paper script sitting where the plate should be. Both men get up and pull out the chair for me with an exaggerated flourish.

"Thank you," I murmur, grateful for the dim lighting as the blood rushes to my face.

"About time," Bernie says. "I was about to die of starvation."

Tara snorts and finishes what's in her glass. "I think it would take a little longer than that. Lacey, have you met the rest of this illustrious cast?"

"No, she has not," Bernie cuts in. "I'll do the honors. I'm Grace, your rival for Darcy's affections. You also already know Lynetta"—Tara waves her empty glass—"and your best pal Emma."

Val grins and ducks her head.

I feel dizzy and overwhelmed, although I get the gist of this introduction game.

"Bernie," I start to ask, and am immediately interrupted by a loud chorus of "Drink!" and everybody else at the table picks up a glass and swallows.

"Come on, Lacey. Drink up." Geoff nudges a glass a little closer to me. "Anytime one of us slips and uses real instead of character names, we all take a drink."

I swirl the glass, greenish liquid over ice cubes with a frosted rim. Thomas did not approve of alcohol, and my only drinking experience consists of the occasional glass of wine when it's offered at somebody else's home.

"What is it?"

"Your favorite," Lance—no, Darcy—says beside me. "Lime margarita on the rocks."

I take a careful tiny sip. Salt, followed by lime and something sharper. It tastes good, and I take a bigger swallow.

"All of your drinks are on us tonight," Bernie says. "Bottoms up."

"And dinner is on me." Lance hands me a menu.

"Oh, Lance, I couldn't—"

"Drink!" A laugh goes around the table, and everybody does so. For a fraction of an instant, I'm embarrassed, but then I realize that the laughter isn't aimed at me, and they are all delighted to have the excuse to drink.

"Lacey," Lance intones in an exaggerated theater voice, covering my hand with his and gazing into my eyes meltingly, "your pleasure is my pleasure. The waitress will be back in a moment—what would you like to eat?"

He's acting, I remind myself. None of this is real. But even so, his touch, his eyes, light up sensations in my body I'd thought were history. I shift my eyes away from his, so entrancingly blue, and to the menu, an unexplored treasure trove of tastes. Thomas and I ate out rarely, and when we did, it was never something exotic like Mexican food.

I scan the unfamiliar names and choose something called "camarones a la diabla," not because I like shrimp so much as that I like the way the words sound in my head.

"You should meet the rest of these people," Lance says after the orders are given and fresh drinks arrive for everybody, including an alcohol-free cocktail for Val, because she's going to work from here. I have barely touched my first margarita, and now a second is waiting for me.

Already the unfamiliar warmth of the alcohol is settling in. I can feel myself relaxing into this group that seems to want nothing more from me than that I pretend to be Lacey.

"That guy over there"—Lance points at Geoff—"is your ex. And this is your son, Lyndon. He's not drinking tonight, of course, because he's underage."

A thin, fragile-looking teenager with a face that will be beautiful when his acne clears gives me a sweet but hesitant smile. I smile back at him, and he says, "Hey, Ma. Can't I have just one drink?"

"Behave," Val says, elbowing him, and he snort-laughs, then blushes and drops his eyes.

"Down at the end is Jayce, who oversees all of the clothes we will be wearing. And DeeDee, our supplier of furnishings and all other things needful, otherwise known as props mistress."

"Drink!" Bernie cries.

"What? Neither of them has character names."

"Even so. You shall refer to them as 'Props Mistress' and 'Costume Maven.'"

"Fair," Tara says, burying her face in her glass and drinking half of it.

"Let's play a game," Geoff suggests, and the rest groan.

"Is there drinking involved?" Tara demands.

"Always. What do you take me for? Two truths, one lie. Guess wrong, and you take a drink."

"Can we guess wrong on purpose?" Bernie grins impudently. "I'll start. My nickname when I was six was Pip-squeak. I was a ballerina until I pulled a hamstring. My favorite movie is *Die Hard*. Miss Lacey, find the lie."

I take a motivational swallow of my own drink, surprised to discover that I'm almost at the bottom. "Ballet. I don't exactly see you as a ballerina."

"Drink!" Bernie cries, triumphant. "I was an amazing ballerina."

Try as I might, I cannot picture Bernie up on her toes doing a pirouette or wearing a tutu. And then I notice that the others are all thumbing through their scripts and realize my error. It's not Bernie who was a ballerina, it's her character in the play. Grace. My rival. "I wish I could have seen you dance," I say, swallowing the last of my drink.

"Ha! You did. You tripped me—oh, it was quite by accident, I'm sure, and down I went. And you wonder why I'm getting in the way of your little romance."

The hostility feels real. Does Bernie have a thing for Lance? Have I offended her?

"Hey, Bern," Geoff intervenes. "Liz is new here. Maybe go easy."

"Liz? I know no Liz, or Bernie, either. Drink up twice!"

"Hear, hear!" Tara says, slamming her empty glass down on the table.

"Refills?" the waiter asks.

"All around," Tara agrees. "We're just getting started. Your turn, Lacey."

I flick through the script, speed-reading for information. "My husband left me for another woman. My son is gay." Even as I say the words, I want to call them back, guessing that the boy who is playing my son really is gay. But he doesn't seem to be bothered by the statement. "And, let me see, I own a pound dog named Nebuchadnezzar. Darcy, find the lie."

"Well," Lance says, considering. "The dog hates me, so it's hard to forget his name. And your son came out of the closet last week. So, the lie is that your husband left you. You left him."

"You know me so well," I murmur.

"And I'm only just beginning," he replies. Something in his voice, his eyes, makes me pick up the glass and drink again without prompting.

"Easy," he whispers, under cover of laughter from the others as Tara delivers her truths and a lie. "If you're not much of a drinker, those go down way too easy."

"My lips are tingly," I confess.

"Drink lots of water, and let's get some food into you." He reaches for the chips and sets them in front of me. Pours more water into my glass.

I watch his hands, entranced by the way he serves me as if it's the most natural thing in the world, not as if he's making some sort of tit-for-tat point he'll expect me to pay for later.

"What does your husband think of you getting into this whole drama thing?" he asks. "I mean really. I'm asking Liz, not Lacey."

I drop my eyes and twist the ring on my finger, imagining Thomas's scathing reaction to my behavior.

"He died. Awhile back." I try to make it sound like it's been years, not just a few months. I don't want to see Lance's eyes and face close into sympathy as he locks me up in the widow box.

"Divorce, for me," he says.

I try to read his face, assessing the damage, unsure why we are talking about our no-longer-here spouses.

"Hey, you two lovebirds." Bernie's voice cuts through the chatter. "Are you having your own personal conference over there?"

"Jealous?" Lance asks, fully Darcy again, claiming my hand in his own.

The warmth of him, the sensation of it being the two of us, together, a partnership of some kind, fills and feeds me more than the giant plate of food that arrives a few minutes later.

Chapter Eleven

Colville shuts down early, and when I leave the restaurant, Main Street is mostly quiet, even though it's just past eight. Tara, Bernie, and Lance are still inside the restaurant, but the others have all departed. A few cars are parked on the street, outside the bar and the theater, but there's very little traffic. A single car passes, the sad wail of a country song loud and clear through the open window. On the far side of the street, a man with a backpack moves quietly, a dog at his heels. The world feels big, simultaneously empty and full of adventure.

Both head and heart are full to the brim, and my brain is processing, processing, trying to make sense of it all. The laughter, the games, the feeling of being included and part of something new and a little daring. Bernie's raw jokes. Tara's sly humor. Lance's arm brushing against my shoulder. His hand on mine, those eyes, the way his lips curve when he's laughing, the blue of his eyes, and the tan of his skin.

Dangerous territory. I have no business thinking about a man this way. And if I were thinking about a man, Lance wouldn't be the man for me to be thinking about.

What kind of man would I be thinking about, then? I ask myself as I turn the key in the ignition. *Better question yet—what kind of man would be thinking about me?*

And that answer brings me back to reality. Am I okay to drive? I have zero experience with alcohol and driving. How many drinks would it take to go over the limit? I stopped at the bottom of that second drink. My lips no longer tingle. I had no trouble walking to the car or getting my key in either the lock or ignition. And I certainly drank less than some of the others who have climbed into their own cars and driven away.

If I don't drive, what then? Colville doesn't have taxis or buses, and I will walk before I'll call Abigail to come and get me. It's only a few miles from the restaurant to my house. There's hardly any traffic. I pull my car out into the street, taking it slow and extra careful, just to be safe.

I make it halfway home without incident, and when I hear a siren and see red and blue lights in my rearview, I pull over to let the cop go by, wondering if he's responding to an accident or a crime, and hoping nobody is hurt. But the lights stop right behind me. My heart ups its tempo. I've never been pulled over for anything. Never had a ticket.

What did I do? I've been watching the speedometer, and there's no way I exceeded the limit. I've carefully stopped at all of the stop signs. Abigail reminded me to renew my tabs, and I put the sticker on my license plate all by myself, a little moment of pride and satisfaction. Thomas had always taken care of these things, and it felt good to do it myself.

The officer is already at my window, and I roll it down.

He stoops to look in at me, then past me, checking out the passenger seat, the back seat, the hatch. I imagine him godlike, seeing all, even the candy bar wrapper stuffed into the cup holder in the console. I can't see his face, which is shadowed, but his physique is more Kentucky Fried Chicken than Gold's Gym.

His face, illuminated by a streetlight, is round cheeked and shockingly young—Abigail's age, maybe. Certainly no older.

"Ma'am, do you know why I've pulled you over tonight?" Not even a hint of a smile. He is serious, a man on a mission, embodying every stereotypical policeman in every cop show I've ever seen.

What if he knows I was drinking? Can he smell the alcohol on my breath?

I manufacture a smile, keeping my breath shallow and my tone light. "If I knew that, Officer, I would not have done whatever it is."

Immediately I see my mistake as his jaw tightens and his expression hardens. He is too young to be teased, fully invested in his own importance.

"Your right taillight is out, ma'am."

Nerves and relief set me babbling. "I didn't know that. I'll get it fixed at once. Well, maybe not at once because I'll need some help. And a bulb or something. Can you tell me where I would get a bulb?" When I was married, cars fell into the realm of male responsibility. Thomas got the oil changed, the tires rotated, scheduled all of the service checks a year ahead on his calendar. I wasn't to bother my head with automobile maintenance.

The officer doesn't answer my question. "License and registration, please." He shines a flashlight in my eyes, so bright, and I cover them with my hands. Even so shielded, I can see the light moving as he searches the interior of my car again, as if he suspects I'm harboring some kind of contraband. Seriously? Do I look like a drug dealer?

My heart kicks up the tempo another notch. A burned-out taillight is still an infraction, and I am still in trouble. I manage to get my wallet out of my purse and find my license. But by the time I reach over to open the glove box for my registration, my hands are shaking so badly I fumble and drop everything—maintenance reports, receipts, random papers, registration, and insurance—all cascading onto the floor.

"Sorry, sorry. I'm so sorry. Just a minute, I can be so clumsy."

I scrabble around in the dark, trying to gather them up, but my seat belt won't let me and I have to sit up straight to disconnect the latch. It takes two tries, and by the time I finally manage to scoop up the stack, tears of humiliation and anxiety are blurring my vision and spilling down over my cheeks.

"Have you been drinking this evening?" the officer asks.

The question is ludicrous, the answer preposterous.

Because, yes, I have been drinking. I'm also the widow of a pastor. I'm supposed to be an example for the church members, the community, my daughter. I can't get a DUI. The gossip would swamp me, embarrass Abigail.

Maybe I should beg for mercy. If I let my tears flow freely, if I play helpless, plead for another chance, maybe he'll let me go. The words hover on the tip of my tongue. "My husband died. I'm so lost, bewildered, and confused, I don't even know how this happened. I never drink, but I was out with friends . . ."

I sense that this officer would like that; it might soften him, give him the opportunity to play the magnanimous man in power.

But I can't make myself do it. I'm so tired of being that woman. Instead, I square my shoulders, look directly into his eyes, and confess. "Yes, sir. I have been drinking."

I offer no excuses. No explanations. Just the truth.

"Please step out of the car."

He opens the door. My knees are wobbly as I swing my legs out and plant my feet on the cracked asphalt. Cold air swirls around me. Above, the sky blazes with stars. I've never felt so alive, so aware of the vastness of the universe and my own small place in it.

The officer calls me back to myself and the little drama I've driven myself into.

"I'm going to give you a field sobriety test. Do you understand what this is?"

"Yes, Officer." I mean it politely and respectfully, am surprised by the tinge of sarcasm that sneaks into my voice. His condescension chafes. I should probably call an attorney, but where would I find one?

We have several in the congregation, but I'd rather be arrested than call one of them to come rescue me.

So I consent. I follow his moving finger with both eyes, right, left, up, down. I walk in a straight line, heel to toe, turn, and come back. The whole time, I burn with humiliation. What if somebody sees me, performing like a circus monkey, spotlighted by streetlights and headlights and red and blues?

I imagine Annie, eyes bright with the pleasure of juicy gossip: "Did you hear about Elizabeth?"

Earlene, wisely resigned: "As the good book tells us, a widow left to her own devices will fall into evil."

Kimber, shocked: "Was she really, you know, *drunk?*" with whispered emphasis on that last, dreadful word.

And maybe I am drunk, because as I imagine the fuss, laughter wells up inside me, as unpredictable and out of my control as the gust of wind that nudges me one direction and then another.

"Stand on one foot, please, and count to ten."

Despite the wind, despite the looseness in my knee joints and the way my legs are shaking, I turn myself into a human flamingo. By the time I'm done, I'm shivering not just with nerves but with cold, wrapping my arms around my body to try to get warm.

"Well, you've passed," the officer says grudgingly. "But I'm still going to ask you to take a Breathalyzer."

I very nearly roll my eyes at him, as if I'm a teenager and not a respectable middle-aged widow. I've passed all of his tests. The drinks have worn off. This man wants me to fail, has been enjoying my humiliation. Confident now, I agree to the Breathalyzer. I'll be safely below the limit, and then it will be my turn to be condescending.

His expression as he reads the score signals my mistake. That's a fist-pump face, a celebration-waiting-to-happen face.

"You blew a .08," he says.

I stare at him, confused. ".08 is the limit, right? I'm fine."

"You're supposed to be *below* the legal limit," he explains, his words slow and emphasized as if I'm hard of hearing or short on intellect. "At or above means you are driving under the influence."

"What happens now?" My mouth is so dry, it's hard to speak. I picture myself arrested, handcuffed, locked up in jail, camera footage playing on some reality TV show.

"I'm going to write you a ticket. You'll go to court for sentencing. You'll be required to spend a night in jail at some point, but not tonight if there's somebody to come pick you up."

"So I can go home?"

"Yes, but you'll need to call somebody to take you. You won't be driving."

I won't be driving for a long time, I think, the panic rising. I can't be in the play after all. I'll be dependent on Abigail or members of the congregation to take me everywhere, even the grocery store. I'm trapped right back in my old life, only worse.

And who am I going to call, now, tonight?

Earlene? Val? She's at work, and I don't know if she can slip away. Whatever I do, I won't, can't, call Abigail. Not after everything that has happened today between us. I take a breath, focus on immediate questions.

"What about my car?"

"It will be towed. Unless you have somebody who can pick it up for you."

"Look, I live a few blocks from here. Can't I just walk home and pick my car up tomorrow?"

"I can't allow you to wander around while inebriated," the officer says.

"I'm not exactly inebriated—"

"Call somebody, or I'll need to take you in."

I recognize this tone, this expression. He wears it differently than Thomas, but the two men bear a striking resemblance in this moment.

He's enjoying his moment of power. If I don't call Abigail, he'll get to handcuff me and stuff me into his car, all while feeling self-righteous and important. The whole idea of it sets my teeth on edge, but I did this. I drank. I drove. Now I will be punished.

Headlights come up the road, and I cringe, wondering if my car or I will be recognized. A pickup truck slows, then pulls over and stops. The door opens.

"Remain in your vehicle," the officer barks, his hand resting on his service weapon.

"Teddy," a familiar voice says, calm and easy. "Don't shoot me."

Lance gets out of the truck, looking from me to the officer and back again. "What's going on?"

"Traffic stop," the officer says. "Everything under control. You can be on your way."

"You okay, Liz?" Lance asks.

My breath is tangled up around my heart. I nod. I will not cry, I tell myself. I will not, I will not. But my body doesn't listen to me.

"You know this woman?" the officer says, his voice edged with disgust.

"I do. We spent the evening together, in fact. What's up?" Lance saunters toward me, casual. "Problem with the car?"

"Problem with alcohol," the cop says. "I'm writing her up for a DUI."

Lance comes to stand beside me. He doesn't touch me, just makes it clear by his positioning that we are an alliance. "She only had a couple of drinks over dinner. Can't believe she's over the limit."

"She blew a .08." The officer says it as if I'm a drooling derelict.

"Maybe you could test her again," Lance suggests. "Hate to screw up the life of an upstanding citizen over a mechanical error."

"I did pass the field sobriety thing," I say.

"Huh," Lance says. "Must be a quiet night, hey, Ted? Doubling up on the tests and all."

"The Breathalyzer is more accurate."

"But still a field test," Lance protests. "We know there's a margin of error. By the way, how many drinks did you have last weekend at Northern Ales? Pretty sure I saw you walk out of there and get directly into your car."

I hold my breath, feeling the tension of unspoken threats and repercussions crackling in the air.

The officer retrieves the Breathalyzer from his car, his movements stiff. Lance nods at me, encouragingly, and I blow into the little mouthpiece again.

"Look at that. .06," Lance says, watching. "Touchy machines."

Two cars drive by, slowing, and I feel the gaze of unseen eyes staring.

The officer draws himself up to full height, his jaws so tight the words can barely squeeze past his teeth. "Given that you passed the field sobriety test and that Lance can vouch for your character, I'm prepared to let you off with a warning."

Shored up by Lance's presence and a new understanding that is growing inside me, I don't grovel or even thank him. "So I can go now?"

"Your taillight is still out. You'll need to leave your vehicle here either until daylight, or until it's fixed."

"I'll give you a ride home," Lance says quickly. "Okay if she moves her car off the road and into the parking lot, Ted?"

"I guess."

My knees start shaking when I sit down and turn the key, and I'm overly aware of both men watching me. It feels like when I took my driver's test, only the stakes are higher. Still, I manage to pull off the road and into the parking lot without incident.

I grab my purse and my phone. My script. Lance is waiting when I get out of the car. He rests an arm on my shoulder, warm and strong. "Let's get you home. Night, Ted. Be careful out there."

He walks me to his truck, opens the passenger door for me.

"Sorry about the clutter." He scrambles to clear a space for my feet from a litter of empty coffee cups, bank receipts, and junk mail.

"It's fine," I say, and mean it. There's something comforting about the clutter. The truck smells of coffee and sweat and hay. A good, warm smell.

As soon as we're both in, he starts the engine, turns the heat on high.

"Ackerman's an asshole," he says. "You okay?"

"How do you know him?"

"I'm a volunteer EMT. We bump elbows." Lance shifts into gear and eases us out onto the street. I watch Officer Ackerman's car fade into the darkness.

"He was just doing his job. I shouldn't have been driving." Shame threatens to swamp me, all of my momentary courage dissolving. "Drunk driving is a horrible thing. I could have killed somebody."

"You weren't drunk. You were under the limit. Ted is known for his zeal, especially when it comes to women."

I remember that look on the officer's face, the similarity to Thomas, and I'm rocked by a sudden epiphany. This officer, this man, hated me because I was a woman. He enjoyed humiliating me and used his authority to do it, just as Thomas did under the authority he claimed as a man of God. He used the church and the apostle Paul as a smoke screen for his dislike, his fear, of women. Used it to wear me down, to make me smaller, to keep me in the place he assigned to me.

A truth spins in the maelstrom and floats to the surface of my consciousness, jagged, hard edged, and bloody.

Thomas stole my life because I am a woman, and I let him do it.

The edges grow sharper.

He did it to Abigail, too. I need to find a way to free my daughter from indoctrination.

I need to find a way to free us both.

"You okay?" Lance asks, glancing at me.

"Thanks for the rescue." I'm so incredibly grateful, but I also hate feeling like a damsel in distress. Hate that now I'm indebted to him, the feeling of being a helpless woman sheltering behind a big strong man.

"My dear Lacey," Lance declaims in shocked theatrical tones. "If anyone was rescued, it was me. I wanted only to bask in the pleasure of your company."

His tone eases me into laughter, but still the camaraderie and fun of the evening is ruined.

Lance drums his fingers on the steering wheel but otherwise keeps silent until he pulls up into my driveway.

"Well, this kinda sucks," he says.

"Only kind of?" I laugh a little. "Thank you again. You have rescued me from a life of crime."

"Look. Liz. If you were Geoff, I'd have done the same. Shit happens. Friends help each other."

I pause with my hand on the door latch.

"So I'm not just a damsel in distress?"

"Well, if I was a hundred percent honest, it's more fun to rescue a damsel than a bro. But if I had rescued Geoff, he'd probably be asking me if I could help him pick up the car and fix the taillight. And then, you know, maybe go get a beer."

"I think I may not drink again. Ever."

"Okay. A coffee, then. Geoff is extraordinarily fond of coffee."

I can't help laughing. I'd meant to bail the minute the pickup stopped moving, but instead we sit there looking at each other. Maybe I could go out for coffee. Not as a date, but as . . .

"Uh-oh."

The front door opens, and Abigail stalks over to the truck and yanks open my door.

"I hope you're proud of yourself."

"Abigail, this is Lance. Lance, this is my daughter." I enunciate the words, a rebuke, a reminder that we are not alone.

"Driving drunk, Mom? What were you thinking? As if this morning's behavior wasn't bad enough!"

"Technically, I wasn't—"

Abigail cuts me off. "Don't bother to try to lie to me. It was on the scanner. Everybody in town who has one is going to know that you got pulled over for driving drunk. Earlene already called and—"

"Oh God." I bury my face in my hands.

"Right. The whole church will know." She redirects her fury on Lance without pausing for a breath. "And I suppose we have you to thank for all of it. Do you get off on preying on vulnerable women?"

"Abigail!"

I'm not sure I've ever heard this particular tone of voice come out of my own mouth. Abigail stops with her mouth open, eyes wide. Apparently she hasn't heard it, either.

"That will be enough."

A moment's hesitation, and then my strong-willed, infuriated daughter actually turns and stalks up the driveway and into the house.

Lance's eyes follow her. "Rather a fierce guardian you have there."

"Yes. She's moving back home to take care of me."

"God have mercy."

"She was rude. I'm sorry about that."

"Don't be. See you at rehearsal?"

I can't help noticing that all talk of beer, coffee, or taillights has evaporated. I don't want to go inside and face my daughter. I'd rather stay right here. But if I'm going to rescue her, if I'm going to stop being a damsel in distress, I'd better start facing up to my challenges.

"Good night, Darcy."

"Good night, Lacey. I'll see you on Tuesday."

Chapter Twelve

April 9, 2019

Dear Inner Liz,
Now what? It all seemed so clear for a minute the other night. Stop being a victim. Get a life. Rescue Abigail. But how am I supposed to do that? She's lived, slept, and breathed the Church of Thomas doctrine since she was a baby. Her belief is enmeshed in her love for him and her disdain for me, and I don't know that it's even possible to change that. All I can think to do is build a life for myself, but I don't even know where to start. So many years of burying myself under what was expected of me that I don't even know what I want.

Small things, I guess. I passed off my church responsibilities to Felicity. Her husband has temporarily taken the pulpit, so I figure she can temporarily be me. Poor girl. Earlene and the others will eat her alive. Yes, I feel guilty. But I did it anyway.

Just Say Yes got me thinking about how frequently I say no, and I'm trying to shift that. Of course, I'm not taking it as far as Lacey does, but every time I catch myself

saying, "I can't do that," I ask myself why. Why can't I?
Maybe I'll get a bracelet or go way over the top and get a
tattoo. WWLD. What would Lacey do? That would keep
the gossips busy for a while, don't you think?

"That's a wrap!" Bill says, clapping enthusiastically. A hubbub of voices fills the theater until he waves for silence.

"Not bad at all. Thursday night we'll be working on blocking out scenes in the first act. Not everybody will be onstage, but you still need to be here if at all possible. You can always get with a partner and go over lines; in fact, you're encouraged to do that. Then, Saturday, we'll be working on the music. Good night, drive safe."

Another round of applause, and everybody starts to drift toward the door, breaking up into little clumps of two and three. Val had to work an evening shift and isn't here tonight, so I walk between diminutive Tara and amazon Bernie.

"What's up with the DUI?" Tara asks.

I glance over my shoulder at Lance, walking right behind us. My toe catches and I stumble, but Bernie's hand steadies me.

"How did you hear about that?"

"Well, you know. Word travels."

"You've got, like, zero alcohol metabolism," Bernie says. "Probably you need to drink more. Want to come out tonight?"

Their easy acceptance eases my shame, but only a little. "Thanks, but I may never drink again."

"Oh, don't be that way about it," Tara says. "Everybody knows Ackerman is a dick. Good thing Lance lives up your way."

"Knight in shining armor to the rescue," Bernie says.

Heat rises to my cheeks, and I'm grateful for my new hairstyle and the way I can let it screen my face.

When Tara, and then Bernie, peel off to go to their own vehicles, Lance moves up beside me. I'm overly conscious of his presence, can feel every movement he makes as if there's some sort of weird echolocation between us. I feel like I suddenly have three hands and three feet and don't know how to manage any of them. Can't think of what I should say.

Do I apologize to him again for Abigail's rudeness? Thank him again for rescuing me? Talk about the weather?

When we reach my car, it's even worse. I have to look at him now because I have no excuse not to. His eyes are intent, his lips . . .

Do not think about his lips, Liz. Do not.

His lips are not too full, not too thin. One of his hands rests on the roof of my car, his body poised right at the edge of my personal space boundary.

Almost as if he wants to kiss me.

My breath gets tangled in my pulse, as if both my lungs and my heart have forgotten their business. Heat travels through my body, not just my face but other parts low in my belly, stirring a long-dormant desire.

I turn my back, open my car door, afraid of what he might read in my face. "Well, I guess I'll see you on Thursday?"

"Unless . . . ," he says as I settle into my seat.

My heart, my body, are out of control. I put the key in the ignition, turn it.

He leans down to look at me. "I'm assuming you fixed your taillight on your own, but we could still grab that coffee."

"Now?" My voice sounds high, breathless.

"Right. It's late for coffee. Okay, how about dessert? We could run our lines."

"I can't. I don't . . ."

I see the wall go up. He's still smiling. He's still looking at me. He hasn't moved. But there's an infinitesimal thinning of his lips, a shift in his body tension, a distance in his eyes. He straightens. Slaps the roof lightly with the palm of his hand. "Of course. I understand."

But he doesn't understand anything. How could he?

What would Lacey do?

Lacey would probably get out of the car and kiss him. I'm not going to take it that far, but I say, carefully, "Lacey, on the other hand, would be delighted to meet Darcy somewhere for dessert."

For a held breath, I think it's too late, that he's already withdrawn his offer.

But then he says, in the voice he uses for Darcy, "Where, my lady?"

"Anywhere but Rancho Chico."

He laughs out loud, not a Darcy laugh, more of a Lance guffaw. "Not much open at this hour. How about that South Main place?"

Dessert sounds decadent.

Dessert sounds like a date.

But running lines is more like homework, and I find a consensus between myself and Lacey. If anybody sees us, the explanation is right there. We're in a play together. We're practicing our lines. South Main is a sports bar but also a grill. Which is both safe and not safe. Church people go there. We could be seen.

"What are you thinking?" he asks.

"Gossip."

"You mean like Tara knowing about your traffic incident? I swear on the grave of my mother that I didn't say anything."

"Is your mother even dead?"

His lips quirk up on the right side. "No. But her grave will be sacred to me. You can count on that. She'd haunt me."

"Church gossip runs even faster than theater gossip. And it's . . . harsher."

"If you'd rather just go home, I understand. I'm sure your daughter is expecting you."

Mention of Abigail turns on my rebellion switch. The smile that curves my lips is part Lacey, part Liz, and there's nothing of Elizabeth in it anywhere.

"My daughter has temporarily gone back to Spokane. And I'm sort of all primed for dessert now. Unless you don't want to be seen consorting with an almost felon."

"Oh, I'd love nothing better than to be seen consorting." The emphasis he puts on "consorting" amps up the heat in my body, both wonderful and alarming. I love the way that look alters the expression on his face. His pupils darken, his lips soften. "It just occurred to me that you might think I'm taking advantage of the situation. You don't owe me anything."

"I think I like being taken advantage of, in this case," Lacey says on my behalf.

"I'll meet you there."

I follow him, parking beside his truck in the parking lot.

We take seats across from each other in the brightly lit restaurant. The TVs are on, and a large and noisy group monopolizes the space. It's far from a romantic environment, and I relax, neglecting my script to linger over the menu. I opt for chocolate cake. Lance orders an ice-cream sundae. When the waitress walks away with our menus, Lance reaches across the table and covers my hand with his.

It's a big hand, strong. There are calluses on the palm. It makes my own hand feel small, protected. My heartbeat is so loud in my ears, I'm sure he can hear it. I don't know what to do, can't think of what to say. Dates with Thomas revolved around the youth group. Did he ever take me out to a restaurant? Did anybody?

I risk a glance up at Lance, only to find him looking at me. "I thought we were going to run lines."

"Mmmm," he says, studying my face. "What if I brought you here under false pretenses?"

"As in, this is a date?"

"And if it is?"

"I guess then I suddenly get all kinds of nervous and try to remember my date questions." I only half know what I'm saying, completely flustered by how much I like the feeling of his hand over mine, the discovery of an almost dimple at the intersection of his left cheek and chin, those gold flecks in his blue eyes.

"You have date questions?" The almost dimple deepens with his grin.

Inner Liz, long repressed, rises to my rescue with a flash of mischief. "I do. Starting with: 'Can you believe Mrs. J is grading us on the curve?' And ending with: 'Can I borrow your notes from chemistry?'"

Lance laughs, and it turns out I love his laugh as much as his eyes and his smile.

The waitress shows up just then with a tray, and Lance withdraws his hand and leans back in his chair. I miss the warmth of his touch, even as I'm relieved and can't help glancing over my shoulder to make sure nobody has seen us.

"You need to update your questions." Lance plunges his spoon right into the middle of his sundae. "It's been that long, huh?"

With his eyes averted and his attention on ice cream, I summon the courage to ask, "So what do you do when you're not seducing hapless women in community theater?"

"I'm a farmer." He spoons ice cream into his mouth and makes a sound of pleasure that brings heat to my cheeks and drops my eyes to the slab of chocolate cake before me.

"How much weight do you want to gain?" Thomas says in my head. *"Empty calories, Elizabeth. And fat. Think of your arteries."*

"You're the one who had the coronary," I retort.

"What's that?" Lance stares, his spoon paused halfway to his mouth, a drip of caramel and melting ice cream curving dangerously over the edge and about to succumb to gravity.

I press both hands to my cheeks, embarrassed. "Bad habit of living alone. Talking to myself."

"Sounds like you were talking to somebody else." His spoon resumes motion just in the nick of time, reaching his mouth before that treacherous drip can escape.

"Honestly? I was having an internal argument with my husband. Thomas. The dead one."

"I assumed you only had the one," Lance replies gravely, but his eyes are laughing.

"He would have objected to the foolish extravagance of this dessert."

"He's not here. You are."

"Exactly. That's more or less what I was pointing out." I dig my fork into the cake, choosing a piece that has plenty of frosting and ice cream. My taste buds explode with sensation. Warm, cold, creamy, chocolatey goodness.

"I'd say you enjoyed that," Lance says around a mouthful of ice cream.

"I haven't had dessert like this in about as long as I haven't been on a date."

"Is this a date?"

A thrill of shame jolts through me before I see that he's teasing, and I scramble for the dropped conversation thread.

"So you're a farmer and an EMT both?"

"Farming is full-time, EMT is volunteer." His voice is clipped, as if I've asked him something he doesn't want to answer. He swallows a bite of ice cream and opens his script. "Better at least spend a few minutes on this so you don't have to lie about your presence here."

"Okay." Reading lines is safe, but my relief mixes with anxiety. I feel like I must have said something wrong, but asking about careers is supposed to be the safe question. His shift of mood confuses me, and as I scan the first scene, I realize I can't possibly say these lines here, to this man. Not over dessert in a scenario that is definitely more date than business. Flirtation and innuendo all seemed perfectly light-hearted and fine when I was reading the script alone. But this . . . this is different.

"What's the matter?" Lance asks.

I keep my head bent to hide my face and tell him part of the truth. "It occurs to me how it'll look if we're heard saying some of these things to each other out of context."

"Ah," he says. "Good point." But he doesn't let me off the hook. "Is it all a matter of location and listening ears? Or something else going on?"

I glance up at him. His face is quiet, listening, and I gain the courage to tell him.

"Maybe I shouldn't have taken the role. It's too . . ."

"Close to home?" he asks when I don't finish the thought.

"That and, well, my husband was a pastor. He would have disapproved of this play and my role in it wholeheartedly. As does my daughter."

"Are you so very religious, then?" Lance leans back a little in his chair, getting comfortable, not distancing himself.

My free hand adjusts my fork so that it's perfectly aligned next to my plate. "Not so much. I married the faith, so to speak. You?"

"I believe in God, but I'm not big on organized religion. I figure whatever He and I have to say to each other is between the two of us. Don't like the idea of a go-between." He leans forward, touches my wrist with his fingertips. "Liz, your feelings about the script are a good thing."

"They are?"

"Of course. It means you're getting into character. *We* are getting into character, and the Lacey-Darcy relationship is becoming a real thing. That's all how it's supposed to be."

"You think?" In high school productions, I got into character and I had crushes on some of the boys I acted with. Maybe Lance is right and this is normal and all part of the gig.

"You've already said yes to the play," Lance says. "You're already in. Sounds to me like doubt talking. The creative person's demon, right?"

"You're not wrong."

His eyes are intent on mine, and I can tell he's thinking about saying something else, but right then the waitress shows up with our bill in hand. "Anything else I can get you two?"

"Liz? A drink for the road?" Lance's eyes crinkle up at the corners, and I can see that he's not laughing at me, just sharing a joke.

I stick my tongue out at him, a ridiculous act, as if I'm five instead of almost fifty. "I'll take a rain check on that one."

He puts cash on the table, and we walk to the door in silence.

Outside, it's begun to rain.

For a moment I hesitate, shrinking back into the warmth of the restaurant, and then Inner Liz takes over and I dance out into the dark, free and unfettered, stretching my arms wide and lifting my face to the sky.

Thomas would be scandalized, but Lance only laughs. I slow my steps as I near my car, clicking open the locks, then turn to look at him.

"Thank you. For the cake. And for . . . the practice."

"A huge sacrifice in service of the play, remember?"

He's standing very close, not just on the edge of my personal space this time, but inside it. Not quite touching, but if either one of us leaned forward, even an inch . . .

His eyes are looking into mine. He's going to kiss me. Right here. Right now. My heart beats wildly, in panic or anticipation or both.

"Your script is getting wet," he says, breaking the moment. "Mine, too. Good night, Liz."

And there's nothing for it but to get in the car. He closes the door for me, waves, and ducks into his pickup truck.

My body is all want, every nerve ending I possess trying to reach through my car door, through the rain, to touch his hand, his arm, his lips. Lacey wouldn't wait to be kissed. Lacey would do the kissing.

Slam of door. Start of engine.

What is wrong with me? I start my own engine and manage to stop myself from glancing over at him to see if he's looking back at me, but I can't help watching for his headlights in my rearview mirror.

~

Halfway home, my phone starts buzzing with texts. I ignore it. The last thing I need is to get pulled over again, this time for distracted driving. But as soon as I pull into my driveway and park, I take a look.

Val: I heard you went out with Lance???

Liz: Running lines. No big deal

I wait. Little dots form, then vanish. Silence. I'm rain damp and cold and dash into the house. Still no response from Val.

An ugly little thought niggles its way into my consciousness. Does Val have a thing for Lance? Could she be jealous? I take off my shoes and hang up my coat before my phone buzzes again.

Val: Just—be careful, ok?

Liz: What is that supposed to mean?

The phone rings.

"Listen, I only have a minute," Val says when I pick up, "but I don't want you to take this wrong. This is not a texting conversation."

"What's wrong with Lance?"

"There's nothing wrong with him. He's a great guy. Just . . ."

"Just what? If you like him, you should go for him. We were just running lines. Nothing happened."

"Me? God no. I am not in the market for a man right now. Look. I'm glad the two of you have connected. But you're vulnerable, and he's . . . emotionally unavailable. Or at least that's the gossip."

"You mean he's what? A player?"

"Noooo, not that." But she drags the "no" out in a way that means she's considering the truth of the word. "Bernie says he's always very clear that he's not looking for a long-term relationship. He has flings with women sometimes, but they never last long."

"He had a fling with Bernie?"

"No! That's not what I'm saying. She's just the conveyer of the gossip. And maybe that's all it is, and maybe the two of you were just

90

running lines. And that's great. I just don't want you to get hurt. Look, we'll talk more tomorrow, okay? I really have to get back to work."

She hangs up, and I'm alone with the fragments of my once beautiful mood.

Do I want there to be something more between me and Lance? I can't deny the way my body responds to every little touch, the way my heart races every time he looks at me. I twist my wedding ring on my finger, feeling as guilty as if I've indulged in an affair. Thomas might be dead, but I see him everywhere I look. Nothing in this house is mine, save my new clothes, my journal, and my books. It still looks like he lives here. It still feels like he lives here.

The ring on my finger is a fetter, a symbol of ownership rather than of love. I twist it over my knuckle and pull it off. In my palm, it's a small thing, a plain gold band. I carry it to my room, wrap it in a tissue, and tuck it into my bedside table.

A thump at the back porch reminds me that I am neglecting the one responsibility I have voluntarily assumed. I open an envelope of tuna. Moses and I are now on a twice-a-day tuna schedule. He's also much tamer than he used to be.

When I open the door, he doesn't run, just sits there in the middle of the porch, wet and bedraggled, miserable in the rain. Before I can set down the bowl, he walks right into the house and wraps himself around my ankles, purring and meowing.

"You can't come in here," I tell him. "You're dirty. You're wet. Thomas would . . . Right. That doesn't matter, does it?"

Forget Thomas. What would Lacey do?

I close the door. Set the bowl down and watch as Moses buries his face in it and begins gulping down food.

While he eats, I fetch a towel from the bathroom and tentatively begin drying him, expecting him to bolt. He keeps eating, purring extravagantly.

Well, then.

I fill another bowl with water. When I bring it back to him, he is chasing the food dish around on the floor, trying to lick up every last bite. He sniffs at the water, then laps a little, delicately for a cat who looks so much like a gangster. And then, without a word or a by-your-leave, he pads down the hallway, into the living room, and curls up in Thomas's recliner.

"You mustn't. You're filthy," I begin, and then I break up laughing. I hate that chair, which is pure petty jealousy on my part. Thomas bought it for himself, with no thought about practicality. He wanted it, so he bought it, all the while relegating me to a stiff, uncomfortable armchair we bought at a yard sale.

"I guess it's your chair now," I tell the cat. "Although I suspect Abigail will have plenty to say about that."

Abigail.

What time is it?

Ever since she went back to Spokane, she's been calling me three times a day. In the morning to make sure I've made it out of bed alive, midday to make sure I've stayed that way, and at night to make sure I'm not out partying in some den of ill repute. If I've missed her bedtime check-in call while feeding the cat, she'll be having a fit.

Sure enough. It's fifteen minutes past ten, and I have three missed calls and a series of texts. She's probably already called Earlene to come over and check on me. I type in a text:

I'm good. Home. Will head to bed.

About five seconds later, the phone rings. Moses transitions from curled into a ball to crouched and ready to run faster than I can find the answer button.

"Are you okay?" Abigail demands. "And where have you been? Earlene says you were out late."

The edge of panic in her voice hits my guilt button, which is anatomically approximate to my rebellion and anger buttons.

"I really wish you would leave Earlene out of this," I retort. Moses startles at my raised voice, and I dare to smooth his fur, drying already, so soft under my hand. "Hush, shhhh, nothing to worry about."

I take the phone into the kitchen where the conversation won't disturb him.

"Don't hush me! There is everything to worry about," my daughter scolds. "I pictured you lying in a ditch somewhere. I'm trying to work, Mother! I don't have the energy to be worrying about you."

"Then don't worry. And I wasn't hushing you."

"Is somebody there with you?" She sounds scandalized, and I can't help laughing.

"Just Moses."

Silence and some heavy breathing and then, "And who is this Moses person, exactly?"

"A cat, Abigail. A stray. He just came in."

"You have got to be kidding me. What if he has diseases? Rabies, even. You can't just bring in a stray like that!"

"Well, I seem to have done so."

"And you wonder why I'm moving home! You're impossible. What am I supposed to make of your text?"

"That I'm a grown woman, safe at home—"

"'Silly dead to bed.' What is that even supposed to mean?"

"I have no idea what you're talking about."

"That's what you texted! 'Silly dead to bed.'"

Laughter bubbles up, clearing out the anger and the rebellion. My poor baby girl. She started trying to control the world when she was just a toddler, hands on her tiny hips, ordering me about. I did my best to quell it, but her father didn't help, and all I managed to do was put a veneer of politeness over her demands.

"Abigail," I tell her, very quiet, very focused. "Autocorrect got me, that's all. I'm home. Safe. Not drunk. Not suicidal. Okay?"

"I hate that you're there alone."

Voices in the background cut her off. "MVA is here, Abigail. We need you in trauma."

"Mom, I need to go. Please be careful."

"I'm fine, Abigail. Go save lives. I love you."

The phone goes silent, and I toss it onto the table with so much force that it skitters over the surface and very nearly over the edge.

Thoroughly riled up and agitated, I'm no longer anywhere near sleep. I put the kettle on, make myself a cup of tea, and turn back to the problem of the cat. Much as I can't admit it to Abigail, she has a valid point. Moses could have any number of diseases. Plus, I don't have a litter box and don't know whether he's litter box trained if I did have one.

When I go to evict him, though, he's fallen asleep, curled in a ball with his damp tail over his nose, and I can't bring myself to throw him back out in the rain.

"I assume you'll let me know when you need to go outside."

Moses says nothing. I watch him sleep while I sip my tea, honored that he has found enough trust to sleep in my presence. And when my cup is empty, I fetch a blanket and a pillow from the bed and curl up on the floor beside the chair, letting go of Val's texts, of Abigail and her words, one by one. In the end, when I drift away, what remains is a pair of beautiful blue eyes, the taste of chocolate cake, and the unexpected pleasure of stroking a purring cat.

Chapter Thirteen

May 4, 2019

Dear Inner Liz,

Abigail is moving in today, and I am the worst mother on the face of the planet. I love her. I would die for her, and I totally mean it about finding a way to free her from the life Thomas and I locked her into. But just between you and me, I don't want her to move in with me. I can't tell her that, of course. My own mother made me feel unwelcome in our house. When I married Thomas, she completely cut me off. I can't help wondering whether my life would have been different if I'd felt like I could go back home. So obviously I won't do that same thing to my own daughter.

Still, I've prayed that there wouldn't be a job opening here in Colville, but of course there was. And that she wouldn't get that job, but of course she did. God isn't going to do anything to fix this mess. It's all up to me. Which is fair, I guess, since I helped to make it.

Maybe, without Thomas in the middle, I can figure out how to mend our relationship. I'd like to believe that. But I am so afraid it will be otherwise.

Another guilty secret honesty moment. I'm afraid she'll see how I feel about Lance, and I don't even want to think about her reaction. I'm being careful, thanks to Val. No more dessert nights. But he texts me, off and on. We've run lines together on Skype, both safely tucked into our own spaces. And when we're together onstage? Sparks! Fireworks! I worry that everyone can see it, but so far they seem to think it's all good acting.

Anyway. The facts are these: I have an unseemly crush on Lance. Abigail is moving home. And there is going to be trouble, because she wants the Elizabeth-and-Thomas version of me, and I'm not going back to that. Not ever. Not even for Abigail.

I'm in Abigail's childhood room putting clean sheets on the bed, and caught up in memories, when somebody knocks at the door. I check my watch. Still too early for Abigail or anybody else to show up. The theater group heard about her moving home, and a work party formed and took on a life of its own in much the same way a forest fire creates its own atmosphere.

Probably Val, I guess, although these days she tends to breeze in without bothering to knock.

"It's open!" I shout.

I smooth the quilt back up over the bed and line up the pillows perfectly, one small thing I can do to make Abigail happy, because she is not going to approve of her welcome-home party.

"Elizabeth?"

I whirl around to see not Val but Earlene, and my heart sinks. I am never in the mood for Earlene, but this morning I'm seriously tempted to tell her to just go away. There are things I want to do before Abigail gets here, and I really don't have time to sit and listen to the old woman's gossip about neighbors or her lamentations about how Thomas's replacement is turning the church into a playground for liberal heathens.

"I'd love a cup of tea, if you're making any," she says, my cue to drop everything and give her my full attention.

Sharp words rise to my lips, but I swallow them down. She's a lonely old woman. Her husband died years ago and her children never visit. Her entire life is the church, and she is what I could so easily become if I don't get my act together. So I manage a smile, for once because I choose to rather than because Thomas would have expected it.

"Sure, why not? I was ready for a break anyway."

While I brew tea and set out a small plate of the muffins I've baked for this afternoon, Earlene regales me with stories from church.

"Electric guitars and drums, can you believe that? Not just with the youth, which is bad enough, but in the *sanctuary*. Some of the members have transferred to other congregations, and we've had a flood—a literal flood, I tell you—of new people coming in. It's a travesty. I've been a member of this church for fifty years, and nobody will even listen to me. Pastor Steve—so disrespectful to call a man of the cloth by his first name—what good can come of that? Pastor Steve encourages them. When I tried to express my concerns, he listened, but I know he didn't really hear me."

I set a cup of tea in front of her, along with the sugar bowl and a spoon. "That must be very difficult."

Earlene measures three heaping spoonfuls into her tea and stirs, then levels me with her gaze.

"You are neglecting your responsibilities, Elizabeth."

I sigh. This is, of course, the real reason for her visit. "They are Felicity's responsibilities now."

Earlene waves that away. "She's a child, and she's too . . . lax, if you know what I mean. People need to see you showing up and doing good works. Living a godly life."

I break a little piece off my muffin, and then another, laying them on my plate instead of eating. My appetite is long gone, lost in the bitterness of Earlene's words, but I need something to do with my hands.

"I'm taking a break from church."

"Dangerous business." Nothing wrong with Earlene's appetite. She slathers butter on her muffin and takes a big bite. "I've been thinking. You should find yourself a good man. It's not good for you to be alone."

"I'm not going to be alone. Abigail is coming home. Today, as a matter of fact."

"Another unmarried woman," she says dismissively. "I've always felt I have a duty to you, as you haven't a mother to guide you, and especially now that your husband is gone."

All of my misguided sympathy dissipates. I should have locked the door, but it's way too late. Earlene is already quoting scripture at me.

"As the apostle Paul wrote, 'I advise these younger widows to marry again, have children. Then the enemy will not be able to say anything against them. For I am afraid that some of them have already gone astray and now follow Satan.' Of course you're not precisely a younger widow," Earlene explains. "But I do fear for your soul, Elizabeth."

"It's a little late for me to have children," I protest, choosing my safest line of defense. I could argue that I'm not following Satan until the cows come home, but it would be pointless. Earlene would remain firmly convinced that I'm straying in that direction.

"You are not too old to fall into sin," she admonishes. "You have stopped coming to church and to prayer meeting. I saw that man drive you home late at night. I've seen you coming and going at all hours, your face all made up like a streetwalker."

I flush, but can't help laughing a little. "Stage makeup. And Lance gave me a ride that one time. It's not like he came in and spent the night."

"All of this gallivanting must stop. A woman needs a godly man, and there are several widowers in the church who would do. For the good of your own soul, Elizabeth."

"For the good of my soul," I repeat when I manage to catch my breath. "What about you? How come you never married again?"

"I was never tempted to stray into temptation," she says virtuously. But there's a hint of something in her eyes that tells me maybe it was more than that. Maybe no member of the fold was interested in spending his life being managed by her. Either way, I've had about enough of her meddling.

I get to my feet and carry both of our teacups to the sink, signaling the end of this ridiculous conversation.

"I was thinking of another cup," Earlene protests.

"And I was thinking the apostle Paul had something to say about widows marrying so they have something to do other than gossip. If you like, I'd be happy to help you select a nice eligible bachelor to help you with that little problem."

Earlene's lips press together, her nostrils flaring. "You are still grieving, and such outbursts are to be expected, I suppose." She gets stiffly to her feet. "I shall pray for you."

She closes her eyes, and I realize she means to pray now, right this minute. And I decide I've been prayed at one too many times already in my life.

"Save your prayers for someone who wants them," I interrupt. "Right now, I think you should leave."

She gasps, shocked at my rudeness and my irreverence. "This is what comes of socializing with unbelievers. Are you listening to yourself, Elizabeth? What would your husband say?"

"He can't say anything. He's dead. Now, if you don't mind, I have a very busy morning with much to do."

Her face is set in an expression that reminds me of the illustrations of a martyr going to the flames in yet another of the picture books Thomas saw fit to purchase for our daughter.

I precede her to the door and hold it wide open. She stops at the threshold, and I hold my breath, afraid she will change her mind and refuse to leave me alone with my temptations. But she has been trained as thoroughly as I have to show good manners, and she can't help reading my clear signals. She steps out onto the porch and then turns back to deliver a parting line.

"You cannot prevent me from praying for you, and I refuse to let you push me away." With that, she marches across the street and I pull the door shut behind her, locking it this time.

"Shit! Now what do I do?"

My exclamation startles me into a burst of shocked laughter. Maybe I have been hanging around Val and the others too much. But I am *so* going to pay for my little outburst to Earlene. She will already be on the phone relaying our conversation, telling everybody I am so far gone I have refused to be prayed over. Which means, of course, that the prayer chain is commencing in about five minutes, with my name moved to the top of the list.

Why, oh why, did I let a lonely, bitter old woman get to me? It was the Bible text that pushed me over the edge. Thomas was fond of the apostle Paul, quoting his advice about women at me all the time. Beneath my accepting veneer, it always rankled that the voice of a man from so deep in history could still have so much control over my life. How I wear my hair. My obedience to my husband. "God's words," Thomas would have said had I dared to argue. "Paul wasn't just a man, Elizabeth, he was the voice of God."

Secretly, in my dark heart and in my morning journal, I'd questioned whether the man might have taken license to slip his own opinions into the messages from God. That whole passage about widows is particularly repellant, implying that the only way to prevent us from gossiping and fornicating is to keep us properly married and under the control of a husband.

Which is what happened to me.

I try the thought on, like an unfamiliar dress in front of a mirror, one that fits perfectly as if tailored for me, even though it's a color and style I wouldn't have chosen.

Who was I before Thomas?

Who was I before I became a mousy, self-effacing, martyred-for-my-own-good woman? What was I going to be, or do? For a moment of free fall, I can't even remember my life before Thomas, as if I emerged into the world ready formed to do his bidding, like Eve in the Eden story, shaped from Adam's rib for the sole purpose of being his companion.

Memory drops me back to a school counselor's office.

I've been called in for something. What? Why?

The counselor's elbows are on her desk, her chin resting on open palms. She's smiling. I'm not in trouble. I feel like—I feel like the first day of summer vacation, the time I spent it with my cousin in the country. Like possibilities and freedom.

The rest of the memory is missing, and I want it back. I focus in. It was high school. Senior year. Before or after I met Thomas? It would have to have been before. My stomach feels like unraveling knitting as the rest of the memory comes clear.

I'm sitting in an algebra class, head bent over a math book, alternately wrestling with equations, which are not my thing, and daydreaming about a theater production I plan to audition for.

A knock at the classroom door. A head pokes in.

"Elizabeth Lundgren? May I see you in my office for a moment?"

Heads swivel in my direction. Some curious, some hostile. My stomach drops and twists as I pack up my books. What have I done, said, left undone? My father's philosophy is "Trouble at school, double at home." It wouldn't be the first time his belt came off and connected with the tender skin on the backs of my thighs and behind my knees because I've missed homework or smart-mouthed a teacher. He pays little attention to me as long as I don't cause him trouble, but a note from school is always a catalyst for what he calls "correction."

I follow the woman down the hallway, my anxiety ratcheting up a notch when we veer left into the counseling services office rather than right into the principal's domain.

"What did I do?" I ask as soon as I'm perched on the edge of the folding chair on the student side of her desk.

"What did . . ." The woman's well-shaped eyebrows rise in an expression of bewilderment. "I was just wondering what your plans are for college."

"I don't—humanities, probably. Teaching? Social work, maybe." Really, I have no idea. I love drama, but that's not something I can make a career out of. It's not like I'd ever be movie star material. I can see my life to the end of high school and then nothing, as though everything ends then. Probably I'll get a job at McDonald's or some other fast-food place. My parents didn't go to college. My stepbrother, eleven years older than me, worked at the lumber mill for a few years after high school, and eventually went into real estate.

"You do plan to go to college." The woman's eyes are warm and quizzical.

She makes it feel safe to be myself, my real self, the one I conceal below the surface. "Honestly, I don't know. My family isn't going to pay for it."

"Well, that's the thing, isn't it? Your teachers tell me you are very bright. Your grades are excellent. Mrs. Valen says your thinking and writing skills go well beyond the usual high school vapidness—those are her words, not mine."

I return her smile, amused. I can hear Mrs. Valen using that word, "vapid," to describe most of the students in English. I agree with her, in secret. It's amazing how so many of them complain about reading books I find amazing, how they miss the point of things that seem so clear and obvious to me.

"And Mr. D says you're one of the best drama students he's ever had. But here's the thing. You've never taken the SATs, or availed yourself of any of our services. If you start now, it's not too late to get some good scholarships. They are a lot of work, but they could put you through college. I really do think you ought to go to college, don't you?"

"Yes." My voice comes out small and squeaky. It annoys me. I sit up straighter, meet those kind eyes directly, and say, louder this time, "Yes!"

"Good! I'm glad to hear that. Let's get you set up to take the SAT test. I'll give you a study guide. And I'll find some good scholarship applications, all right?"

"All right." When I walk out of her office, I feel different, like I take up more space in the world.

Myself, *I think, with a little awe and wonder. This is the real me, this smart girl who is going to college.*

Now, so many years later, I find that I'm weeping for the girl I was. What happened to her?

I did take the SAT, and I got a good score. Started working on the scholarships and then . . . what happened next?

Thomas, that's what happened.

Thomas, and God, and the ubiquitous apostle Paul.

"Oh, you foolish, foolish girl," I whisper to myself.

I chose Thomas and did my best to live up to his expectations. Now here I am. Widowed. Perpetually at war with my only child, with nothing to show for any of it but guilt and regret.

Even genuine grief eludes me. I keep trying to summon up sorrow, remembering all of the years Thomas and I spent together. I feel his absence keenly, keep running my mind over it, the way my tongue kept poking at the place a tooth used to be when I had one extracted. Missing Thomas is like missing a tooth, but a tooth that ached.

If I'm honest, what I feel is more relief than loss.

And when I think of Abigail, my beautiful, brilliant, misguided Abigail, plunging into the same mistakes I made, sacrificing her own dreams for what she sees as duty, I feel anger that borders on rage. Some of it is directed toward Thomas; more of it at myself. I taught her all too well how to go along with her father's wishes instead of asserting her own. And now she's coming home to martyr herself and make sure both of us stay in this familiar trap.

My always-vivid imagination shows us twenty years down the road, empty and bitter. Polite on the surface, loving and hating each other underneath. I'll be just like Earlene. The walls press in on me, and I flee the house and Thomas and my impending future, taking refuge in the backyard.

Screened by hedges, tucked into a green and rather overgrown world, I can breathe again. Stripping off my shoes and then my socks, I focus on the grass cool and damp beneath my bare feet. It needs to be mowed, but I like it this way. Dandelions have dared to intrude now that Thomas isn't here to poison them, and my heart lightens at the sight of their bright-yellow heads. A squirrel cusses at me from up in the big maple.

One hand on the tree trunk, peering upward, I catch sight of him, his red tail jerking with every unholy exclamation he utters. "You and me, buddy," I tell him. "We have got to watch our language or we are both of us going to the bad place."

The squirrel scolds louder, disappearing higher up the tree in a flurry of waving branches.

I envy him that, his freedom to climb so easily, to leap from limb to limb. I want to climb after him, to disappear up into the branches and look down on the world below, unseen. But this tree isn't climbable. All the branches are out of reach. I put my arms around it, lean my cheek against the cool bark, breathe in the scent of pitch and leaves.

Moses meows and flops down not far from my feet, stretching luxuriously. His fur looks healthier since he's moved into the house, and his bones are less obvious. The vet gave me some deworming pills and some drops for mites in his ears. He's tamer, but still wary and easily startled, so I lower myself slowly into the grass.

"Here, kitty, kitty." He slouches toward me like a street hoodlum, climbs into my lap as if he owns it, and begins a loud, rattling purr. I touch two fingers to the top of his head. He purrs louder and I stroke his cheek. He presses his face into my palm, leaning into the caress. I have a weird sensation of the world breathing along with me, as if I can hear the grass roots growing down into the earth. The bright dandelions all around me that have taken root in the hostile environment of Thomas's lawn glow like brands of courage. The squirrel starts up another harangue, such a tiny creature, so courageous, really, to be shouting down at a human and a cat.

And an idea comes to me. Daring. Preposterous. Inspiring.

What if it's not too late to get a degree? There's a community college in Colville. I feel an expansion in my rib cage, as if there's more room to breathe. I'm not dead yet. I don't have to be an Earlene. The world is full of possibilities.

Thomas edges back into my head.

"Go ahead, take an evening class to keep your brain from rapid aging, if you must. But it's too late to do anything else. You'll look ridiculous taking classes with a bunch of teenagers."

Maybe an online university, then. I could take writing classes. Maybe I could write a novel. Or a play. Doubt sneaks back in, not bothering with a Thomas voice this time. *Who do you think you're kidding, Liz? What would be the point?*

And then I touch my wrist, the place where I imagine a WWLD tattoo, and smile. I can say yes to one class, at least. Maybe, just maybe, it's not too late.

Chapter Fourteen

Tara and Bernie arrive first, rattling up the street in a battered pickup that looks like a tree fell on the box at some point. Between them, they lug a cooler into the yard, full of ice and drinks, mostly beer. Bill shows up next, eager to show off his new wife, twenty years younger and clearly adoring. Geoff brings chips and dip and a slow cooker full of tiny wienies in some sort of spicy sauce. Val has ordered pizza.

And Lance—well, Lance isn't here.

I tell myself maybe he's working. It's a Saturday, after all, and it's spring. Farmwork must be busy this time of year. When my phone rings and I see his name on the caller ID, a completely inappropriate thrill runs through me, and I step away from the group happily drinking pre-moving beers on my front lawn.

"Hey," I say into the phone.

"Hey. You may have noticed my absence."

"I may have."

"I'd like to be there."

"Well, then. Come on over. The party is just getting started."

He laughs. "Let me guess. Bernie and Tara brought the booze. And Geoff brought the snacks."

"You sound like you know these people."

"How is your daughter likely to take to this gathering?" he asks.

"Not well." I shiver a little.

"Given our last interaction," he says, "I thought maybe it was better if I don't pour gasoline on the fire."

"Abigail can be terrifying." I try to say it lightly, even though I feel suddenly about a hundred pounds heavier. "I can see why you wouldn't want to—"

"Actually, I was thinking about her. This has all got to be extremely difficult for her. I figured the shock value of the others would be more than enough."

"The more the better. We will catapult her free of her prejudices. Come join the fun. If you're available."

There's a pause, during which I hate the phone. I can't see his face, can't see what he's thinking. And in that space, I decide to tell him the truth.

"She's moving home because she thinks it's her duty."

"Take care of Mom?"

"Yes, only it's not her idea, really. It's her father's voice talking to her from the grave. And it's not so much to take care of me as to keep me—contained."

"Well, that's a clusterfuck," he says.

Part of my brain does its usual defensive, screeching language-alert maneuver. *Bad word. Straight to hell.* The other part delights in the sound of this word, and the perfection of two words coming together with the end sum of this perfect description.

"If you'd rather not face her, I totally get that, or if you have better things to do—"

"Me big strong man," he says in a caveman voice. "I can take it. On my way." The call ends, and I stand there with the phone in my hand, smiling at nothing.

Lance and Abigail arrive simultaneously from opposite directions. He parks in front of Earlene's house. Abigail's got a U-Haul trailer hitched to her car, and she stops right in the middle of the street. Either she's considering the problem of how to back the trailer into the driveway, or she's seen the welcoming committee and is contemplating an escape.

"You made it," I call out, walking toward her car. An inane thing to say, as I'm sure she'll point out to me later. "Do you need some help backing in?"

She doesn't even look at me, too busy glaring at Lance and the rest of the welcoming committee. "I can do it."

Lance parks and walks over to me as she begins her first attempt, the trailer clearly not going where she intended it to.

"I don't suppose she'd like some help with that," he says.

"Don't even think about it."

Geoff gets up off the lawn and ambles over to the car, beer in hand. "Hey," he says into the open window. "Turn the wheel right if you want the trailer to go left."

Even from a distance, I see the unmistakable jutting of her chin, and I feel a sudden rush of empathy. If I were her, I wouldn't want anybody telling me how to drive, either. And I'd be overwhelmed and put off by this cloud of strangers watching, criticizing, offering advice.

Abigail is on trial number three when Earlene's front door opens and she stalks across the street with all the dignity of an offended heron.

"What's the matter?" Lance asks. "You look like you've seen a ghost."

"Worse," I mutter. And then gasp in horror as a convoy of familiar cars comes into view. Kimber. Annie. And Felicity and Pastor Steve.

"You know that word you used?" I ask Lance. "The swear. Is there a term for a whole group of clusterfucks? Like how there's an unkindness of ravens? A murder of crows?"

"A tornado of clusterfucks?" he suggests. "What's up?"

"A collision of worlds. The Church of Thomas is about to meet the Theater."

"That bad?" he asks.

"Worse. Hide me." Lance does the absolutely worst possible thing he could do and puts a supporting arm around my shoulders. He means it in a friendly way, but my body wakes to his touch. I want to melt into him even as I want to cringe away, knowing how my church crew and Abigail will take it.

Pastor Steve joins Geoff, both of them offering up advice.

"We're going to need more pizza," Val says as the others get out of their cars.

"We're going to need the National Guard," I tell her, watching the church ladies close ranks. They clump together at the edge of the lawn, shooting hostile looks at the interlopers. Each one of them is armed with a covered casserole dish. Earlene marshals her troops, leading the charge directly to me and Lance. Pastor Steve walks beside Abigail's open window, giving her directions completely contrary to what Geoff is shouting from behind the trailer.

"I could have backed it in five times by now," Lance says.

"Hush." I ease out from under his arm and step forward to face the prayer warriors. "Hey, everybody! I had no idea you were coming to help. You can take those dishes right on into the house. The door is open."

Felicity shifts her Tupperware to her left arm and gives me a hug. Kimber looks disapproving and says nothing. Annie grins at me, and then turns to assess Lance. "Who is this, then? Are you going to introduce us?"

"I'm Lance," he says easily. "Here to help with heavy lifting."

"Us, too," Bernie calls from her seat on the lawn. "Well, we're mostly here to drink and eat pizza, but also for heavy lifting."

"Earlene didn't tell us you would have . . . company," Kimber says.

"Let me introduce you." I walk over to a midpoint between the two groups.

"This is Tara." The tiny woman holds up two fingers in a peace sign. "Yo," she says. "Good to meet you."

"And this is Bernie. You know Val, and you've already met Lance. That guy over there is Geoff, and the happy couple is Bill and Tracy."

"But who *are* they, is what we want to know." Earlene might think she's whispering, or maybe she wants her voice to carry. Either way, she could offer lessons in voice projection.

"Friends from community theater." I project my own voice on purpose, making sure everybody can hear me. "Community theater people, these are members of my husband's church. Earlene, Kimber, Annie, and Felicity."

"Anybody want a beer?" Bernie asks. "We brought plenty."

Earlene's mouth sets in a line of disapproval. "Moving and booze do not mix."

"Booze is what makes moving tolerable," Bernie retorts.

Abigail finally manages to get the trailer into the driveway, crooked, but off the street and with only one wheel on the lawn. "Good enough for government work," Geoff says, signaling two thumbs-up.

"Let's get this show on the road." Pastor Steve dusts off his hands as if he's responsible for the parking success. "You want to direct traffic, Abigail?"

I can guess what Abigail wants. She'd prefer to carry in one box at a time and unpack it before bringing in the next. Everything neat, everything orderly, everything under her control. But surely even she can see that it won't go down that way with this group of eager box carriers.

Stiff as an indignant cat, she opens the trailer, revealing rows of identical boxes, neatly and perfectly stacked. Bernie whistles. "You are either one tight-ass packer, or one of those minimalists. Surprised you didn't just rope it onto the top of your car and forget the trailer."

I know she left furniture behind, that she took a few items to Goodwill. Even so, Bernie has a point. Minimalist is great when it's a philosophical choice, but I suspect Abigail's restraint in acquiring possessions is more of an ingrained habit.

"Everything goes into my old room," Abigail instructs. "The one on the right, just past the bathroom."

"Got it, boss." Tara grabs a box marked "textbooks," and as she slides it out of the trailer, Abigail hovers, hands outstretched to help. But the tiny woman lifts it easily and heads up the driveway as if she moves boxes full of books every day. Bernie follows, and then the rest kick in, like a line of ants carrying matching box-shaped bread crumbs.

Which, of course, creates a traffic jam. Geoff and Pastor Steve arrive on the porch just as Tara and Bernie are emerging, with Lance and Annie right behind them. Earlene, who is clearly here in a supervisory capacity only, smooths one hand over her skirt and glances down at her modestly heeled pumps, as if wondering whether she's expected to participate.

Val pulls out her phone and initiates an order for extra pizza.

"They need a traffic director at the door," Felicity says to Earlene. "You'd be good at that." She flashes dimples as she says it, all sweetness and light and spun sugar, but there's a flicker of something stronger in her eyes. Maybe I've underestimated her and the church won't eat her alive after all.

Earlene takes to the suggestion like Moses takes to tuna, ordering everybody around as if it's her God-given right.

I carry in a box, mostly to keep myself busy. I pause when I set it down, seeing the room with new eyes. The pink coverlet and matching curtains are an expenditure I'd talked Thomas into the year our daughter turned twelve, arguing that God loved beauty and our daughter deserved a pleasant space of her own. No clutter anywhere, no knick-knacks or decoration. There never had been, I realize with a pang. I never had to get on her case to make her clean her room. It was always painfully, perfectly neat.

A huge framed print of Adam and Eve hangs over her bed. They are clothed in animal skins, looking wistfully back at Eden, blocked by a terrifying angel with a flaming sword.

"Hell of a picture," Lance says, setting down a box with a little grunt of effort.

"I've always hated it."

And feared it. I've had dreams about that angel. What was the effect on a small child left alone with him in the dark? I should have fought Thomas. If there had to be an angel on the wall, it should have been a guardian angel. There are a million pictures like that, of angels shepherding children through danger. Why didn't we hang one of those?

The answer is acid in my belly. Fear and guilt are great manipulators. Thomas wanted her to feel those things. And I allowed it. I press one hand over my mouth, swamped with regret.

Lance rests a steadying hand on my shoulder, his face a question.

"You two having a private confab or what?" Bernie asks. She's lugging a box that appears to be heavy, even for her, and I step aside to make room for her to bring it in. Lance touches my arm, an unspoken message that I can't interpret.

When I reach the front door, a kid is standing there with pizza boxes piled so high, he can barely see over them. The smell of pepperoni and cheese wafts into the air.

"Let's take them to the backyard," I say.

He follows me through the house, and I help him stack the boxes on the deck. A slight stirring in the hedge alerts me to the presence of Moses, predictably unhappy with the invasion of all of these strangers.

Val was planning to pay for the pizza, I know, but I take care of it before she gets a chance. She's the soul of generosity, but I know her budget is tight. Bernie and Tara come through with the cooler.

"All done," Bernie says. "Figured we'd bring the rest of the party back here. You okay, Liz?"

I glance up at her, surprised at the perceptive question.

"Your daughter is a spitfire. Mine, too. Mixed blessing when she moved back in for a bit. We fought. Fur and feathers flying."

"But you worked it out?"

She grimaces, then laughs. "We still speak, if that's what you mean. She didn't stay long. Kids. Just as much grief as husbands, only you can't get rid of them."

"What's this about getting rid of husbands?" Tara flashes her impish grin. "I always suspected you helped yours along, Bern."

Bernie strikes a seductive pose. "Black widow. That's me."

"I'm ready for a beer." Geoff walks right into the middle of us, clueless when we all start laughing.

"Me, too." Pastor Steve reaches into the cooler and pops the top off a can of Bud. He takes a good long swig, wiping his mouth with the back of his hand and sighing with contentment. "That hits the spot. Thank the good Lord for beer and pizza. I hope you got pepperoni."

I try to picture Thomas, sweaty and laughing, guzzling beer and eating pizza. My mind boggles, failing utterly.

Val appears with paper plates and napkins, the church ladies behind her, casseroles in hand.

I extend an olive branch. "Earlene, that pie looks mouthwatering. How about right over here?"

She still doesn't speak to me, but her posture thaws, just a little, and I know she'll forgive me eventually for our earlier conversation, even though she will never forget.

As everybody starts filling their plates, I think about going to fetch Abigail. She must be hungry. After a moment of indecision, I opt for leaving her alone. This day has been hard enough for her already; if she wants to socialize, she'll come out on her own.

The church people gravitate to one side of the lawn, theater people to the other, but the margins of the groups seem easier, the tension defrayed by shared work and the promise of food. I'm about to ask Pastor Steve to say a blessing, something I know needs to happen, when Bill surprises me by removing his hat and saying, "I'm happy to say grace."

I smile at him, grateful. "Thank you, Bill."

He nods, bows his head, and says, simple and heartfelt, "Dear Lord, thank you for this day and for the company. Bless this house and bless this food. Amen."

Cheerful chaos around getting food and drinks eases any final awkwardness.

Pastor Steve, beer in one hand and plate in the other, crosses the line entirely and settles down next to Bernie. "So, Bernie, is it? What do you do when you're not moving boxes?"

"Real estate."

"She sold my place after my divorce," Tara says. "That's how we met." Then, to me, she says, "I don't know how you live in a house where you watched somebody die."

"It's not easy," I answer, which is the truth, only it's the memory of the living man more than the dead one that is causing me distress.

"Have you thought about moving? This place would go in a heartbeat," Bernie says, looking around with sharp eyes. "It's an excellent location. A family would snap it right up. So close to the schools."

"Is that even allowed?" I laugh to cover the fact that my question is genuine. Moving feels like the violation of an unwritten rule. I hadn't even considered the possibility.

"No!" Val exclaims. "What would I do without you next door?"

"Where would you want to move to?" Bernie persists. "Any ideas?"

She's serious. This is not a theoretical conversation. Bernie's not engaging in wishful thinking or imaginary adventures. She's a businesswoman. She sells houses. I stare at her, an expansive sensation of freedom growing inside my chest. A new house. One that belongs to me, that I can turn into a home.

"I used to dream of living out of town," I say with a quiet sense of wonder. "Maybe a couple of acres. Somewhere quiet."

A movement draws my eyes, and I see Abigail standing on the deck, staring at me, her face stricken. *You wouldn't. You couldn't,* her expression says.

I very nearly rush into apology and explanation: "Of course I'm not going to sell the house, I'm just making conversation. I'd never move from here, not when it's so important to you to keep it unchanged, to preserve all of the memories . . ." But before the words can reach my lips, the truth hits me.

Cutting Abigail free of the past is my first step toward rescuing both of us. It wouldn't be selfish. It would be the right thing to do. All at once, I can taste freedom, can clearly picture moving through a space I love, one shaped by my tastes and my needs. One free of Thomas.

"Say the word and I'm your huckleberry," Bernie says, oblivious to the drama playing out between me and my daughter.

Abigail descends the steps in slow motion and crosses the yard, settling into the grass beside me.

Lance opens the mushroom, onion, and sausage box. "You want one, Liz? Abigail?"

"No, thanks," Abigail says. "Not hungry."

"I'll take one."

Lance drops a gooey slice onto my plate, and I lift it with my hands and take a huge bite of cheesy, spicy goodness.

Pastor Steve opens a second beer and grins at his wife. "I know this is a stretch, but if you decide to move, this would be the perfect house for Felicity and me. No pressure or anything, of course."

Felicity squeals, upsetting her plate as she flings her arms around his neck. "I'd love to buy a house. Could we really?"

He kisses her, both of them laughing. "You'd like that, Bunny?"

"I hate the apartment." She kisses him again.

"Plenty of houses to look at," he says. "I just thought, if you were going to sell anyway, then that would be so easy for both of us."

"We are not selling the house," Abigail protests. "Mom was just daydreaming. She does that." Her tone is dismissive, pushing my rebellion button.

"Feel like giving us a tour?" Bernie is already on her feet, snapping photos of the yard. "I mean, I know we've been in the house, but we haven't really seen it. Just in case the interested parties turn out to be deadbeats. Might as well be ready to put it on the market."

"Oooh, yes!" Felicity crams a large wedge of crust into her mouth and claps her hands.

The whole troupe of them get to their feet, brushing off grass and leaves and converging on the house as if they haven't all just been through it with moving boxes.

"You coming?" I ask Abigail, torn by what I plan to do and the fear of what it will do to our relationship.

"No, I am not coming."

I force a cheerful smile. "Have a slice of pizza. You're too thin." The door bangs behind me, and I pray for a sign that I'm on the right track, and not setting foot on the road to hell.

Chapter Fifteen

May 9, 2019

Dear Inner Liz,
I guess you're not so inner anymore. Wow. Go figure. That's
a revelation. I should be happy about being more . . . me.
But this whole being-responsible-and-creating-my-own-
life thing is getting complicated. I sat Abigail down and
talked to her about my idea of buying a new house. That
went well. Ha. She was cold and pushed the guilt buttons.
I took the bait and got mad, and we had a rehash of the
wax museum conversation.

The Elizabeth part of me wanted to fix it. To give in,
to go along. But I can't bring myself to do that anymore.
She doesn't know that I called Bernie and told her I want
to take a look at some houses. She doesn't know that I've
been researching online universities. No decisive action
yet on either front, but I'm entertaining the possibilities.
I'm telling myself it will be good for her, too, but am I
just telling myself stories so I'll feel better? Am I selfish?

If I gave up everything I want and let her boss me,
would it repair our relationship? We'd have surface peace,

I guess, but it wouldn't be . . . true. I'd be pretending again, being somebody I'm not. And I don't really think that's okay, either. I thought wisdom was supposed to come with advancing age, but that's a joke, apparently. What you get with advancing age is hot flashes and weight gain and children who think you're decrepit.

Tonight's rehearsal is all about music, and Bill chooses to focus on me and Lance, putting together choreography for our solos and duets. Everyone else is supposed to be off running lines, but most of them are still sitting in their seats, watching.

I've come a long way since my involuntary audition. I don't mind an audience; as a matter of fact, having eyes on me onstage makes it easier to slip into Lacey. The stage chemistry between me and Lance is still sizzling, and I've stopped fighting it. I tell myself it's like a roller coaster—a safe thrill with built-in limits. I can allow myself to luxuriate in his touch onstage while trusting that it's not going anywhere else.

There have been no more invitations to run lines over dessert or coffee. When we're offstage, Lance is polite, supportive, friendly. His presence still accelerates my heart and starts butterflies flitting about in my stomach, but we seem to have come to an unspoken agreement not to act on our attraction. I'm fine, I tell myself. This is how it needs to be between us.

But tonight, as I step onto the stairs to climb up onto the stage, Lance follows me instead of vaulting up onto the stage the way he usually does. His hand rests lightly on my lower back, steadying me, and his touch seems to burn through the thin fabric of my T-shirt. I glance up and he is glancing down, and the intensity of that moment of connection drives all reason from my brain. All I can think about are sensitive lips and a strong chin and eyes that seem to see everything I've been trying to hide.

When we get up on the stage, the space seems smaller than usual—either that or Lance seems larger. It's hard to focus, hard to catch my breath. Fortunately I don't need to remember lines.

"Okay, let's block it out," Bill calls, walking up the stairs to join us. "Steph, just play through, will you?"

The pianist starts playing "Say Yes to Me."

"Walk to center stage, and stand facing each other," Bill directs. I close my eyes for a bar or two, invoking Lacey. When I can clearly feel her energy, I raise my chin and let my gaze meet Lance's. We stand there, music flowing over and between us, until Bill says, "Turn to face the audience here. We'll put you each in a separate spotlight until the end of the second verse. Now, turn toward each other again, step closer. Closer. Here we'll go with one spotlight, just the two of you on a dark stage."

There's a slow burn in Lance's eyes, a tension in his body, that wakes a response from me.

"Darcy takes her hands here," Bill says, oblivious, and my hands are engulfed in Lance's strong ones. One small step forward, and my body would be pressed against his. If we stand here any longer, I'm going to take that step, no matter who is watching. It's like he's a magnet and I'm iron and nothing can keep us apart.

"Okay," Bill says. "Let's do it with vocals. Places!"

Singing makes it worse. I can't keep my emotions out of my voice, and I swear I can hear Lance's soul. As our voices twine together in the last duet, we stand so close I can feel his body heat. So close a breath of wind could barely come between us.

When the music ends, I'm not sure if I'm still breathing.

"He needs to kiss her," Bernie calls out from the front row. "He would, here, wouldn't he? I mean, that's the whole point of the song."

"She's right," Tara agrees.

"I think so," Bill says. "It would add so much to the feels the audience is having. A perfect opportunity to seize them by the heartstrings and suck them in. It's not required, but are you two up for a little stage kiss?"

"I am." Lance's voice is deeper than usual, roughened, and his gaze holds that same intensity.

I tilt my head back, breath held.

"Lacey?" It's a request for permission, but he doesn't wait for the answer. His head is already bending toward mine. There is time for me to stop this. To say, *"No, I couldn't possibly, we shouldn't I'm married oh God I'm a widow."* I'm headed for hellfire because I want this kiss, crave it.

Lance's face is so close to mine I can't see his eyes anymore, and I close my own. His hand cups my face, gently, gently, and his lips are not dry or dutiful, they are warm, they are alive and mine also are alive and oh God I have never been kissed like this in the course of my entire existence.

When Lance breaks the kiss, he keeps his head bent so we are looking into each other's eyes, our lips so close we are sharing oxygen, one breath sufficient for both of us, his hand still warm on my face.

Applause from the group jars me back into myself.

I feel woozy, unsteady. Lance grabs my hand and turns me toward the auditorium so we can take a bow. And then he leads me across the stage, down the stairs, hand in hand all the way, never letting go until I collapse into my seat.

Val hugs me. "That was amazing! The chemistry between the two of you is hot!"

Chemistry. Acting and chemistry. That's all this is.

I manage, somehow, to focus on the rest of the rehearsal. To remember to sing in the right places, but everything is a blur except for Lance. He has become the focal point of every scene, every song, every movement that I make.

After rehearsal, Jayce calls me into a back room to talk about costuming and to take some measurements. When I walk out, still a little dazed, the theater is empty, the lights turned down. I walk down the center aisle, my right hand brushing the backs of the seats.

And Lance is still there, in the very back, waiting for me.

I look around for Val, for Bill, for anybody, but there is nobody to rescue me from me.

"Hey," Lance says, just the single word, as if it's natural that he would wait, and we walk out the door together, side by side but not quite touching.

Outside my car, I stop to look up at him. "Good night, then. I'll see you—"

"I want to kiss you. Again. Now."

"Oh."

"Would you mind?"

I should tell him, "Yes, I mind. We can't do this. We shouldn't." But all I seem capable of is gazing into his eyes. Lance lets his hands settle on my waist, pulls my body in against his. My softness meets muscle, strong thighs, hard belly and ribs.

And then he's kissing me, deeper than onstage. I open to it and his tongue touches mine, requesting permission, and the way he strokes and awakens the soft surfaces of my mouth is a wonder.

A low sound escapes him, almost a growl, and my body comes alive in a way it never has before. Need swamps me. I want him to fill all of me, all of the empty spaces. His hands slide down over my hips, pulling me against him so I can feel the pressure of him hard in the soft space between my legs.

I gasp at the intensity of it, the understanding that his need is as great as mine.

My hands explore the skin of his back, the long line of muscle, and a sound I never knew I could make finds its way out of my throat and against his lips.

He pulls away, his breath hard and fast.

"I want you alone."

"Abigail's at home," I murmur, and this voice must be Lacey's because it certainly does not belong to me.

His body stiffens, and I am suddenly Liz again, not Lacey, and shocked at the implications of what I've just said. His hands move to my shoulders and tighten there. His eyes bore into mine, searching for something.

"There's nobody at my place."

"Except you and me a few minutes from now," the Lacey part of me says, brazen.

"You're sure?" He kisses me again, and I let my body answer for me. "Damn it," he says. "I didn't anticipate this. No condoms."

"I am impregnable."

He pulls back a little and looks at me. I flush with awkwardness, rushing to explain. "Years of infertility. Onset of menopause." I need to ask him if he's clean, if he's been tested, but I can't get the words out. He's an EMT. Surely he takes care of his health.

"Get in my truck," he growls, breathless. "I'll drive."

"I'll follow you." I need my own vehicle, an escape route, just in case.

One more kiss, and then he opens my car door for me, waits until I'm settled before stalking away to his own truck. I watch his taillights across the parking lot and out into the street. I hear Val's warning in my head, but it's a distant thing, without power.

My body trembles with equal parts passion and fear.

Lance is sure to be disappointed. I know so little about pleasing a man. It's been years since Thomas has touched me in a sexual way. And when he did, he took what he needed, expecting little from me other than submission.

I drive, torn between anxiety and desire, half expecting God to exact judgment. Maybe I'll hit a deer. Maybe there will be a lightning strike from on high. But if the Almighty has any objection to my sexual liaison with Lance, He's keeping it to Himself.

Lance's truck turns into the driveway of a duplex. I park, but just sit there in the dark. Lance opens my door, his shadowed face looking down at me.

"Changed your mind?"

Mute, I shake my head, but still can't bring myself to get out of the car.

His fingers graze my cheek. "You're trembling. Liz. If you don't want—"

"I want." Before I have time to think, I get out of the car and step into him so the lengths of our bodies are touching, stretch up on tiptoes, and kiss him, my hands burrowing into his hair.

In answer, his hands go to my hips, slide down onto my buttocks, pull up and into him so I can feel the hardness of his erection between my legs.

I gasp at the molten pleasure that overrides everything, all of my doubt, my fear, the guilt I know will follow. Lance's lips find mine, and I open to him at once, letting my own tongue explore his mouth in turn, tentative at first, then bolder.

"Unless you mean to do this on the hood of your car," he says, "we'd better get inside."

I'm not sure that my knees will hold me, but his strong arm around my waist supports me across the yard and through the door.

His apartment is a shock, like falling into cold water. Barren as a monk's cell. A single table. One chair. A recliner in the living room. A TV. The walls are white and empty. No books or photographs. No pets. Something is wrong with this, but Lance starts kissing me again, and I forget about my surroundings.

In the bedroom, fear descends.

This moment, here, with this man, is something the romances I've read have not equipped me for. The real world, so different from the fictional world, can't possibly be the same. I remember my wedding night, the way my new husband took my virginity and destroyed my romantic illusions.

Lance, breathing hard, takes a step back, scrutinizing my face. "If you're unsure, please tell me now."

I might be all kinds of unsure, but Lacey knows what to do. It's her hands that go to the waistband of his jeans, undo the button, lower the zipper.

He's gone commando, no underwear, and his full erection frees itself from the confines of his jeans. Bigger than Thomas. Harder. It will hurt to take that into my body, but I want it all the same.

Lance steps out of his jeans, yanks his T-shirt off over his head. He's naked now, and I'm still fully clothed. I've never been naked in front of anybody, rarely even in front of a mirror.

With Thomas, I wore a long nightgown, bunched up over my hips for the crucial act, decorously lowered afterward. But I'm not wearing a nightgown, and I can't bring myself to strip as he has done.

Lance holds my gaze as he lifts the hem of my T-shirt, peeling it up over my head. I breathe a little deeper, expanding. Lance kisses me just below my ear, down the side of my neck, the space between my collarbones. His hands go to my back, unfasten my bra, then he cups my breasts in his hands.

When he releases them, I mourn the sensation of his touch, but only for an instant as those hands smooth down over my ribs, my belly, my hips.

He moves us backward across the room, holding me against him, until the backs of my knees are against the bed. A gentle shove and I'm sitting on the mattress. He presses me back, swings my legs up. He undoes the button on my jeans, works them down over my hips, and then strips off my underwear.

I'm completely naked now, under his eyes. He's not touching me, just looking, and I feel vulnerable and on fire.

"So beautiful," he says, and then his weight dips the mattress beside me, and I close my eyes and spread my legs to make it easy for him, expecting a hard thrust and a few grunts and this will all be over. He straddles my body; I can feel his erection pressed against me as he kisses me.

But then his lips are on my throat again, sensation overriding fear, my body responding in ways that surprise me.

When his lips find the nipple of my right breast, I gasp, my hands knotted in his hair, desire becoming a pressure, a demand.

"Please," I whisper, only I have no idea what I'm asking for.

My body melts into submission, until his lips move from my breasts to my belly. By the time I guess what he is going to do, an act I have only read about but certainly never dreamed of committing, his tongue is between my legs.

My hands tighten in his hair, meaning to push his head away, surely this is a thing that I shouldn't let him do, but I've become incapable of speech, of movement. A sound forces its way from my throat, and then another, and a wave rolls over me of utter pleasure, shakes me to my deepest places, comes again.

He brings himself back up with his weight covering the length of mine. Again, I brace for him to enter me, but he doesn't, not yet. He finds my mouth again, tasting, kissing. Moves to my throat, my breasts, until that pressure is rising once more, and I beg, "Please, Lance."

When he enters me, it's not a sudden thrust. There is no pain. He presses into me slowly, so that I feel my body stretching, widening, until every nerve ending is awake and wanting, and then, only then, does he slide all the way in. There is no taking. His body is a gift. He finds a slow rhythm, and I'm awed by the way I respond, my movements mirroring his, rocking up to meet him and then away.

The pressure and the pleasure meld and grow.

"Open your eyes," he says. "Please."

My eyes meet his, his pupils so large they almost blot out the blue, the tension in his face almost pain. He drives deeper into me, and I feel all of my defenses give way in a rush as a cry bursts from my throat. My hips thrust upward to bring him even deeper, my hands pressing into his buttocks, and then he cries out, a prayer or a plea, an "Oh my God" on a breath that tears something loose inside me.

A long moment later, I feel the tension go out of him as he lets himself collapse on top of me, both of our bodies sweat slicked, and then he withdraws and rolls beside me, one hand over my chest, his face pressed into my shoulder. I feel the wetness between my legs, the damp spot growing into the sheets, and think maybe I will be embarrassed in a minute. Guilty. Full of regret.

But not now, not yet.

Mostly what I feel is wonder. We lie like that for a long while, drowsing, limbs draped languorously over each other while I breathe in the man smell of him, the smell of sex. Gradually I begin to come back into myself, to draw inward. I reach for the sheet and pull it up to cover my body, start thinking about how to get from the bed to my clothes.

"Regrets?" he asks, caressing my hair.

"I don't know yet."

His hand slides onto my cheek, traces the line of my jaw, and just that simple touch ignites the spark of passion again.

Wanton. Earlene is right. Without a husband to tame me, I have become a wanton widow, and what's more, I like it.

"I should go." But I make no move, can't seem to exert the will to get up off the bed. "What about you, with the regrets?"

"Only this, the thing I should have said in the beginning. I like you, Liz."

"I should hope so."

"But I'm not looking for—"

"Stop." I put a finger over his lips. "Don't ruin it."

"I just don't want you to—"

"Lacey and Darcy," I reassure him. "Not Lance and Liz." It's as close as I can get to saying what I mean, but light comes into his eyes. His lips curve into a smile that I want, immediately, to kiss.

"For the good of the play?" he asks, an undertow of laughter in his voice.

"Getting into our roles. Method acting."

"I could do more research." His hand strays from where it rests on my hip, sliding over my belly, then downward.

A trail of heat follows his fingertips. I shiver, deliciously, but then shove his hand away. "I need to go."

"Is this it, then?"

I caress his face with my eyes, run exploratory fingers through the hair at his temple. "I imagine I'll need more research. To make sure I get Lacey right. I just—need to sleep in my own bed. Before my daughter calls for a welfare check."

Neither of us moves, though, and Lance's eyes crinkle with quiet laughter. "Shall we both get up at once so nobody has to be the first?"

"And a pact not to look at each other," I add. "Keep your eyes on your own clothes."

"Fair enough. Ready?"

"One," I say, "two, three, go." I cheat, lagging behind him a little, just enough to let myself look at him. A little softer in the belly than I'd expected, a little saggier in the glutes. Which isn't fair, at all, because I know my own flaws all too well. Every varicose vein, every bit of cellulite. His eyes meet mine, and I know I'm not the only one cheating. Gathering up my clothes, breathless and laughing like a child, I flee across the room and lock myself into the bathroom to get dressed.

Chapter Sixteen

Before I'm fully awake, I begin my usual slow, careful slide out of bed, careful not to disturb Thomas. It's not until my feet touch the cold floor that I remember he's well beyond being disturbed.

The bed looks like he still lives here, though. His pillow is still in its assigned place. The sheets and the comforter on his side of the bed are smooth and unrumpled. Despite having the bed all to myself, I never cross the line into his inviolate, sacrosanct space.

Last night comes rushing back to me, Lance's warm body and the way he focused on my pleasure before his own. Something violent and bitter rises from the core of me. I hate this bed. It is an indecency that fills me with a rage that goes beyond words or reason.

Break. Burn. Tear.

I drag the sheets and comforter off the bed and throw them onto the floor in a heap. I grab Thomas's pillow in both hands and beat it against the bare mattress. *Whomp. Whomp. Whomp.* Such a small, unsatisfying sound.

How many hours have I lain wakeful in this bed, careful not to move too much, holding a position long past the point of comfort in order to avoid a rebuke?

"You woke me, Elizabeth. I love you, but sometimes you are so thoughtless."

How many times did I lie beneath him, enduring his conquest of my body, waiting for him to finish? How could I get to be forty-nine years old and have no idea of the kind of pleasure that can arise from a simple touch and a little consideration?

A flashback to my wedding night grabs me by the throat.

I stand, shivering with uncertainty, just inside the door of a house I have never entered before this night, a house that Thomas has bought and furnished, a house where I feel like a guest.

"Come, Elizabeth." He takes my cold hand and leads me down the hall to the bedroom. I'm suddenly frightened of him and what is to come. This is so different from explorations of passion in the back seat of a car with clumsy boys. I don't know what is expected of me, and I wait for him to make a move, to show me what to do, but he busies himself taking off his shoes, setting them neatly side by side in the closet. Unknotting his tie. Unbuttoning his shirt.

He glances over at me and smiles. "The dress is lovely, but you may want to remove it. Or at least your underwear."

"Just like that?" I'm shy about the idea of his eyes on me, of standing naked in front of him.

"We're married now," he says, reaching for his belt.

"That's not what I mean. Couldn't we . . . could you kiss me? Touch me . . ."

"What for?"

"Because we love each other. Because it feels good. It would make me feel more . . . married."

He sighs dramatically. "This isn't one of those romance novels. It doesn't work that way. Married people have sex for the purpose of procreation."

"Pretty sure some people enjoy it," I retort, my rebellious self awakening from a long slumber.

"Elizabeth," he says sadly, patiently. "Why are you picking a fight on our wedding night?"

"I'm not—"

"Lie down."

I stare at him from across the room. Home is a long way from here. I have no money and don't know a single person. Slowly, cold and shaking and a little sick, I climb up onto the bed and lie down, still fully clothed. He slides my dress up under my hips, pulls down my underwear.

"Wives, submit yourselves unto your husbands, for this is right," he quotes, pinning me between his thighs.

That was the first time he brought the apostle Paul as a third party into our marriage bed, but it was certainly not the last. An ugly croak tears free from my chest, and I pound the pillow with my fists, accentuating each movement with words. "You. Never. Loved. Me. You. Didn't. Even. Like. Me."

I want to rend the pillow apart with my hands, to scatter the feathers everywhere, but the fabric is strong and refuses to give. I carry it to the bathroom and stuff it into the trash can. A fierce hatred for the bed itself turns the edges of my vision black. It has to go. I will not sleep on it another night.

The mattress is unwieldy. My hands keep slipping and I can't get a proper grip, but I tug on one side, then shove from the other, until I get it up on edge and then drag it across the room and into the hallway. It catches against the edge of a picture frame—a wedding photograph, me in white dress and veil, Thomas in a black tuxedo, both of us looking at the camera with expressions that speak more of getting a driver's license than enthusiasm about a wedding.

I yank, hard. The picture swings wildly, then crashes to the floor.

"Damn it," I shout at the mattress. "Do you have to be so freaking obstinate?"

"Mom?"

Abigail's shocked face appears in her bedroom door.

I scrub the hair out of my face with my shoulder. "This piece-of-shit mattress is going out of this house!" I shout at her. "Don't just stand there, help me."

"What exactly are we doing?" I know the tone. *Don't antagonize the crazy woman, whatever you do.* She grabs the other end of the mattress and holds on to it.

"We are taking this fucking mattress outside." I say the forbidden word carefully, testing it, tasting it. It feels good in my mouth, strong and vivid and right. "Watch your feet, there's broken glass."

Clearly she thinks I've totally lost it, and I expect her to resist. But she decides to humor me, and between the two of us, we drag and tug the flopping, infuriating thing all the way down the hallway and to the front door, where Abigail makes a stand.

"Mom." She grips her end of the mattress and holds me back. "Let's think about this."

"There's nothing to think about."

"What are we going to do? Just throw it out on the front lawn? Like we're having a mattress sale or something? *We are in our pajamas.* There are stains on this mattress. People will see."

"I don't care."

"Mom. Listen to reason. We can buy a new mattress, if that's so important. But where is this one going to go? The trash guys aren't going to pick it up. What about the box spring? Is that coming out on the lawn, too? Maybe we can donate it or something. Be reasonable. Let's put it back—"

"I am sick and tired of being reasonable!"

My whole life, I've been reasonable. Compliant. Subservient. And where did that get me? Maybe I'll spend the rest of my life being irrational, pissed off, and batshit crazy.

"If you're not going to help, just let go and let me do it myself." I jerk at the mattress with all my strength, and Abigail starts moving with me. I wrestle the door open with one hand, sucking in a breath of the cool morning air. The birds are singing. The world is green and fresh and vividly alive.

The mattress sticks on the doorjamb, and I stagger when it comes free. If not for Abigail on the other end, I would lose my balance, fall backward, and probably be found dead later in the morning with the suffocating mattress on top of me.

But her weight serves as ballast, and I catch my footing.

In silence, we wrestle my enemy down the stairs and across the lawn to the curb, where I release my grip, Abigail releases hers, and the mattress settles down into the grass like it belongs there.

I scrub my hands on my pants, stretch out my shoulders and lower back, catch my breath.

Abigail's expression, somewhere between fear and horror, sparks another memory.

I've climbed into bed, exhausted after a particularly long day. All I want is to close my eyes and sleep. Thomas has other ideas. When he presses up against me from behind, grabbing my breast and squeezing, I can barely suppress a groan of dismay.

"Could we not, tonight? Please, Thomas."

"Don't tell me you have a headache."

"No, not that. I'm just . . . Abigail was sick, and I visited three people in the hospital, and—"

"It's your duty," Thomas says. "The apostle Paul—"

"Can we leave Paul out of it just this once? I'm tired. I don't want—"

"You made a vow, Elizabeth. I expect you to honor it."

If I keep saying no, he'll accept it eventually. He would never resort to physical force. But he'll be quietly angry and I'll pay in little ways for days to come. Best to get it over with.

I let him pull up my nightgown and lie still, holding my breath against the discomfort of his thrusting, my face turned to the side so he won't see the slow tears of weary helplessness tracking down my cheeks. And then the door opens, and Abigail stands there in her nightgown, staring.

She's so small, too young to see this, to understand any of it. Her eyes meet mine, and hold. I shake my head, warning her to say nothing, and she backs out of the room, closing the door behind her. After, when Thomas is snoring, sound asleep after his exertion, I slip out of bed to check on her. She's asleep, or pretending to be.

I look at my daughter now, wondering if she remembers, if that moment scarred her. We never spoke of it. I didn't know what to say, and she seemed fine. Normal. And gradually the moment faded into the distance and I let it go, the way I let so many things go back then.

What does Abigail see in me now? I feel like my face is a billboard flashing every emotion, every dirty, humiliating secret of my marriage, for her and the neighborhood to see. I wonder if Earlene is awake, if she will see us out here, two wild women, uncombed, half dressed, ridding the house of an offending mattress.

"We don't air our dirty laundry in public," my mother used to say. Well, I've now done that with a vengeance. Maybe it's not too late and we could drag the mattress back in. A flicker of movement in Earlene's window says otherwise.

I wave in her direction, an exaggerated parade wave, and follow it up with a stage curtsy.

"Now what?" Abigail asks, hands on hips, but it's difficult to look in control when you've been wrestling a mattress in your pajamas. She looks younger, softer, her hair in two loose braids hanging down her back.

"You should wear your hair like that."

"Mom!"

Val's door opens, and she steps out onto the porch, a coffee mug in one hand, an already lit cigarette in the other. She, too, is in pajamas—but hers are slinkier, shorts and a midriff top, a knee-length robe unbelted. Her eyes survey the scene as she exhales a slow ribbon of smoke.

"I'm bringing you coffee," she calls. "You want some, Abigail?"

"Thank you, no. I'm going to have a shower and get ready for work." She stalks into the house, slamming the door with a little extra emphasis.

Val pops out of sight and then reappears with a steaming mug in each hand. My anger is fading, leaving me feeling bruised and exposed.

"What's the plan?" Val stands beside me, the two of us watching the mattress as if we expect it's going to develop the power of motion or magically transform into a large bird and fly away.

"Planning does not appear to be my forte."

"Here. Hold my coffee."

She vanishes back into her own house and comes out with an armful of blankets.

"Val . . ."

"Go get a couple of chairs."

I do as instructed, lugging a dining room chair in each hand to find that Val has covered the mattress with a fuzzy pink blanket. She arranges the chairs on either side of the mattress and drapes a large quilt over the top.

"What are you doing?"

"Are you telling me you don't recognize a blanket fort when you see one? Come in. It will be fun."

I hesitate, but Val is already inside the crazy shelter, screened from the road and the neighbors, and I join her.

"See?" she says, grinning, and I do see.

When I was a little girl, I had hidey-holes everywhere. I figured out how to climb up into the shelf in my closet, above the hangers, and would sit there with my legs hanging down, daydreaming or reading. I built blanket forts that let me feel secret, safe, and touched by magic.

"I used to build these for Lenny," Val says. "He had anxiety for years after we left his dad. I found him hiding under the bed one morning, thought he'd heard his father at the door. I made a fort, and we sat in it together almost all day."

"Thomas never hit me," I say. "Not ever. Not once."

"There's all kinds of ways of making fear." She's not looking at me, but I think maybe she knows and understands.

As for Abigail, maybe if I'd made forts for her when she was a little girl, she wouldn't look quite so embarrassed when she comes out of the house, showered, braided, and back to her carefully constructed persona.

"I am not helping you put it back," she says. "Please have this cleaned up by the time I get home from work."

"Yes, ma'am."

Val giggles, an infectious sound that ripples through me. I press a hand over my lips, but a giggle escapes me, too, and the next moment we're clinging to each other, laughing like kids.

"You two are incorrigible." Abigail stalks off, and I hear her start her car and drive away.

My laughter fades, and I stare up at the roof of this flimsy shelter, trying to figure out what I'm going to do next.

Chapter Seventeen

"Wanna talk about it?" Val asks, rolling over onto her side and propping herself up on one elbow to look at me.

"Not really."

"You slept with Lance, didn't you?"

"Oh my God." I sit up and stare at her, aghast. "What makes you say that?"

"Well, didn't you?"

I close my eyes and will the question to go away. If Val guessed, just like that, everybody will guess. Maybe I'm walking around like one of those LED signboards, flashing a scarlet letter *A* for all the world to see.

Val sits up and grabs my hands. "It's okay, Liz. You're a grown woman."

"It's not okay! How is it so obvious? Will everybody know?"

She laughs. "Don't be silly. I put things together. You came home late last night, and you usually come home right after rehearsal. This morning, you had a sudden hatred for your marriage bed. And, the sparks between you and Lance were so hot last night I thought the two of you were going to start the stage on fire."

I flop back on the mattress again, wishing I had a pillow to put over my face.

Val settles down beside me. "Look, what I said about him before . . . I didn't mean you shouldn't be with him. I just wanted you to be careful. I want you to be happy."

"It was just research. Lacey and Darcy. I'm not expecting him to put a ring on my finger." I say it with conviction, but the truth is I've checked my phone a dozen times this morning hoping for a text or a call from Lance, telling myself every time that I'm relieved he hasn't reached out. I don't think I believe me.

"Why do I feel like it was something more than that?" Val rolls over to look at me, and I try to explain.

"In the bedroom, Thomas was . . . and then Lance . . ."

"Thomas was an asshole?" Val supplies.

"This morning, that feels like the truth. Comparatively speaking."

"So it was good with Lance?"

"It was superlative."

We're both silent with our thoughts for a bit, and then I ask, "What am I going to do with this mattress?"

"I was thinking you could turn it into a yard sale."

"I don't—" I stop. Think about all of the things in the house that I never want to see again. "Can I do that?"

"Free country," she says. "And it's Friday. And yard sale season."

"But we should have had signs up, gotten everything set out. And I don't have that much, really."

"Hang on. I have an idea." She sits up and taps at her phone, lets it ring. "Bern? Yes, I know it's early. If you didn't drink every night . . . Well, fuck you, too," she says cheerfully. "Hey, you know all of those old props we've been agitating to unload? Today is the lucky day. Impromptu yard sale at Liz's place."

Bernie says something that makes her laugh. "Perfect. See you then."

She closes the phone and grins at me. "The forces are now at work."

"Which forces, exactly?"

"The theater has a bunch of extra furniture, costumes, you name it, that they've been meaning to get rid of for years. Bernie's bringing it all over. She'll get Tara to make signs."

"What about Abigail?" A burst of panic hits me, and I sit up to stare at Val with wide eyes. "I didn't think. She wants the house to stay exactly the same, forever."

"Are you going to keep it exactly the same forever?"

"I've been thinking about moving. She's completely opposed." My brain scrambles to catch up with events. Abigail will never agree to change. She'll want to keep every item of furniture, every plate and cup and knife and spoon. I can try to whittle away at that, or I can act on this crazy idea and blast both of us loose from our moorings. Dangerous. But sometimes dynamite is necessary.

"What on earth is going on over here?" Earlene's voice asks. Her face appears in the entrance to our cave. Her eyebrows rise almost to her hairline as she glances from me, to Val, to the mattress, and back again. Her eyes narrow.

"Have you been drinking again?" She eyes my coffee mug as if she suspects that it contains clandestine moonshine.

"We're having a yard sale," Val intervenes. "But once we got the mattress out here, we were overcome by the temptation to make a fort."

"I understand a yard sale," Earlene says after a considering silence. "But a little planning would have been in order."

"It just seemed like the right day," I say, then feel devious and deceitful. "Actually—"

Val's elbow catches me in the ribs before I can fess up. "When inspiration strikes, go for it. It's the perfect day. We've got friends bringing things over to contribute. Do you have anything you want to add in, Earlene? The bigger the sale, the better."

"I do have a few things I've been saving up for a sale of my own. We'll need a cashbox and some change. Do you have all that?"

"No," I confess humbly. "I've really got nothing but the idea."

"I'll be back," Earlene says. "And I'll check with the others."

Val looks at me. "If you want to stop this, you have about ten seconds."

But it's already too late. The decision is made, the fuse is lit. I just hope I don't blow my relationship with my daughter to smithereens.

"Too late to stop Earlene," I say, trying to decide whether what I feel is exhilaration or panic. "It's on."

Val stretches out her tanned legs, luxuriously spreading her bare toes. "How is she so put together so early in the morning? Fully dressed. Every hair in place."

"Sometimes I don't think she's human. I don't suppose we can just stay in this fort forever and always?"

"I wish. But if we don't get moving, somebody is likely to buy this bed right out from underneath us."

A snort-laugh escapes me. "If I survive this, I say we have a sleepover in the backyard."

"Deal."

Together we start hauling stuff I don't want out onto the lawn. It turns out that what I don't want is nearly everything in the house. We remove the dining room chairs and the table. Thomas's recliner. The couch. The hated armchair long ago allotted to me. Most of the china and the silverware, both patterns that Thomas chose and I never liked.

I keep things for Abigail that I know she particularly loves. The teapot and teacups painted with garden flowers, with the luxurious gold leaf on the rim. Her father's watch and Bible. But I thoroughly dismantle our bedroom. The dresser goes, all of my clothes stacked in the closet on Thomas's side to deal with later. Thomas's clothes are the one thing that has already left the house, based on the only good advice I've ever had from Earlene.

"The clothes are hard," she'd said. "Maybe we could take them to Goodwill for you?"

With my permission, she and Annie and Kimber packed them up and hauled them all away. Thomas's suits, shirts, and dress pants had overflowed his half of the closet and overtaken mine. What's left is a cavernous space. My new clothes form a small, colorful oasis in the midst of a selection of demure and boring dresses and skirts, all in compatible mix-and-match colors. At the very back end of my row hangs my wedding gown.

"We totally need to go shopping again," Val says, peering over my shoulder. "Want to get rid of any of those?"

"Definitely the gown. Only, I don't think we can yard sale that."

"Abigail might want it," Val suggests.

"It goes." My voice is low and full of venom. I will not willingly pass any memento of my marriage to my daughter.

"I'll take care of it," Val says quickly. She doesn't ask any more questions, just bundles up the dress and gets it out of my sight.

I stand there staring at a small leather satchel in the very back corner of the closet, wondering how it is possible to forget something while it's hiding in plain sight. I've vacuumed this floor once a week since the day I tucked that bag behind the folds of the gown, knowing Thomas would never investigate that corner. On some level, I've always known it was there while at the same time forgetting all about it.

Like a sleepwalker I move forward and drop to my knees beside the bag, brushing off a haze of dust before opening the zipper. It's like a time capsule, and I remove the items and lay them out on the floor. Two pairs of underwear and a pair of socks. Jeans and a T-shirt and a little stash of money. Everything smells musty. The elastic on the underwear is brittle.

I'd packed it soon after my wedding day, when it was already clear to me that I didn't want the life I'd married into. Asking for a divorce seemed impossibly overwhelming and humiliating—Thomas would quote scripture at me and flatten me under layers of guilt. So I daydreamed about sneaking away some evening while he was out, maybe writing him a letter from the other side of the country. And then . . . Abigail. Morning sickness and hormones and the realization that, other than Thomas, I was all alone in the world with no marketable skills. The decision to stay was so gradual and insidious, I never bothered to unpack the bag.

"Everything okay?" Val asks.

"Fine. This can go in the trash." I stuff the items back in the bag, except for the cash, and Val carries it away.

Truthfully, I feel anything but fine, rocked to the core by this brush with my younger self. But if I've gained one skill in my life with Thomas, it's learning to suppress and disguise my emotions. Taking a deep breath, I shake off the memories and finish with the closet, steeling myself for the most difficult room in the house, saved for last.

Thomas's study.

I stand in the doorway, reluctant to enter. The bookcase is laden with weighty tomes on religion. The desk is solid, authoritarian. The pictures on the wall are of Moses receiving the Ten Commandments from an angry-looking God and Abraham ready to slay Isaac at the altar only to discover that there is a lamb he can sacrifice instead. "I don't think I can touch this," I say as Val comes back down the hall carrying two packing boxes. "It always feels like holy ground, like I should take off my socks and shoes before I go in there."

"You'll feel better once it's done," she says. "Maybe that Steve guy would be happy to have all of the books?"

"Or Abigail. I don't even know how this desk fit through the door in the first place. We'll never get it out." I turn to her. "Maybe we should just leave this room for later."

"Time to tear off the Band-Aid," Val objects, determined. "If you don't clear this room, he'll always still be here, running everything."

I close my eyes for a minute, breathing, picturing Abigail's outrage when she comes home to find this sanctum violated. But Val's right. This was always command central, and I still soften my footsteps and shrink into myself every time I pass it. As for Abigail, she's like Isaac, bound to the altar as a sacrifice. Maybe the only way to free her is to sell the altar out from underneath her.

That moves me into action. "Let's start with the pictures."

"I'm not sure these should really be in anybody's house, but okay." Val lifts the Ten Commandments painting down, holding it gingerly with the tips of her fingers. "I feel like God may smite me for this."

"It's only a picture." But I feel the same uneasiness as I lift Abraham and Isaac down from the wall. Isaac's eyes stare into mine. *How could he do this to me?* Isaac asks. *I'm his son. And what sort of God would ever ask him to?*

Val takes both pictures and heads for the door.

I sink into the leather chair behind the desk. How did it feel to sit here, all-powerful and in control of everything? I just feel small and tired.

"You can't get rid of my desk," Thomas whispers. *"You're a crazy woman. The contents of our lives will sit out on the lawn all day, and then you'll have to enlist help to bring it all back in, put it back in its place."*

I focus in on my anger, letting memories fuel it into renewed energy, and begin emptying the desk. The center drawer, neatly organized, contains pens, paper clips, stamps, a stapler. I pull it out and turn it upside down over an empty box, letting the contents rattle out with a satisfying racket. I repeat the process with one drawer after another. Envelopes, stationery, a three-hole punch. Thomas's planner goes into the trash. The file drawer is locked. I tug at it, jerk it harder. What could he have bothered to lock away? Neither I nor Abigail would ever have dared to search his office.

Probably confidential information about the congregation, in which case I should either shred it or maybe pass it on to Pastor Steve. Where would Thomas have put the key? It wasn't in any of the other desk drawers.

My eyes search the office. The rectangles where the pictures used to hang, unfaded by sun and darker than the rest of the wall. The bookshelf holding an array of heavy books and Bibles in different editions.

King James. New Life. Living. His well-worn personal Bible, the one he studied and preached out of, still sits on top of the desk, something I'm keeping for Abigail.

How many times has he read passages at me out of this book, exhorting me to be a more malleable wife, a better Christian? Now I open it, seeking something other than wisdom, and am rewarded by the discovery of a small key tucked inside a pocket built into the protective leather cover. Sure enough, the key unlocks the drawer, and I slide it open.

Hanging file folders contain neatly arranged white envelopes. What is this? Was he planning a mailing campaign? Surely he would have enlisted the church secretary for something like that.

The folder at the front is labeled 2019. The one at the back, 1988, the year we were married. I choose an envelope from the 1988 file, surprised to see it's unopened and addressed to me. The handwriting is my mother's. I sit for a long time with that envelope in my hands before looking at the others. Two more from my mother. One from the high school from which I graduated. This one has been opened, and I draw out the yellowing paper and read:

> *Dear Elizabeth,*
> *I hope this finds you well.*
>   *I was disappointed to hear that you didn't follow through with college. You are a bright and talented girl, and I thought you might need to know that it's never too late. Contact me if I can help you in any way.*
>   *Sincerely,*
>   *Mona Lutz*
>   *Guidance Counselor*

Tears sting my eyes. I blink them back and tear open one of the letters from my mother.

Liz—I've not heard back from you, so I assume that you are not wanting contact with me. Your father has moved out and I've had plenty of time to think. We didn't do right by you. I'd like your forgiveness, if you can find it in your heart. I've tried to call, and Thomas always says he's given you the message, but you never call back. I won't bother you again—you know where to find me.
    Mom

I can't move, can't breathe, can't anything. I am as frozen as a fly in amber.

Val appears across the desk. "Honey, what is it? You look like you've seen a ghost."

My mouth opens but no words come out.

"Breathe," she says, coming around behind me and placing both hands on my shoulders. "Take a breath."

I do. My lungs fill, and the world turns into sharp angles and disbelief.

"Don't tell me you've found a pornography drawer." She says it lightly, trying to make me laugh, but nothing is funny anymore.

I hand her the letter, let her read.

Her brow furrows in confusion. "I don't understand."

"There are more of them. All locked away. Mom and I never talked after my marriage. I thought she just washed her hands of me. But she didn't." There is a splinter lodged in the vicinity of my heart. "I don't understand. Why would he do this?"

I think of the bag, packed and hidden at the back of the closet. If I'd known I could have gone to my mother, would I have had the courage to leave?

"You can find her," Val says. "We'll track her down."

I shake my head, the back of my hand pressed against my lips. "She died, Val. We didn't even go to the funeral."

Val kneels and rifles through the files, stops short. "Oh my God, that bastard."

I don't even cringe at her language; I'm feeling like there aren't words enough to curse him. "What?"

"Are you sure you want to see?"

"No. I'm pretty sure I don't." But I reach for the envelopes in her hand. How much worse can it be?

As it turns out, a lot. Because these letters aren't about me, they concern Abigail.

Three official envelopes, all from universities. The University of Washington. Yale. Duke. Each has been carefully slit open. I draw out a heavy sheet of creamy paper from the one that says "Yale."

Dear Miss Lightsey,

We are pleased to inform you that you have been accepted into the premed program . . .

The words dance on the page. There's a buzzing in my ears.

I can see it all now, as if it's playing on a giant screen.

Abigail, so intelligent and driven, full of an ambition that she knows will never be sanctioned, applying to universities in secret. I remember her walking into the house after school, asking, "Any mail for me?"

Thomas, who always brought in the post, shaking his head. "Sorry, honey. Were you expecting something?"

"Nothing, Daddy. It's just fun to get mail." But the disappointment on her face was palpable. I'd thought at the time maybe there was a boy. I hadn't even dreamed she was applying to universities.

I bury my face in my hands, rocked by yet another memory.

The three of us sit around the dinner table. Instead of saying grace, Thomas sets an open envelope on the table in front of our daughter. "Would you like to explain this?"

"Me? You opened my letter!" Abigail challenges, stiff with defiance. "Explain that!"

"Watch your tone," Thomas reproves her. "I don't like that you applied behind our backs. Why didn't you say that you wanted to go to nursing school?"

I huddle into myself, furious and powerless at the same time. Abigail should have been a boy. Not because I want a son, but because then she could use her brains, be anything she wants to be.

"I don't like this deception, Abigail," Thomas goes on. "It's not like you."

She lifts her chin, ready to do battle. Her father has never quite tamed her. "I thought you might not let me go. And I am going to college. Once I turn eighteen, you can't stop me."

"I have no objection to you being a nurse," he says calmly. "For a few years, at least, until you meet the right man and get married."

"For real? I can go?"

He nods, and she runs to his chair and hugs him.

It was a compromise on his part. Even then I'd been surprised at his capitulation; now I understand. Better a woman should serve as a nurse than rise to the powerful position of doctor.

"How does a pastor lie to his daughter?" Val asks.

"For the good of her immortal soul," I whisper.

I can't begin to explain it to her, how Abigail's even applying must have felt like a sneaky betrayal to Thomas. How he would have felt as justified in this action as if he were intercepting packets of cocaine.

"Surely you don't believe that shit! I mean, what's so bad about being a doctor? They help people."

"A woman's place is in the home." My voice sounds flat, robotic, reciting the old programming. "They can be nurses, teachers, until they get married. And no, I don't believe it, but he did."

"How do you explain him hiding your mother's letters?"

"She was an unbeliever."

"*I'm* an unbeliever! I can't believe you are defending him!"

I look up at Val, the kindest and most giving human being I know. She is always there for me. She has turned my insane reaction to fantastic sex into a yard sale to help me cleanse my life and start over. She always makes me feel accepted, human, worthwhile.

"He was a good man, Val. He thought he was doing right." Sitting here at his desk where he wrote so many sermons, where he helped so many people, it seems like sacrilege to say anything different.

"Don't take this wrong, Liz, but your husband was a controlling jerk. This is abuse."

My head aches. I rub my temples as the inevitable dilemma raises its ugly head. "Now what? Do I tell Abigail? She idolizes him."

"Oh, honey. I don't know." Val's arms go around me, and I turn and rest my cheek against the softness of her breasts. Firm footsteps sound in the hallway, and Bernie's voice booms, "What exactly am I walking in on? Can I get in on the action?"

"You don't always have to be an asshole," Tara's voice chimes in cheerfully. "Cleaning out the death house is hard work. It always starts with the bed."

"It does?" I ask.

"When the spouse dies? You bet. Same with divorce. Too many memories, too much energy soaking into that mattress. This is why I only ever buy new. So, you want some help with this room? Is this desk going?"

"Yes, the desk is going. Just as soon as I finish emptying the drawers."

"Cool. We'll go sell things for you while you do that. Oh, and that church lady is out there acting like she owns everything. That okay with you?"

"More or less." What does Earlene matter, what does anything matter? My entire life has been a lie.

Val kneels beside the chair, swivels it so we are face-to-face.

"Look. My ex was a lying, sneaking, cheating pile of shit. Men like that want to keep you in the dark. To separate you from everybody, keep you barefoot and pregnant."

"Good thing Abigail was a one-off." I try to laugh but it turns into a sob. "He was supposed to be a man of God, Val. I can't—" And I stop there, frozen. I really can't. It's like my brain has flipped some kind of off switch and refuses to process. All fuses blown. The electrical circuit of emotions and thoughts has gone blank.

I can see Val's hands on my arms, but I can't feel them. "You can wallow later," she says. "I'll help you. We'll get ridiculously drunk tonight and cry over a terrible movie. But you have to finish this now. It's your declaration of independence."

I blink at her, knowing her words make some sort of sense, but with no emotion to connect to, they are just sounds.

"When you can't be you, be somebody else," Val says, shaking me. Her face swims in and out of focus. "What would Lacey do?"

Lacey. If there ever were a giant "yes," this is it. As immobilized as I feel right now, despite all of my blindness and my failures and mistakes over the years, I can say yes now. Yes to shedding the past. Yes to freeing myself and Abigail, one small step at a time.

"Pretend this is a play and you're the lead," Val says. "You can do this."

Pretending to be Lacey allows me to move. Where my legs refuse to bear weight, Lacey gets me to my feet. Where my hands don't know what to do, Lacey's are competent and capable. I remove all of the letters and stuff them into the drawers of my nightstand. Later I will read every single one, but today I am deliberately and irrevocably altering my life.

There is one more thing that I need to do.

I walk into Abigail's room, so neat and perfectly put together you'd think the bed was never slept in, that nobody even lives here. And I lift down the Eve picture from her wall. After a moment of hesitation, I deposit it in the big outdoor trash can. I will not be responsible for some other child living with that burden of guilt.

Eve looks relieved, I think, to be free of a duty she never wanted in the first place.

Chapter Eighteen

May 12, 2019

Dear Me,
Abigail did not take well to my yard sale. Of course she
didn't. Even for me, looking at the almost-empty house is
a graphic and brutal reminder that Thomas is dead. But
I want things to change. Abigail does not. When she first
walked through the door, she thought we'd been robbed
and I had to stop her from calling 911. And when I
explained? Well. I knew she'd be sad. I figured she'd get
angry. Her reaction went way beyond anything I antici-
pated. On the good-news front (?), I seem to have bro-
ken through her emotional containment field and given
her an opportunity to express herself. But the picture she
painted of me and my behavior was devastating. The
words "violation" and "betrayal" are still reverberating.

I guess I shouldn't have done it. Truth is, I wasn't
thinking at all. Just reacting. I felt hurt, violated,
betrayed, and I turned around and did the same thing to
my daughter. Only I didn't mean to hurt her, that's the
thing. I've managed to tear the veneer off the surface of

our relationship and discovered a seething, festering pit. I don't know that this can ever be healed.

Confession time now. As emotionally blown to bits as I am by all of my discoveries and the blowup with Abigail, there is a dark streak in me that is amused. Abigail came home to control me, to do everything in her power to keep me and the house from changing. And then I pull a stunt like this! I guess neither one of us knew I had it in me.

I still don't know what to do about those letters. Do I tell her that her father locked up her dreams in that desk drawer? Because what I've done to the house is nothing in comparison to the weight of that disclosure. Part of me says I should burn those acceptance letters and take the secret to the grave. But what if they mean freedom for her? She's still so young. She could still be a doctor.

And to add fuel to my emotional drama, I haven't heard a word from Lance. No matter how many times I tell myself I don't care, the truth is that I do. How will I ever face him at rehearsal?

I am completely out of courage and lacking backbone this morning. If I could, I might gladly retreat to the safety of my righteous widow persona. But I've blown that bridge to bits and there's nothing to do but move forward. Next step? Find a house. I am moving, with or without my daughter.

It's been a long night. I'm too old for sleeping on the floor, as it turns out. What with aching muscles, my uneasy conscience, and a storm of conflicting emotions, I've been awake more than I've been asleep. Moses approves, though. He shared my dislike of the bed for reasons of his own, but he has spent the last two nights curled up by my feet.

Abigail's voice in the doorway sends him streaking for the closet, the only hiding place left in my room. I'd like to join him. Abigail avoided me all day yesterday, radiating her outrage through the empty house without saying a single word. Obviously we need to talk, but I am not ready. I need a mug of coffee, a shower, and about three nights of uninterrupted sleep before I'm up for another confrontation.

But I'm trapped. All I can do is lie here staring up at my daughter, who I can already tell has not magically forgiven me during the night.

"When I was a kid, I wanted a cat." Her words are an accusation. I'm not awake enough to play the martyr, so I respond with the truth.

"When you were a kid, I also wanted a cat. Your father said no."

"Right," she says. "Blame the person who can't defend himself. You need to get up or we'll be late for church."

I should appease her. How hard would it be to go to church? But the misplaced blame rankles, and the thought of facing a congregation that I know has been gossiping about me feels like mission impossible.

"*You're* going to be late for church," I tell her. "I'm going to be absent in a perfectly timely fashion."

"Mother—"

"Abigail." I try to find my mom voice, but it doesn't work when I'm essentially sleeping in a blanket fort and I sound more like a rebellious child. Still, I aim for dignity, sitting up cross-legged to bring myself a little bit closer to eye level.

"You have to go to church. It's expected."

I hold her gaze, feeling the steel enter my spine. "Expected by who?" I ask. And then: "Or 'whom'? It's probably 'whom,' although you wouldn't ever say 'whom expects it'—"

"Mom! Dad would want you to go. And you know the whole congregation is watching you. Us."

"Then they need to find something better to watch."

"You're an example—"

"I'm done being an example! I'm not going to church today. End of story. In fact, I'm going house hunting."

"You can't sell this house! Didn't you hear anything I said to you?"

"I heard everything," I say, gently now. "And I'm sorry I hurt you. I should have done things differently. Bought the new house before packing up this one. But I am not staying here."

"What about me?" Her hurt is buried under about fifty tons of rage.

"You're all grown up, honey. You can come with me if you want, or you can find an apartment. You have a job."

Abigail takes a breath, softens her voice. "Is this a grief thing? Are you mad at Daddy for dying? Because that's one of the stages. People even get mad at God. It's normal. You should go talk to a counselor, and you should totally come to church."

She's right about two things. I am angry with Thomas, and I am having a serious crisis of faith.

Where she's wrong is that it's connected to my grief over her father's death. It's all about what I have come to understand about our life together.

Thomas was the church for me. He stood in for God, sort of like a small-town middle-class Protestant American pope. So his belief, his treatment of me, knocked God right out of heaven the first week we were married. For years, I've pretended to adhere to his beliefs, which I guess makes me a hypocrite. I'm done pretending. I'm feeling my way toward a different sort of God, and the last place I'm going to find Him is in Thomas's church.

I lie down and pull the blanket up over my head. A moment of silence, and then I hear Abigail stomp away. She doesn't exactly storm through the house, but I have no idea how she manages to rattle silverware so loudly when there is hardly any silverware left to rattle. Cupboards close with emphasis. I shelter in place, not sleeping, just avoiding confrontation, until the front door slams shut at a quarter to nine.

Just enough time for her to get to Sunday school.

I've declared my intentions to move, and now I need to follow through, even though my excitement about driving by some houses is decidedly dimmed by what's going on with Abigail. I'd love some company on this adventure, but Val is working today, and while I'm friendly with Bernie and Tara, we're certainly not on the sort of terms where I would call them on a Sunday morning.

Yawning, I head to the kitchen for coffee and realize that Abigail the martyr has scored a serious point by brewing the last of the coffee and then draining the pot. I wouldn't be surprised if she dumped it down the drain, just to get back at me.

I need coffee. I want breakfast. And I don't want to be the one to make it.

Never since the day I got married have I gone out for breakfast, but this seems like the perfect day to start. In a town the size of Colville, there are approximately three options for Sunday breakfast, if I discount McDonald's, and I am not wasting this adventure on fast food. Feeling thoroughly rebellious, I choose the Acorn Saloon, an establishment Val has informed me serves an excellent breakfast.

Of course, given my almost DUI, if anybody sees me not only skipping church on a Sunday morning but also walking into a bar, my reputation as an alcoholic reprobate will be assured. For once in my life, I don't care. I am a woman who has dragged a mattress out onto her front lawn in plain sight of a notoriously gossipy neighbor. I'm done worrying about the weight of public opinion.

Besides, if I ask, "What would Lacey do?" clearly she would say yes to the promise of a deliciously greasy fried breakfast without worrying what people think. Fine, then. Hopefully Lacey likes coffee and chicken-fried steak, because that's what I'm after.

When I step through the door, I'm surprised to see tables and booths occupied by groups of ordinary-looking senior citizens rather than an evil den full of drunks fallen asleep at the bar. A pleasant-looking man shoots pool at a table in the corner. The music is low-key country and western. I seat myself at an empty four-top, and a waitress brings me a menu and coffee, offering a friendly smile and asking no intrusive questions.

I've come armed with a notebook, my phone, and the newspaper, and settle down to work searching real estate listings while I wait for my food to be served. Bernie wants to take me house hunting, but I want to do some window-shopping before subjecting my still-tentative preferences to her boisterous personality.

"What's a nice woman like you doing in a place like this?" a familiar voice says.

I startle, my elbow bumping my freshly filled cup of coffee and sending scalding liquid across the table.

"Oops, sorry, didn't mean to scare you." Lance grabs napkins from a neighboring booth and tries to stem the flood.

The waitress arrives as if by magic, mopping up coffee with a rag. "Don't you worry, honey. Happens all the time. I'll get you a refill."

"Mind if I join you?" Lance slides into a chair without waiting for my permission. I've been playing scenarios over and over in my mind about how it will be when I next see him, but I never could have dreamed up a moment like this. "I've never seen you in here before, and I'm here nearly every Sunday," he says.

I stare at him in dismay. He probably thinks I knew this somehow. That I'm stalking him because he slept with me. The familiar heat rises to my cheeks along with a little thrill of anger. I have just as much right to eat here as anybody else.

"We were out of coffee," I say with dignity.

"Tragic day for coffee, then." Lance doesn't sound annoyed. If anything, he looks happy to see me. And there are other available tables. My heart rate picks up a little.

"I confess that I didn't feel like cooking. And I'm house hunting."

The waitress appears at this moment with more coffee and my breakfast, which smells amazing. I slide my coffee-soaked notebook off to the side and breathe in the warm comfort smells of fried meat and gravy, crispy hash browns, toast.

"What about you, honey?" the waitress asks Lance. "The usual?"

"Maybe I'll be adventurous and have what she's having."

She laughs as she fills his cup. "You got it. Coming right up."

Her hand rests briefly on his shoulder. Is that a hint of jealousy in the smile she turns on me? I remind myself to be careful. Lance and I are friends; the sex was Darcy and Lacey and has nothing to do with romance.

He wraps both hands around his coffee cup and drinks. "Ahh, that's amazing. Coffee and breakfast."

"You don't cook?" I ask.

One eyebrow lifts. "I do. But not on Sunday morning." He takes another swallow of coffee. Sets down the cup. "I'll admit that I'm surprised to see you here. I figured you'd be at church."

"Yes. Well, I'm taking a break from church. Possibly permanently. Time will tell." I take a bite of my hash browns, trying to think what to say next. We know next to nothing about each other; most of our interactions have centered around the Lacey-and-Darcy connection. I want to slide under the table and stay there. Another kind of blanket fort. Another kind of escape.

He touches my arm lightly, with the tips of his fingers, which short-circuits the conversation topics I've been outlining in my mind.

"Heard you had a yard sale."

My whole body goes hot. What has he heard and what must he think? The fact that the impromptu yard sale happened the morning after he and I engaged in what amounts to stranger sex is not going to escape his notice.

"It was a moving sale," I blurt. "Also, I had no idea that you would be here for breakfast. Also, if I'm going to buy a new house, there is no time like the present."

He looks confused. "I can sit somewhere else if you'd rather?"

I take a breath. "I just don't want you to think I came here because I thought you'd be here. I had no way of knowing."

"Well," he says. "So much for my babe-magnet status. If you don't mind, I would love to eat breakfast with you and discuss your house hunt."

The comment and the smile that goes with it ease my embarrassment, and I find myself smiling back. "That would actually be lovely. I could use a little male input and advice. I've never house hunted before."

"I could even drive you and offer my perspective first hand. Or be driven, if you prefer."

"I'm sure you have better things to do with your time."

"Honestly? Not a thing. You'd be saving me from spending the morning cleaning my apartment."

His apartment doesn't need cleaning, it needs cluttering. And living in. And maybe more lovemaking.

"I'd love to be driven."

"Well, then. Cool. Do you have a plan of attack?"

His food arrives, and I share my list of possible houses while we eat.

The waitress brings one check. "Anything else for you two?"

I'm embarrassed all over again. "We forgot to ask for separate checks," I tell her. "We're not actually together."

Lance pulls out his wallet. "We did eat together. And we are together in a thespian sort of way. So it's only fair if I pay."

"More research?" Lacey again, taking control of my mouth, my eyes, even my hand, which brushes his wrist with soft fingertips.

"Call me a research junkie." He looks into my eyes and smiles, his voice a caress.

A wild and crazy freedom fills me. Here I am, eating breakfast in a bar while almost everybody I know is at church, and I haven't been struck dead yet. What's more, I am eating breakfast in a bar with an attractive man who has once taken me home to bed, and is now offering to drive me around to look for houses in which to start my new life.

Chapter Nineteen

A few hours later, the exhilaration has fled.

"There's just nothing to even say about this." I gaze out the windshield at a house that does, as promised, have a large and spacious yard and a rustic, homey appearance. But said yard is at the moment a sea of mud, and five large pigs root around at the center of it, a dozen bedraggled chickens scratch around the edges, and the odor wafting into my car will most likely linger on my clothing long after I am dead.

"The tree is nice," Lance says, referencing an ancient oak that spreads its branches out over the roof.

I look at it dubiously. It's likely to drop a limb at any moment, and the roof of this house does not look capable of withstanding a puff of wind, let alone a falling tree branch. No, there is nothing redeeming about this house at all. I'd held out high hopes for it. It's small, out of town, fits my budget. None of the others have been right, either, and I feel like a balloon that's been blown up five times, emptied, and left flabby and deformed, neither big and round nor smooth and new. Worse, I'm at the end of my list.

"Well, that's it, then," I say. "Home, James. I will make an appointment with Bernie."

"You sure? You could become a pig farmer. They're very intelligent, really. I'm sure they'd love to be rescued from their current existence."

"Cleaned up and brought into the house, you mean?" I wonder, very briefly, whether Moses would warm up to a pig.

"What else was available in the listings?"

"Nothing of interest."

He's quiet for a minute, watching the pigs.

"You have a perfectly nice house," he says. "Why the move?"

Honesty. My new philosophy. "My life inside that house was not as perfectly nice as everybody thinks. I need a clear break."

His fingers tap on the steering wheel, restless, a complicated rhythm. "I get that. I moved out of mine. After the divorce."

He turns the key in the starter and pulls out onto the road. The camaraderie we seemed to have over breakfast has evaporated, and he's clearly making some kind of point about our relationship. He hasn't touched me once. Not to help me in or out of the car, although he opened the door for me. Not a casual hand on my shoulder, or my knee. And now he's even keeping his eyes to himself.

This is good, I tell myself. Exactly as it should be. I'm not ready for a relationship. So why do I keep wishing he'd pull the car over to the side of the road and kiss me?

My new say-yes philosophy is yielding certain complications. This afternoon I'll have to be Lacey, and Lance will be Darcy, and he'll kiss me—only it won't be me he's kissing, it will be Lacey. And after that I'll go home and have to face Abigail. If she was mad this morning, she'll be worse after hours of people asking questions about her delinquent mother.

Lance drives in silence. I let my arm hang out the window, playing with the air currents and letting the fragrance of springtime wash away the smell of pig. Fields stretch on either side of the car. Little by little, I begin to relax and feel a tiny bit better. Who knows? Maybe what I want is still out there somewhere.

"Why can't I find a house like that one?"

I point at a neat two-story house set back from the road, partially screened by evergreens. Tall trees line the driveway, and there's a beautiful big maple spreading sheltering branches toward a roof that looks like it could withstand a dropped limb or two. A front porch, covered by a small balcony, hosts a two-person swing. Behind the house, on the other side of a boundary set up by fruit trees, lies a large field. The house is white, the roof is green. It's a dream house.

Lance slows. "You like it?"

"I love it."

"Well, good. Now we have a better idea of what you're looking for. Uh-oh. Just what we don't need." He pulls off to the right and rolls to a stop as a cloud of dust signals a pickup speeding down the gravel road toward us. When it draws even with us, the truck slows and stops. The driver rolls down his window and grins.

He's a tall, sturdy man, face half buried in a curly blond beard. "Hey, man!" he says. "Thought you were taking the day off. What are you doing out here?"

"Just out for a drive. What about you?"

"Found the cows in the back pasture; just driving around looking for where they got out." The bearded man peers through the window at me. "Well, I'll be. Am I experiencing delusions or is that a woman?"

"Don't mind Gil," Lance says. "He's socially challenged. We suspect he was dropped on his head as a baby."

"Are you going to introduce me?" the man asks.

"Gil, this is Liz. Liz, my brother, Gil."

"Just randomly driving in this part of the world?" Gil asks, leaning down to get a better look at me.

The tension radiating off Lance makes me nervous, and I start to babble. "House hunting. Me, I mean. Not us. Lance is just playing chauffeur."

"Did you like it?" Gil asks, indicating the little white house with a wave of his hand.

I blink at him, confused.

"She's looking to buy," Lance says stiffly.

"You didn't even show it to her? Come on, man, we need somebody in there."

"What are we talking about?" I glance from one face to the other.

"That house right there," Gil says. "I own it, and it just happens to be available. Shitty renters, once again. Just moved out. No notice. Be happy to show it to you."

"Liz has stuff to do. We were headed back to town." Lance eases my car into a slow roll.

Gil backs up to keep pace. "Rosie will have my head if you don't bring your friend over for brunch."

"We just had breakfast."

"Oh ho!" Gil gives me another look, meaningful in a new way, and my face flushes as I see what he's thinking.

"We met, coincidentally, and happened to have breakfast. At a restaurant." Lance's voice is clipped. "And now we are heading back to town."

"I let you go, and Rosie will kill us both."

"Only if you tell her."

Lance is making this decision for me. Not consulting me. It's shades of Thomas all over again, and my soul rises in a hot rebellion. I lean across the seat so I can look Gil directly in the face.

"Is the house really for rent?"

The corners of his eyes crinkle. "It is."

"Would you sell it?"

The men exchange glances. "Get my lout of a brother to drive you up to our place, and we'll discuss," Gil says. "I'm headed back that way myself."

Lance makes a U-turn and follows his brother's truck. I sneak glances his way in my peripheral vision, but his face is unreadable, the entire surface of him gone as smooth and impenetrable as glass. It seems impossible that the two of us have been naked together, our bodies intimate. We might as well be occupying different planets.

"The family farm," he explains as we turn onto a well-graveled driveway about a mile down the road from the white house. "Gil and my sister, Rosie, run it together. He's divorced, she's widowed, so they just teamed up and moved into the old house together. Makes it easier for them than driving in, especially in the summer."

"But you drive in?"

"Yeah, kind of a pain in the ass during harvest, but I prefer my own place."

We park in front of a sprawling ranch-style house, between a Jeep Cherokee and a Subaru station wagon. Gil pulls the truck in on the other side of the wagon.

A border collie dashes down off the porch, barking, tail wagging with enthusiasm. He presents himself to Lance for exuberant petting before he turns more politely to me. I let him sniff my hands. He licks me. I know little of dogs, but I'm pretty sure the tail wagging and the licking are not meant to be threatening. I pat his nose and stroke his ears.

"Are we friends now?"

"Beetle loves everybody," Gil says. "He's not exactly a guard dog."

"Beetle?"

"Don't ask. Come on."

He walks up the steps onto the porch, opens the door, and vanishes inside. Lance stalks along beside me. He holds the door open and gestures me in. I hang back, looking up at him, uncertain.

"They won't eat you," he says.

"It's not them I'm worried about," I mutter as I brush past him and into a space that reminds me of the cloakroom in elementary school. Coats and jackets hang on hooks on the wall. Rubber mats hold a row of muddy boots. The floor itself is spotlessly clean.

"You'll need to leave your shoes here if you want to be on the right side of Rosie." Lance slips off his tennis shoes and sets them neatly on a mat. "And trust me, you want to be on the good side of Rosie."

A woman appears in the mudroom doorway. She's shorter than Lance, and considerably rounder, but she looks like him all the same. On her, the blue eyes are sharper, the smile lines deeper.

"Don't you listen to him," she says. "I'm the nice one in the family. Kindhearted, easygoing—"

"Ha ha," Lance says. "Also the comedian." But he gives her a hug that is more affectionate than his words.

"Somebody has to keep all of you men in line," she says. "Are you going to introduce me?" Her smile is warm and inclusive, as if she's known me as long as she's known her brother, as if me dropping in, unannounced, is perfectly normal and a delightful occurrence.

"Liz, meet my sister, Rosie. Gil thinks he runs this establishment, but Rosie is the real boss."

I've already followed Lance's example with my shoes, and he picks them up and sets them by his own. They look companionable and compatible sitting there together.

"Well, come in, come in. You'll eat, of course."

"Really just dropped in to say hi," Lance protests. "Like I told Gil, we already ate."

Rosie makes a dismissive motion with her hand. "Hours ago, surely. Come on. The boys have already set you places."

We follow her down a short hallway that ends in an enormous kitchen, bright with the light from big windows. Gil stands by a gas stove, spatula in hand, watching pancakes on a griddle.

Lance gestures at the big table that takes up half of the kitchen. Four boys are engaged in wolfing down pancakes. "Those rapscallions all belong to Gil. Meet Tom, Dick, Harry, and Mo."

"For real?" I ask.

"I'm Mo for real," the smallest boy says with his mouth full. He's not exactly small, just the least manlike. His face is still smooth, his voice hasn't changed yet. "So Uncle Lance nicknamed the others to match."

"Have a seat." Lance pulls out a chair for me beside the biggest boy, at the end of the table, and then sits down in the empty chair across from me.

"I don't want to impose," I say, hesitating.

"Sit, sit," Rosie says. "What's one more person? You want coffee?" She doesn't wait for my answer, setting a cup down on the table and filling it. "Tom, pass Liz the pancakes."

The boy beside me sets down his fork long enough to comply. Mo, at the far end of the table, obligingly sends along the syrup and a dish of butter.

"I could use your help this afternoon," Gil says to Lance, sliding a stack of fresh pancakes onto the serving plate. "Like I said, the cows went through the fence again. Somebody needs to fix that. I've got the boys tilling up the garden, and I'm seeding."

"I need to take Liz home," Lance protests. "Plus, rehearsal this afternoon."

"We'll manage fine without you." Rosie levels a glare at the big blond man. "The cows can stay where they are for a bit."

"Don't let me get in the way." I didn't think I'd be able to eat again, but the pancake is extraordinarily fluffy, thirstily soaking up melted butter.

"Nonsense," Rosie says. "It's not every day Lance has a date."

I glance over at Lance, but his eyes are on his plate and he doesn't register that he's heard this comment at all.

"Bacon?" Gil brings over a platter that has been warming in the oven. He forks two crispy slices onto my plate. "Liz here is house hunting, Rosie. Lance was driving her around."

"Looking at a total shithole," Lance says. "I think it's the Mattson place."

"What are you looking for?" Rosie asks.

"Not much on the market that fits the bill," I reply, ticking off my criteria. "Smallish house, out of town but not too far. At least one tree. Not too expensive."

It would be impossible to miss the mental telegraphing that goes around the table. Rosie pauses in the act of pouring syrup over her pancakes. Gil arrests the travel of bacon to his mouth and returns it to his plate. Even the boys go quiet and watchful, although all of them keep eating.

"It's time," Rosie says. "Don't you think?"

"I'm certainly sick of renters." Gil leans back in his chair and looks me over as if I'm a house he's thinking about buying. Or maybe a horse, or a cow.

"Lance, you should show her the house." Rosie's attention goes back to her pancakes as if they are the single most important thing in the world.

"That's exactly what I was thinking." Gil's hand slaps the table hard enough to make the silverware dance.

"I thought you needed me for fencing," Lance says, tight lipped.

"If Rosie wants Liz to see the house, then you need to show her the house. Rosie is right about everything." Gil forks a bite of pancake into his mouth.

Rosie slaps his hand, lightly. "Hush."

"What's a matter, Rosie? You taught me that when I was three. Made me say the words 'Rosie is always right,' under threat of having my face washed with fresh cow shit."

"You, too?" Lance asks. "I thought it was just because I was the baby."

"Are you kidding?"

The biggest boy laughs. "Wish I'd been around for that."

"Don't you be getting any ideas, son. I think it's time we all got back to work."

Gil gets up and carries his dish to the sink. The boys all shove back their chairs and do likewise. One of them takes my plate.

"You want us to wash them now, or rinse and do them after chores?"

"Dishwasher's empty," Rosie says. "Load 'em up. Thanks, boys. I'll go get the key."

The following flurry and rattle of dishes is alarming. One plate gets dropped and broken, but one of the boys gets a broom and sweeps it up as if this is a regular occurrence. Gil certainly doesn't seem bothered by any of it.

"Nice to meet you, Liz." He shakes my hand. "If you like the house, Rosie and I would be happy to talk terms."

"It certainly looks perfect from the outside."

"Hope you love it. I'm sick to death of bad renters. All right, boys. I'm off. As soon as you finish up here, get back to work, you hear me?"

Lance hasn't moved from the table. He's not eating, although half a pancake is still marinating in syrup. Rosie bustles back in carrying a key attached to a horseshoe by a serious-looking chain. Her brow wrinkles as her gaze rests on Lance. She drops the horseshoe into my hand. "Harder to lose it. Plus, good luck, am I right?"

The horseshoe is heavy and unwieldy. Not a thing to be forgotten in a pocket or dropped without noticing.

"It's amazing the way the boys help in the kitchen," I say as they close the dishwasher, hang up the dish towel, and head for the mudroom.

She laughs. "I figure since I spend as much time outside working as the men do, then they can spend as much time inside doing housework as I do. Already raised and launched my own, and I am not going to feed and clean up after Gil and his crew. You ready, Lance?"

He gets up from his place at the table, lines up his chair with the others. He doesn't look ready at all. He looks like he needs to go to bed and recover from a long illness. "Table first," he says with a smile that is not a smile. "Rosie's rules."

He fetches the dishcloth from the sink and begins to wipe up crumbs and maple syrup spills.

"Last one up wipes up the mess," Rosie says. "Hey, it works. Everybody has some sort of system, I'm sure."

My system involved hours in the kitchen cooking, serving everybody while they ate, clearing the table, washing all the dishes, and wiping down the table. I failed at getting even Abigail to help on a regular basis. As for Thomas, he would sometimes enter the kitchen to get his own drink of water or raid the refrigerator for a snack, but all of the unwashed dishes went into the sink, all of the crumbs remained on the counter.

My mother had cleaned up after my father all the years of my childhood. I'd thought it normal and expected. Now, as I watch Lance go through the practiced motions of wiping down the table, lining up the chairs, rinsing the dishcloth and hanging it neatly to dry, it is somehow the finishing touch on disintegrating my old world and my old life.

"You know, Rosie," Lance says, "if Gil really does need my help. Maybe . . ."

"You know I'm perfectly capable of repairing a fence," Rosie says evenly. "And Mo can help me. Go on, it will be good for you."

She doesn't say this in the tone of *That's all right, run off and play*. It sounds more like she's sending him off on a vision quest or to war, as if showing me the house will be dangerous and difficult. She hugs him, then stands up on her tiptoes and gives him a kiss on the cheek. "It's time, Lance."

He hugs her back, then squares his shoulders and marches down the hall without another look at me. I hear the door slam. Rosie squeezes my hand. "Don't mind Lance; he's touchy about that house. He lived there before his divorce. I do hope you love it."

Chapter Twenty

Lance stands by my car, his back to me. A ray of sunlight touches his hair, burnishing unexpected auburn highlights. Somewhere off in the distance, a mourning dove calls and is answered.

"Hey," I say softly.

He startles, as if I've honked a horn instead of practically whispering. "There you are. Let's go."

As soon as I'm settled in the passenger seat, I say, "Look, if you don't want me to see this house, just say so. Rosie said you used to live in it."

He shifts into reverse, doesn't answer.

Elizabeth would have quietly tolerated his behavior. Liz has a mind of her own. "This wasn't my idea. You're acting like I'm holding a gun to your head."

"Are you sure you want to buy a new house?"

"Sure enough to spend the day looking at them and drag you along with me."

"Window-shopping is one thing. Actually buying is another story altogether. Gil and Rosie will sell you that house tomorrow if you want it."

"And that's a problem for you?" I'm not sure if I'm more hurt or angry at this shift from the kind man he has always seemed to be into this rude and irrational stranger.

"I don't want my family pressuring you into something you're not ready for. How's your daughter taking all this?"

This question throws me completely off-balance. "That's a pretty roomy canvas. Which 'all this' are you referencing?"

"Selling off your furniture. Buying a new house."

"She's not a fan of change."

"Must be hard for her," Lance says. "First her dad dies. And then her mother sells everything in a flash yard sale and buys a new house three days later?"

"What exactly are you suggesting?"

"I'm not suggesting anything."

"Oh, don't pull that card. You think you know what I should do about my life and my daughter's life. Guess what? You don't get to tell me what to do."

He looks surprised, as if he totally doesn't understand my reaction. "Look, I'm just saying—"

"I hear what you're saying. I am not going to put my life on pause for anybody ever again. Not for my daughter. Not for anybody."

"Liz. I'm only trying to say that if I had a daughter—"

"*Do* you have a daughter?"

He doesn't answer.

"I didn't think so. So don't try and tell me how to manage mine."

We say nothing more during the drive. We say nothing when Lance parks the car in the grassy parking area. Inside, I'm seething. He has completely ruined what should have been an adventurous and wonderful day. Much as I love the outside of this house, I don't even want to see it anymore. I just want to go home—right after I hit something. But I follow Lance up three wooden steps onto the porch.

Gil is right about the bad renters. Cases of empty beer bottles are stacked haphazardly by the door, and I nudge one out of the way with my foot so I can insert the key into the lock. Once inside, immediately to my right is a small, open space for shoes and coats. The hardwood floor is smeared with mud. To my left is a laundry room with a washer and dryer and scullery sink. Two black trash bags, open and overflowing, lean against the counter. My nose is assaulted by the smell of mold and sour laundry. I ignore it, focusing on the big window looking out over fields and sky and mountains in the distance. Perfect place to put a litter box and a bed for Moses.

I follow Lance into an open area with a beautifully designed kitchen and a space that could serve as either a sitting or dining room. A bank of windows lets in the afternoon sun. A fly investigates crusted dishes left in the sink. The kitchen garbage is overflowing, and a pervasive rotten smell of meat gone bad and something sweeter, like bad apples, permeates the room.

But the maple tree spreads its branches outside the kitchen window. I can easily imagine myself washing dishes in front of that window, watching birds and maybe a squirrel. It's a small kitchen, neat and efficient, with an island that supplies even more cupboard space, and electrical outlets for appliances.

Lance's fingers skim a drawer pull lightly. "All of the cabinets are designed for maximum storage."

The house is talking to me. It feels unfamiliar and familiar all at once, as if I've walked it in a dream, as if I know the shape of it. It's been gutted, betrayed, wants a new life, just as I do.

Inside, I'm murmuring, *Hush, I'm here.*

My eyes are drawn by the beauty of the wood, the quality of the light. I start opening cupboards, noticing the way every inch of compact space has been taken advantage of, despite the grime that is everywhere.

"Bathroom in the hallway to the right," Lance says, leading the way. "Stairs on the left, as you can see."

The stairs are uncarpeted, crafted out of the same aged hardwood as the rest of the floor. I want to climb them, holding to the wooden banister, to see what's upstairs, but Lance is waiting at the bathroom door.

A bathroom is a bathroom, I'm thinking, but I'm totally and utterly wrong. It's a half bath, and small, but the walls are finished with some sort of glorious wood that is nearly golden and looks so smooth I can't help but stroke it with my fingers. The sink bowl is round and looks like an antique porcelain washbasin set in a stand.

The window is stained glass, jewel-toned light turning everything into a prism.

"It feels more like a chapel than a bathroom." I feel reverent here, more reverent than I do in church, inclined to linger and maybe ask God some of the very difficult questions I've been avoiding.

God will have to wait, because Lance's boots are already thudding on down the hallway.

He waits for me in an airy space where a bank of windows provides a full-on view of the world outside. A low, comfortable window seat is built over open shelving that I immediately envision full of books. I can see myself sitting here to read, looking up from time to time for a view of sky and field, trees and distant mountains. It's easy to ignore the litter of dust bunnies and newspaper on the floor, to see it how it should be.

"Gets a little chilly in the winter," Lance says critically. "And hot in the summer, but it's always wonderful in the morning." He stomps off, and I hear him climbing the stairs.

I know already that I want this house. It feels like it was built for me, belongs to me. I want to love it and bring it alive. Alone in this wonderful room, I stretch my arms out as if to embrace it.

At the top of the staircase, I find an open, cozy nook with a big window and built-in shelves. A railing provides safety from the edge of the loft. I could put a desk in this space. Maybe sit here to write something more than my usual morning scribbles. A story. A play. Anything feels possible.

"At night, Orion is framed perfectly in this window," Lance says. But when I turn to look at him, he's already moved away, his voice shifting into the dispassionate tones of a Realtor selling a house. "Full bath here. Two bedrooms. Small, but plenty of closet space."

"You loved this house," I say, rooted to the spot.

"I designed it—built it myself." He stands at the end of the hallway, his face shadowed, closed. His entire body looks like he's ready and waiting to block a punch to the belly.

"It's beautiful," I say carefully. "Must have been hard to leave it."

He takes a step toward me, stiff, as if drawn by an invisible force he is trying to resist. One step, two, then the rest all in a rush until only a handbreadth separates us. One of his hands cups my chin, turns my face up to his. I want to close my eyes, to hide from the intensity of his gaze. His breath is ragged, as if he's been running, or is in pain. Mine flutters in my throat, shallow and rapid.

"Buy the house, Liz, if you love it. Don't let me stop you. I'll give you Rosie's number." His voice scrapes, like gravel on skin. His head dips closer to mine, his breath warm on my face, but then he withdraws and drops his hand, the walls going back up so fast it makes me dizzy. "We'd better be getting back. There's rehearsal this afternoon."

He turns away, his footsteps heavy on the stairs. I follow, my hand gliding down a satin-soft wooden banister that would never dream of giving me a splinter.

Back in the car, Lance is still quiet, but he no longer looks angry. "About the other night," he says, finally. "I'm sorry, but—"

"Don't be sorry." I don't want him to apologize for the sex. I want him to apologize for today. He's got everything backward.

He glances at me, and then away, before I can interpret what I see in his eyes. "You deserve more. I'm not emotionally very available."

"Good." I project a certainty I don't necessarily feel into my voice. "I'm recovering from one questionable relationship. The last thing I need is another."

"You're really okay with how things are?"

"I'm okay with Lacey and Darcy and doing research for the play." It's an evasion, and I think he knows it. I breathe a sigh of relief when he lets it slide.

Chapter Twenty-One

May 15, 2019

Dear Me,

Abigail has put me in the deep freeze. She comes home late, eats dinner, and goes to her room. In the morning, she eats breakfast and leaves early for work. We need to talk, really talk, but she's all surface right now, hiding behind extreme politeness. I can guess she's going for "honor your father and your mother," but I feel far from honored. More like I'm walking through a minefield. The only way for me to fix this is to apologize profoundly and go back to being the mother she wants me to be, which is the one thing I can't do.

It will be a relief when she finally explodes. Wait, is that true? Because if it is, why haven't I told her that I'm buying a house?

No. I don't want her to explode. I'm a coward.

On Monday I called Rosie and then I called Bernie and then Bernie called Pastor Steve and today I'm going in to sign paperwork. It looks like we have a deal, at least if Steve and Felicity can get a mortgage. I keep catching myself holding my breath and have to remind myself to breathe. This has all been so quick, so easy, so too good to be true, and I'm afraid it's all going to fall apart at any minute.

Lance is a problem. He hasn't been as cold as Abigail, but he's put the brakes on so hard, there are skid marks. There certainly haven't been any more dessert nights, or exploration of Lacey and Darcy. He doesn't want me in that house any more than Abigail will. And there's so much I don't understand. If it was his house, why is his sister the one to sell it to me?

I'm buying it anyway.

But first I have a stupid physical that I want to cancel but decided to keep. Dr. Lerner will want me to have a mammogram and colonoscopy and get a flu shot, and I just want to focus on the play and my new house and finding some way to bring Abigail around.

What happens at the doctor stays at the doctor, or so they tell you. When it comes to the medical record, this is probably true. Staff can get in a lot of trouble for sharing actual test results or diagnoses. But there's no penalty for curiosity, for casually saying, "I saw Elizabeth Lightsey at the clinic today. Poor woman. Such a loss."

So far, I've encountered one receptionist and three patients who are church members. It's like today is a Super Medical Sale for the Church of Thomas or something. Every one of them felt compelled to hug me, to ask how I'm doing.

Now I'm sitting on the exam table wearing nothing but a gown, trying to understand why it bothers me that people know I'm here. Why do I care that people know I went to the doctor? It's just an annual. It's not like I'm dying of cancer or suffering from some sort of unmentionable sexually transmitted disease.

"How do you know you're not?" Thomas whispers in my head. *"Unprotected sex, Elizabeth. That man could have any number of diseases. You could be infected with AIDS or hepatitis and not have symptoms yet. The wages of sin is death."*

Val's gentle warning about Lance drifts into my head. I remember the way the waitress at the Acorn looked at him, her hand falling lightly on his shoulder. How many women has he been with since his divorce? I remember a poster I saw once that said every time you have sex, you are having sex with everyone your partner has ever slept with. How many women is that?

But Lance is a medical professional. An EMT. He would be responsible about these things. Surely I'm fine.

By the time Dr. Lerner steps into the room, I've worked myself up into a full-blown state of anxiety.

He was Thomas's doctor, besides being mine, and we used to come in for our annual exams together. So his face is full of kindness and sympathy as he sits down on his rolling stool by the computer.

"I was so terribly shocked to hear about Thomas's heart attack," he says. "This must be very difficult for you."

"Thank you," I say, which is the simplest answer.

He smiles a professionally understanding smile and shifts his attention to the computer screen. "Is the Ambien working for you, helping you sleep? You look tired."

I look tired because I'm sleeping on the floor, but he doesn't need to know that. "I haven't taken any," I confess. "That was all Abigail's idea. I prefer not to take medications if I don't need to."

"Good, very good. You've always been very healthy, and I see you have no other prescriptions. Let's be sure to keep you that way. I'm ordering a mammogram and a colonoscopy for you. Do you want a flu shot?"

Exactly as predicted, and if I wasn't harboring a secret fear of STDs, I'd roll my eyes. As it is, my mouth is dry and my heart is racing and I'm trying to decide whether to say anything or not. So embarrassing. What will he think about me if he knows I've already had sex with somebody so soon after my husband's death? I try to tell myself his opinion doesn't matter. Dr. Lerner is responsible for my physical health. Nothing more.

My self-talk isn't working.

"We did a Pap last year," he continues, oblivious to my turmoil. "Current guidelines say every five years is fine, so we don't need to do one today unless you have had a new sexual partner."

He looks up then. I look back, frozen. Unable to move or speak.

Dr. Lerner takes off his glasses. Pulls a cleaning cloth out of his lab coat pocket and begins to polish the lenses.

"It's fairly common after the death of a spouse to search out comfort and love with another person."

"It is?" I croak.

He puts his glasses back on and smiles at me. "I see it quite frequently. You would be surprised. Did you know that people of our age who find themselves suddenly single and dating are at a high risk for contracting sexual diseases? Teenagers are better informed. Did you use a condom?"

"We didn't seem to have one handy."

Dr. Lerner nods calmly, as if this isn't surprising or shocking at all. "Of course. You might buy some. Or, if this is an exclusive relationship, ask your partner to get tested. I think we will do a Pap test after all, and I would recommend that we run STD tests just to be sure. Is that okay with you?"

"Great," I say, although I'm thinking about the lab techs who will see my name on a label. The nursing staff who will see the order and handle the samples. I'm suffused with shame.

Dr. Lerner places the stethoscope on my chest, listens to my heart, and I take a breath of relief that we have moved into safer territory. He listens to my breathing and palpates my abdomen before inviting in a female assistant to act as chaperone while he performs a breast exam and the Pap smear.

"When was your last period?" Dr. Lerner asks as I flinch a little at the discomfort of his fingers pressing into the tender tissue of my breasts.

"I don't know," I confess. "Before Thomas died. Six months, maybe? Or seven."

"Hot flashes?" he asks.

"A few."

"So it sounds like you're into menopause, which means pregnancy is unlikely, but there is still a small chance. Have you had any symptoms that might indicate that, other than this sensitivity in your breasts? Unexplained weight gain, fatigue, nausea?"

"None of that."

"Good. Let's go ahead with that Pap smear, then, shall we?"

I lie back, ready to endure the usual indignities, praying that all of these tests will come back normal.

~

When I emerge from the doctor's office thirty minutes later, I feel utterly demoralized. I've been poked, prodded, and swabbed. I've peed in a cup and had my blood drawn. Funny how I felt healthy when I walked into the clinic, and now I feel old, decrepit, and shamed. Despite Dr. Lerner's calm discussion of sexual behavior in women of my age, I feel absolutely humiliated knowing my encounter with Lance is now part of my medical record, that staff members are testing my body fluids for possible diseases.

Thank God Abigail took a job in the hospital instead of here, so at least I don't have to worry about her eyes falling on something she doesn't need to see.

As compensation, I treat myself to a milkshake from Ronnie D's, pure chocolate therapy delivered via straw. I drive myself and my frozen bit of heaven to the park and drink it at a picnic table, letting the spring sunshine flow over me while I lose myself in the world of my current novel. Bella, the main character, has a lot more to worry about than social diseases, and by the time I've read a couple of chapters and sucked up the last few slurps of milkshake, my encounter with the clinic seems far away and much less important than the fact that I have a house to buy.

Bernie's office is on Oak Street, part of a section once zoned for housing but now converted to businesses. There's a *For Sale* sign out on the lawn, with *SOLD* layered over the top in giant red letters. What was once the living room is now a waiting area with comfy chairs and a selection of upper-end magazines. There's a Keurig and a selection of cups in the kitchen beneath a cross-stitched invitation to make myself at home.

I have just enough time to make myself a cup before Bernie takes me back to a large, light-filled room with a solid oak desk and two visitor chairs. All of her usual joking behavior has gone on vacation, and she's pure business, setting a stack of papers in front of me.

"Your buyers have already signed," she says. "They're going to need a mortgage, though, so it will take a little time before we can be sure that will go through. The bank will want an assessment and an inspection of your property, besides background and credit checks and all that. You can apply for a mortgage, too, but your seller has offered a substantially better price for a cash payment."

As Bernie lays out my possible options, including sums of money that seem improbable to me, anxiety starts to creep in, and with it doubt. Before Thomas died, he paid all of the bills, managed the bank accounts, took care of all of our financial concerns. I got a weekly allowance that included grocery money and other incidentals. If I needed more, I always had to ask, to explain why and how I had mismanaged my budget.

"*These are not the sort of transactions you're equipped for,*" Thomas whispers to me now. "*You know you have no head for business or math. Walk away from this foolishness before you lose everything.*"

"Take a breath," Bernie says.

I do as she instructs, then ask, "Does it show that much?"

"Let me guess. Hubs handled all of the money, and this is the biggest decision you've ever made on your own." She grins and leans forward a little. "You're a smart woman. You can handle this. Take your time. Ask questions."

So I do. I ask all of the questions about loans and assessors and inspectors. And then, when I think I've got all of that down, I ask the most important question of all.

"How long will this all take?"

Time is my enemy. Time means Abigail's resistance can wear me down, the way an ocean reduces shell and stone to sand. Doubt and Thomas can erode my confidence. Earlene can continue to spy on me from across the street, pray over me in person, and inform the church about my every movement.

"It varies. Depends how busy the inspectors are. Whether or not you go with your own mortgage or pay cash when your buyer's mortgage comes through. A month or two to close, usually."

Bernie opens a drawer and withdraws a familiar item, a key attached to a horseshoe. "Your seller presented another offer. I want to tell you that I would advise you not to do this."

"Do what?" I can't tear my eyes away from the key to the house. *My house.*

"You can take possession immediately, today, if you are willing to clean up after the renters who were there previously. Sign the papers, and you're in. You pay when your buyer's mortgage comes through."

"And you think it's a bad idea?" I touch the horseshoe, my fingers tracing its arc.

"There's no guarantee that your buyer's mortgage will be approved. However, when I mentioned that to your seller, she indicated that surely you would be able to sell your house to somebody else. She said, and I quote, 'We're sick of bad renters, and we want Liz to have the house.'"

"But?" I lift the horseshoe and settle it into my lap, taking possession of it.

"Does my opinion matter?" Bernie asks. "Looks like you've already made your decision."

"Tell me, anyway."

"I just prefer to have everything lined up to avoid unexpected mess later. It's good business to have all of the boxes checked and the money in hand. This is an unorthodox arrangement, and it makes me nervous. They are just a little too eager to get somebody into that house. You should have it inspected."

What she says is logical and makes perfect sense.

I've spent over half of my life doing things that seemed logical and made perfect sense, and look where that got me. This time, I'm taking a gamble. I'm saying yes to this house and this opportunity.

"Where do I sign?" I ask.

Five minutes later, I walk out of the office a changed woman, on top of the world. Everything is going to work out. My courage will be an inspiration to Abigail, and the two of us will sort things out. She'll go to medical school after all, and live up to her full potential. I have the keys to my castle, and nothing is going to stop me from creating a life that I want to live.

Before doubt has a chance to roll back in, I send a text to Abigail.

Liz: Meet me for dinner at Rancho Chico?

Abigail: Why?

Liz: Because Mexican food is your favorite.

I wait for a long moment, my heart in my throat, watching for the little dots that mean she's sending me an answer. Just when I start to give up, she responds.

Abigail: Okay, but you have to buy me fajitas.

I take a huge breath of relief and hope. If Abigail sees dinner as an unspoken apology, she'll be more open to listening. She'll be a captive audience, and I'll have the chance to make her understand. In my currently elated mood, I can even believe she'll be excited about the house and want to move in with me.

Chapter Twenty-Two

I walk into the restaurant feeling like a gambler on a winning streak. It's my lucky day. I've made a deal to buy my dream house. Things will totally work out with Abigail.

I'm a few minutes early and ask for a table, not a booth, so that we're right in the middle of the room and highly visible. Abigail has been taught to never make a scene in public. She'll have to listen to me, and neither one of us will be able to yell. If she's a captive audience, if she has to listen, I'll find a way to make her understand.

But when she stalks in, perfectly put together as always, despite coming here directly from work, I can feel the edge to her before she's fully cleared the door. She sits down, looks at the basket in the center of the table and then at me. "Were you going to leave any for me?"

"We can get more."

She has a point. There are only two broken chips left in the bottom of the basket. The salsa bowl contains only a little clear juice. I was ridiculously hungry when I got here, happiness fueling an unusually big appetite. I still feel like I'm starving, in fact.

The waiter comes over, and I request more chips and salsa and order an enchilada platter. Abigail peruses the menu with all of her formidable attention, as if we don't already both know what she's going to order.

"I'll take the fajitas. Steak and shrimp. And bring me a margarita." She rattles this off, as if she orders drinks every day, then turns to me with exaggerated innocence. "What?"

"Nothing."

"That is not a 'nothing' face."

Another basket of chips appears on the table, and I snag one immediately. "I've never seen you order a drink," I say, dipping.

"So, you get to have this whole new life, and I'm supposed to be the figure in the wax museum now?"

"That's not fair, and you know it."

"Do I?" She dips a chip with so much vehemence that it breaks into multiple pieces, leaving her with a tiny fragment while the rest floats in the salsa.

"Honey." I put my hand over her free one and squeeze. "I want for you to have a full, big, wonderful life. Do what you love. Live where you wish. Travel."

My phone rings. I have no intention of answering it, but it's sitting right there on the table and my eyes go to the call display. And stay there. It's the clinic calling. My brain spins through various disaster scenarios, wondering which of the many diseases they are calling me about. It must be something horrible to warrant a call after hours.

"I'm sorry, I have to take this."

She shrugs and goes back to eating chips, probably grateful for a pause in our less-than-stellar conversation.

"Elizabeth?" It's Dr. Lerner's voice. His assistant always calls with test results. This can't be good.

"This is me."

"Are you sitting down?"

I feel for my chair with my free hand and anchor myself, bracing for what must be even worse news than I was expecting. I glance up at my daughter, who is staring at me, and I turn away to screen my face.

"Most of the test results won't be in for a day or two, but there is one finding I felt you should know about immediately."

"And that is?"

"It appears that you are pregnant."

"Pardon me, I'm what?"

"I ran a blood test, just to rule out the possibility. Your HCG is elevated to a level consistent with pregnancy."

"But that's not possible."

"I'm sure this is quite a shock," Dr. Lerner says. "Now, there is a slight possibility that the test could indicate a tumor of some kind, but the timing of your sexual liaison is consistent with the numbers. I don't have anybody here to schedule you now, so call in first thing tomorrow and get an appointment so we can discuss your options."

"I have options?"

"There are always options. Goodbye, Liz. We'll talk in a few days." The phone goes silent.

I am frozen. This isn't possible. This isn't true. It's a dream or an elaborate hoax or an enormous mistake.

"What was that all about?" Abigail asks.

I stare at my daughter, aghast. I'm pregnant? This is infinitely worse than gonorrhea, or even AIDS, which is at least a treatable condition these days. Dear God, if I'm pregnant, can I still move into that house? It's half an hour from town in good weather. That's a long way from the hospital.

"Mom?"

I cannot tell Abigail that I am pregnant out of wedlock.

"I won a sweepstakes," I say brightly. "Didn't even know I'd entered."

I hold my breath, sure she'll see right through the lie, but she takes the bait.

"Oh, for goodness sake, Mother. It's a scam! They prey on people your age. Do not give them your address or your bank information. You didn't, did you? Give them your banking information? Or your Social Security number."

"I know better than to give out that information over the phone."

"Don't mail it to them, either. Tell you what, maybe you should just not ever give out any info unless you run it by me first. There are some really good scam artists out there."

Abigail's drink arrives, and I wish it were mine.

Only, if I'm pregnant, I can't drink.

How can I possibly deal with this situation? If telling Abigail is impossible, how do I break the news to Lance?

Abigail reaches across the table for my phone. "I wonder what would happen if we hit call back? Probably not even a working number."

My heart knifes sideways in my chest. I should have put my phone in my purse, should have deleted the call, should have done something, anything, to cover my tracks. Of course my lies were too easily believed, and now comes the retribution.

Abigail scrolls through my phone with one hand while dipping a chip in salsa with the other. She freezes. Our eyes meet and hold across the table.

"Give me my phone, please." I hold out my hand.

"The clinic called you? After six? Why would they call you after hours?" Fear replaces her irritation and anger. "Mom. What are you not telling me?"

"Have a drink," I say. "You're going to need it."

"Mom." She reaches across the table and grabs my hand. "Whatever it is, we'll beat it."

And now, given that she thinks I have some terminal diagnosis, I have to tell her. "Well," I say. "I'm sure it will all turn out to be a mistake, but Dr. Lerner called to tell me that I'm pregnant."

Her eyes widen, then narrow. "Don't be ridiculous. This isn't a joke. Tell me the truth."

"That's the truth. That's what he just said. My HCG is elevated and consistent with pregnancy."

"Maybe it's just a tumor."

"I'm going back for more tests."

She drops my hand as if it burns her, sits back in her seat. "But how is this even possible? Dad's been gone since January. You'd be showing by . . ." Her eyes go round. Her mouth drops open. "You didn't!"

The waiter arrives with two giant plates of food, destined to be uneaten.

Abigail leans forward, lowering her voice with a side glance at the table next to us. "Tell me you didn't have sex with that man."

There is nothing I can say, so I say nothing.

"How could you!" She's moved from shock to outrage.

"As it turns out, that part was really easy."

"Mom!" Abigail slams her hand down on the table, hard enough to jar the silverware. Her face is flushed, except for two little indentations of white in the sides of her nose. "This is how you repay Dad for all of the years he put up with you? By having sex with some guy? I can't believe you!"

"You know what I can't believe? I can't believe that you think your father was perfect and that everything is my fault. Are you completely unable to see what he did to us? How he held us back and kept us small and—"

"I will not listen to you badmouth and diminish him!"

"And I'm done letting you idolize him."

People are staring, but Abigail doesn't seem to notice. For me, the worst has already happened, and I don't care anymore who hears me.

"You know what I found in his desk drawer, Abigail? Letters. Letters that belonged to me and to you, that he kept from us."

Abigail turns a shade paler. "He must have had a good reason."

"Oh, he had a reason all right. To make me feel like I had no other options, and to keep you out of medical school."

"No." Abigail's knuckles, circling her glass, are white, and I'm afraid she's going to crush it, as if we're characters in some overly dramatic B movie.

"There was a locked drawer in his desk. I found the key."

She shakes her head in denial. Her hand around the glass, still raised, has developed a slight tremor, and I reach out and press down on her wrist, gently, and then more firmly, until hand and glass lower safely to the table.

I lick my lips, dry, salty, and go on.

"My mom didn't want me to marry your dad. We'd never been close, but we had a falling-out. She died, and all this time I thought she didn't want to talk to me, but then I found letters she wrote, reaching out. Asking for contact. He kept them from me."

Abigail shakes her head. "He wouldn't have. I don't believe it."

"And you. You'd been accepted to Yale. University of Washington. Duke. Your pick of universities. He hid those letters from both of us."

Her eyelids squeeze closed, her lips quiver. And with that, my anger flees. She is immediately my baby girl again. I want to put my arms around her, to rock her. I want to take everything back, make up another story.

I want to shout at her father. To shake him until his teeth rattle and his perfectly combed hair is awry and he begs for me to stop. But he's dead, and I'm pregnant, and there's no going back to undo any of it.

I watch Abigail pull herself together by sheer willpower.

Her hands open palm down on the table. Her shoulders drop. She draws a deep breath and her face smooths. When her eyes open, there is no trace of tears.

"Why?" she asks.

"He loved you. He thought it was the right thing to do."

"Not him. You." She leans forward, both palms pressing into the table. "Why are you telling me this now? So I'll overlook your absolutely shameless and unacceptable behavior? I'm not going to desecrate his memory like you've done. He was right. He was always right."

Her words cut me, dice and slice. I press my feet against the floor, a reminder of gravity and support in a chaotic world where I have no anchor and nothing to hold on to.

Abigail folds her napkin and sets it on the table. Adjusts her silverware. Twists her margarita glass one turn to the right. She pushes back her chair and walks away from me. Perfect posture, perfectly braided hair, perfect shoes to match her perfect skirt.

"Is there a problem?" The waiter appears at the table, polite but knowing.

"My daughter had to leave early. Could I have all of our food in a box, please?"

"Yes, of course."

My phone rings as I'm getting into the car. It's Val. I stare at it, torn. I want to tell her everything, but that means telling her my news, and I just want to pretend the word "pregnant" doesn't even exist.

"How did it go with Abigail?" she asks as soon as I pick up.

"Disastrous. We got into entirely the wrong conversation. Huge blowup." Tears threaten, and I press my hand over my mouth to silence a ragged breath.

A pause from Val, and then, "So you didn't tell her you bought the house?"

"We got off on a tangent." A distant corner of my mind rolls its eyes at the understatement.

"Shit. Don't hate me."

"Why would I . . . Oh, Val. Oh no. You didn't."

"I did. Oh God. I'm so sorry. I was trying to help, and I know I've made things worse."

I groan. "I'm not sure it's possible to make things worse. What happened?"

"She got out of her car looking like the tortured martyr on the way to the stake—so I assumed you'd told her and she didn't take it well. I just walked over and said, 'Go easy on your mom. She deserves to have a life, too.' She gave me this laser-eyed stare—no offense, Liz, but your daughter can be scary intimidating, and I got all scrambled up and started babbling. I told her how much I was going to miss you, and that I was mad at first when you bought the house so far away from me, but then I realized it was because I love you and it will complicate my own life, and that was selfish and—"

"Oh, Val."

"You're mad. I don't blame you."

"How can I be mad when you just said you love me?" I find myself laughing, a creaky, lumbering sort of laugh. "What did she say?"

"She just gave me that look, the one your husband used to give me, like I was a fly that she was forbearing to squash out of Christian kindness. And then stalked right past me and into the house."

"I'm sorry, Val."

"No, I'm sorry."

"Don't be. She was going to find out sooner or later."

And everybody else is going to find out that I'm pregnant. Unless it is just a tumor of some kind. Maybe a nice little cancer in an early stage. Something operable that hasn't spread. Lance would be sympathetic. My daughter would forgive me and take care of me.

"I have to work tonight," Val says, interrupting my daydreaming. "Coffee in the morning?"

"Absolutely."

I start my engine but still sit there, not sure where to go. I can't go home; I am so not ready to face Abigail again. I want to go to Lance, to have the comfort of strong arms around me, but dear God, I can't tell him about this; we barely know each other. My new house, instead of being an exciting adventure, now feels like a colossal mistake. If I'm pregnant, if I'm going to have a baby, can I live so far from town all by myself? It's too far from hospitals and schools and babysitters and Val, the only support I have in this suddenly very much bigger and scarier world.

"*I warned you,*" Thomas says. "*You can't make your own decisions. Just look at the mess you've made of things. Now what are you going to do?*"

"Right back where I started from," I whisper, leaning my forehead on the steering wheel.

I feel like history is repeating itself. The details are different, but the results are the same. I'm still the same.

Even though I want to remember my pre-Thomas self as independent and self-sufficient, in reality, I was geeky and insecure, always searching for acceptance and love. Neither of my parents had time or emotional energy for me. My father was too busy drinking to care much what I did; my mother was so exhausted from managing everything that she was most happy if I stayed quiet and out of sight.

Drama was my life. I lived, ate, and breathed theater productions. My head was full of epic romances, and I was constantly waiting for my knight in shining armor to show up and rescue me from a life that was far removed from fairy tale. I wasn't having a lot of luck. Most of the boys I knew were as awkward and inept as I was, also looking to be saved by some sort of magic. I had a few dates, experienced some backseat fumbling that stopped short of actual sex, but it was clear that none of them could save me or give my life direction.

I lived vicariously through books and movies. I read everything I could get my hands on, working my way through the libraries at school and in town. But plays—real, live, professional theatrical productions—were my passion. The Shakespeare videos my drama teacher showed us were sterilized versions of the real thing. I wanted to see the scene changes. I wanted to sit in the audience and feel the excitement of a crowd, of the real-life actors onstage.

There were plenty of professional productions in Seattle, but they all cost money. My part-time job at a nearby sub shop barely financed clothes, shoes, and lunch money, certainly not quality theatrical productions. I begged my parents for tickets. My father laughed at my begging when he was sober, and cursed it when he was drunk. My mother, ever the martyr, would go into long soliloquies about how hard it was to make ends meet while Dad drank all the money away, simultaneously deploring my selfishness. How could I even think about wasting her money and my time on watching a bunch of live puppets reciting lines on a stage?

"Go to church," she said, "if you want to hear puppets reciting nonsense."

And so I did. I saw a poster about a spiritual drama troupe hosted by a local church. Admission was free. Unable to talk any of my friends into attending, I went alone. The play was well done, the actors so convincing, that tears poured down my cheeks when the leading lady parted company with her beloved because he couldn't put God first in his life.

And then, when the play was over, a young man walked onto the stage and rewrote the course of my life.

All of these years later, I can still feel that moment like the reverberation of a thunderclap.

The spotlight remains on the heroine while the rest of the stage goes dark. Tears glisten on her cheeks, but her hands are clasped at her breast, her eyes lifted heavenward, a smile touching her lips. Soft music comes up. The choir begins to recap "Just As I Am," a hymn sung during the play.

And then a new circle of light illuminates a young man at center stage. His hair is dark, his features look like my fantasy version of Romeo. He holds his hands out directly toward me. I feel as though his eyes have singled me out in the crowd, that his invitation, in a warm voice, tremulous with passion, is for my ears alone.

"Are you lonely, struggling, frightened of the future? Do you want faith, comfort, and companionship for the journey? Surrender yourself now to your Lord and Savior, and you will never be alone again. He will walk beside

you. Fight your battles for you. Most of all, He holds all of the answers. Are you ready to let go of your own pitiful, selfish existence and step into His?"

Yes, *my heart sighs. Yes, I'm ready, so long as this new existence has something to do with this passionate young man and his melodious voice.*

"I hear you," the man says, his voice almost breaking with emotion. "I know you are ready. Jesus asks us to declare our intention publicly, just like these people in our play. Can you do that? Stand up right where you are."

I rose from my seat, buoyed up by this new emotion, found myself swept forward into the aisle and to the altar. Up close, my spiritual Romeo was even more beautiful, with commanding dark eyes. He took my hands in his and prayed for me, and by the time I left the church, I was utterly under his spell.

Sunday found me back at the church, where it turned out that the young man's name was Thomas and that he served the church as youth pastor. I joined the youth group. I volunteered for anything and everything. All else fell away—friends, my plans for college, even my beloved theater. That last semester, I was too busy helping arrange an evangelistic series to even audition for a part in the spring production.

Neither of my parents had been to college and had no aspirations for me, beyond the expectation that I find a way to be self-supporting. So long as I kept my religion to myself and didn't try to inflict it on them—a mistake I was only foolish enough to make once—they paid no more notice to my church obsession than they had to my drama productions. Of course, they didn't know about Thomas.

Thomas began to rely on me. To ask for my help, to thank me for my service. For the first time in my life, I felt needed. Valued. One evening, after I stayed late to help clean up after an event, he asked me to join him in his study.

He held my hands, looked deeply into my eyes. "I've been offered a chance to serve the Lord in an even deeper capacity," he said, his voice tremulous with emotion.

My heart dropped out of my chest, a slow roller-coaster ride down to my shoes. In the space between these words and the next, I pictured him moving across the country where I would never see him again. Dying in a jungle as a missionary. Serving as chaplain in a war and then expiring romantically from a wound acquired while saving a child.

"Are you going away?" I asked, choking back tears and wondering what I would do without him.

"I've been offered a church! Just a small church, in a small town. But I need a wife." In my mind, I started running the list of eligible women and girls he might choose, but he went on, "Marry me, Elizabeth. Be my helpmeet and my better half. We will serve the Lord together, two bodies with one soul, one heart, one mind."

"Yes," I said without hesitation.

Only then did he kiss me, and surely that was the moment I could have seen that he believed my soul, my heart, my mind, would now belong to him, but that his would never belong to me. Looking back, I can see that he asked me because the position required him to be married, and not because he loved me. Even the kiss was more contract than passion.

But I was only eighteen, so young, so inexperienced, so infatuated.

How fervently I believed that he was my salvation, sent to rescue me. He was my first love. I was filled with pride that Thomas had chosen me—me!—to be his wife. I lived for the times he noticed me, for his smiles of approval, the touch of his hand, the occasional kisses. I missed all of the warning signs and remained totally under his spell until I woke from my dream on our wedding night.

There was never any romance, and he was not a prince. But he did take care of me, and I let him. He made the decisions, managed the details, kept me fed, sheltered, and clothed. And now that he's dead, it turns out my decision-making skills are no better than they were when I first fell under his spell.

"Sad, isn't it?" his voice says. *"You've deluded yourself into thinking you want freedom, but you don't. Not really. Right now, all you want is for somebody to tell you what to do."*

I feel myself sinking under the familiar weight of guilt and futility, but a sudden thought buoys me up.

Yes, I was bad at decisions when I got married. Teenagers are supposed to make bad decisions; it's what they're known for. Parents are supposed to run interference. And if I'm bad at decisions now, it's because I've had precious little practice. Maybe my new "What would Lacey do?" decision-making tree isn't the smartest one in the world, but I've lived more in the last few months than in the last thirty years.

I will gather all of the facts, and then I will make my own decisions about the baby, the house, and the rest of my life.

Chapter Twenty-Three

For the better part of three decades, I've been waking up at 4:30 a.m. It began when Abigail was a baby. I wanted precious time alone with her, the two of us in the not-quite-dark living room, rocking as I nursed her. I didn't want to share her with Thomas in those moments. And then when she was a toddler I wanted there to be an easiness when she woke up, which meant I needed to prepare breakfast and everything Thomas might need beforehand so I would be free to lavish my attention on her.

Later, I spent that precious time with my journal.

But this morning, exhausted by the emotional roller coaster of yesterday, I've slept in. By the time my eyelids flicker open, the room is full of light and Val is standing in my bedroom doorway.

"Sorry to wake you, but I wanted to make sure you were okay."

"I'm fine," I croak. "Just overtired, I guess."

"You don't look fine."

I don't feel all that fine. An ache has settled into my lower back. I feel vaguely crampy. Irritable.

And then I remember. I'm pregnant.

Panic is closely followed by hope. Maybe the crampiness means I'm miscarrying. Maybe all of this will just go away, and twenty years from now I'll laugh and tell the story about the time I thought I was pregnant when I was almost fifty.

"I'll make the coffee," Val says. "Want me to bring it to you in . . . well, not in bed. On floor?" Her laugh lacks conviction, and she looks in no condition to be taking care of me or anybody. Her hair has come mostly loose from a ponytail. She's still in her work scrubs, and there's a brown stain over her left breast. There are dark circles under her eyes, fine lines around her mouth.

"You don't look so hot yourself. Rough night?"

She flops down beside me on the floor, spread-eagled on her back.

"It was a shit night. Shit everywhere. Literally. And then Marcus passed." She closes her eyes and draws a quavery breath.

"Ah, honey. I can't imagine how hard that is."

"It's fine. It's expected, right?" But quiet tears find their way down her cheeks.

"You're a good person, Val." My hand hovers over her forehead, then slowly settles. She sighs, and the tension in her body eases a little as I begin to stroke her hair, frazzled and sticky with products, not soft and smooth like Abigail's. "Those people in the home are lucky to have somebody like you."

"I liked Marcus," she says. "His kids never came to visit. Couldn't even be bothered to come say goodbye. So maybe he wasn't a great father. But I liked him."

We sit in silence, my hand moving rhythmically over her forehead and her hair. Lift. Repeat. It's an exploration for me, this closeness. Her breathing slows and eases, and I think maybe she's fallen asleep. I'm wondering whether to cover her with a blanket or wake her when she asks, drowsily, "Have you patched things up with Abigail?"

My hand stops moving. "Not sure that's possible."

Val's eyes pop open and she scrutinizes my face. "So what did you fight about first? Since you didn't tell her about the house."

"Those letters Thomas kept from her, for one thing."

"She was mad at you about that?"

"Justifiably, really. I used them to distract her from the pregnancy."

Val sits up, wide awake and wide eyed. "Abigail is pregnant?"

I stare at her. Wait a beat. I'm not ready to speak the words out loud.

"Coffee?" I moan and groan my way up onto my feet and into the bathroom to pee, disappointed for the first time in my life to discover that I am not bleeding. In fact, the cramps disappear the minute my bladder is empty.

"Just spill the news already," Val calls through the bathroom door.

"I need coffee. And breakfast. Want an egg?" I head for the kitchen and start the coffeepot, already preloaded, sticking my head in the fridge to hide my face.

"Make it two." Val settles herself on a stool. "Tell me about Abigail."

"What about me?" Abigail pops into the kitchen like an angry genie. "It's seven o'clock. How come there's no coffee?"

"Your mom slept in," Val says. "Probably worrying. I'm so sorry I dropped that news on you last night. I thought you knew."

"Mom's a great one for keeping secrets." Abigail slams open cupboards and drawers, obviously still mad, while I pull out eggs and bread and totally on impulse the jar of pickles. Why fight a craving just because it's ridiculously predictable?

"Seriously?" Abigail snarls. "Are you trying to live out every cliché in the book?"

"Oh, I hardly think this situation counts as cliché." I fish out a big fat pickle and crunch into its cold, salty tang, holding the remains in one hand while I turn on the burner beneath the frying pan with the other.

Abigail slams her still-empty mug down on the counter. "Pardon me for forgetting to stock up on ice cream."

Val stares at us both, then says with the sort of caution you might use if forced to address a maniac wielding a chain saw, "Does anybody want to tell me what we're talking about?"

"Well?" Abigail juts out her chin. "Are you going to tell her or shall I?"

"I think I already know," Val says. She gently puts a hand on Abigail's shoulder. "It will all be okay. You'll see."

"How is this ever going to be okay?" Abigail shouts. "We're talking about a baby! A little difficult to hide the evidence."

"We're not sure yet that it's a baby," I interject. "It might just be a tumor."

"It might what?" Val looks away from Abigail to me and then back again. "Of course you didn't plan this, but it's not—"

"It's not Abigail." My pan is hot, and I turn my back and add four eggs, two for Val, one for me, and another for Abigail. On second thought, I add one more, already counting the possible tumor as an extra mouth to feed.

"You thought it was me?" Abigail screeches. "Pregnant? How could you ever possibly get the idea that I would be so careless, so stupid, so . . . immoral?"

I poke at the eggs with the spatula, even though they're not remotely ready. One of the yolks breaks, and I watch the little yellow rivulets spread into the white and think about a tiny little microscopic egg and a cohort of eager sperm all racing for the prize. Why couldn't *that* yolk have been broken?

"*You're* pregnant?" Val squeals. "You? That's incredible. You told me how you'd always wanted another baby. Now look at you! Your own house and now this. Dreams coming true everywhere you look."

"You don't think I'm a little old for this?"

"I'll be an aunt!" Val says. She puts her arms around my waist and hugs me, spatula and all.

"More like an honorary grandmother!" Abigail shouts. "What is wrong with you two? Surely you can both see that Mom cannot keep this baby."

"What did Lance say?" Val asks.

"Lance doesn't know." I look her directly in the eyes. "Nobody can know, Val. Promise."

"I promise. But you can't hide it forever."

"There's still a possibility that it's not a baby. I have to see the doctor again. More tests."

"My lips are sealed until you give the okay. But if it is a baby, you know I'm totally here for you, right? Driver, hand holder, diaper changer, babysitter."

I hug her. "I know."

"Do you two hear yourselves?" Abigail demands. "Nobody is changing diapers. Mom is fifty!"

"Forty-nine."

She rolls her eyes. "Pardon me. So you'll only be sixty-seven when your child graduates from high school, not sixty-eight. That is so much better."

"Absolutely decrepit," I say lightly, but inside I'm reeling at the math. Abigail is right. I'm already old enough to be a grandmother.

"This is not funny! It's dangerous. It's—against nature. The body isn't meant to do this!"

"You forgot to tell the body that, apparently! What do you want me to do, Abigail? Have an abortion?"

It's a low blow. I know how she feels about abortion. I also know how much she wants this inconvenient, embarrassing, and potentially dangerous pregnancy to just go away.

She takes a breath, lowers her voice to a semblance of calm, and says, "I want you to be reasonable. The health risks can be managed. There are so many people wanting to adopt a baby. Nobody here would even have to know. We'll move you out of town and—"

"What? Send me to a home for unwed mothers?"

"I think those eggs are done." Val turns off the burner and removes the pan. The eggs are more than done. An unpleasant burned smell fills the air.

Abigail doesn't even notice. "It's embarrassing! What do you think? My fifty-year-old mother is pregnant, not even a year after my father dies! People will—"

"Forty-nine. And yes, people will talk. You care too much what people think."

"*I* care too much? You raised me to care," she snaps. "Everything I did, every word I ever spoke, was subject to judgment. 'The congregation is watching you, Abigail. Be an example, Abigail.' And now you're surprised by that?"

"And the solution is what? Send me and my embarrassing mistake out of town, and then you suddenly get a whim to adopt a baby and—"

"Mother! This is not one of your stupid novels. And I am not taking care of your mistake."

I'm out of line, and I know it. I make myself take a breath. And then another. "I'm sorry."

"Good to know," Abigail retorts, still livid. "So we'll start looking for a place—"

"Don't misunderstand, Abigail. I'm apologizing for the way we raised you, nothing else. It was wrong to teach you to care so much about the opinions of others." I lean toward her. "I spent way too many years caring. But right now I don't give a rat's bony butt about what the congregation thinks. I don't know that I cared then. That was one of your father's things."

Her mouth opens, and I hold up a hand to stop her. "I know. You see him as a paragon of perfection. He was human and fallible, Abigail. And he was wrong about women and our place in the world."

Abigail pinches the bridge of her nose.

"Stop trying to shift the blame to Dad. It might have escaped your attention, but the idea of you running around having sex with that guy—"

"Lance."

"What kind of name is that, anyway? Like he's a knight. Or a porn star. Why couldn't you just be—a widow?"

"Like Earlene, you mean? That's really what you want for me?"

Val shovels the ruined eggs into the trash and starts washing the pan.

Abigail and I glare at each other across the kitchen. I remember her sitting at the kitchen table eating cookies and drinking a glass of milk after school. Drawing pictures. Doing her homework. Reading to me aloud while I made dinner.

I can still search out the child she was in her features, in her expression. She was always serious. Intense. Focused. We didn't do that to her, she came that way. But we channeled it. Taught her control, perfection, self-righteousness. I'd like to take it back, but I can't. There's not a decision in the world I can make for her; she'll have to figure it all out on her own.

My decisions now need to be for me. Choices that I can live with for the rest of my life. I soften my voice.

"Abigail. This is my life, not yours. And I'm not making decisions based on who is watching and what they are going to say. Do you understand?"

I think I see a softening in her eyes, but it's gone before I can be sure. "I need to get ready for work."

She stomps out of the kitchen.

I sink down onto a stool, wrung out and exhausted. "Well, that went well, don't you think?"

Val breaks new eggs into a sizzling pan and slots bread into the toaster.

"You have options," she says quietly. "Adoption is only one of them."

"Terminating, you mean? I don't think I could kill a baby, Val."

"You're super early. No heartbeat yet, not really a baby. All you'd do is take a pill and have a heavy period. Not like those horror stories they tell you about ripping a baby apart. No drama. No need to even call it an 'abortion.' And nobody needs to know."

Something about her tone of voice, the way she glances at me sideways and then turns her face away, prompts me to ask, "Have you? You know . . ."

"After I left the Accursed Ex, I realized I was pregnant. I was terrified. I could just barely take care of Lenny. I started having morning sickness and almost lost my job because I was home puking. So. It was the right thing. It was the only thing. But sometimes I dream about a daughter. And then I wonder if I could have managed somehow. Wished it hadn't been necessary to do what I did."

"Would you do it again?"

She hesitates. "Yes? I think so. It nearly destroyed me, but I was further along. Had to go to a clinic and all that."

My heart breaks for my friend, even as it yearns toward the sweet simplicity of this solution. This pregnancy could be just a little speed bump in my new life. Lance would never need to know.

Abigail would remember these last few months as "that time Mom went crazy after Dad died" and not be humiliated by my pregnancy, or obligated to help me care for a sibling she doesn't want.

"It's too early to decide anything," I say as Val slides a plate of toast and eggs onto the counter in front of me. "Tests first. And then we'll see."

Chapter Twenty-Four

May 23, 2019

Dear Me,
According to the doctor, we still don't know anything for sure. All of the tests are back. The ultrasound showed no tumors, but it also didn't show a pregnancy, which the doctor says is normal. We won't be able to see anything before six weeks gestation, and another ultrasound is scheduled for then. Meanwhile, my HCG levels continue to rise and be consistent with a pregnancy, the timing of which matches my very clear date of conception.

Meanwhile, I am not deciding anything. I tell myself this is logical; how can I make decisions until I see the ultrasound and know for sure?

And until I know for sure, I don't need to tell Lance. I can continue to look him in the eye and pretend all is well.

I'm also still moving. Steve and Felicity's mortgage came through. I'm not waiting for the closing date! Val and I spend all of our spare time cleaning the new house, top to bottom. I've hired a moving company for three weeks from now, and bought a new mattress and bed frame to be delivered that same day.

Abigail is threatening to move into an apartment rather than aid and abet me in this insanity. She claims I'm in denial, and the truth is she's right.

I don't need any fancy medical test to tell me I'm pregnant. This morning I puked right after I woke up and then was instantly ravenous. Still eating pickles, over which Abigail continues to be furious. But she's furious in general and alternates between ignoring me and lecturing me about my stupidity in letting this happen.

Today I'm going to paint my new bedroom. And yes, I'm still hoping that this pregnancy will just somehow evaporate. Poof. Gone. As if it's never been.

This baby might not be big enough to show up on an ultrasound, but it's big enough to pour nausea-producing chemicals into my bloodstream and make me want to sleep for a hundred years. Tonight's rehearsal feels like a marathon and I can't wait for it to be over. I'm tired of smiling and pretending nothing's wrong. I'm tired of lying to Lance with my silence.

All I want to do is escape, to sink into a hot bathtub and close my eyes.

Instead, we're working choreography, which is not my strong point. I never was a great dancer, maybe from an inborn lack of grace, maybe because I never had much practice. During my life with Thomas, dancing was one of those forbidden things, inspired by the devil to lure humans into extramarital sex.

Lance is an excellent dancer, which makes it easier, and at least if we're dancing, I don't actually have to look into his face and keep from blurting out my big news.

But my legs feel like they're filled with lead weights. I keep praying Bill will call some sort of halt so I can sit and recover from the exertion, but instead he keeps pushing harder. Only a few weeks to go before dress rehearsal, so there's no time to waste. A cold sweat slicks my body. My heart is racing. I'm beginning to stumble over my own feet.

My willpower keeps me moving until we hit the scene where Lance is supposed to twirl me around three times and then catch me. My balance isn't down with the swirling thing, and the room keeps on going when my body stops. My vision begins to darken from the edges inward. My legs go boneless. For a lingering minute, I hear Lance's voice cut across the music, sharp with alarm.

"Liz!"

The next thing I know, I'm lying flat on my back on the stage.

Lance is chafing my hands. Val has my feet in her lap. A circle of anxious faces peers down at me.

"There you are," Lance says as my vision clears and I look up into his face. "God. You scared me."

I try to answer but my lips don't move. I moisten them with my tongue. Try again. "I'm fine."

"Not sure I'd call this fine," Bernie's voice says.

I start to sit up, but Lance presses me back. "Just lie here for a minute, Liz."

"Let me get up. I'm okay. I promise." I roll onto my side and push myself up into a sitting position. My head swirls briefly, then settles. I feel tired. Weak. A little nauseated and shaky. Nothing I haven't felt on and off for the past week. All symptoms I had with Abigail, even the fainting episode.

Val and I exchange a look. "Did you eat today?" she asks.

I think back. "I think I might have forgotten."

The truth is that I couldn't keep anything down in the morning, and then I got busy working on the new house and then I came to rehearsal. I know better.

"Do you tend to have low blood sugar?" Lance asks. "Has this happened before?"

"Ambulance is on the way," Bill calls, walking up the aisle with his phone to his ear.

"I don't need an ambulance!" I protest.

"Any chest pain?" Lance asks, checking my pulse. "Or pressure in your chest, or unusual sensations in your throat? Your neck? Heart attack symptoms are different for women."

I'm going to have to tell him, and I'm going to have to do it now, in front of everybody.

"This happened a couple of times with Abigail," I say. "I just need to eat something."

I watch Lance's face, the way he's trying to process this comment.

"I've got chocolate," Tara says, holding out a Twix.

"She needs protein, not sugar," Val counters.

"What about the ambulance?" Bill asks.

I turn back to Lance, watching his face as I say carefully, "Tell them it's a false alarm. I've already seen a doctor. I'm just . . . pregnant."

The cluster of faces hanging over me all gasp, nearly in unison. It would be funny if it weren't so tragic. Lance is frozen, eyes fixed on mine, for what seems like forever.

Finally he breathes. Rocks back on his heels. "I'm sorry," he says. "I can't do this."

He gets to his feet and stalks out of the theater, leaving me horribly, devastatingly alone. My knight in shining armor has left me to fight the dragon on my own.

Chapter Twenty-Five

Val practically drags me to the next rehearsal. There are so many reasons not to want to go.

I'm embarrassed by passing out. I don't know how I'm going to get through scene after scene onstage with Lance. We need to talk, but he hasn't answered any of my text messages. When I tried to call, it went to voice mail, and he's never called me back.

"How am I going to manage with Lance onstage?" I ask Val.

"That's why they call it acting," she says, towing me to her car.

"He's going to be so—"

"Fuck him!" Val turns me toward her and straightens my hair. "He's every bit as much responsible for this as you are. Maybe more, taking advantage of a vulnerable widow and all."

"I wasn't . . ." Too late, I see the mischief in her face and stop myself.

"Now. Did you eat? Did you bring snacks and water? Make sure you hydrate like crazy."

"Yes, Mom." I hold up my water bottle in one hand, my baggie full of crackers and cheese and nuts in the other.

"I don't see Lance puking or having to go to the doctor or giving up a single one of his plans. He can just deal with a little discomfort around this freaking play. All right?"

"All right."

But it's not all right. My feelings for Lance run deeper than I want them to. The minute we walk into the theater, my eyes find him in the semi-dark. My heart lurches drunkenly. Val squeezes my hand. "You've got this."

"Thank God!" Bill bellows when he sees me walk in. "Thought maybe we were going to have to cancel the performance. Sorry, that came out wrong."

"Over here, you two," calls Tara. "We saved you a place."

Lance, on the other side of Tara, says nothing, just looks grim.

"You going to be okay to do a full run-through?" Bill asks. "Your health is more important than anything, of course."

I make a little curtsey. "The show must go on, right?"

"As you say," he booms approvingly. "You're a pro, Liz. Well, then, let's get started. Tonight we're aiming for a complete run-through. Might go a little long. Next week we'll be drilling down into trouble spots. And the week after that is tech week—adding in the lights and mics, orchestra and choir, complete costumes and props, the whole shebang. Eat your veggies, boys and girls, because this is where the rubber meets the road."

Lance and I manage okay onstage, but all of our lines fall just a little flat. In the scene where he kisses me, it's very clearly a stage kiss, impersonal and cold. He looks tired, and my ridiculous soft side wants to comfort and soothe him. I harden my heart.

Poor baby, did you have a hard day? Did your little fun adventure end up not so fun?

I make sure I'm fed and hydrated before we get to the dance scene that dropped me to the floor last time. Lance keeps breaking the flow, holding on to me too long when he spins me, putting out a hand to steady me when he's supposed to be turning the other way. When he causes a collision between two other people moving in their proper choreographed positions, Bill calls a halt.

"Everybody okay up there?" he asks as the music goes quiet and everybody stops to breathe and stare.

"Perfectly fine here," I call out.

"Can we just take Lacey out of this scene?" Lance asks, not looking at me. "I'm worried about a repeat performance of last week."

"Maybe we should take Darcy out of this scene so he doesn't stomp all over Lacey's toes," I retort. I want to shake him, slap him, stomp on *his* toes, on purpose. How was I stupid enough to think I was falling in love with this man? He's insufferable.

"I just think you should take it easy a little, given your condition," Lance says.

My eyebrows go up. "And what is *my condition* exactly?"

I see him struggling with himself and realize that we haven't talked and he doesn't know if I'm still even pregnant. Did I run off and have an abortion? He has no way of knowing.

"Fragile," he says after a long, uncomfortable silence. "Unwell."

"I am not fragile. I'm pregnant. No more fainting episodes so long as I remember to eat. If Darcy will stop hovering over Lacey, the scene will be fine."

"Good enough," Bill says. "Darcy, you heard the lady. Stop hovering. Places. Music. Let's go again."

It's late by the time we make it through a complete run of the play, and everybody's nerves are frayed. Bill gives us a little pep talk.

"The first run-through always feels like a disaster. This is normal. Promise. The next couple of practices we'll spend on cleaning up individual acts. Remember to clear your schedules for tech week! Now, go home and get a good sleep and dream of the flawless production we'll have by dress rehearsal."

I'm unconvinced, nauseated, and exhausted.

I'm also still furious with Lance and with myself. How did I fall for him? So many warning signs. That empty apartment he lives in, for one.

And what is a fifty-year-old man doing just working for his brother and sister? No wonder his wife left him. He was probably a dick to her, too.

Bernie pulls me out of my dark thoughts. "When are we moving you?"

I blink at her. "I've scheduled a moving company."

"Why on earth would you do that? We moved Abigail in. We can move you out. Way cheaper."

"I can't ask—"

"Are you kidding?" Tara asks. "Pizza and beer. We are in."

"Can we do it on a Saturday? I'll bring a truck," Geoff says. "Can't imagine you've got much stuff left. That was one epic yard sale!"

"Deal!" Bernie says. "Can't wait to see the new house."

Val grins and shrugs. "You know I'm in."

"What happened to Lance?" Geoff asks. "We need at least one set of muscles."

Everybody goes silent, exchanging uneasy glances. Finally, Tara smacks Geoff's forearm lightly. "You are so clueless."

"What am I missing?"

She sighs and tows him toward the door. "Come with me and I'll explain it to you."

"Lance will come around," Bernie says, always direct. "He's a good guy. Just taken by surprise, I'd think."

"He's not the only one," I retort.

"Point," Bernie agrees. "And you don't have the luxury of running away. Want me to beat him up for you?"

I laugh at that, feeling lighter than I have in days. Maybe I'm not as alone as I thought I was. Val makes me feel even better.

"I had this idea," she says as we're driving home. "Later, when you're further into your pregnancy, you can stay with me for a while if you want. I mean, keep the new house, but come and be closer to town. And maybe let me help you with the baby for the first couple of weeks. Unless Abigail is going to do it."

"You are the best friend ever. I might take you up on that. Abigail is talking to adoption services."

"Are you seriously considering that?" Val asks.

"Abigail is. Same difference."

We laugh at that, but I sober quickly. "She might be right this time, Val. The idea of raising a baby by myself is daunting. It was hard enough when I was eighteen, and I had Thomas. Plus, that bit about being retirement age by the time the poor kid graduates high school? And my budget doesn't exactly allow for a child."

"Did he actually help?" Val asks. "Thomas, I mean. I'm not seeing him changing midnight diapers."

I snort. "Now that you mention it, it probably would have been easier without him."

"So, what are you going to do?"

"Deny everything and pretend this isn't happening?" I sigh. "Or, you know, grow up and have the ultrasound and start making decisions."

Chapter Twenty-Six

June 14, 2019

Dear Inner Me,
Maybe I owe Thomas an apology. I wanted to be out
from under all of his dogma and make my own decisions.
Can I take that back? I thought this whole say-yes-to-life
thing would be a big adventure. Drama productions and
dream houses and fantastic sex.

Not decisions like whether to have an abortion or an
adoption or try to raise a baby on my own.

Yesterday I had my ultrasound. Today I see the doctor
and get the verdict. And then I have to decide. Abigail
has already e-mailed me a link to a site where I can look
at adoptive parents. I clicked it open and had a massive
anxiety attack. All of these hopeful couples begging for
my maybe baby. But I know damn well they aren't all
what they appear to be. Anybody can smile pretty for a
picture and write up a thing about what a wonderful,
loving family they are. If Thomas and I had put up one
of those posts, we would have looked amazing. Which we
clearly weren't.

And if this is a baby, and if I carry a baby to term, and if I keep it, then what about my plan to shake Abigail free from the way we raised her? She'll make herself a martyr to raising a half sibling she secretly resents, and that would be horrible for both of them.

Oh God. What have I done?

I'm dreading this doctor's visit. I'm dreading tomorrow's move. I'm dreading rehearsals and talking to Lance and the minute Abigail gets out of bed. I'd probably still be in bed myself, hiding under the covers, if I had an actual bed to be in. This sleeping-on-the-floor routine has got to go.

Dr. Lerner looks at the computer monitor, reading intently, while I fidget, shuffling my feet, tapping my fingers on the arm of my chair. Finally he swivels toward me and gives me a long look over the top of his glasses.

"Well, it's definitely a baby."

"Oh good. I was worried it might be an alien."

The man has never had a sense of humor. He doesn't laugh, just keeps looking at me in a way that raises my anxiety level to the point where I finally ask the question that's really been bothering me.

"Is it okay? The baby? Is it . . . Down syndrome? I read I'm at high risk for that."

"We can't really tell so early. It's implanted in a good place in the uterus. The heart is beating. But we can't see most birth defects for a long time yet. Trisomy 21—what you call Down syndrome—and some other genetic abnormalities don't ever show up on the ultrasound unless they come with a significant physical problem. Which is why we'll do genetic testing. And an amniocentesis."

"What's the amnio thing?"

"Very simple procedure. We insert a needle through your belly into the uterus and withdraw an amniotic fluid sample that we then send for analysis."

I stare at him in horror. "I don't want to do that."

"Truly it's not a big deal. Most women say that it is painless. You'll want that information so you can make decisions. If the fetus is—compromised—you can choose to terminate."

"No."

His smile disappears. "Elizabeth—"

"Liz."

He raises his eyebrows.

"I've always been Liz. Elizabeth was a Thomas thing."

"All right, then. Liz. Having a baby at your age is entirely possible. Some career-conscious women are doing it these days on purpose. But it's serious business. It's not just hard on your body, your reproductive cells are aging. Did you know that a baby girl is born with all of the ova already formed? So yours have been around for fifty—"

"Forty-nine. Why does everybody insist on adding on that extra year?"

He sighs, patiently. "Okay. Forty-nine years, six months, and, what, twenty-three days? Those eggs are past their shelf life."

"You make it sound like I'm going to give birth to a three-headed chicken."

"The principle is the same. Are you ready to commit the rest of your life to a three-headed chicken?"

"I don't know if I'm ready to commit the rest of my life to the most beautiful and perfect chicken in the world."

He shifts his position, his face going impersonal and even more professional than usual. "We don't do terminations here, as this is a Catholic facility. But if you choose, you can visit Planned Parenthood."

As soon as he says the words, I know termination isn't really an option. Much as I would love to avoid the reality of months of nausea, of sleepless nights, of the embarrassment and discomfort of waddling around with a giant pregnant belly, not to mention the pain of child-birth, I know I can't do it.

I've said the words "the baby." I can no longer think of this inter-loper as an alien or a chicken or a clump of cells. We've crossed that line with this whole beating-heart thing. And if it's a baby, then it gets to live if it wants to, no matter how many heads it has.

I shake my head. "I won't terminate. Even if there are birth defects. So I can skip the needles, right? I mean, there's no point to it."

"Due to your age, I strongly advise that you still have the testing. And then you'll know what you're getting into. Have you considered adoption?"

"It's a possibility."

He nods. "Is the baby's father involved?"

"He is not."

"In that case, you might strongly consider whether you have the resources you will need to raise a child on your own. If you do choose to adopt, the prospective parents may want to have the DNA testing. So take a few days to think about it, but not too long. There is an optimal time frame, so we need to get you scheduled. Due to your age and the potential for complications, I'd also like to refer you to a specialist in Spokane."

"I'd rather deliver here."

"Let's have you at least meet with the specialist once, shall we? I'll have my nurse come in and talk to you about all of these referrals."

The rest of the visit passes in a blur.

All I can think about is that there can be no more denial. It's time to step into the reality I've accidentally created.

~

Maybe it's too late to control whether or not I'm with child, but at least I can decide when and how the news is going to break. First, I text Abigail and Val:

Not a tumor. Definitely a baby.

Val responds with encouragement. Abigail doesn't respond at all.

When I get home, I call Earlene and invite her over for a cup of coffee.

"It's about time you and I had a chat. It's been weeks!" She walks into my kitchen with her nostrils pinched as if she smells something rotten. I sympathize. Coffee doesn't smell good to me today, and I'm wishing I'd thought to make tea instead. Not that this conversation is going to be pleasant, no matter what the beverage.

"How is the knitting circle going?" I ask, setting a cup of coffee down in front of her and launching into the safest topic I can think of.

"It is just not the same. Felicity has no sense of tradition. She is forever trying to change things. She has brought in new people, and they all want to knit from patterns. Can you believe it?" Earlene takes a sip of coffee and makes a face. "Don't you have any sugar?"

"It's actually packed. Sorry. Abigail and I don't use it, and the move's coming up."

Earlene glares at me. "How have I not heard about this? Felicity and Pastor Steve don't move in here until next month. I have heard absolutely nothing about where you are moving to or when."

I blow on my hot coffee to hide my amusement at her affronted tone.

"The house I'm buying is available now. And I decided, why wait?"

"A house?" Earlene asks. "If you had asked me, I would have advised something smaller. Where is it?"

"Colville is a little short on condominiums," I say dryly. "And I'm not living in an apartment. The house is out on Williams Lake Road."

"So far? You will come to regret that, Elizabeth, in a few years. I spend more time at doctor's appointments than almost anywhere else these days. And nighttime driving? Don't even get me started."

"Well, it's a little late now. I'm moving tomorrow."

"You are what?" She sets down her cup in genuine consternation. "There is no time now to organize a moving party. Why didn't you tell me?"

"Actually, Earlene, I have plenty of help."

She's busy with her phone, not listening. "Let me see what I can do. There are one or two people who might be available on short notice. If you hadn't stopped coming to church, we would not be in this predicament. If Felicity knew about this and didn't tell me, I will set that girl straight in no uncertain terms!"

Moving without Earlene's advice and approval is one thing. Moving without allowing her to arrange interference is yet another. She's out of breath, her face flushed, and I touch her wrist to slow her down and allow me to launch the real bomb.

"Earlene. Please don't blame Felicity. She knows nothing about any of this. I do have another matter to discuss—of a confidential nature. I've told nobody at church as of yet. Can you keep this to yourself?"

Her smile is so genuine, I feel slightly guilty over my manipulation. She pats my hand gently. "You can always confide in me, Elizabeth."

I look directly into her eyes and let the cat out of the bag. "I'm going to have a baby."

Earlene's forehead wrinkles, her lower lip presses in against her dentures, and she continues absently patting my hand, trying to process this news.

"Surely Abigail is not—"

"Oh heavens. No. Abigail is not."

"So you're adopting, then? At your age? Are you sure this is wise?"

"I am having a baby," I repeat, enunciating every word. "I'm pregnant. The baby is due at the end of January."

"You're . . ." She stops. Blinks repeatedly. She looks like a robot with some sort of glitch, and I start to worry that I've broken her.

"Are you all right?" I ask. "Shall I get you a drink of water?"

"A baby," she says. "You. January."

My evil self is enjoying this moment more than she should be. "Maybe you could knit a blanket in the circle. Of course, I don't know yet whether it will be a boy or a girl, but . . . are you leaving already?"

Earlene pushes back her chair and gets to her feet but just stands there looking a little dazed. I carry her nearly untouched coffee to the sink, empty the cup and refill it with water. "Here. Drink this."

The water brings her back to herself. Setting down the cup and wiping her chin, she says, "Well, then. I really do need to go get started on finding moving people. I'll let you know."

"One thing done," I say as soon as the door closes behind her. "What's next?"

I spend the rest of the day finishing my packing while simultaneously running lines for the play. Moses disapproves and is whiny and unhappy because I won't let him outside, afraid he'll run off due to the disruption and not come back before it's time to go.

Most of the cookware is packed, so I put together a giant dinner salad for me and Abigail and am just setting it out with a couple of paper plates when she slams the front door and stomps into the kitchen.

"Did you have to broadcast it to everybody?"

"I have no idea what you're talking about. How was your day?"

"Don't you try to evade this! Everybody knows. Five separate patients asked about you and the baby today. Four of them want to know when the wedding is, and the other one offered to pray for your salvation. A lot of expecting women wait until the end of the first trimester to tell everybody. Married women who want babies. But not you. You have to announce it to the whole world—"

"China doesn't know yet," I tell her. "Probably not North Korea, although they do have spies. I understand the microwave might be listening—"

"Mother! This is not funny."

"The microwave thing? I know. It's like *1984*—"

"You are being deliberately obtuse."

"And I have no shame. It would have come out sooner or later. Better now than when I start to show."

Her eyes fall on my well-worn script on the kitchen counter. "I can't believe you are going through with that stupid play when you're pregnant."

"Responsibility. Commitment. It's not like I'll be showing or anything." I change the subject. "Are you all ready for tomorrow?"

"I'm going to ask you one more time to listen to reason. The house is too far from town. If a medical emergency happens, it's going to take too long for anyone to get to you."

"Already packed. Papers are signed."

"You could still change it. You just don't want to. If you won't see reason for yourself and the . . . baby . . . think about me. It's a long drive. It will be ugly in winter."

"About that," I say resolutely. "I want you to get your own apartment. Or move back to Spokane. I can tell you're not happy with this job."

Moses chooses this moment to saunter into the kitchen, meowing, and winds around Abigail's feet. She picks him up and scratches under his chin. He purrs loudly, then meows again.

"Is he hungry?" Abigail asks in a voice I never thought to hear from her. "Poor old baby. Did Mama forget to feed you?" She glances up when I make a sound of surprise.

"Didn't think you approved of stray cats."

"He stopped being a stray when you fed him," she says to me. And then, to the cat, "I'll get you some dinner. I haven't forgotten about you, not like some people."

"I did feed him," I protest. "About an hour ago. He's a mooch."

"He's not going to like the move, either," Abigail says.

"Stop changing the conversation. I want you to move back to Spokane."

"Because I've recruited your cat to Team Abigail?" She says it lightly, but there's hurt in her voice, and I go on, quickly, before it can take root.

"I don't want you to spend the rest of your life taking care of me, or worrying about a baby you didn't ask for and don't want. I'm a grown-up. I'll manage."

"Mom—"

I hold up my hand to stop her. "I promise to give you the chance to take care of me when I'm old and senile. We're not there yet."

"I'm not entirely sure about that." She grabs the ranch dressing out of the fridge and slams it down onto the counter a little harder than necessary. "I can't leave you alone when you're pregnant. Especially way out there. It's only nine months, anyway, because you're going to give the baby up, right?"

"I haven't decided that for sure."

"Don't be ridiculous! How are you going to take care of a baby?"

"The same way I took care of you."

"But—"

"Abigail. Please. Live your own life. Go out with friends. See a movie. Take a trip. Go back to school."

She fills a plate with salad and drowns it in dressing. "I don't have any friends."

"Make some. Or move back to Spokane."

"I don't have friends there, either."

"What happened to that nice boy you were dating?"

"Not motivated. Not going anywhere. Not . . ." She spears a fork into her salad. "You really want to know? I wanted him to be a surgeon.

I pushed him. He's so smart! He could be whatever he wanted. But he said he just wanted to do family practice, that he liked making connections and helping people work through illnesses. But it wasn't enough. I kept pushing him to be more and—oh dear God." She covers her mouth with both hands, eyes wide. "Because I couldn't be a surgeon myself! What is wrong with me?"

"Nothing is wrong with you. You are beautiful, brilliant, perfect." I take both of her hands and plant a kiss in each palm. She stiffens but doesn't pull away. "I think . . . when you're held back from being yourself, from living your gifts, how can you possibly be your best self? If your own life feels out of control, then it's easier to control somebody else's. Only, you can't, you know. Not his. Not mine."

"I don't even know what I want." The misery in her eyes breaks my heart all over again. "I did want to be a doctor, a surgeon, but not enough to go for it. Even then, I had to have known that letters must have come in, right? But I didn't look into it. Didn't ask about my mail, didn't call the universities to check. Didn't apply elsewhere. And now . . . I don't even know what I want."

"You were still a child. And you'd been taught, always, to be less than who you are. We did that to you, your father and I. But you're still young. You're figuring it out now while you have a whole life ahead of you. It's not too late! You can be anything you want to be."

"You think?" She looks terribly young, lost, and frightened.

"I know, my girl."

"If only I knew what that was. I'm honestly not sure anymore."

"Figure it out. Don't wait until you're knocked up and fifty."

"Forty-nine," she says. The moment hangs in the balance, and then the two of us are laughing, and I revel in this beautiful moment of connection, wanting it to last forever.

I hug her, my arms tight against the warmth of her back. "You are amazing and I love you."

"Where did that come from?" But wonder of wonders, she hugs me back.

"That I love you? I've loved you every minute of every day and night since you were born. Even the times I wanted to strangle you."

"Like I want to strangle you right now?"

"Precisely. Love with a side of strangling. I'm starving. Can we put everything on hold and eat?"

"Deal," she says.

We eat in companionable silence, neither of us wanting to risk any conversation that might lead to another fight.

Chapter Twenty-Seven

I wake confused and disoriented. For the first time in weeks, I put out my hand to feel for Thomas's bulk beside me, but instead find only blankets and carpet. There is no mattress, no bed, no Thomas. Even Moses has apparently abandoned me for some softer, warmer refuge.

And then I remember all of the crazy, chaotic details of my life.

I'm pregnant. Lance is avoiding me. Today I'm moving into my new house.

On my way to the kitchen, I check on Abigail, the way I used to do when she was little. She's sound asleep, sprawled in a position that would send me for a trip to the chiropractor if I maintained it for an hour. Moses, the traitor, is curled up across her thighs with his nose buried under the tip of his tail. I tiptoe over and adjust the covers, pulling the blanket up over Abigail's bare shoulder. She looks so young in her sleep, her hair loose around her face rather than pulled back in the severe daytime braids or bun. I bend down and whisper kiss her forehead. She stirs slightly but doesn't wake.

Moving boxes are stacked neatly along one wall of her room, ready to go. Whether she approves of me or the house or not, she is determined to move with me.

It's amazing to me how many boxes of my own there still are to move. The house has seemed so empty since my yard sale, I had thought packing up would be easy. It took longer than I thought, but it's mostly done. I'll make breakfast and stow the few remaining kitchen items in the open box waiting for them. Get dressed and add the clothes I slept in to my suitcase.

I'm not sure how I'm going to get Moses into the carrier I bought. He took one look when I brought it into the house and hid under Abigail's bed for the rest of the day. I'm hoping she'll help me, but there's no guarantee about that. As if I've summoned him with my thoughts, Moses pads into the kitchen and rubs against my legs.

"Breakfast, then?"

He meows, and I scoop canned food into a bowl, then set about making breakfast for Abigail and myself.

Eggs. Toast. Bacon. I'm not crazy about bacon, but Abigail loves it, and I wanted to do a nice thing for her this morning. The sizzle in the pan, the rich, warm aroma, wakens a childhood memory. My mother, on a good day, making me a bacon, cheese, and pickle sandwich. The idea sets my mouth to watering, and I toast my bread, slather it with mayo, and am just neatly slicing a fat, juicy pickle into thin, glistening slices when I sense eyes on my back and turn to see Abigail watching me.

Her nose wrinkles.

"For breakfast? You have got to be kidding."

She heads for the coffeepot.

"Have you ever even eaten a pickle?"

"No. Should I?"

I make another sandwich, cut it in triangles and remove the crust, then carry it to my daughter, who is leaning on the edge of the counter cradling a coffee mug in both hands.

"Here." I hold out the plate. She pokes at the sandwich with one clearly disapproving finger. "Seriously?"

"You are probably the only person in North America who has never tasted a pickle."

I take a huge bite of my own sandwich, saliva surging into my mouth over the salty, crunchy, chewy goodness. It's seriously the best thing I have ever eaten, and my stomach immediately settles and asks for more.

Abigail makes the *yucky* face she used to make when she was six, and takes a small bite, exploring it with her mouth before she really starts to chew. "What was it with Dad and pickles?" she finally asks, as close as she's ever going to come to saying that she likes what she's tasting.

"He didn't like them."

"Well, right." She's staring at me as if she's never seen me before. "I gathered that. But, when I was a kid, I thought they were bad. Like, cigarettes or LSD bad."

I see an opening, a thin sliver of blue sky through heavy cloud. "When your father believed a thing, it became gospel for him. God. Pickles. A woman's place in the world. Medical school."

"Don't," she says.

"You're still young. It's perfectly feasible. I applied to online university before . . . well, before." Another dream to put on hold. I don't have the bandwidth to take a class right now.

"Let's not talk about it." Her voice has an edge, and I back off, protecting our fragile truce.

Together we wash the last few dishes and pack them into the waiting box. Abigail leaves for work. She would have taken the day off if she could, she's told me, but I suspect she doesn't want to be here, to see the last of the memories moved out of her childhood home.

The truth is, I don't want to be here, either. It's harder than I thought it would be to leave this house behind. I keep stumbling over good memories, quiet moments of closeness with Abigail before we grew so far apart. Plus, I'm realizing I should have waited to talk to Earlene until after the move. Church will be buzzing with my new status as a fallen woman. Everybody is going to want to show up to get a glimpse of me. It will be the church version of the paparazzi, out in full force, with nowhere for me to hide. Yesterday, getting this over with seemed like a great idea. This morning, not so much.

Val breezes in, takes one look at my face, and gives me a hug.

"I'm here, ready to do whatever. Just tell me what you need."

I hug her back, hard, wondering how I managed to live so long without a best friend, realizing how much I'm going to miss having her next door. "Don't suppose you've got a spare scarlet letter lying around that I could wear for the day?"

Val laughs. "Somebody leaked the news?"

"I leaked the news. Seemed like a good idea at the time. Earlene threatened to send people over this morning to help."

"That is the last thing you need today. Tell you what. How about you take the cat and scram right now over to the new house. I'll stay here to supervise loading the truck, and I solemnly swear I will not give away your forwarding address to any members of the congregation."

My heart leaps with more hope than I've felt in days. "You would do that for me?"

"That and more."

Moses is hiding under Abigail's bed. He refuses to come out. I have no tuna to tempt him with, and in the end, I get down on my belly and drag him out by the scruff of the neck, his claws snagging carpet all the way. By the time we stuff him into the carrier, Val and I are both bleeding.

"He's never going to forgive me for this."

"Are you kidding? He'll forget all about it the first time he sees a hayfield and realizes how many big, fat mice are hiding there. I'd patch you up, but you're already on borrowed time." Val bundles me and the cat into my car just as Earlene steps out of her house and heads across the street. I wave as I drive by, pretending I don't see her semaphore arm gestures commanding me to stop.

Moses howls. Tears rise and flow unchecked as I leave the house behind. I've spent more than half of my life in that house. What has possessed me to think I can move somewhere else, especially now that I'm pregnant?

Once I'm clear of town, I open the windows to let the fresh air flow in. Under the influence of blue sky, fields, and trees, my spirits begin to rise. When I open my new front door and walk into my house, I feel even better.

Moses has subsided into a sullen silence. After some consideration, I decide to leave him in the carrier. If he gets out now, he won't know this is home. Doors will be open to facilitate the move, and he might run away and never come back. I carry him upstairs and leave him in the loft.

And then I walk through the rooms, turning lights on as I go, picturing where the furniture will go when I get some. What colors I might paint the walls. In every room, I see a little girl playing on the floor. Her eyes are blue, and shaped like Lance's. Dark hair hangs in her eyes. There's a smear of dirt on her cheek, and her grin is crooked, missing front teeth. I see blocks in the living room. Toy cars on the stairs. In the second bedroom, I see an unmade bed, a jumble of jeans and T-shirts on the floor. Crayon scribbles on the walls. Laughter follows me, room to room.

My right hand goes to my belly. Somewhere in there is a spark of life. A tiny magic light of potential. A baby.

What if I keep it?

Abigail will throw a fit if I don't proceed with adoption, and she's probably right. I can't imagine raising a baby by myself. I also can't imagine giving one away.

Shaking off my dark thoughts, I go out to the car and fetch the one box I brought with me. It contains the coffeepot and coffee, essential breakfast preparation items for tomorrow morning, and my luxury expenditure of one-thousand-count Egyptian cotton sheets and a new comforter for the bed that should be delivered shortly.

Somebody has left a vase of wild roses on the kitchen counter, the subtle fragrance filling my nostrils. A housewarming gift from Bernie, I think at first. Or maybe from Lance's sister, who has called to let me know I should come over for dinner anytime, no reservations required.

But the handwritten note says:

Evidence and my behavior aside, I love that you and the house will have each other. Lance.

I stand there with that note in my hand, torn by conflicting desires to press it against my heart and tear it into shreds. Anger wins. How dare he leave me in the lurch and then offer up wildflowers?

Before I can flare up into a full-on blaze, a delivery van drives into the yard. "Up here," I tell the delivery guys, leading them upstairs to the master bedroom.

"Beautiful house," one of them says. "The craftsmanship is amazing."

"Don't make 'em like this anymore," the other guy agrees.

They are right. I can't help but see the loving attention Lance put into building this house. He's everywhere I look, a problem I hope will pass in time.

It only takes them a few minutes to assemble the bed frame and bring up the mattress. As soon as they're gone, I smooth the luxurious, crisp sheets into place, shake out the fluffy duvet. Then I toe off my shoes and lie down in the very middle of the mattress, spreading arms and legs wide, taking up all of the space rather than one small allotted spot on the right-hand side.

I roll from one side to the other, testing the view of the room from different angles. There is no Thomas's side, no Elizabeth's side. Just this wide expanse of welcoming comfort. If the moving crew wasn't likely to show up any minute, I'd just close my eyes and have a nap. Moses meows pathetically from the carrier, and I get up and sit in front of it where he can see me.

"It's for your own good, buddy. I'll let you out as soon as we're done moving. I promise."

I hear a truck engine and get to my feet to see a convoy headed up my driveway. A U-Haul truck followed by a procession of cars and pickups. "Here we go," I say, squaring my shoulders. "Too late to back out of this now. I'm in."

Chapter Twenty-Eight

June 22, 2019

Dear Lacey,
Tonight is opening night for Just Say Yes, *and just for today, my nerves have overtaken all of my other worries. I never had stage fright when I was young, but then I wasn't widowed and pregnant and worried about making a spectacle of myself.*

I'm sad, too. It's impossible to believe that in a few days there will be no more rehearsals. I've built a life around the play and the people in it, as if they're family. We say we will see each other again, but will we? It's so easy to say such things, and even mean them, and then it all falls away.

It's not like I can be in whatever the next production is going to be. But maybe I'll do it again after the baby is born.

It feels like I've been in this play forever. Also, it's responsible for everything. I wouldn't have this new house. I wouldn't have met Lance. I wouldn't be pregnant with his baby and facing the most difficult decisions of my life.

So, Lacey, I'm not entirely sure whether I love or hate you. It's too late to go back now, though, and I've gotten rather fond of this saying-yes philosophy. Maybe it just takes a little practice to figure out when to say yes and when no is a better answer. I still haven't decided what I'm going to do about adoption or not adoption.

I keep telling Abigail we have lots of time. She insists that the sooner we choose adoptive parents and involve them in the pregnancy, the better bonded they will be with the baby. There's probably truth to that, but I suspect she just wants me to commit to the adoption thing so I'm less likely to back out.

Once the play is over, I'll have no more excuses to avoid making decisions and absolutely nothing better to do with my time. And I won't be seeing Lance. We still haven't talked, and I've given up on trying. The last few weeks of rehearsals have been purgatory. Not hell—because I will confess here but to nobody else that there is still so much pleasure when he holds my hand. When he looks into my eyes, I believe that he cares about me, that he's the man I thought he was—can that really all be acting? If so, he belongs on a bigger stage.

I'm pretty sure everybody in town, and probably everybody in Russia and Korea—both North and South—knows by now that I'm pregnant, and this does nothing to decrease my stage nerves. If the theater crowd is judging me, they are doing a fine job of hiding it. Everybody, with the exception of Lance, treats me the same as always. The church is another story. I've had no texts. No phone calls. Nobody has even shown up on my doorstep to pray over me. Even Pastor Steve has only been in contact through Bernie. The silence feels ominous, like an impending storm.

My self-esteem is at an all-time low, and my nerves are a mixture of excitement, dread, and uncertainty. Fragments of lines run through my head and collide with worries about pregnancy and whether I should go ahead with an adoption. I try to focus on the play, but there's plenty of extra anxiety there, too. What if I forget all of my lines? What if I pass out again in front of God and everybody, the disgraced woman lying there for everybody to gossip over?

Val's arm slips around me, and I realize she's trembling.

"Why on earth did you drag me into this?" she asks, under cover of the preshow music playing through the speakers.

"Crazy woman." I hug her, and the two of us cling together for a long moment.

"Maybe it would help to look," she says. "I keep imagining the seats filling up with hecklers and the mean girls from high school. Which is just stupid, right?"

"Come on." I grab her hand and drag her to the edge of the curtain at stage left, drawing it back just enough that she can peer out without much risk of being seen.

"Well?"

"Just people. Not a mean girl to be seen. Oh wait. Uh-oh . . ."

"What?"

"Nothing." But she's got a look on her face that is not a "nothing" look, and she's blocking the edge of the curtain with her body. "Let's go get ready."

"Move, Val. Let me see."

"Liz . . ."

I shoulder her out of my way and take my own time peering out into the crowd.

Earlene stands in the middle of the center aisle, blocking traffic, having a conversation with a couple seated on the aisle. The man and women shift over to the far end of the row, neither of them looking happy. Earlene follows them, the rest of a posse of church people filling the seats behind her. Annie and Kimber. Amy. Pastor Steve and Felicity. The one person I wanted to see out there, Abigail, is missing.

I step back from the curtain with my hand over my racing heart, knees weak.

Val laughs, shaky and high. "They are here out of support. It's good."

"Or it's your mean-girl situation with a religious twist."

"Did you bring your snacks?" Val asks. "Are you hydrated? You look a little wobbly."

"I feel wobbly."

As if summoned by a cosmic pregnancy bat signal, Lance arrives at my side, one hand under my elbow, the other on my waist. "Are you all right? Have you eaten? Are you hydrated?"

Val has every right in the world. Lance does not.

Anger steadies me. I draw a slow, deep breath, and glare at him. He's got absolutely no business telling me how to manage a pregnancy he doesn't choose to be part of. I've worked hard to get myself into a mind-set that lets me work with him onstage. His touch, his solicitous tone, threaten to undo all of that. But the last thing I want to do is create a scene.

"Unhand me, villain," I intone in a Shakespearean stage voice. And then add in a normal voice, "I'm good. Just nerves."

He grins at me. "Picture them in their underwear."

A vision of Earlene in her undergarments flashes before my eyes, and I grimace. "No. Thank you."

Bill marches over. "Places, people. What are you all doing over here?"

"Melting down," Val says.

"None of that. Just picture them in their—"

"No!" Val and I object simultaneously. Then we both dissolve into half-hysterical laughter, and all three of us follow Bill to the greenroom where we are supposed to be waiting.

The laughter eases the tension, but still, when I walk out on the stage for the first time, blinking against the bright glare of the stage lights, my body feels unreal, and for just an instant, my first line escapes me.

But Lance is solid and real and present. Despite his massive failures in the Father of the Baby department, if I fall, I know he'll catch me. If I stumble over my lines, he'll make something up to cover me. As Darcy and Lacey, we are golden. It's only as Liz and Lance that we're so hopelessly messed up. Onstage, Lacey has got this. I channel all of my emotional upheaval into her, and I can feel the audience responding.

After I find the first line, the rest of the play goes smoothly, with only a few minor glitches, and I'm almost surprised when it's over. Lance and I stand alone onstage, holding hands, gazing into each other's eyes. I tell myself one more time that the love and loss I see in his are just good acting. We each take a slow step backward, as we've practiced so many times, our hands separating as the lights go out and two separate spotlights pick us up and the orchestra begins the final song. I'm afraid I won't be able to sing, my voice choked with unshed tears, but when it's time, I'm able to channel all of my sadness and my hope into the music.

And then, it's all over. The houselights come up and people are clapping and we are all taking our bows, alone, as a group, and then Lance and I are taking our bow together, hands linked, and I can't stop thinking that after the run of shows are over I'll never hold hands with him again.

My tears start flowing, but it doesn't matter. I'm not the only one crying tonight. Even Tara and Bernie look suspiciously shiny eyed when they hug me backstage, and Val is openly weeping.

"I've loved this so much," she wails. "I can't believe it's almost over."

"So be in the next production," Geoff suggests. "I'm auditioning. Tara and Bernie are always in."

"I'll be sitting out the next couple." I wipe tears away with the back of my hand. "I'll miss you guys."

"Hey, you don't get away from us that easy," Tara objects. "We'll be, like, babysitting and stuff. Right, Bern?"

"Right on."

Evan, the quiet boy who plays my son onstage, grins at me. "I'll claim the after-school shift. I'm a great sitter. Took care of my sibs when Mom worked evenings."

And now I'm crying again as everybody comes together in a circle for a group hug. Everybody except Lance, who is nowhere to be seen.

We're broken apart by a familiar, demanding voice. "Where is Elizabeth Lightsey? We want to talk to her."

I have just time to stand up and scrub my sleeve over my eyes before Earlene appears, followed by the rest of her people.

"Don't worry, we've got your back," Val says, and then Earlene is shoving a wrapped parcel into my hands.

"I know it's customary to bring flowers, but we wanted to give you this."

Felicity hugs me, package and all. "That was brilliant, Mrs. L. You made us all cry."

"I certainly did not," Earlene objects.

"She did," Annie whispers, winking.

"It's so awesome that you all showed up," I say, surprised by how touched and happy I am to see them here, even Earlene.

"Open your gift!" Felicity reminds me of a child, eyes wide with excitement.

I tear open the wrappings and stand blinking at the object in my hands. It's a knitted baby blanket in a patchwork of rainbow colors, every square vibrant and a different texture.

Felicity actually bounces in delight. "We made it in the knitting circle! Don't you just love it?"

"I do love it. This is . . ." I clasp the soft blanket against my chest and stare at them all through a brand-new haze of tears. "It's beautiful."

"We all made different squares," Kimber explains. "And then Felicity sewed them all together."

Annie rolls her eyes, but she's grinning. "Will the wonders never cease, right? Miracles are alive and real."

"It was so much fun, we're going to make all of them this way." Felicity beams at me. "Even Steve made a square. But we didn't actually include it."

"It was pretty crooked," the pastor says, laughing. "But it was fun to be part of the circle."

For just a minute, I feel left out. Maybe this new, reformed knitting circle would be something I'd want to be part of. Earlene brings me back to my senses.

"Next time we will be much more structured. We'll abide by a color scheme and—"

"You don't have to control everything," Annie butts in.

"Oh, come on, you two, not tonight," Steve objects, but I know the bickering will only escalate from here.

"Hey," Tara says, coming up beside me. "That blanket is so adorable! Excuse me for butting in," she says, "but I need to borrow Liz for a minute." She tows me off to the side. "Just wanted to let you know the cast is meeting at Rancho. You're coming, right?"

"Wouldn't miss it. No drinking games for me, though."

"Of course not. You and the baby can drink something disgustingly healthy. And be our designated drivers if we need them."

Earlene and Annie are still bickering, and I say my goodbyes with more relief than regret. Felicity hugs me as I'm leaving and whispers, "Can I call you sometimes? For advice?"

"Not sure I have any advice to give."

"Well, just moral support, then."

I laugh at the rueful expression on her face. "You are already miles ahead of anything I ever managed to accomplish. But yes. Of course. Call me anytime."

The party at Rancho Chico feels like a letdown. Maybe it's because I'm emotionally drained, or because I am the only person who doesn't drink, aside from my stage son. Maybe it's because Lance is conspicuously missing. Whatever the reason, I excuse myself early.

Abigail is asleep on the couch, our first joint purchase for the house. Moses is asleep on her feet. He still hasn't forgiven me for the carrier, and the minute he sees me, he gets up and stalks away, looking indignant. A book is open on Abigail's chest, *The Handmaid's Tale*. Nothing like a little light reading on a Saturday night. She looks so peaceful, I don't have the heart to wake her; I just close the book and set it to one side. Then I cover her with a blanket and drag myself up the stairs to my room.

I am so bone tired, I can barely keep my eyes open long enough to remove my stage makeup before I fall blissfully into my lovely new bed and drift into a deep, dreamless sleep.

~

When I wake, Abigail has already left for church. But she's left a plate of peanut butter and crackers by my bed, along with a glass of water. A doc at her job told her protein before I even get out of bed will help with the nausea, and it does seem to be working.

Downstairs, the coffeepot is loaded and ready to go.

I slip into a sweater and carry my coffee out onto the porch. It's still cool, but the sun is warm. I sit in the porch swing, soaking in the fragrance of grass and wildflowers, listening to the birds. I love that I have no neighbors close by, that I can sit out here in my pajamas without bothering to comb my hair.

Despite the caffeine and a good night's sleep, the peaceful rocking makes me drowsy. I set down the mug and let my eyes drift closed, soaking up the spring sunshine and the birdsongs, letting my overtaxed brain just drift in and out of a light doze.

"Hey, sleepyhead," Lance's voice says, and my eyes pop open.

He's leaning on the porch railing. I assume he's looking at me, but the sun is directly behind him, casting his face into shadow.

I gasp and straighten up, wiping the back of my hand across my mouth in case I've been drooling.

"I didn't mean to startle you." The glow behind him highlights the lines etched in his face, the dark circles under his eyes. "You looked so peaceful."

My hand goes automatically to my uncombed hair, and I wrap the sweater more closely around me, remembering the pajamas and feeling resentful that he's caught me at such a disadvantage. We need to talk when I'm fully dressed—maybe in the elegant cocktail gown I don't own, with diamonds at my throat and a bodyguard standing by.

"Did you need something?"

"I came to talk."

Gathering up all of my newfound determination and decisiveness, wearing it like armor, I say, "Do tell."

"Please don't be like that."

"Like what, exactly, Lance? You're finally ready to have a conversation, so you just show up and assume I'm good with that."

"I was completely blindsided. I think it's reasonable that I took a little time—"

"*You* were blindsided. Funny thing—I don't have the luxury of just ignoring the fact that I'm pregnant. It's kind of up front and in my face."

"Maybe you should have thought of that sooner."

"Me? What about you? Maybe only one person can carry a baby, but this wasn't an immaculate conception."

"You told me you couldn't get pregnant, when clearly you . . ." He stops, shifts his weight.

"Go on," I urge him, thoroughly angry now. "When clearly I what?"

"Where do I even start? The odds of a woman your age getting pregnant are astronomical. Were you on fertility treatments? There you were, pretending to be so innocent and inexperienced, and all the time—"

"Oh my God! You think I did this on purpose? What insane woman wants to be pregnant at this age?"

"You wouldn't be the first woman to loop a man in."

It's all so ridiculous that my outrage finds an outlet in a burst of laughter. Lance folds his arms across his chest, a muscle in his cheek twitching rhythmically.

I cross my own arms and glare at him. "First, I don't need a man, not that bad, anyway. Second, if I did need a man, getting pregnant is certainly not the way I would hook one."

Lance turns away, looking out across the field behind him. "I'm sorry if I misjudged you."

"Now there's a heartfelt apology. Is that why you came over here? To accuse me of tricking you into—what, exactly?"

"Marriage." He turns back toward me, taking off his ball cap and twisting it in his hands. "I came over to ask you to marry me."

Now I'm speechless. I rock back and forth on my swing trying to think of something, anything, to say.

"It's the right thing to do," he says after a long silence.

"Right for whom?"

He flinches, and I soften my voice. "Listen. Lance. Whatever you thought, you were wrong. I tried for years to have another baby after Abigail and couldn't. I'm well into menopause. When I said I couldn't get pregnant, I believed it, only apparently I was wrong."

"You didn't seem like the sort of woman who would do that sort of thing," he admits.

"And you didn't seem like the sort of man who would jump to an assumption like that." I don't add the "apparently I was wrong" clause, but it hangs between us as clearly as if I had. Is it ingrained in all men to believe that women are temptresses? It's Eve with the apple all over again, luring Adam to his fate.

Lance's lips twist into a rueful half smile. "So no to marriage, then?"

"A definite no. You can cross that one off your to-do list."

"I'll help," he says. "Financially. Or anything. Cooking. Cleaning. Plowing snow out of your yard in the winter. Rides to the doctor. If you need all of that. If you're not . . . God, I'm bad at this. Are you going to . . . end it?"

"Get an abortion, you mean? No. I . . . can't."

"Thank you," he breathes. "I know I don't deserve an opinion, but a baby . . . a new person that's part of both of us. I'd like it to have a chance to live." He paces the length of the deck, his boots clomping. "Your health, though. That's the most important. Are you . . . can you . . ."

"The doctor says that while the risks are higher for a woman of my age, most of them are for the baby. I'll likely survive. Abigail wants me to find an adoptive home. She's approached an agency. I'd need you to take a DNA test and sign papers."

He blinks, twice. Rubs his face with his hands. "I might not be the father?"

"Oh, you're definitely the father. Legally, though, you have to prove it's yours before you can sign away your rights."

"If you keep it, we could raise it together," he says very softly.

"Apparently we can't even have a conversation without fighting. Not sure raising a child together is such a good idea. Also, if it makes you feel better, there's still a high possibility of miscarriage."

The muscle in his cheek twitches. His face works with emotion, and he turns away and rubs his sleeve across his eyes. "Liz. I'm not usually this much of an asshole, I swear it. I feel like I'm stuck in a character role I can't shake loose of."

I want to walk up behind him and put my arms around his waist, lean my cheek on his shoulder, giving and receiving comfort. I harden my heart and clamp my teeth together. I'm the wounded party here. Not him. I will not say I'm sorry or soften any of the words I've spoken.

He sucks in a long breath. "I know I should have come and talked to you right away. Every morning I'd wake up, pick up the phone, and say, 'Call Liz,' and then I'd find a hundred reasons to do it later. Truth is, I've been an emotional wreck. Didn't know what to say or how to say it. Couldn't trust myself not to behave like I just did again today. It's like, when Rachel left me, I put every single emotion on lockdown. And then you being pregnant—it blew all of that containment to smithereens. I realized I've processed absolutely nothing. I guess all of those emotions didn't disappear; they just hung around waiting for me, and now they've all blown up at once."

"What do you want from me, Lance?"

He makes a sound that might be a laugh or a sob and turns to face me. "Tolerance? The chance to make it up to you. If you can possibly find it in your heart to let me, I'd like to be part of this."

"The morning sickness part? The part where I have to go through labor and then give the baby away and have nothing to show for it? That part?"

A spasm of grief crumples his face. When it passes, he says, "All of the parts. I know women suffer more, and it's not fair. I'm volunteering for bucket-holding duty. I'll drive you to the hospital. Hold your hand. Do whatever I can to help. If you'll let me."

Tears flood my own eyes. I want to trust his words, want to slide into his arms and open my heart to him, but I can't. Actions speak louder than words; I learned the truth of that one the hard way. My focus now needs to be on building my life and nudging Abigail into building hers. On getting through this pregnancy and making the hard decisions.

But I also won't kick him in the teeth. I need some of what he's offering. It will take the pressure off of Abigail. "If you'd help around the house, that would be great," I tell him after a long pause. "Mowing and upkeep and all that. I'll let you know if I need any rides. Let's start there and see how it goes."

"Thank you," he says. "For that. And for . . . you. You're an amazing woman, Liz. I'm honored to be your baby daddy." His eyes are still wet, but his old smile slips back into place. He puts his hat back on his head, touches his fingers to the bill in a mock salute, and walks off across the field in the direction of Rosie and Gil's.

I follow him with my eyes, letting my own tears flow now. He's a tiny speck in the distance before I realize I'm resting one hand protectively over the place where a baby is growing. "I'm sorry, little one," I whisper. "I'm sorry."

Chapter Twenty-Nine

September 28, 2019

Dear Lacey,
Such a mess you got me into.

It frosted last night, and it's too cold to sit on my beloved front porch swing.

But I love my new comfy chair in the living room. One for me, one for Abigail. Together with the couch, we now have lots of places to sit.

We also have amnio results, since the adoption agency insisted. All DNA came back normal, so no three-headed chicken after all, though the doctor did remind me that some defects can't be detected until birth, despite all of the testing that they do. Twenty-two weeks today, and this pregnancy is no longer theoretical or mythical. Val dragged me out shopping again, this time for maternity clothes. I can no longer fit into the jeans we bought in the spring.

My body has turned traitor, a sagging, aching, creaky mess. I dread the months I still have to go and can't imagine lumbering around at nine months pregnant. I feel like my hip joints will collapse under that amount of weight and I'll cave in like an abandoned barn.

All of that glorious freedom I was just beginning to feel has vanished into a list of can't do because of the baby. Can't drink. Can't plan trips. Can't be in the theater production that's in rehearsals right now. My journey into saying yes to things has hit a serious snag.

And yet. Moment of truth. I'm glad this little creature is hanging on to life. Time to stop saying "it" or "the baby." He. A boy. At least, that's what my last ultrasound said. I can feel him moving, swimming inside me like a little fish, and I'm amazed, when I let myself be, that Lance and I, in that one act, created somebody new. But those are dangerous thoughts, because we're steaming down the adoption trail. Our top-running candidates are coming over this afternoon. They want to "meet" the baby early. Talk to it and whatever. Which can't be anything but awkward, and I wish it could happen without me.

Lance is coming. He's been around a fair bit lately. Mowing the yard. Weeding and watering the flowers I planted. Fixing things that I can't see need fixing around the house. Replacing light bulbs. He added three extra smoke detectors yesterday. And every single time he's here, he brings me wildflowers. He just puts them in a jar on the table without a word, not putting me on the spot of having to say something or feel an obligation.

It's no safer to think about Lance than it is to think about the baby. So because physical activity is already getting uncomfortable and thinking is dangerous, yesterday I started writing a play to keep my mind busy. It's a stupid little thing, and I cringe at every other line. But maybe that's normal for a beginner, I don't know. Seems like everything I thought I wanted is complicated.

Note: I would never go back. If Thomas were magically resurrected, this time I would not stay.

There are three of us and three of them.

Team Adoption is made up of Michelle and Gordon Walker, the want-to-be parents, and Joyce, the representative from the adoption agency. Michelle and Gordon are thirty-one and thirty-five, respectively. She is five foot five and weighs 150 pounds. Her eyes are blue, her hair is blonde, and she's an elementary school teacher. He is an accountant. Five foot ten, 175 pounds. Hazel eyes and brunette. They live in a clean, well-maintained bungalow in Spokane Valley. Michelle will stop teaching and stay home with the baby. They would like to homeschool. I know all of this because of their profile on the adoption site.

It's a warm afternoon, and Abigail serves iced tea before we settle down for business.

Joyce, somewhere around my age but very thin and athletic and stylishly dressed, is clearly not a woman who would fall into the predicament of a midlife out-of-wedlock pregnancy. She smiles brightly and inclusively at all of us, radiating professional warmth and cheer.

"Well, let's get acquainted better, shall we? This is your chance to ask questions about things that are not in the profiles. I am here only for moral support and to facilitate. Elizabeth? Is there anything you would like to know? Parenting style, political beliefs, that sort of thing?"

"Call me Liz, please," I answer. And then: "Political beliefs? Really?"

"It's very important to some," Joyce says in a soothing tone. "Especially in an open adoption, where the birth parents have agreed-upon levels of contact with the adopting family and the baby. That is another thing we will want to discuss."

Gordon reaches for Michelle's hand and squeezes it. A comforting gesture, probably, but I remember having my hand squeezed that way as a warning to keep my mouth shut. Or as a reminder that Thomas was the decision maker. They have chosen to wear matching T-shirts with a logo I don't recognize: *BT*. In my head, I translate it as "the Baby Takers."

Lance and Abigail and I should have logos of our own. "The Baby Growers," maybe. This could be a reality show taking place in my living room. I remind myself that I am voluntarily giving my baby away, not defending it from adversaries, but emotions are what they are and I can't shake this one.

Abigail and I are ensconced in our new armchairs, the Baby Takers are all on the couch, and Lance has brought in one of the kitchen chairs. I'd thought meeting here would give me a home turf advantage, but it just makes me feel exposed. I can see them judging my still-half-furnished house behind polite expressions, determining that I'm clearly destitute and that's why I'm prepared to give away my baby.

Michelle glances up at Gordon, silently asking a question, and he nods, giving her permission, or maybe just reassurance. Either way, given the go-ahead, she leans forward a little, worrying her bottom lip between her teeth. "Is there any history of alcoholism or drug abuse? Not to judge, of course, but it can be a genetic trait?"

Lance's eyes find mine. He shrugs, and answers first. "I've never had a problem. My mother uses substances off and on. Psychedelics, mostly. LSD, mushrooms, pot, peyote. Very little alcohol. I don't know that she's an addict. She says she's questing for alternate realities."

"Are you sure about alcohol?" Gordon asks. "Pardon me for this question, but I noticed from your disclosed history that your mother is half Native American. And alcohol can be a problem for . . . your people."

"As I've said, alcohol has never been a problem for my mother or for me." There's a warning in Lance's voice, and Joyce dives in before things have a chance to escalate.

"I don't believe there is a genetic component to the use of psyche-delics. Liz? What about your side of the family?"

My childhood raises its ugly head. I feel defensive and embarrassed, like I did all through high school whenever the subject of my parents came up. But it's a fair question, really. I keep my answer short and to the facts. "My father was an alcoholic. My mother was not. I don't know about my grandparents or other family members. I drink rarely and have never had a problem." Abigail's eyes flick toward me, and my brain darts off down a legal rabbit hole. Am I lying? There was that almost DUI. That counts as a problem. Is that on record somewhere? Could these people unearth it if they tried hard enough?

Lance risks rolling his eyes at me, and I can't resist smiling at him. We'll get through this grilling, somehow.

"But nurture can overcome genetics, surely?" Michelle asks. At least I think she's asking. Everything she says has a questioning inflection. "We'd be homeschooling? And our love and prayers would surely be stronger than any genetic predisposition?"

"Of course, my dear." Gordon beams at her, and then at all of us. "We have so much love to offer a child. And prayer can overcome any less-than-optimal genetic background, a blessing, as we all have sinned and fallen short."

"What about the two of you?" Lance asks pleasantly. "Any sub-stance use, by yourselves or your families?"

Gordon sits up straighter. "I've tracked our genealogy all the way back to German ancestry, in my case, and English, in Michelle's. Our ancestors were successful, industrious people. And our parents and grandparents were social drinkers only."

I notice that Michelle lets him answer for both of them—also that her eyes drop to the floor, the fingers of her right hand rolling the hem of her T-shirt. Maybe there's a little something in her own background that Gordon doesn't know about.

"We were so relieved that the DNA testing was normal," Gordon says. "And that the baby is a boy!"

Lance's jaw tightens. "Why, exactly? Does it matter?"

"To carry on Gordon's family name?" Michelle says. "Although it would be wonderful to have a little girl, too." I hear the wistfulness in her tone and soften toward her a little.

"How do you feel about having contact with the baby, and with us?" Gordon asks. "We feel it would be in his best interests. So many adopted children feel lost and abandoned and then go seeking their origins. It might be best to just be open about that from the beginning."

"What are you thinking?" I ask. I'd thought about open adoption, torn between conflicting fear of never knowing what happened to my baby and the ongoing heartbreak of seeing him without being close to him.

"We would invite you to join us for Christmas and Thanksgiving," Gordon says. "Possibly for birthday events. It's one reason why we insisted on meeting in person, to see if we are . . . compatible."

"God." Lance's expression is pure horror. "So we'd be like, what? Distant relatives? Showing up for holidays with pockets full of gifts? What is the child supposed to call us—Aunt and Uncle?"

"Grandma and Grandpa." I swear Abigail says this, but when I swivel my head in her direction, she's sitting quietly and nobody else seems to have registered the comment.

"Well, of course it couldn't be Mom and Dad," Gordon says. "So Aunt and Uncle are possibilities."

I feel a knot forming in my throat. Tears fill my eyes. I can't imagine being Aunt Liz to a baby I've carried in my body and given birth to.

"These decisions are very difficult," Joyce soothes. "There's no rush. You'll need time to think and process your emotions. These are just some possibilities to be negotiated."

My hand finds its way protectively to my abdomen, and again I apologize to the little one inside. *I'm sorry. You are not a commodity to be negotiated over. This is not a trade agreement.*

"Would you mind telling us your reasons for giving him up? So we know what to tell him when he asks?" Michelle has tears in her own eyes.

I pinch the bridge of my nose with my fingers, reminding myself to breathe. What are my reasons? They no longer seem valid. Adoption is meant for women who can't care for a baby. Too young, too broke, too addicted, whatever. You don't just give a baby away because it's inconvenient. So what if I'm old enough to be his grandma? Grandparents raise children all the time these days. What do we tell him? Your mom was busy finding herself and creating a new and interesting life where there wasn't a space for you?

Abigail answers for me. "We've all agreed that my mother is not in a position to raise a baby. She's single and approaching retirement, with only a small fixed income. We feel a baby should have two younger, healthy parents who will be around to raise him."

Lance has had enough. He surges to his feet, the chair skittering away behind him on the hardwood. "My apologies, but I don't agree. Liz and I would be in a position to raise this baby if we did it together."

"Don't you dare back out of this!" Abigail snarls at him. "Sit down."

His gaze meets mine, then flicks away. "I'll still sign if that's what you choose to do. But I won't sit here like we're trying to reach some NATO agreement. And I won't be part of any fucking open adoption. I'll raise the boy and give him my best if we keep him. If he goes, I am not visiting him for Christmas."

He stomps out, leaving a shattering silence in his wake. Abigail is seething. Michelle weeps softly, burying her face in Gordon's shoulder.

"Well," Joyce says, far too brightly. "As I said, these conversations are hard and emotions do run high. I recommend that everybody just take a few days to cool down and think about all we've discussed. And then if you want to meet again, we can make that happen. I know it doesn't feel that way, but this is just a little bump in the road. Many adoption agreements are worked out after similar conversations."

Gordon hugs his wife tenderly, in a way that makes me think I may have misjudged him. He strokes her hair. "We'll figure it out," he says. "Don't give up yet."

Michelle roots around in her purse for a tissue and blots her eyes and blows her nose. "I'm sorry, it's just so . . . I do want a baby so badly."

I offer her a tentative smile. "When I was your age, I desperately wanted another baby."

"But at least you had one," she says, and my emotions sway another direction. Here is a woman whose heart is breaking because she can't have a baby. And here am I with a baby I am completely unprepared to raise. It makes perfect sense that we should make this transaction, but it feels utterly wrong.

Joyce rises to her feet. "Let's go, shall we? And then we'll discuss another meeting in a day or two."

Gordon clears his throat. "We'd like to say a prayer before we go, if you would permit us." It's a request, not a demand, but still I hesitate.

"Of course," Abigail says. "That would be lovely."

"Our Father," Gordon begins. "You know all things and we bow to Your will, but You have also told us to ask for whatever we need. I ask now that You bless these two people who have conceived this child, Elizabeth and Lance, and that they might find forgiveness and healing in You. I ask that you will bless this unborn, innocent child, that you will guard him, protect him, and see him delivered safely and raised in a home where he will be surrounded by Your love . . ."

His voice is earnest, sincere, but I hear Thomas's inflection on the words, implicating the deep sinfulness and shame of a child conceived out of wedlock, urging me to confess, to make a gift of my child to a family who might, with emphasis on "might," be able to counteract his origins and still save his soul. I feel like I'm being prayed at, manipulated. It's only my imagination, I tell myself, over and over, but I don't believe it.

Years of practice allow me to contain my emotions. I shake hands politely with Joyce and Gordon. Michelle hugs me, murmuring, "I can't imagine how hard this is for you. But if you can find it in your heart . . . I will love your little boy so fiercely." I return her hug, saying nothing.

Abigail sees them out, and I collapse into my new chair, so wrung out and limp I seem to have no bones left in my body.

"Well?" Abigail asks, returning and flopping down in the chair beside me. "Apart from Lance's meltdown, I thought that went well. I think they're still open to the adoption."

My head leaned back, eyes closed, I murmur, "The question is whether I am."

"Mom. You can't be serious. They are perfect. Lance is such a wild card! What could have possibly possessed him to react like that?"

"I felt the same way he did, Abigail. I just didn't say anything."

"You what? What is wrong with you?"

Her tone pierces the heavy fog of fatigue that is weighting my limbs and numbing my brain. I sit up and look at her directly. "What's wrong with me is that I'm a human being. I can't imagine watching my child be raised by those people. Can't begin to wrap my mind around how heartbreaking it would be to visit him as a casual stranger."

"You'd know you had done the right thing for him! That you'd done your best to put right a wrong and—"

"There's the rub. Right there. I don't believe what Lance and I shared was sinful. What I did wrong was not using birth control. This family is too . . ." I struggle for words.

"Too what, Christian? You want him raised by atheists?"

"I want him raised to understand that men and women are equals. That the man doesn't make all of the decisions and say all of the prayers. That the woman can be a doctor if that's what she's called to do."

"Please," Abigail protests with a groan. "Not this again."

But I'm not listening. In my mind, I replay the entire visit. Yes, Gordon was kinder and gentler than Thomas. But Michelle deferred to him in every comment, every move she made. She couldn't even make a statement without turning it into a question.

I do not want my baby raised like that. It would be Abigail all over again, only this time with a boy. He'd be raised to believe he's better, just because he's a man, that he has the right to make all of the decisions, that women are created for him.

And then the truth hits me, as invigorating and in my face as a bucket of icy water.

I want this boy to be raised by me. This new me. Not the old Liz, or the old Elizabeth, but me. This woman who had the courage to say yes to life in the first place.

"God, Abigail. I don't think I can do this." I'm on my feet, reaching for my phone. I really need to talk to Lance.

Chapter Thirty

I wait for him on the deck, needing the fresh air, the feel of sunshine on my face. When I called, he was at Rosie's, and it only takes a few minutes for him to drive up and park in the yard.

"Can I sit?" he asks.

"I won't bite you," I answer, and he settles down in the porch swing beside me.

"Look, I'm sorry. I know I went off—"

"I would have, if you hadn't."

He turns his head to look at me. "Really?"

"The Bible's got hell all wrong. That meeting was worse than flames and pitchforks."

Lance sighs, leaning back, stretching out his legs. A relaxed pose on the surface, but I can feel the tension radiating off him. "Maybe some other couple will be better."

"Some other couple will be horrible in a whole different way."

"God," he says, and it sounds more prayer than blasphemy. "What a mess we got ourselves into. I need to tell you something, Liz. Something I should have told you a long time ago. About my son."

"You have a son?" My hand goes to my heart. I've had enough shocking revelations for one day.

"Had," he says, his eyes on the horizon. "Gwyn. He would have been twelve this August, if he'd lived."

"Oh, Lance."

"He was stillborn. You'd think the grief would be less when I never even had a chance to know him. But . . ." He swallows, shifts his weight. "Well. Rachel was so excited about that pregnancy. So hopeful. Ten miscarriages, years of fertility treatments. Every time we lost a pregnancy, it killed her a little more, killed us a little more. I begged her to stop. No more babies. We could adopt. We could be cat people or dog people. We could try to get back to the way we were together before she'd gotten so desperate for a baby. I told her it didn't matter to me. She said if it didn't matter to me, then I didn't love her.

"But I told her I was done, anyway. Couldn't stand to watch the cycle anymore, her terrible, wrenching hope when she'd miss a period, get a positive test. Her utter despair when she miscarried. I just couldn't do it. I stopped . . . well, I wouldn't be with her anymore in that way.

"We fought. She said if I loved her, I'd want her to have a child. That I'd see how much she needed this. She accused me of cheating on her. She wept, she ranted, she stopped eating and bathing. I took to hiding medications, locking up knives. I was scared to leave her alone, but being with her was a nightmare.

"We were already in debt from the fertility treatments. I took out a second mortgage on the house. And then, God help me, I finally agreed to try again. This time, just like that, we got pregnant. It was like magic, or maybe an answer to all of her prayers. I was afraid to hope, braced for the inevitable miscarriage, but then she made it past the first trimester. She felt the baby move, a first-time milestone for her.

"The two of us began to heal. She was happy again, alive. By the time she was twenty-four weeks, it was almost like all of those miscarriages hadn't happened. The doctor was optimistic. The baby was viable—preemies that age had been known to survive. Everything looked great. We started preparing. Bought a crib. She was knitting baby clothes. Singing around the house.

"Money was a problem, but I kept that worry to myself. I'd always been self-employed on the farm. Gil and Rosie and I had equal shares and made decent profits, but I couldn't afford good medical insurance. I was broke and in debt from paying for fertility treatments and the specialist. Rachel was supposed to have the baby in Spokane; everything was normal, but she was considered high risk because of all of the early losses. We were planning to stay in a hotel for the last few weeks of her pregnancy, close to the specialist, but she went into labor early. We panicked.

"I drove her into Colville as soon as the contractions started. They were strong by the time we got there, too late to stop them, too late to drive to Spokane, but the doctor reassured us. Thirty-two weeks, babies do great these days. Rachel was so excited, so happy, so trusting. 'Get ready to meet your son,' she said to me. I . . . kissed her . . .'"

He stops for a minute, and I swallow back a sob. I put my hand over his, and he laces his fingers with mine and squeezes. Takes a deep breath.

"They put her in a room and put a monitor on, and there . . . there was no heartbeat."

"Oh, Lance. Oh God. I'm so sorry."

He shakes his head. "She wouldn't stop hoping. She said there was something wrong with the monitor. And the nurse said sometimes it's hard to find a heartbeat. So they got the ultrasound . . ."

He withdraws his hand from mine, leaning forward and burying his face in both hands. For a long moment, there's only the sound of his ragged breathing, a bird singing in the distance.

"The baby was dead. We . . . she . . . had to go through all the agony of labor, with no reward at the end. It destroyed her. When we buried that tiny baby, we buried us, too. There was nothing left between us. She left me a week later. And then the rest of the bills started rolling in. I couldn't pay the mortgage, was facing bankruptcy. Rosie and Gil bailed me out. Took over the mortgage, bought out my share of the farm. They would have just given me money, but I couldn't—I'd already lost everything else, my pride was the last thing I had left. The only thing.

"I didn't want to live here after, anyway. The memories haunted me. I loved this house when I built it, but everywhere I looked, I just saw death. I told myself it was appropriate for renters to trash it. And then—"

"And then I came along. Why on earth didn't you tell me all of this sooner?"

"Instead of just being a dick?" He laughs, shakily. "You came into my life like an earthquake, Liz. Shook everything up, and all of the skeletons I'd buried came tumbling out into the open."

"I can see how me moving in here would have hit you. And the pregnancy—God. No wonder."

He shifts his position to look me in the eyes. "You may have noticed I live a . . . minimalist sort of life."

"Is that what you call it?"

"When Rachel packed up and drove away, even before she filed for divorce, there was nothing left of me. At first I really did nothing but drive the tractor wherever Gil told me to. Eat when Rosie made me. Sleep whenever I could. And then little bits of life crept in. I love my nephews. I started volunteering for the ambulance, and it felt good doing something for other people. I earned my EMT, started working that job part-time. And then the community theater happened. Can't remember why I decided to do that first play, but I loved being somebody else onstage. I liked the easygoing community with the theater people, so I did another play. I dated a few women, but it was very casual. I never let anybody get close.

"Then you walked onstage with me for that audition, and I felt like I'd been shaken until my teeth rattled in my head."

"Sorry?"

He laughs, for real this time, and some of the tension goes out of him.

"It was a good thing. You woke me up. I looked around my apartment that night, and for the first time in twelve years, I realized that I have deprived myself of anything resembling a home. That night I brought you in—"

"Just research," I whisper. "Casual sex. I know."

"Do you actually believe that?"

The passion in his voice sets me to trembling. I can't hold his gaze, letting my head and my eyes drop to my hands where they're twisted in my lap.

"Is that all it was for you?" he asks. "Casual?"

I shake my head. Try to find the right words to tell him. Be brave. Be the new Liz. I take a breath and force myself to meet his gaze, his eyes so blue, so intense, they seem to be staring straight into my soul.

"I tried to tell myself that. You were . . ." I swallow, let my eyes drop again. I can't look at him and say what I need to say. "Thomas was my first. My only. And he . . . he didn't . . . I didn't . . ."

"Oh my God." He sounds stricken. "That was your first time outside of marriage? I should have—"

"You were utterly perfect. I was so furious afterward, with Thomas, that I'd been married for thirty years and never knew it could be like that. But then you got all—"

"Weird." He still looks aghast. "And then I turned into an asshole. You must have thought it was because you had sex with me. That I'd gotten what I wanted and lost interest."

"Crossed my mind." I try to smile, but my lips are trembling.

Lance puts his hand on my cheek, turns my face up to look into his. "It was the opposite. After twelve years of being locked up tight, not wanting anything, all of a sudden I wanted everything. You. A relationship with you. Three kids and a house and a dog. It terrified me. I didn't know how to be normal around you, so I just stayed away until we bumped into each other at the Acorn."

"And then I found the house. Your house."

"I wanted you to have it. I wanted you to be happy, I saw the way you lit up. The way you noticed all of the little things I'd done to make it special. Rachel never—she never understood the house. It was just a house to her. Any house would have done. She didn't care about the yard or the land. All she wanted in the world was the one thing I couldn't give her. After I showed you the house that day, I forced myself to go back and walk through all of the rooms again. To try to picture happy things, to remember how I felt when I was building it. I was coming around.

"And then you collapsed and blurted out the news. I was shell shocked. All of this grief and rage about the baby and the divorce came boiling up, and I turned it on you. Can you ever forgive me for being such an asshole?"

"Are you going to be around to be forgiven?"

I hear the hitch in his breath, feel his muscles tighten. He shifts his position and gazes deep into my eyes, as if he's trying to read my soul. "If you'll let me," he says, and the emotion in his voice makes me want to fling myself into his arms.

But I'm not ready for that. Neither of us is ready for that.

"If I were to keep the baby, you would help me?"

"Are you saying what I think you're saying?"

The hope in his eyes is too bright, too much, and I have to look away. "I can't let somebody else raise this child. I realized that during that horrible interview. But it's not just my baby, and not just my decision. We'd have to figure out how to raise him together."

"The marriage offer still stands."

I shake my head. "Not that. We would raise the baby as friends. As partners. Neither one of us is in any shape for a relationship beyond that."

He cups my face in his hands, tilts it up toward his. "Liz. I think I love you. I don't know if I can do that."

I can hardly breathe with the memory of kissing him, the desire to do it again. But, very gently, I turn my face away, freeing myself from his touch. "You barely know me. I don't even know me. This is not the time to make a relationship commitment. For either of us, Lance."

"Liz." He reaches for me, but I draw back, out of reach of his hands, afraid that if I let him kiss me again, I'll melt and say yes to anything.

"As friends. Or not at all."

The moment that follows trembles on a balance point that will change the course of my life, one way or another.

Finally he nods. "Deal." He holds out his hand and I give him mine. We shake, a strong, businesslike gesture, but he holds my hand longer than he would need to and I can't bring myself to pull away.

Which is how Abigail finds us. She lets the door slam shut behind her and glares at us both, as if we're teenagers caught out in a forbidden tryst.

"What is he doing here?" she demands.

"I invited him over to talk." I keep my voice calm and level, letting my hand rest in Lance's instead of snatching it back. "Sit down, Abigail. I've come to some decisions."

"Pretty sure I don't want to hear anything either of you have to say right now."

"I'm not going through with the adoption."

She sighs, gustily, and crosses the deck to lean on the railing. "Look. I get that you didn't like this couple. I heard what you said, and you have a point. But they aren't the only ones. We can find somebody more compatible."

"Abigail. I am not adopting the baby out to anybody. He is my responsibility." Her mouth opens, and I raise my hand to silence her. "Don't. There are women my age raising babies all over the country.

You know what I realized during that fiasco? He's mine. Or Lance's and mine, I should say. We created him. We'll raise him. End of story."

"So what now?" Her voice rises. "You're going to let this . . . this man . . . move into the house? I am not living with the two of you. I can't even imagine what Dad would say about this!"

"Your father has nothing to say about this. He's not here." A bubble of laughter rises at the insane idea of Thomas and Lance and Abigail and I and a baby, all living happily together under the same roof.

The laughter is definitely a mistake.

"You think this is funny?" Abigail demands. "I don't even know who you are anymore. And I tell you what. If he's moving in, I'm moving out."

"I'm not planning to move in." Lance's tone is calm. Understanding, even. "I'm sure this is hard enough for you already."

"You have no idea how hard anything is. Either one of you. I can't *do* this. I've tried, but I just can't." She stalks back into the house, slamming the door behind her.

"I'm sorry," I say in the reverberating silence that follows. "She is rather opinionated."

"Thank God for that. Imagine if she was like that Michelle person, all tentative questions, like she's asking for permission to exist in the world."

He's right. Abigail is strong. Resilient. She's learning to express her emotions.

I heave myself up onto my feet. "I should go check on her."

"And I should get some work done." He stands there, facing me, close enough that I could so easily step into his arms.

But I've made my choice, and I stay with it.

"Thanks for telling me about Gwyn. And how you feel about the house."

He shrugs. "Should have told you sooner. See you soon." He drops a kiss on my cheek, and I watch him walk to his truck before I go back inside to make peace with my daughter.

At least that's the idea, but I see at once there will be no peace in the immediate future. There's a suitcase open on her bed, and she is stuffing clothes into it without bothering to fold them. Strands of hair have come loose from her braid. I watch as she throws a pair of shoes in on top of a skirt, then crams in three sets of nursing scrubs.

"What are you doing?" I ask, alarmed.

"What does it look like I'm doing?" Her face is hidden from me, but her voice is blurred with tears and her shoulders are shaking with sobs.

"Abigail. Honey." I put my hands on her shoulders, but she shrugs me off.

"Don't touch me."

Sinking down on her bed, I close the suitcase, preventing the addition of an armful of underwear. "We need to talk about this."

"Do we?" She faces me, defiant and tear streaked. "What is there to talk about? My opinions don't matter to you. You're going to do whatever you want no matter what I think. And I am not sharing a house with that man."

There are so many possible responses, and my answer is going to matter. I leave the Lance issue alone and zero in on what I guess to be the problem.

"Your opinions matter very much to me, because I love you. But that doesn't mean I'm always going to do what you think I should do. You're my child, Abigail, not my mother. You don't get to tell me what to do."

"If I asked you, would it be different? If I asked you to stop having any contact with Lance?"

"He's the father," I say, a little helplessly. "He has a right to be involved."

"If you adopt out the baby, his involvement isn't with you. Don't you see? If you loved me, you'd do this for me."

"Abigail. Please. It's been a hard day. Let's both just take some time to calm down, and then we'll talk. All right? You don't have to make any decisions today."

"You've already made your decisions, and you sure didn't take time to think them through. Please leave my room."

"Honey . . ."

"Get out!"

She glares at me, hands on hips, vibrating with hurt and anger.

I do as she asks, pausing in the hallway to say, "Don't forget I love you."

She closes the door in my face.

Chapter Thirty-One

October 5, 2019

Dear Munchkin,

It's just you and me in the house now. Abigail spent the week in a motel, and today she moved the rest of her stuff into an apartment. It's a formal protest against the way I'm living my life, her version of a peace march or whatever. She said she'll talk to me when I break off all contact with Lance.

I feel . . . gutted. Defeated. I wanted so much to fix things between us, but I can't do that by sacrificing you. She's grown up and gets to make choices. You didn't get a choice in any of this, so you're just going to have to deal with the choices I make for you.

And then probably hate me for them later.

Is that inevitable? Val's son doesn't seem to resent any of the choices she made, but then Val is Val. I miss her. Today, with the house so empty, still so sad about Abigail moving out, I miss the theater people. Today I even miss the knitting group and Earlene.

Town is a long way away and winter is coming. The maple in the yard is crimson and leaves are starting to fall. Soon there will be snow and driving anywhere will be dicey. I love this house, but the idea of taking care of it by myself . . . all of the maintenance that a house needs . . . is terrifying.

Lance has stopped in every day, and I know he'll help with things, but whatever this is between us is tentative and not permanent. Am I brave enough for this? I guess I'd better be. Steve and Felicity are all moved into the old house and there's no going back.

Would I undo this for a chance at the old life?

Still no.

November 10, 2019

Dear Munchkin,
Abigail still holds resolute. She dutifully calls to check in, once a week on Sunday mornings, to make sure I'm alive and taking care of my health. Have I seen the doctor? Done the recommended screenings? Am I ready to talk to another adoptive couple? Am I through with Lance?

I haven't seen her since the day she left. She hasn't told me where her apartment is.

Somehow I have to fix this, if not for me, then for you.

You need to know your sister. She needs to know you.

On the bright side, at least she's living her own life right now.

God help me, I think maybe I'm going to need to go to church.

It feels like years since I've been here, rather than just a few months. The church looks smaller, a little shabby. It's time for a new coat of paint. The parking lot needs to be repaved. But the grounds have been beautifully mowed, and there's a new sign out front, one of those LED things with a cute slogan that Thomas would have hated and that seems like a finger pointing at me: *If God seems far away, guess who moved? You can come back anytime.*

I'm not coming back, just visiting, but everybody will rejoice over the sinner returned, and I'll have to let them, keeping the truth that this is a one-time event to myself. There might be a different church in my future, but there is way too much heartache and hypocrisy tied up in this one for me. I'm here because this is the one place where I know I can find Abigail, aside from interrupting her at work. If I corner her, she'll have to talk to me.

I park in the lot, then sit in my car and second-guess this decision, cringing at the thought of the stares and whispers that will follow in the wake of my obviously pregnant belly. Maybe I should just call Felicity to ask for Abigail's new address. Or hire a private investigator.

Too late. Annie pulls in to the space beside me, smiling and waving. With a sigh of resignation, I turn off the ignition, pocket my keys, and get out of the car.

Annie hugs me, then steps back to look me over. "Well, look at you and your baby bump."

"Um, thanks?"

She hugs me again and laughs. "You look great. Hey, think of it this way. You and your baby daddy bought poor Marjorie some slack. She got her divorce, got married, and moved out of town in peace while everybody talked about you."

I have always liked Annie, partly because she didn't bore me, but the gossip jars me, even though there's no malice in it.

"Come on," she says, starting for the door. "The others will be excited to see you."

I trail along behind her. When I imagined this all in my head, I came in late and lurked in the back. In my imaginary plan, everybody was so entranced by the sermon, they didn't turn around, didn't make trips to the bathroom or slip outside for a forbidden smoke. I latched on to Abigail when she walked out after the sermon and insisted on talking.

Now, dragged along by Annie, I see how utterly improbable that whole scenario was. Annie is going to triumphantly present me to the entire congregation, as if she'd gone out into the highways and byways and rescued me from my life of sin.

What happens is worse.

We walk through the front door and run, literally, into Abigail, who has her phone to her ear and isn't paying attention to where she is going. "Oh," she says, eyes widening with surprise. She drops her phone into her purse and stares at me. "Mom? Thank God. I prayed for this moment."

She flings her arms around my neck.

This is bad. She mistakes me as the prodigal mother, come to her senses, which was not what I had in mind at all. She doesn't give me a chance to clarify. A worship team is gathering on the platform at the front of the sanctuary, signaling that the service is about to begin.

"Come on, I already have a seat saved and we can make room for you." Abigail twines her cool fingers around mine, and I follow her up the center aisle, almost to the front row. I can feel all of the eyes on my back, and the only reason I can't hear the whispers is because the band has started in on a praise song. The guitars, keyboard, and drums drown out everything.

Abigail pauses by the third row from the front. This is our pew, the place we always sat when Thomas was preaching, but today a young man occupies the seat at the end. There's an Abigail-size space on the other side of him, and I realize with a rush of embarrassment that this is where she expects me to sit. There isn't room for me, certainly not for both of us, and I already feel conspicuous without either trying to crowd into a spot where I don't fit or lumbering back up the aisle again, this time looking at all of the faces that are looking at me.

The young man politely gets up to let me in. The family on the other side of the empty space sees the dilemma and all crowd farther down the pew. There's nothing for it but to walk in and sit down, feeling like one of those people who come into the movie theater late, talking on a cell phone and balancing three buckets of popcorn while everyone else is trying to watch the movie.

Abigail and her friend are able to cram in beside me, the three of us wedged like sardines in a can. Immediately I need to pee. *Good luck with that,* I tell my bladder. *We are stuck here for the duration.* The music team is good, and under other circumstances, I would enjoy this part of the service, but I am anything but relaxed and receptive. Abigail is so happy that I am here. She'll be thanking God for my change of heart, and then I'll have to tell her the truth—that coming to church has everything to do with her and nothing to do with God—and she'll be angry and disappointed and hurt all over again.

Memories crowd and jostle me almost as much as Abigail and the sharp-elbowed woman on the other side of me. Thomas preaching his interpretation of the word of God while I sat here, obediently, my entire job to look pious and make sure Abigail behaved. Church services were long and stressful. Inwardly, I was seething in resentment.

Today, despite my resistance and anxiety, the music gets under my skin, pulls me in. I realize I'm singing, Abigail's alto harmonizing with my soprano, and it's the music that carries a new truth right into my shivering soul.

I'm mad at God for what Thomas did.

As if to emphasize this point, Pastor Steve gets up to speak. There's no hellfire and brimstone, no judgment, no oration. He just talks, simply and from his heart, about loving each other, sprinkling in stories of a God who would have been a stranger to Thomas. A kind God, a loving God, one with a sense of humor. He ends with a benediction:

"The Lord bless you and keep you; the Lord make His face to shine upon you and be gracious unto you; the Lord give you peace."

I blink back tears, knocked completely off-balance by the thought that I'm unjustly blaming God for things that might not be His fault. But that's a thing I'll need to deal with later. Right now, I need to navigate walking down the aisle, finding the bathroom, and having a chat with Abigail.

One bonus to sitting up at the front is we get to walk out first. The downside is that everybody watches us, hands reaching out to shake mine as I walk. So many familiar faces, but a lot of new ones, too.

When we make it to the foyer, the young man stays right by Abigail's side, as if they're connected by strings. He's wearing jeans and a casual button-up shirt open at his throat, no tie. His hair is long enough to graze his collar. He looks easy, open, comfortable in his own skin, and my uptight daughter smiles up at him with an expression I've never seen on her face before.

"Josh, this is my mom."

"I can totally see the resemblance." He smiles at me, wide and genuine, and holds out his hand. His handshake is warm, firm, his eyes clear and steady.

"I can't believe you're actually here," Abigail says. "God does answer prayers."

This is my chance to tell her why I'm really here, to un-answer her prayers with the truth. I hesitate, searching for the right words, and settle on a more pressing problem as a means of escape. "I really need to use the restroom. It was lovely to meet you, Josh. You'll wait for me, Abigail? Maybe I could take you out for lunch."

"We'd love that," she says, which was not what I had in mind at all. I don't really think Abigail will want Josh to be present for the conversation we need to have.

I encounter Kimber and Earlene, heads together, discussing some issue or other. Needing the restroom is a great excuse for keeping our exchange short, and after hugs all around, I extricate myself without being dragged into their conversation.

Most of the congregation has already cleared by the time I take care of business and give myself a pep talk in the mirror. Abigail and Josh are waiting just inside the front doors. His head is inclined toward her, and it's clear he hangs on every word she is saying. Her expression is animated, and she's so engaged with him, she doesn't notice my approach until I'm right beside her.

My throat tightens at the sight of the two of them together, a complex emotion washing over me. This is what I want for her, I remind myself. To be happy. To have a good life, not to be taking care of me. But loss is right there, side by side with the joy, protesting that if she's in love, maybe she'll leave me for good, releasing the duty without us ever finding another and better form of connection.

"How about I buy lunch?" Josh says, beaming a smile at both me and Abigail. "Since today is special. Where shall we go?"

Pastor Steve strides over at that moment, Felicity at his side. She hugs me, and then Steve puts his arm around me and gives my shoulders a gentle squeeze. "Welcome back! I knew you'd find your way, given time."

My Elizabeth self shakes off the dust and rises to the occasion with a practiced smile. "It's so good to be here. I enjoyed your sermon. And I like the changes to the music."

He grins. "So glad to hear that. We've lost a few of the older members."

"But so many new people coming in!" Felicity glows with enthusiasm. "Mrs. L., maybe you could come back to the knitting circle. We have new members and it's so much more open. You could make something for your own baby."

Abigail's lips tighten, but she holds her tongue.

I look at the four of them, and a new sort of responsibility settles on my shoulders. They all want to celebrate because they believe I'm transforming my life and will be coming back to church regularly. And as much as I would love to let them keep believing that, to have their celebration and be joyful, I need to be true to the newly emerging Liz.

"I'm so sorry," I say, my eyes seeking Abigail's and pleading for understanding. "I won't be coming to the circle, Felicity. I'm only here today because I need to talk to Abigail, and I knew I'd find her here. So if all of you could excuse us for a few minutes, we need to talk."

An awkward silence falls. Feet shuffle. Felicity leans into Steve for support.

And I pray, silently, for my own sort of miracle. *Please open Abigail's heart to me. Show me what to say, how to fix this.*

It's not my day for miracles. Color rises to Abigail's cheeks at the same time as her lips thin and her chin comes up. She's hurt and disappointed and angry, but doesn't want to make a scene.

"Well," Pastor Steve says, his people skills rising to the surface. "We should let the two of you talk, then. It was good to see you, Mrs. L. And you are always welcome."

Felicity hugs me again, just as warmly as the first time, and the two of them walk away hand in hand.

"You want me to stay?" Josh asks Abigail.

She ignores him, all of her energy focused on me. "So nothing is changed, then? That man is still living with you?"

"He's not living with me. He has never been living with me."

"But the two of you are planning to raise a baby. And you're not even remotely sorry about any of this, are you?"

I turn both hands palm up and hold them out to her, empty of any explanation that she is going to accept. "I didn't get pregnant on purpose, Abigail. I want to make things right with you, but it's too late to take that back. What can I do?"

"Give me my mother back."

I let my hands drift back to my sides. "I'll always be your mother. But I can't be who you want me to be."

Tears well up in her eyes. "I have to go," she says, her voice breaking. "Don't do this again."

"Abigail, please . . ."

But she is already marching away, head bent, arms wrapped around her chest. I've never seen her like this, and it breaks me wide open, tears of my own pouring down my face.

Josh looks stricken, glancing from me to Abigail's retreating back. He touches my shoulder lightly, as if wanting to offer comfort, then turns without a word and trots after Abigail, slipping an arm around her waist. To my surprise, she doesn't pull away, and the two of them walk together and get into a car that I don't recognize, Josh in the driver's seat.

I wait until the car is out of sight before walking out to my own.

"See what you've done?" Thomas whispers as I wipe my eyes and turn the key in the ignition. *"You want to blame me for her unhappiness, but really it's all you. You're the one who could fix it, but you're too selfish, caught up in the temptations of the flesh."*

"Just shut up!" I say out loud.

I'm sick to death of him hanging out in my head.

As much as I've grown and changed, despite the fact that I'm carrying Lance's baby and have bought my own house and make my own decisions, still, Thomas crawls into bed beside me at night and follows me through the house in the daytime, criticizing and commenting. Despite all of my efforts to shake him, he clings to me, bits of Thomas interwoven with bits of Liz.

He's still at the center of everything, spilling toxins into my life so that I'm always in cleanup mode.

I don't want his poison to infect my unborn child.

Turning left instead of right, I head for the cemetery instead of toward home. I've been back only twice since the funeral, assuaging my guilt by knowing Abigail takes flowers on a regular basis. I'm not even sure why I'm going there now, other than a vague notion that I need to stand by his grave in order to somehow break the hold he has over me. If this were one of my fantasy novels, there would be a magic word to break a spell, but I know life doesn't work that way.

When I park, I look around for other visitors, grateful that I seem to be alone. The last thing I need is to trigger a new round of gossip. Even so, when I reach his grave, I stand there feeling stupid and awkward. He's not here. His body is decomposing. His soul is wherever souls go. And the only memories tied to this place are of shock and exhaustion and the first guilty glimmers of freedom to come.

It feels stupid to talk to him, overly theatrical. He's not going to hear me and certainly not going to answer. But maybe this little ritual isn't for him at all. It's purely for me. So I clear my throat and say what I've come to say.

"You need to let go of me." My voice is loud in the silence, and I crane my neck to be sure no other mourners are listening. "You had all of me, everything I am, for over half my life."

"No. I never did. There were always parts of you I couldn't get to."

The words are so clear, I scan my surroundings again, half expecting to see a Thomas-shaped ghost standing behind me. I feel the hairs rising on the back of my neck.

It's true. I hid Liz from him, but I kept her alive. There were the journals I wrote in the mornings while he was still asleep. The bits of poetry, the scenes of plays. The books I read. The thoughts I hid away.

"Always the actress," Thomas says. *"Always playing a role. I knew it, but I couldn't break you of it. Eve, the temptress, living in my house. And in my heart."*

"I'm not acting anymore. And I want you to leave me alone."

"I did love you, Elizabeth."

"Not me," I whisper. "It wasn't ever me you loved. Only what I chose for you to see."

"I did love you," he says. *"As much as I was able."*

A new question rises. Had I—Liz—ever loved *him*? He created Elizabeth out of his need for the perfect wife, and I let him do it out of need for . . . what? Safety, security, meaning?

My own fault weighs me down. I chose to marry him. I let him create my reality. And it was easier, safer, to let him make all of the decisions. To tell me who to be and how to be that person. To let him dictate how to raise our daughter, how to spend my time.

There were so many moments, back in the beginning, when I could have broken free but chose not to. I abdicated responsibility for my own life long before I was so enmeshed in his reality that I could no longer see my way to freedom.

Grief overwhelms me, and I sink to my knees, weeping. Not for the man who is buried here or for the life that I had with him, but for the girl I once was, so young, so eager to latch on to security and structure that what Thomas offered seemed a gift. I weep for the years I lost, for the understanding that I never loved him and he never loved me, and especially for the way I let him step between me and Abigail.

"Not this time," I tell the baby inside me, along for this emotional ride. "Nothing comes between you and me. Nothing and nobody."

"I did what I thought right," Thomas says, his voice nothing more now than the faintest echo.

"I forgive you," I whisper. "Now let me go."

Silence follows. My knees hurt and my nylons are soaked from kneeling in fall-damp grass. I feel empty inside, scraped clean. It hurts, but it's a good hurt. Like I've cleaned out an infection and maybe now I can heal.

~

I buy myself lunch at Ronnie D's, a decadent hamburger, fries, and milkshake. Pure comfort food. When I get home, Lance's truck is parked in the yard. This is nothing unusual these days. He comes and goes freely, much as Val did at the old house. Most mornings we have coffee together. I'm usually happy to see him, but not now. Not with the graveyard still clinging to me, with so many feelings to sort and sift and process.

As soon as I open the door, I smell paint fumes and know he's upstairs working on the nursery, a project the two of us started earlier this week. Maybe I can sneak up to my room and change before I talk to him. I don't want to tell him about Abigail or that I've been visiting Thomas. I don't want him to know I've been weeping. I actually consider getting back in my car and driving away, but apparently today is all about facing up to people and emotions.

"Liz?" he calls. "That you?"

"Yep. Be right up."

Lance turns when he hears my footsteps in the hall.

He holds a small brush loaded with gold paint, ready to add stars, the finishing touch to the mural he's creating of a whimsical, friendly moon shining down on trees, owls, and forest animals. He's delightfully rumpled, unshaven, wearing paint-stained jeans and a T-shirt with holes in it. It makes him look young and vulnerable, and my heart swells with love that rapidly evaporates into guilt and irritation at his first words.

"Where the hell have you been? I was worried."

"Out." *Good one, Liz. Nice, casual evasion.*

"I called. Texted. You didn't answer."

"I'm fine." I turn my back and head for my room. "I'll just get changed and come and help you."

"You don't look fine. Did you fall? Are you hurt? Is the baby—"

"Oh my God." I turn around and come back. "No, I didn't fall. I can honestly take care of myself and the baby for a few hours. Stop hovering!"

"Do I pretend that I can't see you've been crying and that you have mud and leaves on your knees?"

I look down, processing, realizing I walked into a restaurant in this condition. All the fight goes out of me.

"What happened? Talk to me."

Lance crosses the room and puts his arms around me. I lean into the warm strength of him, breathing in paint and clean male sweat and something else that is purely Lance and has no name. It's comforting to be held like this. It makes me feel like I'm not all alone against the world.

"I really don't want to talk about it," I say, my cheek resting against his chest.

His hand strokes my hair. "I wish you wouldn't block me out."

"I don't block you out."

His silence is eloquent, and after a long moment, I sigh, and admit, "Okay, fine. I'm blocking you out. I went to church. To see Abigail. It did not go well."

"I'm sorry," he says, and I know he means it. He cups my chin in one strong, warm hand and tips my face up toward his. I recognize that look in his eyes, but before I fully register what it means, he's kissing me and I'm kissing him back. Something new and fragile blossoms between us, something different than the Lacey-and-Darcy sexual exploration, something sweet and beautiful.

I look up at him with wonder and new hope.

He blows it all to smithereens.

"Marry me, Liz."

All at once I'm cold and shivering, even though I'm still circled in the warmth of his arms.

"It doesn't have to be tomorrow," he says in answer to my expression. "We can wait until after the baby is here. He can be the ring bearer. We'll tie it to his pacifier."

I want to say yes. I want to follow this new emotion, see where it leads. But bits of Thomas are still clinging to me. I thought I loved him. I chose to give up my own life to be part of his. I don't want to make that mistake again.

Steeling myself for the hurt in Lance's eyes, I whisper, "I can't."

His breath snags on something sharp in his throat; his gaze stays locked on mine. "You still don't trust me. What do I have to do?"

It's not him I don't trust, it's me. I don't trust that I'm strong enough, yet, to be me, to stay me. I don't trust myself not to be possessed and consumed by a man, the way I was with Thomas. The baby growing inside me is already enough to reshape my life a million times over. But I don't know how to tell him any of this.

I press the palms of my hands against his chest, partly to push him away, partly to feel his solid strength. "You don't have to do anything. Just . . . don't push me. I can't—"

"You could. You can. Anytime you want to. That's how it's done, Liz. You take a risk. You make a decision."

"Then my decision is no."

"Well, that makes it clear." He drops his hands, turns his back, and begins cleaning up the paint supplies.

"Lance, please." I feel desperate now, a pressure cooker of hurt and fear. "It's not you I don't want. It's . . . marriage. The whole two-people-shall-be-one-flesh thing. There was barely anything left of me when Thomas died. I'm working to be me, but I'm . . . already symbiotic with this baby. How can I figure out who I am if I let myself get lost in you? It wouldn't be fair. Don't you see?"

He places the lid on the paint can, pauses with his head bent, his hands on the rim, then slowly tips up his chin to look at me. He looks weary, defeated. "I'm not Thomas, Liz. I'm not like that."

"I know you're not. I just . . ." My voice breaks and the tears come in a flood. I'm too tired, too frightened, to hold them back. Lance won't leave me now, because he's a good man and he'll be there for the baby. But I've just ruined any hope of the two of us together.

"Oh hell." He turns back to me and draws me into the circle of his arms while I weep, one hand stroking my hair, but I can feel the chasm between us. He won't ask me again.

Chapter Thirty-Two

December 24, 2019

Dear Munchkin,
Merry Christmas, little one.

Christmas Eve, and it's just you and me. Rosie invited me over, but I'm already having dinner with them tomorrow, and I was there for Thanksgiving, and being with Lance is . . . difficult these days. He's kind and considerate and always available to help—but he's also carefully and politely distant. So things are awkward with us, and worst of all, I miss my Abigail.

This is the first Christmas without her. We are so hopelessly cut off from each other. I can't believe that I'm writing this, but I even miss Thomas. Christmas was all about family. It softened him, somehow. He was more indulgent toward Abigail, gentler with me.

And now I've gone and made myself cry.

Ah, Munchkin. Next year this time, you will be big enough to crumple wrapping paper and crawl into boxes. You'll have your nephews to play with you, and your auntie Rosie and uncle Gil will love you. You'll be your daddy's whole world. But you're missing out on a sister.

It's past my usual bedtime, and I've allowed myself to become a blubbering, self-pitying mess. Besides being alone on Christmas Eve, I'm physically wretched.

My back aches. My hips ache. I've got heartburn. My breasts hurt. I'm exhausted, but if I go to bed I know I'll just lie there awake, trying hopelessly to find a comfortable position. I thought I was miserable when I was pregnant with Abigail, but this is ten times worse. The small person growing inside me is also restless tonight, squirming and kicking, trying to make more room.

"Easy," I whisper, my hands stroking my belly. "We've got another five weeks to go."

Next week, after Val gets back from visiting her son for the holidays, I'll be moving into her place to stay until I deliver. Everybody, including me, is unhappy about me being so far from town. Lance has begun sleeping on the sofa at night so I'm not here alone, although tonight he's off celebrating Christmas with his family, as he should be.

So I am utterly alone, with my unborn child and my phone for company. Even Moses has abandoned me, annoyed by my frequent changes of position. He's dozing in Abigail's chair, signaling his disapproval even in his sleep.

I'm watching *It's a Wonderful Life* and lying to everybody by text message. They don't know I'm weeping. The beauty of texting over calling is that it's easy to pretend to be fine. In response to Val's check-in and Merry Christmas text, I reply that I'm indulging in eggnog—no alcohol!—and watching Christmas movies. I tell Lance that I'm perfectly happy and all is well and he should enjoy his family. I text Abigail, something I've taken to doing daily although she never responds, and tell her I miss her.

A knock at the door startles me.

Lance and Rosie and Gil all have keys. Val is in California. The knock comes again. Irrational fear creeps up my spine. I'm alone and about as capable of self-defense right now as a capsized tortoise. Moving as quietly as possible, I make my way down the hallway and pause with my hand on the deadbolt. No peephole. No window in the door.

"Who's there?" I call.

"It's me."

I fling open the door. "Abigail? What on earth?"

It's snowing, big, fat flakes clinging to her dark hair. She's also not wearing a jacket, and her eyes and nose are red from weeping. I grab her by both arms and drag her into the house, closing the door behind her to shut out wind and snow. "Honey, what's happened?"

"Nothing," she says, but a little sob slips past the word, and I know it's a lie.

Bedraggled as she looks, she's still Abigail, so I don't try to hug her, even though that's all I want to do. "Come in and get warm; you're shivering. You want a cup of tea?" I lead the way into the living room, and Abigail scoops up Moses and buries her face in his fur. He makes no objection, purring happily at the attention.

I fix her a cup of tea with lemon and honey, the way she likes it. All the while, my heart is thumping with a combination of worry over what must have happened to bring her to me, and joy at having her home.

"It looks good in here," she says, accepting the mug and cradling it in both hands, blowing to cool it.

"All Lance's doing," I answer, then want to bite off my tongue for mentioning him. He brought in a little tree for me and we decorated it together. A wreath hangs above the fireplace, in which there is no fire because bending down to make one just felt like too much trouble.

"I was worried you wouldn't have a tree," Abigail says, her lower lip trembling.

"Abigail. Honey. Tell me what's wrong."

Tears overflow again and slide down her cheeks. She bends her head over the cat pooled bonelessly in her lap. "I was alone, and it's Christmas."

"Me, too," I say, my own tears rising to match hers. "I missed you so much."

"Josh went to his folks in Seattle. I was invited but I had to work today. And again the day after Christmas. And everything was all wrong. Everybody else was with family. You texted me, and I knew I needed to come . . . home." She stops short on that last word, her chin jerking upward so she's looking at me, wide eyed and surprised.

"You have a home with me anytime you need one."

Abigail sips tea, regaining her usual composure after this unusual display of emotion, and scrutinizes me. "You look very—pregnant. You're what, thirty-five weeks? You should not be way out here all by yourself. Or is that guy living with you now?"

I can't help smiling. That's my girl.

"Lance has not moved in, but he does sleep on the couch sometimes just in case something goes wrong."

She focuses on her tea mug as if it's of absorbing interest, and finally says slowly, "I should have been here. Maybe I don't like your choices, but I shouldn't have cut you off like that. I'll stay until after the baby comes."

It's as close to an apology as I will ever get from her, and the grace of it brings me to tears all over again.

"And now I've made you cry," she says. "That's not what I meant to do."

I wave her not-quite-apology away, laughing. "I'm pregnant. I cry about everything. And you don't have to stay unless you want to. Lance hovers. His sister is right down the road and can be here in five minutes."

Abigail glances up at me, almost shyly, and says, "I want to be here, if you'll let me. You're the only mom I've got."

Those words are the best Christmas miracle ever, and I smile at my daughter through a haze of tears while silently whispering a prayer of thanks to the God I might believe in after all.

~

It's almost impossible to believe that in two days I'll be thirty-seven weeks. Christmas and New Year's have passed quietly and surprisingly peacefully. Tomorrow I'll be moving into Val's house for the last few weeks, all of us agreeing it would be best for me to be closer to medical care. Abigail has already packed my things, and in the morning, Lance will drive me into town. Tonight, though, we're having a party—a part-housewarming, part-baby-shower event that Val has been planning for weeks. My part in it—from guest list to what will be happening—has been nonexistent. I have no idea who is coming, what we're eating, or what we'll do when everybody gets here.

The doorbell rings, and I prepare to heave myself up out of my comfy chair to answer it, but Abigail waves me off and practically floats down the hall. So light. So graceful. So not a whale out of water, floundering and flailing to get out of the recliner.

So wonderfully and miraculously present in my life.

I hear voices in the entry, and Val appears, brushing snowflakes off her shoulders with one hand, carrying a gift bag printed with multicolored elephants in the other. "Don't bother getting up, Liz. You just sit right there. I'll hang up my own coat, and Abigail and Lance can help me get the food set out."

She leans down to hug me, smelling of cool air and snow and cinnamon gum. The promised arrival of the new baby has inspired her to stop smoking about five times in the last five months, and she's taken up gum chewing to help her kick the habit. She wants to babysit for me, wants the baby to sleep over at her house, wants me to come and stay with her until the baby is born. She knows I'll put my foot down about tobacco exposure no matter how much I love her.

"You okay?" she asks, brow furrowed with concern as I let out a little gasp.

"Fine. Baby kicked me. Plus Braxton-Hicks."

"Those can be intense," she says, heading for the kitchen.

They've been intense for a week now, but this one feels different. Deeper, more intimate, an ache in my lower back and pelvis at the same time. But it eases and I let it go. Tonight is for celebration and hope, not worry and fear.

Tara and Bernie come in without knocking, both with their arms full of oversize, brightly wrapped packages. Both of them still have their boots on and leave a trail of melting snow behind them.

"Thought the snow might have kept you away," Val says, helping them arrange the packages in the corner of the room, while Abigail grabs a towel and wipes up my precious hardwood.

"What's a little snow to keep us from a party? Food. Drinks. We're in."

More footsteps in the hallway, and to my great surprise, Earlene appears, minus her boots and wearing slippers, with a tray of cookies in her hands and a gift bag hooked over one arm. "Huh. You people again?" she says with a side glance at Tara and Bernie, but there's no energy behind the complaint. "You're melting on Liz's floor."

"Oops. Sorry." Tara bends to unlace a pair of furry mukluks. "We were bearing heavy gifts."

They trail back toward the door, shedding bits of snow and leaving slushy footprints. Abigail follows with the towel.

"Where's that man of yours?" Earlene demands, setting her gift with the others.

Lance pops out of the kitchen like a summoned genie. There's a smudge of flour on his face, a flowered apron tied around his hips.

"Your wish is my command," he intones, lifting the tray from Earlene's hands. "Do I see peanut butter cookies? Be still, my heart."

"When are you going to make an honest woman out of Elizabeth?" Earlene unravels a scarf from around her neck and peels out of a down jacket that makes her look like the Michelin Man. "For the sake of the baby if not for propriety."

Lance juggles the tray onto one hip so he can assist her with her coat. "You'd have to ask Liz." He says it lightly, pretends to meet my gaze, but his smile isn't real, and he's looking at my forehead, avoiding eye contact.

My back cramps up again, a deep, long spasm. I worm my right hand behind me, pressing against the unhappy muscles. I hear new voices in the coatroom, and then Geoff, Pastor Steve, and Felicity all come in together in a flurry of gift bags and food trays. Rosie is right behind them. She sees me battling gravity and the chair and comes over at once to give me a hand up.

"You okay?" She surveys my face, and I work hard to plaster on a smile to hide my discomfort.

"Fine. Just sat too long." Now that I'm on my feet, my back is easing, but the low, heavy pressure in my pelvis continues.

"You're sweating." Her cool hand brushes my forehead.

"It's warm in here. Shouldn't have put that last piece of wood on the fire."

"Warmed up a bit outside," Rosie says, collecting an armful of coats. "Just enough to make for freezing rain."

"Turning into a skating rink out there. I hit the brakes and nearly slid off the road." Geoff settles into a folding chair with a plate already loaded with goodies. "If I hadn't been closer to here than home, I might have gone back."

"Sleepover!" Bernie sings out. "And no work tomorrow. Hope we brought enough beer."

"Roads like that, nobody's drinking," Tara objects. "I mean it, Bern."

Everybody exchanges looks.

"Maybe we should go back now before things get worse," Steve says. "Although I'd hate to miss your party, Mrs. L."

Lance switches on the scanner, something he bought me soon after I moved out here. Everybody this far out of town needs one, he'd said. In the summer I can check for fire news. In the winter, road conditions. With a crackle, it immediately comes to life, with the dispatcher calling out ambulances and law enforcement for a multiple car wreck on Highway 395, between here and Colville.

"Guess us Colville folks aren't going anywhere for a while." Earlene sighs. "Kettle Falls you can probably still get to."

"You're here now," Val proclaims. "Have food. Let Liz open her gifts at least. The sand trucks and snowplows will come out and it will get better."

Another pain grabs me. I'm good at denial, but this is rapidly getting real. I'm in labor, I have a house full of people, and the roads are terrible. I need a minute to plan, to decide what to do, to pull Lance aside and clue him in.

"You sure you're okay?" Rosie asks.

I wave her words away, and as soon as I can find my voice, I offer up the best distraction I can think of. "Want to see the nursery first? Lance finished the mural."

I've uttered words of power. Even though there's a din of tongues wagging and three different conversations going full steam ahead, the room falls silent and everybody turns to look at me, even Geoff, even Pastor Steve.

"I'm half afraid to see the standard you've set," Steve says, laughing. Felicity snuggles up against him, and he kisses the top of her head. Her eyes are shining, and she asks, "Shall we tell them?"

"Your call."

But there's no need now, of course. A hubbub of "Congratulations!" "When's the due date?" "Is it a boy or a girl?" follows as everyone converges on the stairs.

Tara is in the lead, but she stops on the first step and turns back to me. "Wait. It's your nursery. Come on, Liz. Give us the tour."

"You all go on up. I feel like the Little Engine That Could every time I climb up there these days."

My back is spasming again, the intensity of that deep inner pressure cranking up another notch. I'm not sure my legs are going to hold me upright through this one.

Lance, at the foot of the stairs, takes a step toward me. Nobody else moves, as if they've been given some stage direction that reads: *Freeze in place and stare at Liz.*

The pain releases, and I'm about to reassure them all that I'm perfectly okay when I feel an odd little pop and water gushes out between my thighs. Warm wetness runs down my legs, soaks through my pants, puddles onto the floor. Before I can fully register what has just happened, the next contraction grabs me, low and deep, a fist squeezing, twisting, and it's all I can do to stay on my feet and breathe.

Hovering over the fear and the pain is a random thought: *Water isn't good for hardwood. I should mop that up.*

And then, finally: *Oh my God, my water has broken.*

Abigail is at my side before I can draw another breath. "Clear," she pronounces, as if it's a diagnosis. I just stare at her, trying to process, not entirely sure I haven't just peed my pants.

"Clear is good," Abigail says. "No meconium staining."

Everybody is still staring. Embarrassment floods me. I don't even ask what meconium is. All I can think is that the stairs are blocked by onlookers and I need to go up and change my clothes. "Wipe it up," I tell her. "Before it ruins the floor."

"I'll start the truck," Lance says. "Get your jacket."

"But we're having a party."

"No," Abigail says. "We are not. Nix the truck, Lance. We should call an ambulance."

"It will be faster to get her there in the truck."

"And safer in an ambulance. The baby is still early."

"What about that wreck?" Rosie says. "I don't know that you'll get through."

"What do you want to do?" Lance asks me. His face is impassive, but his voice is tight with anxiety.

"Truck," I say. "They know you. They'll let you by."

He nods. "Either that or they'll put you in a cop car or ambulance on the other side of the block." He vanishes out the door as Abigail takes my arm on one side and Rosie steadies me on the other.

"How long have you been having contractions?" Abigail demands.

I think back to what I thought were Braxton-Hicks. "Maybe an hour? But they weren't so—" I can't finish the sentence, wracked with another spasm of pain.

"These are super close. Last one can't have been much more than two minutes ago." Abigail sounds more like a frightened child than a nurse. "I'm calling an ambulance. I don't care what you and Lance say."

She's already dialing.

"I need to change," I insist, but Val is already at my side with a clean pair of sweatpants and a hand towel to stuff inside them. "Everybody into the kitchen," she orders, shooing them like they're a flock of sheep. "Go eat things. Liz, you can change right here."

"I'm sure there's no urgency," Earlene says. "Labor takes hours. I was in labor for three days with my first . . ." Her voice trails off as Steve and Felicity propel her away and into the kitchen, taking her stories with her.

For once, Earlene's story of pain and suffering sounds comforting, but it's unlikely that I have three days before this baby arrives. My labor with Abigail was terrifying in intensity, and so short we barely made it to the hospital in time. A nurse delivered her twenty minutes after I was admitted, three hours from the time I felt the first contraction.

"The floor," I say to Val, as if it matters.

"You change. I'll get the mop."

I feel exposed, changing in the middle of the room, but the idea of walking anywhere seems overwhelming and we might as well keep all of the mess in one place. I strip out of my soaking pants and underwear, and another contraction hits before I can get the clean ones on.

Over the edges of the pain, I hear Abigail's voice talking to dispatch.

"How long? There has to be something sooner, the baby's early and she has a history of . . . Yes, I understand. All right."

She hangs up the phone and comes to help me. As soon as the contraction passes, she holds my pants for me. I lean on her bent back and lift first one leg and then the other. "That didn't sound promising."

"Ambulances are all out on calls," Abigail grinds out between clenched teeth. "Couldn't even tell me when they could get somebody out here. I guess we'll go in Lance's truck after all."

Pain slams into me again, and I don't have the breath to do anything but hold on to the promise that this contraction will end and I'll have a break.

"Remember your breathing," Abigail says, her cool hand on my belly. "In through the nose, out through the mouth."

"Fuck breathing," I want to tell her. Would, if I could speak.

"That escalated way too fast," Rosie says. Her usually calm face is tight with concern.

"I'm not so sure the truck is a good idea," Lance says, coming in from outside. "The windshield was iced over, and I fell on my ass twice walking back to the house."

"Best to just stay put until the roads are sanded," Rosie says.

Another contraction hits, and it's all I can do to keep from screaming. I squeeze Abigail's hand until I feel the bones compressing, try to breathe, but this time I can't; I'm just lost in the pain.

"Do we have that kind of time?" Abigail asks.

"She can't have the baby here," Lance says. "I'll put chains on the truck. Gil can drive ahead with the tractor, maybe that will break up the ice."

"All the way to town?"

"If needed."

I want to tell Lance not to worry. The house isn't cursed. This baby will be fine, born alive and well, but the pain hits me again and fear comes with it.

"I don't think we have that kind of time," Rosie says. "I don't think she's going to make it to town."

"That's not possible!" Lance's voice is sharp with anxiety. "It can't happen that fast."

Another contraction hits me. All the breathing in the world doesn't help this time. I scream with the onslaught of agony. My entire belly is being clamped and squeezed, not in a fist anymore but in the jaws of a machine.

Through my own whimpering, I hear the conversation around me.

"I'll check on the ambulance." Abigail's voice.

"She can't have the baby here." Lance sounds desperate, panicked.

And then Rosie again, the soul of reason. "Women had babies at home for centuries. Go put the chains on the truck, Lance. Val, can you get some blankets to put on the floor? She needs to lie down, and we're not dragging her up the stairs. Abigail, turn the oven on low and put some towels in to warm."

Everything becomes a blur. My friends settle me on the floor, hold my hands, encourage me. And then Lance is back, uttering soothing words, but his eyes are full of fear. Another contraction hits me, and when it eases, Lance is there with a pan, holding my hair away from my face while I vomit, and then everything is lost again in an eternity of pain that waxes and wanes but never really goes away.

"You're doing great," Rosie says, her face swimming into view.

How is the baby doing? That's the question I need to ask, but I know there won't be an answer. How can anybody tell? No monitor here tracking the little one's heartbeat.

"No ambulance yet," Abigail reports. "But the snowplows and sand trucks are out."

"Hey, honey." It's Val now, hanging over me. "You can do this." She stays with me through a tsunami of a contraction. When it eases, I croak, suddenly remembering the party, "Please tell me everybody left."

"Nope. All congregated in the kitchen. Pastor Steve prayed over you and the baby. And then Earlene told God exactly how your labor is supposed to go, in no uncertain terms."

A tiny bubble of laughter finds its way out of me, but the truth is, I'll take all of the prayers right now, even Earlene's. I add one of my own.

Please let the baby be born healthy. And let me live to be its mother.

But then the next contraction hits, and a guttural noise tears my throat as my body bears down, hard, without warning.

Abigail's face appears in my line of vision, eyes wide. "Breathe! Pant, like a puppy. Do not push!"

But my body is doing its own thing now, and I have no control over it.

"Rosie!" Abigail yells. "I think the baby's coming!"

"I'll be right there!"

"Oh my God. Come now! I can see the head!"

My daughter kneels on the blanket at my feet, shoving my knees up and anchoring my feet with her own body to keep them there. I'm in too much pain to even register embarrassment that she's pulled down my pants and is staring at a part of my body that is definitely not meant for her eyes. My body is pushing again, and now, instead of somebody telling me to pant, Rosie's calm voice says, "Push, Liz. Push. Harder! Lance, get behind her and sit her up a bit, so she's leaning back on you."

"You do this," Abigail cries. "I've never delivered a baby."

"Me neither," Rosie answers, still calm. "Since your hands are already there, you get to do the honors."

Abigail's eyes are wide, frightened. "I thought you knew what you were doing!"

"It's not rocket science," Rosie says. "I've helped a midwife a few times. Delivered plenty of calves. No great mystery about birth. Keep a little counterpressure on the head so it eases out slow. There you go."

Lance slides in behind me and lifts my shoulders, pulling me back between his legs so I'm supported by his body. I grab on to both of his hands and squeeze, pushing again, releasing a sound that is somewhere between a grunt and a scream.

A rush, a slither, my body forced wide open with a flare of pain.

A sudden easing.

"Oh my God," Abigail cries, somewhere between terror and ecstasy.

She's holding a baby in her hands. It's tiny and wet, streaked with blood and smeared with something white and creamy. *Vernix,* my brain tells me. Like the name of anything matters.

The baby isn't crying.

Lance is weeping silently. I can feel his every intake of breath, the shaking of his body.

"Slap his little feet, Abigail." Rosie dashes into the kitchen, returning with a stack of warm towels. She takes the baby from Abigail and starts rubbing it dry, vigorously. "Come on, little guy. You can do it."

Now that the pain is gone, that tiny face is my whole world.

I see the minute it scrunches into a frown. See the mouth open. The intake of air. And then an indignant cry, moving into full-on outrage. The bluish-gray body turns red. The tiny hands clench into fists and wave, the legs kick.

"There you are," Rosie says. "Keep crying, little boy. Here, Abigail, tie the cord off with these."

My daughter's hands, usually so steady and competent, are trembling. She's weeping, has to rub her arms across her eyes to clear her vision as she fumbles with a couple of twist ties and the slippery cord.

Rosie cuts between the ties with a pair of scissors, and then she lays the crying baby facedown on my chest with a warm towel over both of us.

Immediately the baby's strident wailing protest changes, softens. His body molds to mine. My heart expands, too big for my chest already but still growing. I'm half laughing and half crying, already overwhelmingly in love with this tiny new person. I peel back the edge of the towel so I can get a look at him. A perfectly proportioned face. All fingers and toes present and accounted for.

"He's doing great!" Rosie says, beaming.

"Where is that damned ambulance?" Lance demands.

"Probably stuck in a snowdrift. Easy there, little brother. Mama and baby are doing fine. Liz, let's see if the little guy will eat something."

At that moment, a new cramp hits me and I gasp.

"What is it?" Lance's hand squeezes mine again, too tight.

I feel a new pressure low in my belly. A gush of warmth between my legs.

"She's bleeding!" Abigail's voice is sharp with alarm.

"Just the placenta coming, honey. It's okay. See, here it is." Rosie's hand moves to my belly, digging in a little, feeling for something. "There, see? No more bleeding. Her uterus is nice and firm. If we can get the baby to breastfeed, it will help to keep her from bleeding. And be good for the little guy, of course."

She gets up and lays a clean quilt down behind me, covering it with towels.

"Here, scooch back onto this."

A minute later I'm propped up against Lance's strong warmth again, his arms around me. The baby's cheek turns toward me, his mouth opens, and I guide him to my breast. When he latches on and begins to suckle, a collective sigh goes up from all of us.

"He's gonna need a name," Lance murmurs.

"I guess I can't call him Munchkin forever."

Abigail, her face tight, is busy bundling up bloody blankets and towels.

"I think Abigail should name him," Lance says.

She freezes in the middle of shoving the placenta into a trash bag. Her eyes meet mine. I wonder if she remembers all of her demands for a baby brother when she was a child, the ridiculous names she came up with, some half nonsense, some completely made up.

When the laughter rises into her eyes, and then her lips, I know she does. "Very brave of you," she says. "What if I name him Yertle?"

"He'll be mercilessly teased. Lance was bad enough growing up."

Rosie steps out of the room with her phone pressed to her ear. She returns a moment later. "The wreck is cleared. Road's been sanded. Ambulance on the way."

"Do I have to go?" I ask. "Why couldn't we just stay here?"

"So long as it's safe, you should go get checked out, you and the baby. He seems fine, but he is a little early."

Abigail comes to sit beside me. Her fingers reach out to stroke the baby's tiny cheek. "He's doing awesome. I can't believe I . . ." She chokes on the next word. "Just so you know, if you . . . if I needed . . . it wouldn't be a burden to take care of him." I hear the love in her voice. Not even an hour old, and already we are all under this little boy's spell.

"You want to hold him?"

She hesitates, then lifts the tiny body into her own arms. His eyes are wide open, staring up into hers. "Oh," she breathes, as if she's just obtained enlightenment. And then, a minute later, "He looks like Lance."

"I think he looks like you."

"What's your name?" Abigail asks Lance. "Your full given name, I mean."

"Can't I take that with me to the grave?"

"Lancelot Gawain Arthur Marshall," Rosie says, laughing.

"You're making that up."

"I wish," Lance says. "My mother has always been . . . a geek, to put it mildly. Seriously into cosplay. And Arthurian romance is more real to her than her real life. Including me. So. Yes. Lancelot. Please don't use your naming powers to inflict that one on the little guy."

"At least she didn't name you Percival." I can't help laughing at the expression on his face, or wondering what is wrong with me that he is the father of my baby and I've never even asked his middle name. Or names.

"You laugh," he says, "but it was very nearly Galahad. Would you have still made a baby with me if I was a Galahad?"

"Eww," Abigail objects. "Sitting right here. The baby's name is Gavin. Like Gawain, only in modern English. Lance can pick his middle name."

Her choice stuns me, both because she's chosen to acknowledge Lance in this way, and because Gavin is so close to Gwyn, the name of the baby that died. I'm not sure how Lance will take it, if the name will hurt him, if . . .

"Thank you." He clears his throat. "I love it."

"So?" Abigail demands. "What's his middle name going to be?"

Lance glances at me out of the corner of his eye, and says, very carefully, "I was thinking about Thomas."

Again, a silence falls over us. "Mom?" Abigail asks. "I know Dad wasn't perfect, especially not to you—"

"Gavin Thomas Marshall," I interrupt, rolling the name on my tongue. Looking down at the baby to compare it with the reality of him. "It fits."

Chapter Thirty-Three

January 7, 2021

It's been months since I've picked up this pen. Who has time for journals with a little boy to raise and a household to run? I've just recently begun to feel like I have a brain again.

Truth is, I haven't felt the need of it.

I've been too busy living.

Not that I won't keep a journal again, but you, my little book, are a story that is done.

Liz

"Where's my baby?" Abigail sings out before she's even made it into the room. "Is he really walking? I can't believe I missed his first steps! Stupid day job."

Gavin crows with delight at the sight of his adored big sister. "Baba!" He drops the toys he's been playing with and holds up his arms, expecting to be picked up and spun around the room.

She drops to her knees and holds out her hands to him. "Oh no, you don't. You walk over here like the big boy you are."

Instead, he crawls directly into her lap. Abigail hugs him, smothering his face with kisses, and both of them break into delicious laughter.

"I can't believe he's almost one! How's the party planning?"

"Out of my hands. By the time Bernie and Tara are done, it will be a birthday extravaganza like this town has never seen."

I hit save on my work and close my laptop, reveling in one of my favorite moments of the day. The bond between my children is a beautiful thing. I love watching them together, so I delay mention of the long white envelope waiting on the end table beside me. It's the sort of envelope that threatens to change everything, but change is inevitable. And good. Even if it brings some heartache with it.

"Something came for you today."

Abigail sobers at the tone of my voice, staring at the envelope I'm holding out to her. It's addressed to Miss Abigail Lightsey. The return address is official—the University of Washington.

"I was going to tell you," she says slowly.

"Just open it."

"I don't know if I want to." She holds the envelope gingerly, as if it might explode. Normally, she's a neat letter opener, slicing carefully at the fold with a knife, but she takes a breath and tears the envelope open.

The time it takes for her to read seems like an eternity.

"I'm in," she says, glancing up at me, her face full of indecision and worry. "But I don't have to go. I know you need help with Gav and—"

"You need to have your own life," I say evenly, tamping down a rush of grief and loss. This year has been a gift, the chance to build the relationship the two of us never had, but I still want Abigail to live her own life.

"But you need me to babysit and help." Her voice wavers.

I know she's torn. She loves her little brother, but she hates her job. Plus, Josh has moved to Seattle, and the long-distance relationship is a strain. Going to UW would bring the two of them back together. She needs to go, and I need to help her make that decision.

"The babysitters are clamoring for turns. Lance spends hours with him. Val would move in if I'd let her. Tara and Bernie threatened to kidnap him the other day if I didn't give them a turn soon. And Gil's boys are over here all the time, not to mention Rosie and Gil."

Abigail sniffles. "I missed his first steps, and I live in the same house. I don't want him to grow up without me."

"You also don't want to spend the rest of your life working at this job. We'll visit. We'll FaceTime. Go be near Josh and become the surgeon you always wanted to be."

"About that." She glances up at me, then away. "I don't think I want to be a surgeon."

"But you applied to medical school."

She runs to retrieve her brother, who is trying to crawl underneath the sofa, where Moses is hiding from grabby little fingers. "I'm thinking I'll be an obstetrician. That way, I still get to do some surgery and . . ." Gavin twists and arcs his back in her arms, howling a loud protest, and she sets him on his feet, holding his hands so he can walk. "Well, that moment when Gavin was born was the best moment of my life. I was the very first person to ever touch him. And the way he changed everything, for us . . . I want to be part of that for my whole life, I think."

Now both of us are sobbing, which is out of character and suddenly funny, so in a minute we are laughing and crying all at the same time. Abigail walks Gav close to my chair and then lets go of his hands, hovering close to steady him, but he gets his balance and totters toward me, babbling with excitement.

Abigail claps her hands as I scoop him up and hug him.

"Well," she says. "You'd better get dressed if you're going out. And I'll clean up a bit. Looks like a tornado hit."

"That tornado's name is Gav." The room doesn't look at all like the *Better Homes & Gardens* serenity my imagination pictured when I first walked through this house. It's a mess. There's a playpen where I planned to put a decorative table. The floor is cluttered with a toppled pile of durable cardboard books we'd been looking at. Gav's beloved plushy ride-on tractor lies on its side. Two of my kitchen pans plus lids that he'd been using as drums and cymbals earlier are right in the middle of everything. It's amazing how much easier it is to raise a baby when I'm not trying to keep a perfect house.

Abigail has lightened up in some ways, but she's still an obsessive neatnik. Fine by me. I prefer to divide my time between playing with Gav and making slow progress on a new play that Bill has promised to put on with the community tribe, even if it's just for fun and without an audience.

Leaving Abigail to clean up the mess and supervise the baby, I go upstairs to change.

There is one thing still lacking in this life I'm creating for myself, and I've concocted a daring plan that makes me feel like I'm vibrating from the inside out. I've even bought new clothes for the occasion with some help from Val—a pair of nice slacks, boots with heels, a long knit tunic over a black silk camisole.

I make half turns in front of the mirror, trying to suck in my belly and tighten my butt. Postpregnancy bounce back is not a thing that happens to a woman my age, but it could be worse.

When I come downstairs, Lance glances up at me from where he's playing on the floor with Gavin. His eyes widen appreciatively.

"Wow. Was I supposed to dress up?"

"You're perfect."

"Are you sure? You could go to the opera in that, and I'm Colville casual."

I grin at him. "Colville casual works fine."

Half an hour later, we sit across from each other at the sports bar. He's drinking a beer, but even though I'm no longer pregnant or breast-feeding, I'm sticking with water. I'm driving, and my one episode with an almost DUI is going to last me for the rest of this lifetime.

"So this is the big surprise?" he asks suspiciously. "I mean, I know this place has memories, but we've been here a lot since our first date."

"It wasn't a date."

"I thought it was." His tone of voice, the intensity in his eyes, raises a hot flush to my cheeks. I haven't heard that from him since the day he asked me to marry him. This is perfect timing, encouragement for what I'm about to do.

"I knew it was a date," I confess. "Just . . . it was easier to pretend to be Lacey. I needed her. She was a free spirit who could do whatever she wanted. She gave me distance from my old life, from all of the rules. But . . ."

The words I want to say stick in my throat. What if, instead of breaking down the wall I erected between us, they create more distance? What we have as friends and co-parents is good, and what I'm about to do will disrupt the delicate balance we've established.

"But?"

He's looking at me the way he used to look when he wanted to kiss me. It makes it hard to think.

"But." I swallow, make my eyes meet his. "It wasn't Lacey who fell in love with you. It was me."

My heart is hammering so loudly, I'm sure that even the waitress can hear it, that she'll ask me to turn down the volume so I don't bother the other patrons.

"You love me," he repeats, as if he's tasting the words. I don't see shock or dismay on his face, and that gives me the courage to keep going.

"You asked me before if I would marry you. When I said no, it wasn't because I didn't love you, just because I was still all tangled up. I didn't trust my feelings."

"And now?" His voice is husky, those eyes looking right through me.

"Here." I draw an envelope out of my purse and hand it to him. "This is for you."

Lance opens the envelope, his forehead creasing in a puzzled frown. He glances up at me.

"Flights to Vegas?"

"Not just flights." I can't breathe, waiting for him to see, watching his face for the reaction.

He removes the plane tickets from the envelope, sets them on the table in front of him.

Then he withdraws a sheet of printer paper, unfolds it. I watch his eyes move, know word for word what he is reading, beginning with the header: *Vegas Wedding Chapel Vacation Package.* It seems an eternity of waiting for his reaction, and my head is light from lack of oxygen when he finally looks up at me.

"Breathe," he says. "Before I have to come over there and resuscitate you."

I follow his command, and when the buzzing in my ears recedes, I say, "I knew you'd never ask me again. So I figured it was up to me. If you still want to."

He says nothing, and I plunge onward, filling the silence with words.

"When you asked, it wouldn't have been right. I didn't know who I was. I needed to figure that out, to be sure that I knew how to be me. That I wouldn't be . . ." I pause, looking for the right word.

His lips quirk in the hint of a smile. "Assimilated? Like the Borg in *Star Trek?*"

"Exactly. Not because of you, because of me. And the baby, and everything. I loved you then, I just wanted things to be right. No false pretenses. No marriage of convenience. But if you've changed your mind, if you don't feel that way anymore, I'll understand."

Lance looks down at the paper in his hands and then back at me. "Are you sure about this?"

"Look, if this is out of line, you can just forget it, okay? Last thing I want to do is ruin what we—"

"Liz."

He stretches his hand across the table and closes his fingers around mine.

"Of course I want to marry you. But—Vegas? Eloping in Sin City? Our friends will kill us. Are you sure?"

"Absolutely! I do not want a church wedding. Can you imagine Abigail and Earlene and Bernie fighting over how the service should be? It would be a disaster. I thought we could just slip away, the two of us, and get married. Commit the sin and ask forgiveness later. They can throw us a party."

"You in Vegas," he says.

"I'm not talking an Elvis wedding. There are chapels and—"

"Yes," he says, his fingers squeezing mine. "Now, can I ask a favor?"

I've run out of words and look my question at him.

"Can we get out of this place so I can kiss you properly?"

We've already ordered, and I almost get bogged down in propriety. You don't just run out of a restaurant. But I can't sit here across from him another minute. I get to my feet and start walking. He follows, his hand warm on the small of my back. But as soon as we are outside and clear of the door, instead of kissing me, he gets down on one knee in the snow, right there in the parking lot. It's dark, but the streetlights illuminate us. He turns his face up to mine, digging something out of his pocket.

"Idiot. I already asked you."

"My turn. Fair play, and all that." There's a ring on the palm of his hand. It glows, softly luminous. Not a diamond. An opal, all shifting colors with fire at its heart.

"The minute I saw it, I knew it was yours. It's like you. Who you are shifts a little with light and perspective, but at the center, you are always you. Liz."

"And you just happened to have it with you?"

"Been trying to get my nerve up to ask you again. I carry it around with me."

"I don't know what to say," I whisper.

"All you need to say is one small word. It starts with *y*."

"Yes. Of course, yes. Now will you get up from there?"

He slides the ring on my finger, but before he can get to his feet, a car pulls into the parking lot. The window lowers and Tara's head pokes out. She whoops out loud. "That looks for all the world like a proposal!" she shouts. The catcall from the driver's seat can only be Bernie.

"Run for it," Lance says. He scrambles to his feet, grabs my hand, and the two of us dash for my car. We slide in, laughing and breathless. He kisses me, then breaks away to ask, "That's small-town living for you. What are the odds? Can we bump up the date on those tickets? Leave tomorrow?"

"It would cost us."

"Worth it."

My phone buzzes. Lance's chimes about two seconds later. Text messages come in fast and furious.

Val: Hey, do you have something you want to tell me?

Abigail: I can't believe I just heard the news from Bernie of all people. I live in your house! I'm your child!

Rosie: About time.

Pastor Steve: I just heard a little rumor—if it's true, I'd be honored to perform the service.

"We're in for it now," Lance says. "They'll never let us elope."

"We could drive. Leave right this minute. Forget clothes and everything and just go."

"We do have a small anchor."

"Abigail will take care of him. We can call her when we're well out of town." But I know full well it's too late. The hounds will track us to the ends of the earth if we try to run. And now that I'm thinking about leaving Gavin for a week, I know I can't do it anyway. Lance knows it, too.

"It was a fun idea," he says. "But I kind of like the idea of Gavin as ring bearer."

I lean back against my seat, accepting.

"Regrets?" Lance asks, reaching for my hand.

"Never. You ready to go home and face the music?"

"One more kiss to fortify me."

After considerably more than a single kiss, I pull out into the street and head toward home and a life beyond anything I ever dared to dream. I don't need Lacey anymore to guide me. From now on, all decisions are up to me, and I plan to say yes to every good thing that comes my way.

ACKNOWLEDGMENTS

I am grateful to so many people for their part in the creation of this book.

First, as always, thanks and much love to my Viking, for moral support, tolerating long brain absences when all I could think about was the story, and also that all-important continuity read. Also to my sons—your excitement over my success is a huge energy boost on hard writing days.

Thank you to my wonderful agent, Deidre Knight, for being as excited about the premise as I was.

I am incredibly fortunate in my editors. Much thanks to Jodi Warshaw, my acquiring editor at Amazon, and to developmental editor Jenna Free, who always pushes me to go deeper into both story and characters. As for copyeditor Michelle Hope Anderson, you are an absolute delight to work with, and I love the way you shine up my words without altering my voice.

Kristina Martin and Barbara Claypole White—I owe you both for your courageous read of an exceptionally rough draft and for all of the helpful and encouraging input.

To all of the wonderful, supportive people in the League of Legendary Writers—thank you for helping me stay on track. You all inspire me on a regular basis.

And a special vote of thanks to the people who helped me get my facts straight. Liv Stecker, thanks for your insights into community theater. Thanks to Sara Wheaton for going over EMT and ambulance procedures and Kellie Rice for sharing your professional knowledge around the logistics of a DUI.

Readers, you make my writing world go round. Thank you for your love of books—without you, this book would never have been written.

ABOUT THE AUTHOR

Photo © Diane Maehl

Kerry Anne King is the *Washington Post* and Amazon Charts bestselling author of *Closer Home, I Wish You Happy, Whisper Me This,* and *Everything You Are.* Licensed as both an RN and a mental-health counselor, she draws on her experience working in the medical and mental-health fields to explore themes of loss, grief, and transformation—but always with a dose of hope and humor. Kerry lives in a little house in the big woods of the Inland Northwest with her Viking, three cats, a dog, and a yard full of wild turkeys and deer. She also writes fantasy and mystery novels as Kerry Schafer. Visit Kerry at www.kerryanneking.com.